D0414108

SHEEPSHAG

Born in Liverpool in 1966, Niall Griffiths now lives in Wales and is also the author of *Grits*.

ALSO BY NIALL GRIFFITHS

Grits

Niall Griffiths

SHEEPSHAGGER

V

VINTAGE

Published by Vintage 2002

14

Copyright © Niall Griffiths 2001

Niall Griffiths has asserted his right under the Copyright,
Designs and Patents Act, 1988 to be identified as the author
of this work

First published in Great Britain in 2001 by
Jonathan Cape

Vintage
Random House, 20 Vauxhall Bridge Road,
London SW1V 2SA

www.vintage-books.co.uk

Addresses for companies within
The Random House Group Limited can be found at:
www.randomhouse.co.uk/offices.htm

The Random House Group Limited Reg. No. 954009
www.randomhouse.co.uk

A CIP catalogue record for this book
is available from the British Library

ISBN 9780099285182

Penguin Random House is committed to a sustainable future for
our business, our readers and our planet. This book is made from
Forest Stewardship Council® certified paper.

Printed and bound in Great Britain by Clays Ltd, St Ives plc

BREAK THEIR TEETH, O God, in their mouth: break out the great teeth of the young lions, O Lord.

Let them melt away as waters which run continually: when he bendeth his bow to shoot his arrows, let them be as cut in pieces.

As a snail which melteth, let every one of them pass away: like the untimely birth of a woman, that they may not see the sun.

Before your pots can feel the thorns, he shall take them away as with a whirlwind, both living, and in his wrath.

The righteous shall rejoice when he seeth the vengeance: he shall wash his feet in the blood of the wicked.

So that a man shall say, Verily there is a reward for the righteous: verily he is a God that judgeth in the earth.

Psalm 58

Then the world seemed to me the work of a suffering and tormented God. Then the world seemed to me the dream and fiction of a God; coloured vapour before the eyes of a discontented God . . . The creator wanted to look away from himself, so he created the world. It is intoxicating joy for the sufferer to look away from his suffering and to forget himself. Intoxicating joy and self-forgetting – that is what I once thought the world.

Nietzsche, *Thus Spake Zarathustra*

I am the man for which no God waits
For which the whole world yearns
I'm marked by darkness and by blood
And one thousand powder burns

Nick Cave, 'O'Malley's Bar'

—HELL OF A boy, Ianto, wasn't he.

—Hell of a boy's right, aye. Straight from-a fuckin place he was if yew ask me, like.

—Nah, he wasn't. No demon him, mun. He wasn't put yer on this earth fully formed as a murderer, like, he –

—Murderer? Just a murderer?

—Yeh, and the fuckin rest, mun, and the fuckin rest.

—. . . he had a birth and childhood and upbringing like us all. Only his was all fucked, like.

—No excuse.

—That's easy for yew to say, tho, innit? I reckon Ianto's childhood would've turned Mother fuckin Teresa into a murderer, mun. Tellin yew. Would've turned anyone fuckin crazy, that would've.

—That's bollax. Hundreds, no, fuckin *millions*-a people have a shitey upbringing and they don't turn into killers, do they? Yewer talking fuckin rubbish, mun. Shite. Jesus, if that was the case yerd be murderers all-a fuckin time, mun, all over these fuckin islands. Left, right and bastard centre.

—I agree.

—Yeh, well, yew fuckin would, Marc, wouldn't yew. Creep.

—No, Griff's right, mun. Under fuckin Thatcher? Major? The poverty, the repossessions? All that shite? New fuckin Labour's no bastard better, either. So, fuck, by yewer reasoning, Danny, we'd all be fuckin murderers. Awful fuckin lot uv shitey upbringings in-a past couple-a decades, mun.

—Says you, yeh, with yewer dad a bastard doctor. What the fuck d'*yew* know about poverty?

—Well, I reckon-a whole argument is far too simplistic. In Ianto's case, like.

—What? Bollax, mun. What was yewer verdict, Griff? 'Fuckin sicko pervert', was it? An that's not simplistic, like?

—Ah, it's all just fuckin wind, mun. Just talk, like. Useless.

I

Solves fuckin nothing. What's happened's happened an yer's fuck all we can do about it.

—No, but we can try an understand it, can't we? Try an, like, y'know . . .

—Why, like? What for? What's-a fuckin point of that, then?

—Because Ianto was a fuckin mate, that's why. We all knew him. How many of us ever suspected that he'd be capable of doing what he did?

—No mate of mine, that cunt. No fuckin way. Never did like him, me.

—Nor me.

—Aw, Jesus fuckin Christ. That's complete shite. Yewer just saying that cos yew know now what he was really like, what he did. Yew all fuckin liked-a boy before he died and before yew found out what he did. We all did. He was a mate. Don't fuckin deny it.

—I fuckin well *will* deny it, mun. Are yew deaf? Watch my fuckin lips: I. Never. Liked. The fucker. Get it that time, did yer?

—Fuck sakes. This is getting us fuckin nowhere. Going round in bloody circles yer we are.

—Well, enlighten us then, Danny. Go on, tell us-a truth. Yew seem to know all about it, like, and evidently we don't so go on, fill us in, cos I'm dying to fuckin know, we all are. Tell us about Ianto. Tell us why he did what he did.

—I don't know why, Marc. That's the whole fuckin point of talking about it, like, so we can reach some kind of understanding. Foolish fuckin hope tho when a shite-fer-brains like yerself is in on-a conversation, like.

—Fuck off.

—And anyway, even if I *did* know, what would be-a point of tellin yew because yew never bloody listen to anybody except yewerself and yewer own fuckin bigotries an self-deluded bullshit. Might as well talk to-a bastard wall, mun.

—Or shut the fuck up. Yeh, that's a good idea, innit? Just don't say another fuckin word on-a subject. Or anything else, for that matter.

—Alright then. I won't.

—Right then.

—Good.

—Yew pair-a childish fuckers, aye.

IANTO IS FIVE.

Playing in the knee-high ryegrass which encroaches on the heather and forces that lilac bloom further up the mountain, in the lee of which he plays with two small stones, pebbles smoothed into almost globular roundness by undying winds and inexhaustible drizzle and the calm collisions of the lapping waves of the inland sea this dingle once was an unthinkable time ago, now evaporated leaving this landscape of breathable seabed, past and over all dream or fancy or even all knowing. Ianto has found these small stone marbles dotted with microfossils, perished in an age when all life only crawled or swam and he is banging them repeatedly together, crash and apart, crash and apart, the 'pok' sound of their repeated meetings whipped by the wind over to where his grandmother wrestles with washing among struggling vegetables in the scrubby front garden of the old and falling whitewashed farmhouse, her lined and liver-spotted hands attempting to fight on to the nylon line the wind-snapped and billowing dresses long washed-out, woolly socks more hole than substance and heavy shirts long gone shapeless and out at the elbow and the swallowing adult jumpers and corduroys she dresses baby Ianto in, on whom she now keeps one milky eye once bright and blue, the colour dictated by her blood. The little person playing under the swell of the mountain's foothills is but a speck against the giant rise, engrossed in the repetition of crash and apart, crash and apart, some rock-grit on his fingertips and handbacks and small shock lightly throbbing in the sinews of his hands, his control over the violent and instantaneous contact crash and apart, crash and apart.

The high bleating of a lamb in distress sounds behind him unfamiliarly and frighteningly close and he turns to see the small animal newborn-white hobble on wobbling legs towards him, the black rag of a raven wheeling away in the wind from its nodding head, black carrion bird, he who in these mountains hops rapid and beak agape and red-rimmed eye drilling at the newly born or newly deceased. Ianto squats silent and watches the lamb come, hears its cries echoed by those of what must be

4

its mother, standing scared and uncertain on an outcrop of rock away where the dingle begins its downward rush to the estuarial waters. The lamb comes bleating through the dried and tangled ryegrass, the wind lifting the innocent quiff of white curls away from its eyes where Ianto can now see there are no eyes, only holes, dark sockets red-frothed with cords hanging loose like impatient scavenger worms. Blood has leaked and darkened the cheeks and masked the little lamb, which now stands calling and helpless in Ianto's face, its senses in this world of plunged pain and darkness leading it towards the nearest large living thing. Nothing it can see and nothing it can feel but for the sky-brought fire in its face. Well-fed corvine in the twisted branches of the bare tree above cackles, the feathers on his blue-black breast puffed and riffling in the wind. Loose-lipped Ianto turns his head to look up at the bird and there is something in the act of his looking which is not there when he looks, something which turns his head on the fulcrum of his neck with promises quickly betrayed. Something within him but not without. Something in him dashed against the ancient world, which now comes at him like a whirl of swords. The lamb cries and cries again, the dark and bubbling holes in its face expanding into howling voids which begin to draw little Ianto in and he reaches out young-fingered and desperate to fill those awful weeping gaps with his plaything pebbles, to put something where there is nothing, to bring substance upon emptiness. The stones sink softly into place and for a moment the lamb stands stone-eyed, but Ianto's developing and unchecked motor functions carry his fingers further forwards and the stones and then the chubby thumbs themselves sink with a suck and squelch deeper into tissue and crunch through cartilage then wetly into brainmush and the lamb falls instantly limp on Ianto's hands, all life gone in a blink of his eyes blink blink blink with the coming horrored waters as he tries to shake his burden off, both small arms pumping frantically at the shoulders, demented puppeteer with a barking-bird audience, raven craning its thick black neck to the strange hybrid below, the Iantolamb. Dead weight pulls Ianto groundwards, the lamb's head following every movement of his arms as if in nightmare, death-biting limpet-clinging lockjaw cemented, and he calls out in no known word and his grandmother's white head swings like an eland scenting lion. She drops her washing and it tumbles into the furrowed mud of the potato drill and she runs towards her grandson bobbing old and determined over the uneven ground. Ianto sees her coming and cries

5

out again and tries to raise his arms jerking the dead lamb off the floor and clammy liquor races down his crawling skin and now at last he can scream, a long high scream of terror of blackness come sudden down on to his head, one with the gathering wind and the raven hopping and excited on his branch beak gaping hard consonantal bird-shriek, black-bellied and wet-heavy stormclouds massing above the mist-hackled mountain crest like a colossal black cap over all this, this endless drama of tiny deaths played out in miniature among mountains.

Ianto with the lamb, dead on his young hands. The old woman scrabbling stiff-limbed towards him. He is five, Ianto is.

—WHERE WAS IT he was born, Ianto? Llanidloes, was it?

—Nah, Llangurig.

—Well that area anyway. Inland, like. Farms and mountains, fuck all else. That's all there is yer, just farms and mountains.

—And lakes.

—Couple-a lakes, aye. Bleak fuckin part of-a country anyway, mun. Nothing to do out yer 'cept drink an shag, stuff yewer face full-a mushies during-a season like, just trip yewer fuckin life away on-a hillside just for something to fuckin do. To take yewer mind away from yer hard an boring existence.

—The suicide rate out in those places is massive. Hangin from-a trees like fuckin Christmas baubles they are, come wintertime like. On certain nights all's yew can hear are the bangs of people blowin eyr own heads off. Honest. They all –

—Which is what happened to Ianto's dad, like, that.

—What?

—Shot himself in-a head, mun.

—Bollax. That was Ianto's grandad, he was-a one who topped isself. Ianto's father, like, well, nobody really knew who he was. He –

—Including Ianto's mam.

—Probly her own fuckin brother, aye.

—Yeh, or her own bleedin father.

—Ianto used to call his brother 'dad'.

—Yeh. Him an his dad an his brother added up to less than three people.

—He was probably a traveller, like, one-a them gyppos who used to have a camp out by Newtown. They'd go back every winter, help with-a spud picking an stuff, earn a few quid, then fuck off on eyr travels again. Ianto's mam probly met him in the fields or at one of-a dances or something, had a knee-trembler in an outhouse or up against a tractor, something like that.

7

—Yew seem to be unduly interested in-a sex life of Ianto's mam, Llŷr.

—Probly ad her isself, dinny.

—Fuck off, Marc. She was a hopeless pisshead who died when Ianto was about elevenish or something. Drank herself to death, like. But before that, see, before she died like, Ianto was already living with his mam-cu, had been since he was a nipper. Mam didn't want him, see. Interfered with her drinkin, like. His granny was more of a mother to him than *she* was. Nice old biddy, far as I can remember. She used to come up to-a school –

—Jesus, Ianto never went to fuckin *school*, did he? I can't believe that that half-wit ever went to school. No way.

—It's true, Griff, he did.

—. . . she'd come up to-a school with Welshcakes for us all at dinnertime, like, an a great big jar of home-made jam. Fuckin lovely it was. We'd all dip the cakes in the jam an cover our faces with it, thirty sticky red kids runnin around sticking to each other as if we'd been glued. Sarnies, too, she'd sometimes bring a big plate-a them up an –

—Oh aye, I remember that. Cheese ones, a great big mound-a them covered in a tea-towel like to keep away the flies. Used to have two dinners, I did, whenever Ianto's granny came up, me own an whatever she brought. Used to fuckin love that, I did, two dinners.

—No wonder yew were a fat little get, yew.

—I think she was lonely, like, that's why she did it, out yer on her own in that little farmhouse when Ianto was at school. No company like. No other houses for fuckin miles around. Must've been horrible for her to live like that, on her own in-a place where her husband of thirty years I think it was topped himself like. Horrible way to live mun.

—I thought he . . . hang on, someone told me that he did it in that disused silver mine, y'know where we found-a bodies? That's what someone told me, that he went in yer with a borrowed gun like and blam.

—Nah, I'm tellin yew, he did it in-a shed. I know.

—What shed?

8

—Well, yeh, there used to be a shed which Ianto's granny knocked down, to get rid of-a memories like. That's where he did it, in that shed. With that knackered old gun that Llŷr's got now.

—Shite. I got that gun off me dad.

—Yeh, who got it in turn off Ianto's mam-cu. She didn't want it in-a house, see, after what happened, so she offered it to someone in-a pub like an that someone was yewer old man.

—Don't believe it.

—I'm tellin yew, it's true.

—My dad got it off his dad, who used it in-a war. First one, I think.

—He didn't. It was Ianto's grandad's. My dad was yer when your dad bought it off Ianto's granny. I remember it clear as fuckin day.

—Fuckin cursed that gun is, mun. Evil, like. Get rid of it if I was yew, Llŷr. Which I thank God every day I'm not like.

—Knob off Danny.

—Me an fuckin all, mun.

—Well, anyway, whose ever's fuckin rifle it was or is, that was Ianto's childhood like, just him and his grandmother out in that old farmhouse where her hubby shot himself.

—The silver mine! Fuckin tellin yew mun, the silver mine! Have yew not been listenin to a word I've fuckin said?

—All right then, Griff, the silver mine, fuck, what does it really matter? I mean the point is like that that house had been in-a family for generations like, hundreds of years, its walls an floors were all on-a wonk. Yew'd feel pissed in it, yew would. Dizzy like. It was built ages ago when that law was around, y'know that law which said something like if you could have four walls and a roof with a fire going in-a hearth between sunrise and sunset then yew wouldn't have to pay for the land, something like that . . .

—Yeh.

—Which was why it was all on the slant, like, cos it was a rush job. Tidy age it was like. Ianto's family had always lived in that house. Back when they were using fuckin oxen to plough and hunting fuckin wild boars for their tea Ianto's ancestors were livin in that fuckin farmhouse.

9

—Yeh, which makes it even more fuckin unfair that those cunts can come along an repossess the fuckin thing. Weren't even theirs to fuckin repossess. Bastards.

—Yeh. Fuckin disgusting that was.

—Fuckin shame.

—Yeh, but really it was Ianto's granny's fault, wannit? No, no, it was, I mean, she put it up for collateral, didn't she? Remember: she needed a new tractor an some other farm machinery like an she was skint so she got a tidy loan using that house as security. The farm, if you can call it that like, just fuckin scraps of plants and animals really, the farm was losing money and she thought that more up-to-date machinery would make it more profitable, a going concern again, like, so she could get rid of it at a tidy price. So that's what she did, she offered the house as collateral, got the loan, bought-a gear, an fuck all happened. No bastard improvement at all. Just carried on going downhill.

—Still fuckin disgustin tho. Been in that family for generations, that house had. It was fuckin *hers*, mun.

—Yeh, I know. I'm not sayin it's fair or anythin like, I'm just sayin that that's the way things are. That's how they work in this fuckin world like. I mean yew've got to pay the loan back somehow, haven't yew? Nothing for fuckin free in this world, boy, nothing for fuckin free.

—Don't fuckin agree with that at all. Can't take someone's fuckin home from them. Specially not one that'd been theirs for all those years. Not fuckin right, that.

—I know, but what the fuck can yew do? That's the way it works, mun, right or wrong, that's a way it bastard well works.

—It was that that did for Ianto's granny, wannit? Losing that house, like, that's what killed her, I reckon.

—Well it definitely had something to do with it, yeh. Altho she was an old woman by that time like. I mean yeh, she had the heart attack an keeled over an died when-a bailiffs came like, but she must've been in her late seventies, early eighties like. Old woman. An she'd worked on that poxy little farm all her life, single-fuckin-handedly even for the twenty or so years before she died. Can't've been easy for

10

her. An I'm sure fuckin Ianto weren't much bleedin help like.

—Fuck no.

—Those fuckin bailiffs, mun. Fuckin Ianto should've let us know they were coming. Would've been up yer with a fuckin basie I would've aye.

—I don't think Ianto was arsed, Griff, to be honest. What was he doing on the day his granny was made homeless? Remember? Lying in his own puke in-a squat, that's what he was doing. His poor granny up yer on her own.

—Yeh but he still should've told us. Any excuse to kneecap a bailiff, mun, any fuckin excuse . . .

—Yeh. I would've gladly gone up there with me gun.

—Oh Jesus no, Llŷr, seeing that fuckin gun again probably would've killed the old biddy straight off. That would've knocked her stone bastard dead that would've aye.

—Died anyway, tho, didn't she?

—What happened to Ianto after that? Is that when he . . .

—Well, that was it, wannit? What the fuck could he do? Poor bastard, no home, no family, he was fucked. Alone and fucked. Lost, he was like, that's what he was. An orphan with nowhere to live. Poor fucker.

—'Poor fucker?' Too fuckin soft yew are, Danny, aye. Too fuckin liberal.

—It was still no excuse.

—For what?

—For what he did.

—Well maybe not, no, but fuckin imagine it mun; yewer in yewer early twenties, yewer not-a fuckin brightest of people like –

—'Not the brightest?' Fuckin *backwards* that cunt was, mun. Thick as fuckin pigshit, like.

—An twice as bastard smelly, aye.

—. . . an all of a sudden yew've got absolutely fuck all, no family, no home, no money, nowt. Yewer mam's dead, yewer granny's dead, yewer grandfather's well dead, yew never knew who yewer dad was, yew've got absolutely fuck all in-a whole wide world. What the fuck d'yew do like?

—Yew survive, that's what yew fuckin do. Yew never fuckin give in. Yew do all yew fuckin can to survive an get one over on those fuckers.

—Yeh, an that's what Ianto did, innit? Went to live on-a streets. In-a squats.

—And in my fuckin cottage.

—And in yewer cottage, Llŷr, aye. Which is all he could do, just get his head down wherever he could like, doing what he could to survive. He tried, at least.

—Kept going on about that fuckin house, tho, dinny? Always goin on about that fuckin house he was, d'yew remember? On an on an on.

—Yeh. As if it was some kind of fuckin homeland or somethin like, some fuckin promised land he'd been exiled from.

—Well it was, if yew think about it. I mean –

—Shite. Homeland be buggered.

—Got on my fuckin tits, he did, to tell yew-a trewth, going on an on like that.

—Went up yer with im once, I did. Just to look at-a house like. Don't know why really, he just said he wanted-a see it again an I just tagged along like. Bored I suppose. It was a fuckin disaster, I'm tellin yew. Wish I'd never fuckin gone, altho if I hadn't've Ianto probably would've ended up dead or in prison that night.

—Shouldn't've bloody gone then, should yew? Would've saved a shit load of fuckin trouble if yew hadn't've gone up yer, Llŷr boy. Would've saved every fuckin one of us a whole lot of bastard bother.

—Not to fuckin mention a certain pair of hillwalkers like.

—An a certain schoolboy.

—Yeh.

—Borstal boy, not schoolboy.

—What's-a fuckin diff? Young lad either way.

—Yeh, a fuckin disaster it was.

—Most things were with Ianto. Who was that feller in the legend who turned everything he touched into gold? Well, Ianto was the opposite; everything *he* touched turned to cack.

—Not only touched, either; all he had to do was fuckin *look* at something, mun, an that'd be it, bing, brown an mingin. Fuckin walkin disaster area that twat was I'm tellin yew.

—Yeh.

—Yeh. Cursed, he was, I'm fuckin sure of it, mun. There was always something not quite right about him, wasn't there? Even when he was a kiddie like.

—Yeh.

—Always something, I dunno, just not quite right. Can't quite put me finger on it like. Just not, y'know, just not fuckin *right*.

DUSK, SUMMER, AND Ianto leads Llŷr and Llŷr follows up the steep downrushing dingle, Llŷr's cottage and the estuary behind and below them now afire in the sinking sun, a wet immensity washed in mild pink and harder orange intensifying in strata down the darkening sky to meet the eye-searing seething scarlet where the mudflat pencils a thick line against the sky, bisecting the far furnace of the setting sun. Llŷr is panting, wheezing, occasionally coughing up phlegm shellfish which he spits out into the brittle ryegrass, where they cling to stalks like cuckoo-spit or odd land-molluscs unshelled. Ianto climbs steadily up the steep slope using his feet and long hands, prehensile and balanced like one unused to other forms of locomotion, say bipedal, upright.

—Jesus, Ianto mun . . . I'm buggered . . . how far now?

Ianto shakes his head wordlessly and pulls himself onward. Upwards.

This vast land they climb, its peaks and its plains like furniture designed by and for some titanic race was wind-stripped and rain-flayed of anything soft and yielding aeons earlier under a low young sun. There is nothing of any comfort here, all soil upholstery slashed and ripped and torn off and scattered horizonwards, tumbled over the world's edge in clods and slabs, leaving just mud and protruberant close-packed stone in dense sharp ridges underfoot, squamous and scutellated like a reptile's back or the feet of a falcon. Ordovician country, named after the dark squat tribes it once sustained. Rock reinforced by lava flow and pumice to bulge and swell into mountain, quondam islands in the sea once here and now marked with the spiral and circle of petrified brachiopod and trilobite and conodont, languid graptolites drifting after plankton frozen in one instant of their incessant trawl and now caught stalking for ever. It is a land now as it was then, vast and rough and repellent and ragged; it must be scrambled up and through, upright motion

14

is abhorred. You must dirty your knees and knuckles to let this land lift you up.

—Fuck's sake, Ianto, mun . . . should install a fuckin escalator out yer aye . . .

Ianto crests the dingle and stands panting, sweat cooling on his brow and face. He climbs up here fairly regularly but is not yet and nor will he ever be accustomed to this vista, this long and powerful prospect; the swooping dingle and the spread estuary beyond, the roof of Llŷr's cottage below button-sized and gapped like a kicked mouth in the small copse of largely moribund trees edging the thin ribbon of road. A space too huge for the eye to drink, the eye must dart and flicker bat-like to take it all in. Ianto stands and surveys like a poor lord, sees the mound to his right and across the valley the knee-shaped swell, on the far side of which the entrance to the disused silver mine stands like an attentive grave and which is topped by the circle of standing stones, ancient and dark and glyphed with strange shapes, incomprehensible messages of man's hand and still older imprints of living and easier forms caught in cold stone when it ran and flowed like mud. Only the stone's crowns can be seen from this location and smaller than toes at this distance, but Ianto nevertheless squints their way, his matted light brown hair tossing lankly in the breeze. Nondescript Ianto, remarkable only in the prominence of his ears and upper front teeth; average height, underweight, nothing like the grotesque troll the newspapers will later depict him as, no similarity with the hulking hirsute beast image that the collective fears and neuroses will be fed. They will dig up an old mugshot of him taken after a pub brawl and that is how he will be apprehended in the public imagination, huge and bruised and bulging with blood. Scruffy skinny spotty Ianto, tiny in this vastness.

Llŷr climbs chest-heaving beside him, bends forwards hands-on-knees to wheeze air into his labouring lungs and dribble sticky oxygenated spittle into the grass. Ianto looks at his heaving back, then looks away to the lightning-blasted blackthorn on his left, the charred and twisted harbourer of sight-stealers and vision-killers; he glances at this once and then again and then turns away to take in the nearby house, the farmhouse, the

15

place of his odd childhood, the basic superstructure of which brings back memories sharp and sudden, but which now has sprouted a patio french-doored and a small gazebo to the left of the small garden, spaceship-like and to Ianto alien, incongruous. There is a smoothly tarmacked drive and a corrugated carport, shining cars parked and one huge humped motorbike and a barbecue pit, around which people mill and talk in shorts and T-shirts and sandals and thin bright dresses and trouser-suits, untucked loud shirts and dark expensive sunglasses. Baseball caps and straw hats. The smell of cooking meat fills the sunset and sets two buzzards to wheel high overhead. A sturdy wooden table supports vats of salad and garlic bread and stacks of canned beer and a coppice of bottles, brown, green, clear for the spirits amber and transparent. Phil Collins sings about another day in paradise beneath the high and happy chatter, accents traceable only to a vague South of England locale, where none seem to have been or go but from where many originate. The valley wall steeply barren rises up behind the house, the party; Ianto remembers it as being an imposing presence of menace when he was a little boy, but it now looks like nothing more than a convenient natural windbreak, fortuitous shelter from the wind, which perennially whines if not howls up here for the pleased partiers in its lee.

Llŷr draws himself upright, breathing more easily now, and spits again. Neither he nor Ianto have eaten in some time and the barbecue smells are wringing their bellies and undamming their saliva. Beneath the lightly moaning wind and the chatter and the music sounds can be heard from inside them like the rumbling of distant boulders dislodged. Thunder dragging itself over the horizon. High overhead the buzzards mew and whistle.

—Bloody hell. Llŷr shakes his head in mild disbelief. —Yew'd hardly recognise-a old place now, would yew, eh? Bloody hell. Lost all its fuckin character it has, yew ask me. Looks like a fuckin holiday chalet or something. That barbie smells fuckin great, tho.

Ianto says nothing, just stands and stares, the salt wind off the estuary far below ruffling his dirty hair and slapping the collar of his brown-checked shirt against his cheek. There is a slight and

16

subdued undercurrent to one side of the party's conversation now, a sly gatecrashing murmur; people have begun to notice them standing there, Ianto and Llŷr. Heads are half-turned their way. Grins are beginning to falter.

Llŷr shrugs. —Well that's it then, Iant. We've seen it. Nowt more to see. Might as well go back down. Altho I might bastard add that it's a long fuckin way to come for fuck all, like.

Ianto doesn't move.

—C'mon Iant, yer's bugger all else we can do. Can't look in any windows or anything with all those bloody people yer, can we? Have to forget it, mun. Come up again some other time, hope they're all out. Nothing else we can do.

A small voice: —Bastards.

—I know they are, Ianto, I know they are. It's fuckin unfair like but yer's fuck all we can do. Too many of-a cunts. Just got to put up with it, mun. Just let it go, like; it's some posho fucker's second home now innit and yer's fuck all we can do about it, mun. Don't have to like it, but that's-a way it is. Just got to let it go aye.

Ianto darts forward three quick steps. Llŷr takes his shoulder.

—What the fuck're yew doing? Can't go over yer, Ianto mun, place int fuckin yours any more. C'mon, let's go back down. Go-a pub, eh? Have a few bevvies, chill out like. Just take it easy, eh?

Ianto shakes his head, shrugs Llŷr's hand away. The cast of his face is determined and set. And he talks, now; Llŷr has heard Ianto talk so seldom that he has forgotten the sound of his voice and indeed there is a general consensus amongst their friends that Ianto's usual taciturnity has something in it of the pathological, but now he talks, in a voice rusty with disuse:

—I just want-a stand on-a fuckin soil, mun. That's all I want-a do. Fuck all wrong with that, is there, just standin on-a fuckin soil? Fuckin dug in that soil when I was a kiddie I did. Buried stuff in it like. Used to bury coins in yer, I did. Yeh, yer's my money in that fuckin garden, mun, and I want it bastard back. My rightful fuckin belongings in yer there is.

This is the longest speech Llŷr has ever heard Ianto make. Conversation in the garden has ceased now and people are openly staring and some muttering is going on. Women in sunglasses fingertip tresses of hair back behind their ears. Tumblers and cans and thin-stemmed wineglasses are held at chest height. A man at the barbecue wearing a sombrero and a plastic apron patterned as a Manchester United home shirt holds a pair of tongs gleaming with grease. Another man, beard and belly and knee-high socks and long floral shorts below a motorcycle leather approaches the white slat fence which marks the garden, topped with barbed-wire tinsel even though it stands barely three feet tall.

—Can I help you, lads? This *is* a private party, you know. What is it you want?

Llŷr shakes his head and tries to gently lead Ianto away.

—No, it's alright, mate. Just my friend yer, he, he used to live yer, see, when he was small, like. Memories an that y'know. It's alright. C'mon, Ianto mun, eh.

The bearded man has been joined by others. One of them, hair gelled tightly back skull-clingingly into a ponytail above aviator sunglasses is grinning very widely like a shark and revealing a gobful of very white and very long teeth. He holds a bottle, an almost-empty wine bottle, dark green glass and thick base.

—That's enough now, I think, this man says. —Time for you two to leave, I reckon. Private party, private land. You weren't invited up here, you're not welcome up here, so you might as well both just go.

—Yeh . . . c'mon Ianto . . . let's leave these people to eyr party now, eh . . .

Ianto jerks his arm out of Llŷr's grasp. His eyes blink rapidly and his jaw works as if he's chewing gum, and with a plummet Llŷr can see what's coming and he doesn't want Ianto to do it, but he cannot help noticing at the same time how very small Ianto looks, how thin and pathetic in the world, how reed-skinny and impotent he is in his spots and torn and mucky clothing standing here among the mountains before these clean and moneyed people, occupiers of his childhood. His voice is high and shrill and as taut and stringy as the protruberant sinews in his neck tight as harpstrings, the throbbing blue veins at his temples:

18

—Get out of my house! This is *my* fuckin house! This is my fuckin house and yew people have no business in it! Trespassing yew are! TRESpassing! On my fuckin land!

His hands clenched anally into small fists at his sides. His left knee jerking with each stressed and shouted word.

—My family have lived yer for hundreds-a years! Thousands! Leave now and we'll do no more about it! Just fuckin give it back!

The man in the tropical shorts looks back over his shoulder.

—Jessica, get the dogs.

The man with the sharky grin grins even wider, chuckles:
—Oho, that's the *one*, and swings his leg over the fence holding the barbed wire down with both hands. Someone else, cropped grey hair, jogs over to join him, holding a poker.

—Jesus fuck, Ianto. Leg it, mun!

Llŷr grabs Ianto mid-swivel and they both stumble over in the grass. He sees for an instant in perfect close-up focus a tiny lilac flower black-mottled at petal-edge perhaps with smuts from the barbecue and then he is up and running limbs pumping a bellows in his chest and Ianto is behind him leaping over spiky tussocks and still yelling:

—We'll be back, yew bastards! Yew thieving bastards! *My* fucking house! *My* fucking garden and I want yew bastards out!

Jeering laughter in response.

—Any time, sheepshaggers! We'll be waiting!

A lot of mixed laughter as if every partygoer there without exception is amused, tickled. And a male voice, that accent:

—Run back to your hovels, peasants! Bloody Welshies don't even know how to look after your own country! Should all still be living in caves!

Yet more laughter. Llŷr and Ianto tumble down the dingle towards the sea, two tiny tumbling leaping figures down the huge descending slope, new moonlight climbing and blueing their flight towards the dark flat of estuary and the far hills beyond it and the rising night above speckled silver with stars newly returned. They stumble downwards until they come chest-heaving to rest against a kennel-sized and kennel-shaped rock pointing perpendicular from the steep grassy slope, lunar-surfaced, dotted with small fossils ammonite-carousels and splattered with yellow lichen gone grey in the fading light. Curlews call lonely across the mud flats beneath and a bat flits through the orbit of the two heaving figures, banks and returns again quick leathern flap and then flits away. The sun is a sliver of crimson visibly sinking, disappearing below the world's end as if cowering away from the rubbed coin of the climbing moon.

—Fuck's sake Ianto . . . Llŷr is draped across the rock panting, lank damp hair in his eyes his full almost African lips agleam. A pendulum of spit swings from the lower. —What the fuck did yew go and do *that* for? Near got us both beaten bastard well up yew did, yew soft twat. What-a fuckin hell were yew fuckin playin at, mun? Only fuckin two of us, Christ . . . fuckin loads-a them . . .

Ianto stares into the middle distance, breathing heavily through his nose, and shrugs his small shoulders. Says in a small voice little more than a mumble: —Just want my fucking house back, that's all. Got nowhere to fuckin live an that's my fuckin house. Those bastards use it as a second home like for eyr holidays an I haven't even got *one*. Not fuckin fair it's not. Cunts.

There is a jerking sob in his voice. This is the second longest speech Llŷr has ever heard Ianto make.

—I know it's fuckin not, mate, but that's how it works, see? Those without money like, ey have things taken away from them an given at a price to those who've got money. Way of-a fuckin world, mun. Fair or fuckin not it's how-a world works. *I* don't like it, *you* don't like it, but yer's fuck all we can do. It's just-a way it fuckin is, mun. Fuckin awful like I know, but . . . yew've just got to live with it, mun. Don't have to like it, just accept it. Drive yew bastard mad otherwise, see.

He squeezes one nostril shut with a finger and snorts a string of snot out the other and it glistens on the rock like glue.

—An anyway, I've told yew, all's yew've got to do is go in-a DSS and tell em yew can't find anywhere to live an they'll help yew out. Put yew in a B and B or somethin. Duw, yew might even get in one-a those new flats on Queen's Road. Smart flats them aye, handy for-a pubs, a shops, a beach . . . worth a try, innit? Can't do any harm like.

Ianto does not answer. He folds his arms across his chest and looks up at a large bird flying overhead in the darkness owl-silent and owl-intent, white-bellied and deadly. Llŷr looks up at it also and takes aim at it with an imaginary gun, tracks its path through the stars his elbows resting on the rock and pulls the imaginary trigger: —Boom . . . have to bring me gun up yer sometime I reckon. Some good shootin up yer, boy, aye.

Ianto says nothing. The features of his face are lost in the falling darkness.

—Aw c'mon mun, cheer up eh? Fuck em all off, mun, eyr nothing but wankers. Utter fuckin wankers. Tell yew what we'll do: get some of-a boys from Meibion up yer to torch-a fuckin place, how does that sound en? Sound good?

A shake of the head from Ianto. —Sounds fuckin stupid. Place wouldn't even *be* yer then, would it? Never fuckin get it back then. Just a pile of ashes.

—Ah Christ. Llŷr rubs his face in both hands. —I was only fuckin messin anyway. An besides, a Meibion boys don't do that any more. Eyv given it up.

He reaches out to where he estimates Ianto's head to be in the thick night and ruffles his hair and then surreptitiously wipes the palm of his hand on the leg of his jeans.

—What're we going to do with yew, Ianto, eh? What ARE we going to do with yew?

He lights two cigarettes and passes one to Ianto. Smoking in the windy darkness, silent, two red eyes lifting and falling. Glow-worms courting. They finish their cigarettes and stub them out on the rock and flick the dead bent butts away.

—Where now then? Pub is it? Ianto nods and they head carefully off down the dark dingle.

And two nights later and Ianto is back. Hungover head-achey after forty-eight hours' no-sleep drinking amphetamine-dabbing in pubs and bedsits and squats and pubs again, Ianto is back standing at the fence in the furthest reaches of the rhomboid of yellow light thrown out by the kitchen window, through which he can see two men and two women sitting around a big circular table, their heads thrown back laughing. One of them is the man with the beard and the long socks; Ianto remembers his fat and white and puzzled knees bared beneath sock-top and shorts' hem. The high moon pours cold down on Ianto's head, the insides of his ears wind-stung and wind-waters spilling from his eyes and rolling down his icy cheeks and he knows how it would be inside that kitchen, how warm and how safe, the log fire in the grate and the expensive whisky they're sharing and how it would be with him were he in there with the immense world-cupping knowledge comfort of living on and in his ancestral land his feet on the same soil his far forefathers dug in for their sustenance and ploughed and harrowed by hand, further back even to when barelegged ragged men with Ianto's same blue eyes laid traps on rain-strafed mountain tops for boar and for beaver, fought bears and wolves and shaggy-tank aurochs with tree-spear and stone-axe, built stone houses beneath snowlines and waterfalls and were the only knowers of this mad land. Which they can't feel, these new owners, ignorant of the particular preterite here, its knowledge and possible belonging, they can't feel that connection in their blood; although, which burns in Ianto more, they behind the double-glazing in the fire's glow and the whisky and their arm-touchy gestures and their head-back laughter don't seem at all perturbed or attenuated or even at all bothered by this lack. We want for nothing, this tableau behind glass and safe from wind and rain says; everything we could ever need is right here with us. We want for nothing. We have it all.

Ianto stands and stares. Fresh indulgence-pimples on his cheeks throb in the cold night wind and harden into callosites. Weak rain frost-dots his brow. There is a stone in his right hand, petrified apple, which he raises over his shoulder as if to hurl, then lowers then raises again then lowers again. As if in rehearsal. His top teeth gnaw his lower lip. He imagines raising a high-powered rifle, Llŷr's perhaps, and sighting along it into the kitchen; boom, and the top of the bearded man's head explodes against the wall in a burst of black-streaked red. The man, skull crunched away like a soft-boiled egg topples slowly sideways still smiling in that dimly lit way he was a moment before as he listened to the blonde woman's blatherings opposite him, who now gets the second round through her right cheek and out her left, her face following the bullet's trajectory through itself in a nano-second, her nose and chin rushing through the hole in her cheek and exiting the other cheek in a small sideways geyser of bursting blood and splintered bone. The other two, the man and the woman, are standing up now staring horrified at the holed window and Ianto can toy with these; he sights on the man's ample paunch, worn like a well-stuffed wallet, and fires, turns his torso from crotch to navel into one smoking hole; the man is thrown back into the roaring fire, where he instantly whumfs into flames, his hands reaching out of the blaze, his bones delineated black as if in the death-ray of a Martian. The last one, the other woman, is now standing and screaming and Ianto can hear her high-pitched alarm through the neat round holes in the double-glazing, can see her clutching her face, her mouth an anguished oval into which he aims and fires and she is yanked back against the Aga like a puppet, limbs flailing, reaching behind her with her well-manicured hands, groping at the severed ends of her spine extruding through the shredded flesh of her nape, once sunbed-tanned now torn and scorched with cordite. Ianto pumps bullets into her chest, three before she falls, her breasts exploding through her print dress, then he takes over the house and buries the bodies in the garden to fertilise the carrots and cabbage and beans he plants and repairs the window and mops the kitchen free of blood and lives very very happily ever after.

Stone raised, stone lowered. Teeth gnawing the lip. One of the men is pouring whisky into the four glasses; one of the women covers her glass with the flat of her palm and the man lifts her hand away grinning and holds it there while he fills her glass with whisky, or brandy it could be or cognac, something anyway amber in the firelight and warm and smooth and soothing. Ianto takes out a crossbow and fits a bolt into it; ah, but this is a special *explosive* bolt and he fires it through the glass and into the whisky man's chest, where he has time to stare down at it in shock protruding from his sternum for a

23

few seconds before it explodes and in an eyeblink the room is red, all over the window, dripping from the lightshade and the long hair of the women. The other man leaps upright and grabs the women protectively in his arms and then there is a bolt in the back of his skull and then his head is gone, the stump of his gold-chained neck spurting blood into the faces and open screaming mouths of the women, who both get it in quick succession, one in the belly and one in the face, the first standing with her arms outspread staring down at the place where her midriff used to be, now a smoking cave, intestines slobbering to the polished slate floor in steaming blue loops.

Stone raised, stone lowered. The wind whistling around Ianto's head. One of the men is acting out a story now, or part of a story, walking exaggeratedly across the kitchen floor, arms pumping and goose-stepping. The others watch him and grin, waiting for the punchline, and all they know about the Molotov cocktail tossed through the tall picture window is that they are suddenly aflame, running madly and ricocheting off each other and the walls and slipping in the viscous pools of melted flesh and fat, which is running off their frantic burning bodies on to the slate floor, grabbing at each other in terror and panic and dripping fiery gobbets of muscle and fat in their clutching hands. One of the women grabs at the hand of one of the men and the skin of his whole arm sloughs off in her fingers like a long lace glove. Eyes melting. Faces running down chests, red skulls screaming, still alive in unimaginable pain.

Stone raised, stone lowered. Ianto's breath is heavy in his chest. And all four faces are at the window now, pressed against the glass staring out at him and palm-framed to reduce the reflection. Ianto yelps and drops the stone and runs, kicking up water in the ruts of the dirt track, which takes him over a gate in one bound and along a pass between the humps of two low hills behind the house, his house, a voice following him borne along on the increasing wind:

—Who's there? Who's that? Show yourself!

And then the barking of a large dog and Ianto runs faster, whimpering chest, bursting legs pistoning, a dribble of piddle running hot down his left thigh. Through mud and tangled

24

bracken he flees bats whizzing past his ears insects pinging off his inflated cheeks and he falls headlong over some log rotting beneath the knotted grass, his hands sinking in softness and his face stung in sneezewort and tormentil. He knows where he is, where he has fled to; the bog, the peat bog, in which he as a child would get mud-caked and sodden and play with toads and newts and lizards and even on occasion snakes. Confidant to the reptile he was, familiar of warts and forked-tongue-flicker, known to the slitherer and the slider and the lurker in quags. Still is: that property will never leave him, not until death itself swamps him and muds him and turns him slow to slime and slop, which is when such strange relations will be reinforced and nothing other or less.

He lies supine in the bog, panting, listening through the wind for any sounds of pursuit, of which there seem to be none. An owl screeches somewhere and he covers his mouth with a trembling hand to dampen and possibly still the heft of his breath. Listening carefully, senses finely attuned to any sound foreign or discrepant or any heavy ground pressure which may rock the bog beneath his back. There is nothing, nothing but the wind and the hiss and trickle of the mire beneath him, yet he continues to lie there anyway like some giant salamander, swamp-soft and bog-safe, his rushed breathing slowing. Smelling the methane leak and escape around and under him, seeing the stars blink weakly high above. Shooting stars and orbiting satellites. God how the night sky sometimes slides. Feeling the light rain on his skin cool his heated cheeks and dilute the acid in his guts.

Ianto lying on his back in the bog. Snake-silent and lizard-still. And the moon has moved some distance across the soot sky before he hauls himself upright again, the back of him saturated and smelly and tentacled with hanging and dripping stems and stalks and leaves. Chickweed has bound itself around his legs and toadflax has infiltrated the laces of his trainers as if seeking a mate. He pulls a crumpled blue flower of bugloss from his drenched head and lets it fall back down to the mock ground. He has slept here in this swamp a moment's exhausted slumber, more of a passing out, and could not in truth have remained awake had he even wanted to and rain falls heavier now on his already wet head. He stretches, joints cracking, and pulls himself over towards the higher and drier ground, stalking and scrambling and sodden silent among rocks ridged and never shaped separate to how they are now before rain and before wind when there was only rain and wind and nothing else or more. Standing unsteadily upright, the peat bog stretches below him struck silver in parts by the moon and blue and grey, all the pale shades of failure and of blame. He looks down on this for a moment, then like a creature bog-born and engendered by mud and moisture, conceived of filth and fly, he drags himself over to where the ground solidifies and rises up again, shallow valley baby-glacier carved when the moon was other and the night sky was else, when house-high horned beasts were sucked lowing into this slurping swamp and rock rang to their bellows.

A soft rain on his face, hair lifted in the wind. Here where he is no outcast, here where he is not vagrant. In this place between water and earth he coughs and mutters as if in response to some fancied inquisitor:

—Fuckin *belong* yer I do . . . my fuckin land . . . *my* fuckin land . . .

He pulls himself up to his full height and stands in the pale rain and looks. His sparrow chest out-thrust. This land has always been his and always he its; take one from the other and it will wither. Before Ianto was this land was, forming and flowing and forever awaiting its wearer. And almost as proof, jack-o'-lantern shows himself in the middle of the mire, rises slowly from the sizzling marsh, some messenger of methane made from the rancid aftermath of some battle long forgotten, some steel-hewn bone leaching its mulch, the compost of long-rotten warriors. This bog a wet necropolis for man and for beast. The heat of corruption and that of the earth's innards themselves the searing scorched genesis of this delicate and fragile pale flame, which as Ianto watches sputters and worms itself into some soft substance, some vague shape, gossamer-ghost drifting through the veil of rain, reaching tendrils towards Ianto like serpents of smoke offering greeting or yearning in anguished loss. Silent writhing above the clinging earth, above the standing stagnant pools mantled brown and brackish, soft-snaking around

26

stalks and low vines and clumps of flowers turned colourless by night. *Ignis fatuus*, floating phantom lantern guiding Ianto up on to the drier land he mounts as if triumphant, arms spread in the drizzle. Lilac pilot gently popping against the drier rise, exhausting its fuel and folding in on itself with a barely heard hiss and sizzle, little blue light gone. Odd spectre gone, strange shape of nothing gone.

Ianto stares out at the darkness and the scribbles of rain and grins. Marvel at what dreams may rise from blight and canker. From putrefaction, from decay. His perpetual grin in the always rain which is mirrored in the moon, cratered and cracked and battered but never to be reached.

IANTO IS SEVEN.

On his child knees on the moorland, witness his spittled mirth as the living lace threads his unwrinkled muckied fingers; just one muscle, the viper coils his young hand, squeezes his forearm tighter than any protector, tickles his soft and sunburned skin with the trailing tip of its tail. Ianto grins to see its tongue flicker, to feel the warm-giving smoothness of its crawling bellyscales. Should he know the cargo this creature carries, the pulsing sac of poison, he would do no other; he loves the black diamonds, the content and curious blackberry eyes in the grey and glabrous head. Any toxin here seems neutralised in the serum of his delight, his trust, the ease of his movements, the softness of his touch. One chubby fingertip strokes the serpent's head; briefly the peppercorn eyes close, as if in feline pleasure. Raggedy small boy down among the heather and the foxgloves, enraptured of snakes. See his blue eyes glaze.

And young Ianto it is who would tumble with the cubs of badger and fox, who would with the polecat low-slink deadly silent into the rabbit's den. Who would dart with the hare across the snowy heads of hills. He who would loll in the sundew's sweet quicksand, who would find on the merlin's plucking block the treasured severed wings of bird and moth, one precious-speckled the other blood-nibbed. Ianto it is who would soar wing-to-spread-fingered-wing with raptor, with passerine, low over the forest canopy, over the bog and over the sands, high over the surging mountain, meteor-quick over dingle and sea. It is he who would flick and shimmer with the bomb-round trout under the old stone bridge. Of mountains, mud and mire is this young Ianto made. Fern-fronds his hair, stream-spume his drool. Night-time anthracite the pupils of his eyes. Snake-twined and standing to inherit this splitting earth.

—HE COULD, ERM, actually talk tho, couldn't he?

—What? Of course he could fuckin talk.

—No, I mean, he wasn't slightly dumb, or mute or whatever it's called, was he? I mean . . .

—'Slightly dumb?' What the fuck're yew wittering on about now, mun? '*Slightly* dumb?' Duw, yewer either dumb or yewer not, yer's no in between. No 'slightly' about it. That's like being 'slightly' dead; yew can't be. Yewer either one or the other. Fuck's sakes . . . av yew yerd this twat?

—Never heard stupider.

—Daft arse.

—No, I mean it's just that I hardly ever heard him say anything. Yew could sit in a pub for hours with him and yew'd be lucky if he said ten words. Never said fuck all. He'd laugh, like, and make other noises, but words . . . just didn't seem to be part of the fucker.

—That's cos he was fuckin thick.

—Well, that depends on how yew wanner define 'thick'. Personally, I don't know whether he was, in the normal sense of-a word like. I'd say he was more of a . . . dunno. Fuckin enigma. Mystery, like.

—Watch what yewer sayin now. Yewer on dangerous fuckin ground yer, Danny boy.

—Well I'm not fuckin *praising* the cunt or anything, I'm just tryin to work im out, y'know, see what drove him an stuff. I'm not fuckin *praising* Ianto, mun. I'm just sayin that, y'know, that the word 'thick' doesn't really do him justice. D'yew know what I mean? It seems to somehow, a dunno, sum im up the wrong way like.

—What word would yew use then?

—'Different.' That's what I'd say, that he was 'different'. Still fucked up like, oh yeh, still sick, an a fuckin pervert, but I'd still say 'different' rather than 'thick'. Cos that's not what

29

Ianto was. 'Thick''s what yew'd use to describe someone like PhuhphuhPhil, or Ikey or someone.

—I'm tellin im yew said that.

—Boy's in Swansea jail. I think I'm safe.

—Ikey – a thick cunt. Wait'll I fuckin tell im, mun.

—Yew could never tell what was goin on in Ianto's head is what I'm tryin-a say. A closed book, he was. An enigma, like. A puzzle. Which is why it was such a fuckin shock in-a end like . . . I mean, be honest now; did any of yew ever think Ianto would do something like that? Ey? Did yew?

—Didn't fuckin surprise me, mun, to tell yew-a trewth. I always said he wasn't right, that fucker. Always said yer was something wrong in is head. Like that fuckin song he used to sing all-a fuckin time . . .

—Which one?

—The one about the Eskimo girl?

—No, not that one. A one about eating the worms.

—Oh aye.

—Yeh, eating-a worms an everyone hating him? That one?

—Yeh.

—Oh bollax, mun, yer was fuck all wrong with that! A kiddie's song, like, that's all that was! We used to sing it at the school! Just a little song, like. Funny as well. Used-a make me laugh. That's all that was, mun, a fuckin children's song. Nowt sinister.

—Yeh. I used to sing that meself. Just a little song, that's all.

—About how he was going to go an suck the juices out of worms cos nobody liked him? Doesn't sound particularly fuckin funny to me, mun. Sounds fuckin crazed that does, aye.

—Aw fuck sakes, Marc. Sense-a fuckin humour? Heard of it? Yewer just thinkin that because Ianto did what he did, then yew can see wrongness in fuckin *everything* he did before that. Which is shite. I mean, if yew yerd *me* singin that song, or Llŷr, or Griff like, yew wouldn't think twice, would yer? Just a funny little song, yew'd think, just a funny, strange little kid's song. That's all. And I, personally like, reckon that Ianto never really grew up. That was his problem like. Most of him stayed being a kiddie, which is what him singin that song shows, that part of

30

him stayed always in his childhood. He used to sing that worm song all-a time up at the school like. It was as if he couldn't really grow up, or didn't want to, like. Refused to become an adult. He wanted to stay a kid for ever.

—Aye, an yer's a word for that.

—Which is?

—'Off his fuckin head.' It's madness. Fuckin madness. Not right in-a fuckin head that like, remainin a kiddie all yewer fuckin life. Pure fuckin insanity like.

—Aw Jesus Christ.

—No, it's fuckin true. None of us want-a grow up, do we? We'd all of us like to stay young with ar mams, no bills, no jobs, no fuckin courts, no fuckin responsibilities. Be just fuckin dandy, that would. He –

—Aye but that's the fuckin point, Marc, see? Ianto, he didn't have any of those things when he was a nipper. Didn't have a mam or a dad. He was working out in-a fuckin fields when he was about six or seven, younger even, picking the turnips an the spuds. His childhood wasn't-a same as yours, growin up in a nice big house in Newquay. *Your* dad was a doctor. Ianto's was, what was he, a fuckin *ghost*.

—Piffle. Absolute fuckin piffle. Yewer all just making excuses, that's what yewer doing. Making excuses for *that* sick bastard.

—Christ. He was a friend, remember?

—Not any more.

—No, of course not any more, how can he be? He's fuckin dead. But he was a mate before he, y'know, before we found out what he was really like. What he'd done. An yew should never forget that.

—D'yew want-a know what I reckon? I reckon Marc's just jealous cos of Ianto's relationship with Gwenno. Yew can see it in his eyes mun.

—Don't talk shite, Llŷr. I, I never fancied Gwenno.

—Bollax! Yew shagged her! That night up at Llŷr's!

—Yeh, but I was never fuckin in love with her like. Not like fuckin Ianto was.

—Yes yew fuckin well were. Yew were obsessed with her, mun. We all remember it. Yew wouldn't leave her alone.

31

—'Wouldn't leave her alone?' Fuck off, mun. Never got a chance to talk to her cos Ianto was always yer first, sniffin around.

—See!

—Gwenno was the only one he'd ever talk to, really, wasn't she? Remember like?

—Aye, which was a shame, cos she couldn't stand the fucker.

—Again! See? Jealous!

—Nah, I don't think it was like that. It was Roger she couldn't stand. Ianto she didn't mind. Said Roger gave her the creeps.

—Gave everyone the creeps, him.

—Too much death, mun, too much death. Been to too many fuckin funerals for a feller my age I yav.

—I think Gwenno just found Ianto a bit, well, odd. Y'know. Peculiar, like, that's the word she used, peculiar. She spoke about it once when we were both out pickin mushies together like. Just me and her.

—When did yew –

—Aw man! The green-eyed fuckin monster yer!

—Altho she did say as well like that she saw a certain kind of gentleness in him.

—Who? Roger?

—No, Ianto. I remember her saying those exact words. When we were lyin on ar backs in the heather after we'd just made love.

—Ha! Look at-a fuckin face on Marc!

—Don't cry, mun!

—I'm only messin, Marc. Never touched Gwenno. Not after yew'd been there, ug.

—Knob off.

—Never saw Ianto in one of his fits, tho, did she? When he'd go mad like . . . rage. Like the time after that rave in that fuckin commune thing. That house.

—Aw yeh. Pure fuckin nuts he went, dinny.

—Mental.

—But it was like, y'know, he liked animals an stuff, couldn't stand to see one of em harmed. Strange. Like most psychos, most

32

murderers like serve their like apprenticeship killin animals, but Ianto . . . I dunno. Odd.

—Yeh. There was one time when me an him were out with me gun, and –

—Christ, Llŷr, yew an that fuckin gun. In love with that bastard thing, yew are. Yew'll be marrying that fuckin gun next, yew will.

—Stickin yewer dick down-a barrel.

—Fuckin valuable weapon, that. Took it to a dealer I did.

—I think that's why it was such a shock to find out that he did what he did. To me, anyway. Cos yer was a gentle side to im like. Ripped-a fuckin guts out of me it did, I must say.

—Gobsmacked.

—To say the fuckin least.

—Would never have imagined it in a million years, me.

—*I* fuckin would've. Never fooled me, that fucker didn't. No way mun. Knew it all afuckinlong, I did.

—Well why didn't yew do something about it then, Griff? Why didn't yew stop him before it was too late? Ey? Why-a fuck didn't yew do that?

—Cos it wasn't my job. That's not me. Haven't even got enough time to do what I *should* be doing, let alone stop some other cunt from causing chaos. That's not my fuckin look out, mun. No fuckin way.

—Jesus.

—Fair enough, I reckon. Fair e-fuckin-nuff.

33

RIFLE HELD IN the crook of his overcoated arm Llŷr leads Ianto into shelter away from the relentless sizzling drizzle, up against a huge fin of grey rock which erupts from the hilltop like the back of a giant shark, sudden and full of threat. Delicately they walk, soft steps and whispering, as if this huge granite sail is some slumbering beast they are at pains not to arouse. They find a small stone shelf jutting at head-height and hunker under it, looking out at the never-ending rain through drenched ropes of lank hair hanging in their eyes. The hem of Llŷr's overcoat has been trailing across the moor for two miles or more and now sports a frill of crushed flowers and thorns and burrs and dead insects and the small soft eggs of shit, sheep and rabbit. Ianto steps out into the rain to look back and up at the citadel of sharpened stone that is affording them harbour; vast clam shell, its edge serrates the silvery winter sun, whose weak light drifts milky and murky on to the sodden planet beneath. Ianto looks and sees it, the small rain on his face, then steps back into shelter again alongside Llŷr.

—Pig of a fuckin day, Ianto, eh?

—Yeh.

—Hate this fuckin weather I do. Rain rain fuckin rain. No bastard let up aye. Have to start gathering wood to build us a bleedin ark, won't we?

—Yeh.

Llŷr leans and spits. —Two by two, that'll be us. Do it different this time, tho, cleanse-a fuckin planet like, leave some of the fuckers out yer to drown. Cats, can't stand those selfish fuckers. Rats as well. Squirrels, just fuckin vermin ey are, mun, cute be buggered. Eyr rodents, just fuckin rats with fluffy tails, that's all. An foxes; snidy cunts. Sly, like. Leave them out as well, aye; let-a bastards drown, that's what I say. No, on second thoughts bring em aboard, bring em all aboard; give me some decent fuckin target practice aye,

34

somethin to do when I'm bored like. Pick em off one by one.

He tucks the rifle tight between his elbow and ribs and rubs his palms together, chattering his teeth.

—Fuckin freezing. Giz a swig of that whisky, Iant.

Ianto takes a half-drunk bottle of Bell's from the inner pocket of his dirty anorak and they both take two deep swallows each, hissing through bared teeth as the liquid burns their throats, then Ianto puts the bottle away again. Llŷr squirts thin saliva through a gap in his front teeth and it streaks a lichened rock at his booted feet.

—I'll tell yew what I'd like to see now, Ianto; fuckin English army on manoeuvres. We could hide behind a rock and ambush-a cunts, give em a *real* taste of battle, eh? Good practice for them it would be. Or, no, what'd be better, the fuckin English rugby team out on a trainin jog like, yeh, I'd take fuckin Carling's knees off one at a time I would. Laugh at the cunt floppin about in a mud. Be fuckin great that would aye. Just gradually pick away at him till he's nothing but a trunk. Stand im upright, take a good run up, convert the twat over Cader Idris.

Ianto laughs, his top teeth protruding over his lower lip and his eyes disappearing in crinkles. He almost *yuks* when he laughs like a hillbilly caricature, his epiglottis jumping and spittle shining on his chin, veneering the pimples. It pleases Llŷr, to see Ianto laughing.

—Good lad, Ianto.

They drink from the whisky bottle again and stand in silence for some time, then Llŷr points at a bird hovering at house-height before and above them in the ever-falling grey rain. Long-tailed and still, vibration in the wing-tips almost too swift for human perception.

Llŷr points. —See him, Ianto? The kestrel? See him hovering?

Pure hawk, pure skyborne being, the completeness of its aloft existence matched only in the world over by the focus of its hunt, the concentration of its search in the sliding drizzle knitted when scaled it leapt from branch to branch and ran bipedal over a volcanic beach to bird and bird only, raptor

35

entire. Nothing of anything other than pure hawk in its still high scour, its frozen flight. Hanging so still above the damp landscape as if on wires heaven-rooted, it is paradigm of hunt and harry, paragon of patience and plummet and rend and survive.

—Daft little fucker, aye. Should know yer's better predators than im round yer, shouldn't he?

Llŷr raises the rifle to his shoulder and sights along the oily barrel blue-shiney in the wet. Eyes wide Ianto watches him and watches the kestrel, eyes darting one to one. Llŷr's cheek squashed up against the wooden stock. He pulls the trigger the report swallowed by rock and by rain and sodden air, sharp stink of cordite in Ianto's face and instantly the bird is falling broken all-shapes leaving a hole in the sky which seems to Ianto to scream.

—*Got* the fucker! Fuckin marksman me, Ianto, aye! If I haven't taken-a bastard's head clean off I'll be disappointed in meself cos that's what I was aiming for. C'mon, Iant.

They squelch over the waterlogged moorland to where the kestrel is curled crippled against a rock dotted with dark coins of its blood beginning to run in the rain. It lies on its back with one shattered wing held skywards and feet clenched like two scaly spiders faking death. Breast feathers eddying around a crude hole, curls of down whirling like motes above the charring and the spillage, chest heaving, red-rimmed beak ajar to reveal the grey tongue and the dark eyes open and alive in the steely sculptured head now rapidly losing its gloss, its lustre once unique now becoming common and ever-seen. Carrion already this bird is, looking up, tearing bill widening with each tortured breath, dying.

Llŷr prods it hard with the barrel of his gun and the clawed feet open and then close again.

—No more hunting for you, mun, eh? Let's see you hover *now*, yew clever little bastard.

—It's still alive, Ianto says. Voice croaky with disuse. —It must be in pain. Yew've got to kill it now, yew have.

—What, an get me bastard hands torn open? Fucks. Still give yew a nasty rip, this little fucker would. Beak on it, mun. *I'm* not ringing-a fucker's neck. Yew do it, mun, yew want it dead. I'm not fucking going to.

—Give me the gun.

—Yew *are* joking, Ianto, I hope. Ammo costs money, y'know. Give me a bullet and I'll give yew the rifle. He'll be dead in a minute anyway, Duw, what's-a fuckin rush?

Russet breast now porridged in drizzle and in blood. All bird life in an instant smashed against this small rock on this ever-wet wailing waun, going away, the gimlet lasers of its eyes fading like the light of a setting sun seen through the stained glass of an abandoned church now flocked only by ruin. World robbed of bird in one twitch of the finger.

Ianto says the only thing he can: —Yew fucking bastard, yew are. Yew are, yewer a fucking bastard.

Llŷr looks at him, surprised. —What, me? What the fuck's up with yew?

—Yew fucking bastard.

—Aw, Ianto, man, it's just a kestrel. Yer's thousands of em round yer. Don't be like that, what the fuck's up? Not as if it's a *rare* bird or anything, it's just a fucking kestrel. An anyway, what about all-a little mice an voles it was going to eat, eh? What about them then? It's dog eat fuckin dog in this world, mun, yew know that. Survival of-a fittest like, that's what it's all about. An what's stronger than a man with a gun, eh? Tell me that now. Duw, I can –

Ianto turns his back and walks away, head down through the rain. Llŷr calls after him a few times then shrugs and spits and he too walks away, gun-tucked, in the opposite direction. The fallen falcon dies and within an hour is gone, scavenged, dragged in some jaw to some dark and secret burrow and plucked and torn and devoured. And as he has done for years Ianto just walks away into the place where the ground swells and swells and never ceases swelling, where the flagstone-heavy sky sags and trees cannot grow and lightning flash-totems the mountain tops, stilting from peak to peak high-stepping and bone-white. And in the evening of that day Ianto stands tiny above a deep valley, the silent watcher on high and how really does he differ from bird, from bush?, thin silver ribbons of river and road far

37

below between the whitewashed nubs of scattered houses and he watches shadowbreak like a tide of ink rush down the valley seawards, pushing the light, bright light running, valley swells illuminated momentarily then dark green on green in bands of now golden now dying light. Buzzards soar below him on spread wings, swoop low through heather and then rise again under a dark sky holding an ocean over these mountains, the big birds swinging towards the valley's end and wheeling beak-to-heel through a rainbow's wild fires.

The rain falls again. Ianto walks. That's all he does.

That night he dosses drenched and bedraggled on a weed bed in an abandoned hovel semi-roofed in a clutch of old pine, makeshift dwelling kinned with that one in which he was conceived nearly thirty years ago. Raftered half-roof and three tumbling stone walls in which his unlucky conception was made, small stone shack shocked by thunder and lightning rapid lethal and eye-searing. Old home in which he sleeps and like that in which his life first ignited, now abode to weed and spider, vole and bat. Ianto's unfortunate genesis. Ianto the unwelcome get of some huddled coupling, quick and mistimed. Idiopathic Ianto defined by no date or place of birth nor lineage nor pedigree only this poor place rain-battered and holed by hail.

He squats against the sturdiest wall and drinks what remains of the Bell's while the rain clatters around him and he sleeps foetally on plants with whiteness drifting through his lying head. From navel to outcrop was Ianto's connection made and sustained unbreakable, unbroken. Twig-ribbed he will stride heart booming through valleys where grass sprouts under his enduring mirth. He walks these mountains in the lightless hours with the confidence of one who could recount if he cared to that these vast black star-gulping shapes belong to him and him alone, and nothing he cares for he is not grudged walking untouched across these crests where the rain will drill the rock and the thunder will pluck pines like daisies and dam the rivers with rootballs the size and shape of sheds.

Spider legs awaken him, meek tickle on his cheek. He brushes at his face and sits and stretches joints cracking like snapping wood, a great whoop of air sucked through his yawn. Rubbing the nape of his aching neck, knuckling mucus crusts from his eyelids. There is an old animal skull gone green in the debris on the floor, cobwebs in its empty eye sockets and cocooning the ribbed curved horns, some strange and splendid feast for a spider with palps of steel. Ianto pushes with his foot it and the detritus around it to one side to bare a small patch of packed earth, black beetles scuttling, and he drops his stiff jeans and squats over this made space and shits. Curious blue fritillary flitters around his head as he strains at stool, alights on his tensed shoulder to spread and dry its delicate wings for a moment then flutters away, out through the ruined northern wall into the morning sunlight. Ianto watches it go then stands and wipes with dock leaves, swearing as nettles puncture his arse crack, then he places the old skull and a chunk of rotten wood over his steaming dark coils, burying his spoor as an animal would, covering his tracks and individual stench as a wild animal would. He steps out into the sunshine with his usual after-sleep melancholia, missing someone he's never met, lonely for what he has never known or could indeed ever know and drops to all fours and rubs his stubbled flaking face in the refreshing cold dew of the grass. There is a taste in his mouth like wet ashes. His belly rumbles and he has not eaten for two days, just drunk at mountain streams jaw-to-jaw with sheep and cattle, and he watches a buzzard atop the hill crest above him swoop and rise and fly off with some small thing clutched in its talons, and his belly rumbles and squirts again and he knows that he is hungry and for a moment knows not where he is and he looks out over the valley scratching his stinging cleft and taking his bearings from the natural landmarks of wood and scree and glittering lake and distant blobs of high-ground cairn, and he thinks for a moment then descends towards the dull grey vermiform road on the valley floor below.

He is at Llŷr's cottage in an hour. Peering through the smeared windows he can see no crashed-out bodies, no embers in the fireplace or smoke from the chimney or any sign of life other than insect among the empty receptacles and dirty dishes and discarded clothes. Cold hearth. Empty house. He steps back and throws clods of earth at the bedroom window, bellows Llŷr's name with that 'll' sound he has never, since he first began to speak, been able to wrap his tongue around:

—Cer-leeeeeeer! Cer-leeeeeeer!

There is no response. He imagines Llŷr mid-binge in a pub or room somewhere or gleefully and without compunction or even stint blasting birds from the sky, carcasses hung by claw from his belt and droplets of blood and ferns of feather seesawing down around his head. Ianto toys with the idea of breaking a window or forcing a door so he can get at comfort and clean water and maybe food, but he decides against it since he more or less lives there too and would be made to pay for the repairs, so he throws one last clod at the pane leaving a greasy smear of soil with a small pink worm wriggling in it half-squashed against the glass and heads off between irregular rows of beech and mountain ash and over the tumulus atop which the megaliths stand steaming in the sun and past the door-sized dark opening of the disused silver mine where, as a child, he knew a dragon slept. He passes the tentacled rootball of the fallen tree beneath which Ikey Pritchard is rumoured to keep his stash and traverses a slow and shallow brackish stream and walks on to tarmac again and follows the road down into the nearest village and the small shop in the small square, two poppy wreaths propped up against the war memorial and the Gogerddan Arms at this hour closed. He goes into the shop and summons the shopkeeper with the door's ting. Fat man white-smocked and guardedly suspicious because he knows Ianto, has had dealings with him on numerous uncomfortable occasions in the recent past.

Ianto nods. —Shwmae.

—How do.

Ianto busily scours the single aisle, doing his daily shopping, that's all he's doing for his necessary purchases. That's all he's about, he's just shopping. Everybody does this: they need certain items to see them comfortably through their days so they go to the shop and they buy those things. These simple rhythms of normality. He puts bread and crisps and cheesy crackers and chocolate up on the counter, then goes over to the refrigerated display and puts a packet of bright orange processed cheese with the other goods, the shopkeeper watching him, watching him.

His hand hovers over the selection of Ginster's pies and pasties and Scotch eggs, then he shakes his head and his hand drops then suddenly raises again and grabs a Curried Chicken Slice and he takes it to the counter and stands there with the food between him and the shopkeeper. He is smiling, Ianto is, but still emanating this air of efficiency, of diurnal chores being carried out with aplomb.

—Will that be all?

Ianto misses the sarcasm in the merchant's voice. —That's it, yeh. Oh wait, no, I'll tell yew what, put a bottle of Bell's with that as well an twenty . . . erm Lambert an Butler I'll have. They're the cheapest, aren't they. Treat meself today, aye.

He smiles at the man, who rings up the charges on his till stern-faced. Turns to Ianto his head inclined now so that he has to look up through his thick eyebrows and the lenses on his spectacles and the deep furrows on his forehead.

—Sixteen pounds ten.

—Diolch.

Ianto begins to pocket the items.

—Going to get paid for them then, am I?

Ianto freezes with the cheese at his chest.

—Erm, my tab like. That's alright, innit? I mean I can fit these on?

The shopkeeper sighs deeply and takes off his glasses and rubs the bridge of his nose between forefinger and thumb. He replaces his spectacles and shakes his head slowly, sadly almost, then takes a battered yellow exercise book from beneath the counter and licks the end of his thumb and flicks through the dog-eared pages until he reaches the relevant entry.

—Here we are. Your friend owes nine ninety-nine. That's for a bottle of vodka he came in for last night, *after*, I say, *after* he'd cleared his outstanding bill. You, though, owe me twenty-seven pounds and sixty pence.

He stares hard at Ianto, who coughs and shuffles his feet on the scuffed lino.

—Am I ever going to see any of this money? When do you intend to clear it? Three months old this account is now, bear in mind.

41

Ianto scratches his head, looks up. —What number did yew say?

—Twenty seven sixty.

—With this stuff yer?

—With that stuff there, yes.

—So, erm, what is it without this? I mean what was it when I came in?

The man folds his arms across his wide chest. —Eleven pounds and fifty pence. Three months old this account is now.

Ianto gives the man his profile. Shows his sharp nose and low brow and prominent epiglottis. Staring at a board layered with pinned packets of peanuts and the one next to it tubed with Pepperami sausages, thinking, cogitating, working things out.

—What day is it today?

—The twenty-third. Although I don't see what that's got to do with anything.

—No, I mean, what day? Of-a week like.

A large theatrical sigh. —It's a Tuesday. Why?

—Well, I'm thinking see, I could come back in this arvo like and pay half the bill. That'd be alright, wunnit? I've got to get into town like, but then I can get the bus back out see and pay half the bill. How much was it again?

—Oh good Lord.

The man begins to separate the goods into two piles. To the left he places cigarettes and whisky and chocolate and crisps and cheese and crackers, leaving on the right the loaf of sliced white and the Curried Chicken Slice.

—There you go.

He indicates the right-sided pile.

—You can take them. That's today's dinner. Give you the fuel to get into town so you can pick up your money and come back out here to pay me your bill. Which is now a round thirteen pounds.

He begins to replace the items on the shelves: transaction over. Ianto pockets the pastie and carries the bread, swinging it by its topknot and turns and heads towards the door but is waylaid by the rack of newspapers and magazines by the ice-cream cabinet, bright and glossy offerings of things he needs which are not and

42

could never be food. His eyes scan the blared black headlines, zigzagging up over the comics and the hiking and hillwalking monthlies and the style magazines and up then vertical to the four-item selection of soft porn. He tucks the bread under his arm and reaches up and takes down *Men's World*, the cover of which shows just his type and there is an instant soft squeeze of his lungs, the heavily made-up eyes and bright auburn hair snub nose and thick lips, three-quarter profile to camera showing the round brown globes of her arse and the studio lights creamy-gleaming on the tensed tanned muscles of her back. NONSTOP SOPPING FANNY FRENZY says the cover and there is a small whimper in Ianto's throat as the smooth pages slide and whisper over his fingers as he searches for the covergirl's set.

—Going to buy that, are you? Don't look if you're not buying. This isn't a bloody library.

Getting up to feverish Ianto flicks the pages looking for the auburn hair, his dick beginning to grow in his jeans and his throat dry.

—Oi! What've I just said?

The shopkeeper comes around in front of his counter and strides down the aisle towards Ianto and removes the magazine from his flicking hands and replaces it top shelf.

—That's enough now. You've got your stuff, now go on, clear off. And I want that bill paid in full this afternoon, d'you hear me? Thirteen pounds and I want it before close of business today or it's the law. Not running a bleeding charity.

Ianto turns redfaced and walks out and considers throwing something through the shop window but doesn't, but does store plans to do so late one night in the near future, and walking fast he crosses the road and enters the small park, duck pond and roundabout and single set of goalposts, and he goes into the public lavatories cistern-gurgling and cool and goes into the cubicle locking the door behind him and places his food on the tiled sill of the frosted-glass and cobwebbed insect-husks-hanging window away from the pissy germ-crawled floor and drops his jeans and lifts the lid of the toilet and wanks into the open bowl, ten long tugs is all it takes the groan summoned from deep, deep within him and his semen plops on to the

43

shit-smeared porcelain and into the oval of water reflecting his loosened face and he imagines his sperm balled in tresses of auburn hair quivering and blue-tinged like the clutch of some mythical bird. When he's finished he pulls his mangled foreskin still cicatriced pink back over the head of his dick, the wafting odour reminding him of how long it is since he last bathed and he opens the cubicle door and goes over to the sink to wash his hands, but in the icy water the droplets of sperm on his fingers stick to his skin like scum so he wipes them away with a harsh paper towel which he bundles up and tosses into the urinal and then directs with his piss through the soap-cake slalom and over the fag-end chicane and up against the squat spider-like brass drain cover which it bobs against and bobs against as if seeking escape. ARMITAGE SHANKS, the urinal says, they always say ARMITAGE SHANKS, or less frequently TWYFORDS, which Ianto thinks might also be the name of some moorland somewhere in southern England but he's not entirely sure.

He takes his food out into the park, where he finds a patch of sunlight to sit in on the banks of the small pond. He wolfs the pastie in four huge bites and a third of the loaf dry and claggy and stodgy on his tongue and teeth and the waterfowl gather around him, mallards and moorhens and one lone coot, and he breaks the remaining bread into small lumps and tosses it into the water and watches the birds squabble. There are some ducklings in the feathered fray, fist-sized balls of brown down and whenever one of them succeeds in catching a piece of bread an adult bird hammer-pecks its back and head and tiny vestigial wings until the food is dropped and appropriated. One is grabbed by its reed-thin neck and submerged, held under by the black beak of a female adult and it does not rise again.

Ianto stands and wipes his hands on his filthy jeans and leaves the park and follows the road until he reaches a sign at a junction telling him that Aberystwyth can be found nine miles to the left, so he heads off in that direction along the roadside verge thankfully not too muddy in today's sunshine with his head hung down and his thumb out. Moor-walker, beach-creeper, walking at the roadside dirtied and unwashed with his thumb held out to the passing cars. Upland-scrambler, mountain-leaper, treader of

44

heather and stone-strider. Shadowflit half-glimpsed searcher of forest and of cave now walking the roadside thumb stuck out and all the cars ignore him bar one, which beeps yet does not stop and there are grinning faces in the receding back window all signing thumbs-up at him and Ianto wills them to overshoot the next corner and crash through the barrier and out and over the steep valley side, ricocheting through trees and exploding in mid-air. Wills upon them some immense trauma and who can deny that, who can gainsay his need for the same sky to ceiling them as it does him? Neither dark of night nor light of day nor rain nor hail nor sunbeam may stay this wasted walker, whom the cars ignore their chrome and paintwork fiery in the unaccustomed sun. He walks one mile, two before a Little Dragon twelve-seater Town Link Trumpton mini-bus whines to a stop beside him and the doors hiss and swing open.

—Needing a lift?

—Yeh. I can't pay yew, tho, cos I've got no money. Why I'm hitching, like.

—Ah, yew've already paid, mun. Get on.

Nice young smiling driver and Ianto boards gratefully and gazes out the window of the otherwise empty bus. A brood of old women get on at Capel Bangor and converse in the local language, of which Ianto understands no more than a handful of words. The journey to Aberystwyth is quick and uneventful and Ianto thanks the driver and means it as he alights. He can smell the sea here, taste its salt on his lips.

—Dim probs, mun. The driver scratches his blond beard. —Hate to see a boy walking, I do. Used to do it meself, aye. I know what it's like when no bugger wants to stop for yew.

Ianto smiles and thanks him again and waits for a gap in the traffic and darts over the road to the Job Centre. It is hot inside and there is a queue. The person directly in front of Ianto turns nose-wrinkled to scowl his way, probably at the smell of him, and Ianto just returns his stare and the man turns away again. Middle-aged waiter jowly and becoming fat now with the cessation of his work. Holding in his hands now a thin blue booklet where once he held what, some tool perhaps, some lever. Ianto glares at the angry red boil on the back of the man's

45

neck, some small grey hairs sprouting through the inflamed skin, and wills it to burst but it doesn't. The man is called to one of the desks and Ianto stands aimless, biting at his thumbnail.

—Who's next, please.

Shite. Ianto wanted the pleasant and lenient young man with the flat-top and the glasses but instead he's got the black-bobbed battleaxe. Officialdom, how it unsettles him; the irrefragable opprobrium, the irrepressible disapproval.

—Can I help you?

Ianto approaches the desk.

—Just signing are we?

He can see the bridge of her nose crinkle as his stink reaches her and can almost hear her thinking: Good Christ, he reeks. He does.

—Yeh.

—Do you have your ES40? Your signing-on book?

—Erm, no, I don't, I'm sorry. I've forgotten it. Left it in the house I yav.

She pulls a face. —What's your name then?

He tells her.

—National Insurance Number?

—Haven't got a clue. Begins with NM tho, I think. Yeh.

—Address?

—No fixed abode.

She taps a few buttons on the computer keyboard and retrieves information.

—Erm . . . you're of no fixed address.

—That's right, yeh.

—Then what do you mean you left your ES40 at home?

—At a mate's house, I mean, I left it yer. Staying at a friend's house see, but I didn't sleep yer last night like an when I went round this morning he wasn't in. So I couldn't get my card, see.

—Does he not give you a house key then?

Ianto shakes his head.

—Perhaps he should.

—Well, yeh, but he hasn't.

—Maybe you should ask him for one then. Might be a good idea.

46

She studies the computer screen. —How's the job search going? Anything we can help you with?

Ianto's lips hang open as he thinks, the tip of his tongue making some small tapping sounds on the backs of his bottom teeth.

—What kind of work do you usually do?

Tap tap.

—I see here that you last worked two years ago. Erm, potato picking was it? That was for two months on a Mr Evans's farm in Llangurig.

—Yeh, in-a fields I was like. It was just with-a seasons, see. He only needed me for . . . erm . . .

—Seasonal employment, yes.

—An I saw im last week like an he said that he might need me again this yur. Maybe. The crop last yur was bad cos of-a weather an-a blight like so he dint get much out of-a ground, but cos of-a mild weather this yur yer's no blight.

—So he may need you to work for him again, then?

—Yeh.

—Well, fingers crossed.

She fetches Ianto's file and pushes it across the desk to him and he takes up the pen and makes his mark on the relevant line, which is all he can do.

—Come back any time after three and we'll have your cheque for you.

Ianto glances up at the clock: just past one.

—Ta.

He leaves and walks the busy dinnertime streets of the small town stopping to talk to one of the *Big Issue* vendors he is acquainted with and past the pubs, many of them now closed for refurbishment in anticipation of the student custom at the end of the summer. Rubble-filled skips outside and Radio 1 in the dark and dusty interiors. Smell of meat and onions from the kebab shops and vinegar from the chippers setting his belly arumble again, strong and unusual spring sun and exhaust fumes baking him in his unwashed clothes stiff and sour and the caked muck begins to liquefy and pool in his insteps and armpits and perineum and run down his back and itch on his head and

47

he scratches at his scalp then studies his fingernails now rimed with a scurf of yellowish scales. On to the promenade, where the sea glitters like an open drawer of polished cutlery and where student stragglers delaying their trips homeward mill and eat ice-creams and talk too loudly and hold discussions above their rucksacks clustered on the flagstones between them. The sun comes back in a large silver star off the window of the funicular house atop Constitution Hill. Ianto cadges a cigarette off a workman relaying the flagstones anterior to the bandstand then walks out on to the jetty to smoke it, watching two girls in shorts and T-shirts too young to be students maybe fifteen, sixteen, playing in the breaking waves, their school uniforms in twin humps on the shingle. They come out of the water thin material clinging sweeping their wet hair back over their heads and they catch Ianto staring and one of them sticks a pink tongue out at him and the other holds out the middle finger of her right hand erect. Ianto grins and wants to say something to them, anything, some small contact but can think of nothing so he takes a last drag on the cigarette, which now smoulders on to the filter, and flicks the end out on to the sea. The coal detaches from the filter in mid-flight, spins away at a right angle like a rocket splitting pod from thruster once out of the stratosphere and trails smoke to the water, where it dies with one little hiss. The filter bobs on the waves, poor lure. The girls have gone, probably under the boards of the jetty to dry off and dress away from leering faces and Ianto imagines it under there dark and cool with the thick salty stench of rotting seaweed and the feel of their sea-slick calves cupped in his palms and his own smell rises to offend his nostrils and he walks the long walk hands-in-pockets to Tan-y-Bwlch, the south beach, across the jagged volcanic landscape until all town sounds have died away and there are no signs of human commerce except for a clear plastic barrel wedged between rocks. He strips to his scrawny white nakedness, a greasy black band belting his waist and he soaks all his clothes bar trainers in the sea then lays them flat across a large flat rock to steam and dry in the sun. Then he wades out stiff-nipple deep into the cold ocean and rubs all his body vigorously with his hands under the water

48

until he is marooned shivering in a small slick, rug-sized patch of sea befilthed and moted with skinflakes and twists of hair. He takes a deep whooshing breath and ducks his head under, roughly massages his scalp and wiggles his index fingers in his ears then surfaces again a bloom of silver spray from his upturned lips like a strange and small cetacean, sea-mammal pale and emaciate. He thinks of the splashing schoolgirls, their gleaming skin, and he reaches down under the water to manipulate his penis, but the salt stings the old wounds even now the old injury stings with the salt water so he leaves the sea and walks ashore, skinny and adrip and scab-kneed and boil-backed, no one's notion of a being from the water and he lies spreadeagled under the sun, which is now obscured with cloud, and he begins to tremble but he stays like that until the sun has reappeared and his skin has dried and tightened and his clothes have too, more or less, and he can climb back into them which he does. He knows that in a few hours' time his garments will be fluffed white and stiff with salt and his hair will be bristled like a yardbrush and his skin will crack and flake, but for now he feels cleansed and hugely refreshed, the stink sloughed off him in slabs and that will suffice, for a short while he has a new-feeling body to live in and that will surely do. He stands at the shoreline and watches the seagulls for a moment, hears their plaintive cries, sees a cormorant plunge from a protruding rock and rise to gulp head heavenward a glittering fish which he can't quite make out at this distance but just knows will be violin-shaped. He raises his hand and waves to the far black feeding bird as he would at a multitude cheering for him alone. Chanting his name. A white butterfly dances across the breaking waves then rests spread-winged on a dry rock. At his feet a lone bee rises from a pink cluster of thrifts buzzing and ungainly in its pollen jodhpurs, flying upright like a faery, like an angel. He watches it go.

He leaves the beach. Back into the town-sounds again and into the grounds of the ruined castle where sitting with their backs to the ancient battlements are a couple of people he knows, vaguely; Scouse Colm and short-haired Margaret, sharing a bottle of red wine. He approaches them.

—How's yerself, Ianto?

49

—Alright.

—Up ter much?

—Just off to pick up me giro like. Waiting for me it is, in-a Jobbie like.

—Yeh?

—Yeh.

—Counter payment is it? No fixed abode like?

—Yeh.

Ianto stands above them, staring down. Margaret squints out at sea and Colm looks up shielding his eyes from the sun with his hand shelfed against his eyebrows.

—What're yis after?

Ianto shakes his head. —Nothing, like. Just waiting for me giro. I'll, erm, I'll be in-a pub in a bit. Cambrian.

Colm shakes his head. —No ta. Wer off ome ferrer long an derty shag, arn we Mags?

Margaret laughs and Ianto looks, liking her laughter.

—Eeyar, avver bang on tha.

Colm offers the wine up to Ianto and he takes it and tips it to his lips. It tastes better than he could ever have imagined, albeit too warm and diluted with spittle.

—If we change ar minds we'll comen join yer. The Cambrian, yeh?

—Yeh.

Colm holds his hand up for the bottle and Ianto returns it and wants to stay, so he just stands there looking down, the sun behind and above him.

—Tara then mate, Colm says. —Avver good one.

Margaret smiles. —See ya, Ianto.

He walks away not thinking anything and goes back to the Job Centre and picks up his cheque and cashes it in the Post Office and loves the moneybulge in his hip pocket which he hopes is completely dry now and will not wet the notes. He buys fish and chips from the Dolphin takeaway and shares them with the pigeons on the benches in the square by the nightclub, then leaves the ketchup-streaked tray for the town birds to peck at and walks down Great Darkgate Street and meets nobody he knows and up Terrace Road and meets nobody he knows and into the Cambrian Arms, where there are many drinking people none of whom he knows not even just to say hello to. He buys a pint of lager at the bar and takes it over to a corner table with a window looking out on to the busy main road and the train station and he stares out of this at the passing people, sipping the pint, taking it slow, savouring it, cold and sharp and lovely, much needed. The first of many.

IANTO IS EIGHT.

And he actually saw with bulging eyes the lightning reach spindle-fingered down from the dishwater sky of the dying day to clout the tree, heard the sharp splitting crack and now stands with ozone in his nostrils and his hair erect watching the tree burn, the awful lilac leaves and the crackling exoskeleton of electricity blue and white and purple crawling and hissing and spitting like snakes across the branches denuded and twisted in the flames like claws, arthritic fingers, all the attitudes of agony attendant on the plundering of flame. Little Ianto stands awed before this blazing blackthorn, feels the tremendous and terrible heat on his face sizzling through the rain, evaporating droplets in mid-fall so that they vanish at Ianto's eye height in little hissing puffs of greasy steam. His young cheekbones and lips shine orange and red and the burning tree is replicated in miniature in each of his widened pupils, the tiny fires of his face. This sizzle and crackle and snap of boiling sap all the words that Ianto needs or even desires to hear and the hen harrier circling, rising on the thermals above the flames long-tailed and lethal, all the guidance he could comprehend ever and could want or pray for nothing more than this taloned plunger from wet skies or moonlight leading him in the dance on the slab of smashed bone, showing him on to the stone dark with blood long-spilled and he small boy following glad.

—An I remember this one time I didn't see him for weeks. Fuckin weeks, just up an off ee was. Wasn't at Llŷr's, no one ad seen im in-a squat, I'd ask people in town if they'd seen im like an they'd all say no. Just seemed to av vanished. Well, I thought, that's it – fucker's dead. He've fallen off a cliff or done too many pills or drowned in-a sea or been battered or somethin, like, I just thought ee was dead. Never thought I'd see im again. Got used to the idea. An then one day weeks after I'd last seen im I go into-a Fountain with Gwenno like an a couple of er mates an yer ee is, up at-a bar, half lashed an drinkin a beer as if ee'd never been away. No change in im whatso-bleedin-ever.

—Typical fuckin Ianto that.

—Yeh. Bloody typical.

—I asked im where ee'd been like an ee just shrugged. 'Out an about, like, yew know.' That's all I could get out of im: 'Just out an about.' With a fuckin beard down to is neck, like, and a bastard smell off im like ee'd been sleeping in a fuckin midden.

—Probly ad, like, knowin that fucker.

—Yeh. Wunt put anythin past that twat me, mun, no.

—Just fuckin like him, that was. Take isself off like, no word to no one. Just up an off, just fuckin like him that. Always doin it ee was. No explanation nor fuck all, he's just yer one minute an gone the next. Like a fuckin ghost.

—Yeh. Wouldn't see im for days.

—Weeks even.

—Which was probly when he was doin is, yer know . . .

—Is stuff.

—Yeh, the fuckin pervert. His dirty sick nasty perverty fuckin stuff.

—Well no, not always, because if that was-a case then almost every fuckin tourist to this country'd be brown fuckin bread, wunney? Cos Ianto would disappear all-a fuckin time. Thousands of fuckin times. An if each time ee did so ee fuckin topped some hiker or something then yer'd ardly be any fuckin tourists left, would there? I mean I reckon, right, that out of every given month, Ianto would on average spend two weeks in-a town like, y'know in society, with people. Two weeks. That's half his whole fuckin life. Anny other half spent wanderin over-a mountains or doin what ee did. Fuck knows what he used to do. Should've been born a fuckin fox, ee should uv.

—Aye, or a wolf. If they were still around like.

—Or a wild cat, if yew got em in Wales.

—Or a hawk.

—That's enough now, Jesus Christ. Sound like David fuckin Attenborough yew cunts do.

—No, a hawk's good, or an eagle, somethin like that. Like, y'know, a bird of prey's a same as Ianto was; yer's like, a sort of capacity for chaos at odds with their, erm, loneliness, it seems. Y'know, like –

—Oi!

—Jesus, Danny. There's clever aye? There's fuckin *stupid* more like. Christ.

—Never heard yew talk like that before, yew thick twat.

—Be writing a fuckin *poem* next, yew will.

—Yeh, well, I've been fuckin reading, haven't I? Should try it sometime, yew should. Might even fuckin learn something like.

—Yeh yeh.

—Mouthy get, yew.

—Alright, fuck's sakes. That's enough. Bunch of fuckin kiddies yew are, aye. Shut yewer gobs or I'll crack yewer heads together an send yew to bed without any tea.

—It was like after that rave. Remember that rave?

—Oh yeh, *that* one . . . which fuckin rave, mun? Which specific one out of-a thousands are yew talking about like?

—That one when Ianto fucked off afterwards.

—Ah. Narrows it down to several hundred, that does.

—The one when Gareth OD'd an died?

—Erm, I don't know if it was that one . . . can't really remember like . . .

54

—Gareth died at a rave did he?

—Yeh, the soft twat, in-a back of a van. Comes out of jail that very fuckin day an to celebrate OD's on meth. Carked it. The prick.

—Overdose like. Bump, that's him.

—It might've been-a same one, I don't know, I can't remember. I'm talking about the one when Ianto wrecked-a house in-a morning. When he went doofuckinlally.

—Oh Christ, aye! *That* one!

—Yeh, I remember it. Burnt the fuckin gaff down dinny. Went bastard berserk like.

—Weren't-a fuckin only one, tho, was ee?

—Went mad in-a house then fucked off for ages. Didn't see him for yonks after that like.

—All that bleedin billy he was using, aye. Sent im off is trolley. It would anyone, that amount. Billy for fuckin breakfast, like. Eyes on stalks, teeth ground down to stumps. Fuckin crazy, boy.

—Yeh. I remember, ee was grinding is teeth so fuckin much that when ee spat it would be all gritty like, have little white lumps of grit in it.

—The enamel off is teeth like. Jesus Christ.

—The coppers said, they reckoned that that was when ee did is first like, that time. After that rave, like. They reckoned they dated it back to then.

—Don't see how. How can they do that?

—Fuck knows. Forensics, mun, innit? Amazing what those cunts can do like.

—No, it was the lad, like, the young lad, Ianto's victim. On-a day he was reported missing like. Simple. No fuckin lab work or anythin like that, just simple fuckin common sense. That's all yer is to it, mun.

—Schoolboy, wanny.

—Who?

—The lad oo Ianto murdered like. Schoolboy ee was.

—My arse. Yew make it sound like –

—Fuck off Danny. He was fuckin sixteen years old.

—Yeh, but he was from-a borstal. He'd been done for raping

55

his mate's sister, it said so in-a paper. Fuckin freak ee was, a nonce like. That's what ee was doing yer, he'd come on an Outward Bound course for borstal boys an got lost or something. He was a bad fuckin boy. A rapist.

—He was fuckin sixteen. That's-a school age, mun. He was just a fuckin kid.

—Yeh, but yewer making it sound like he was this innocent angelic child or somethin an it wasn't like that at all. He was a fuckin nonce.

—How the fuck do *yew* know, then? Right there with im, were yer?

—No, but I read the papers.

—An they don't tell-a fuckin trewth. Yewer only gettin half the story. Girl might-a been asking for it, yew don't know. Willing like. An then said she was forced cos she regretted it or she wanted the attention, something like that. Happens all-a fuckin time, mun.

—Yeh.

—The boy was sixfuckinteen, that's all that matters.

—A schoolboy aye.

—Sixteen. Sixfuckinteen.

—Jesus. Yew sick fucker, Ianto, yew were. A schoolboy, Christ.

—Jesus.

HUNCHED OVER THE white-lined record sleeve balanced on his knees and with a fiver tubed into his nostril Ianto snorts the amphetamine, one line, two, and sits sniffing back, with his face beginning to burn and his eyelids jumping, and stares at the stolen expensive TV on which a panel discussion on imminent Welsh devolution is under way and has been for some time. Stern men underlining their points with vigorous hand gestures and women with crisp hair. Ianto can't hear what they are saying above the pounding techno elsewhere in the squat and the boom of blood in his skull, but inside him somewhere he can sense that events of moment and of import and no small consequence are beginning to unfold before his eyes and in the unknown world around him and that, sitting on this landfill floor marooned in fastfood cartons and empty cans and bottles and overflowing ashtrays and encrusted clothing and a supermarket trolley and a Rolls-Royce hubcap and record sleeves and small clear hinged cassette boxes and an oily engine part like a giant black heart, with strong sulphate asizzle in his face and searing its way down his gulping throat, that he is being drawn in by powers unimaginable and unstoppable and that history itself is stirring, reaching out to drag him into its orbit, its maw, and he, one small wrecked person, can do nothing utterly but surrender to the part assigned in some never-to-be-entered office in some marbled and columned building in some never-visited city somewhere to him and only him. Re-enfranchisement, re-empowerment, respect: Ianto can just make out such words if he presses his hot forehead against the TV screen, the tiny filaments on his flickering face prickling in the static. Re-enfranchisement and re-empowerment and rebirth and renewed respect. Such words.

—Ianto!

Danny's head peers around the door, grinning and excited.

—Not still watching that crap are yew? It's all bollax, mun, devolution won't change a fuckin thing. Still be answerable to

57

Westminster. Still be in their fuckin power, mun, always fuckin will be. If yew got a fuckin big saw an separated the country down Offa's Dyke an let us float out to sea we'd still be in their fuckin power. Never change, mun. Anyway, listen, get yewer arse in gear bach, we're all set to go like. How're yew feeling?

Ianto stands and swallows and says: —Devoluted.

Danny laughs. —Devoluted, aye? That's good enough for me, mun. Good whizz, yeh?

They leave the house and climb into a car, which stands engine-revving at the kerb and in which more techno thumps. Marc is driving with Griff upfront next to him and Ianto and Danny squeeze into the back seat alongside Llŷr, whose face is grin-split, cheek muscles juddering with uppers and the golfball-sized gum-clump in his mouth, teeth and cheekbones working frantically.

—All set yew two then, aye? Should be a good fuckin night this should. Yer's crews comin up from all over-a fuckin country, mun, Cardiff, London, Brum. Full-a Scousers an Geordies an Jocks an Paddies it'll be, fuckin spot-on like, hundreds, thousands. Fuckin ace it will be. Spank DJ's an-a Eternal Cru, yer's four fuckin marquees like and I'm going to have-a best time-a me bastard life. I'm off me fuckin face already, mun, I am.

—Eternal Cru, Danny sneers. —And other fuckin trust-fund junkies. Other wasters sponsored by mummy an fuckin daddy.

He sniffs, hard.

Nodding, Llŷr points at the cassette player. —This fuckin Derrick May mix. Tellin yew, mun. Fuckin *tunes*.

Marc turns the music up even further and the car's whole superstructure rattles and buzzes with the bass and Ianto feels it buzzing in the bundles of nerves behind each of his ears and a bottle of warm vodka is passed around the car, the air thick with smoke and sticky with the different synthetic fruit smells of four types of gum. They drive out of the town past the harbour, over which the sun sinks red, bouncing off masts and cabin windows, scoring in the surface of the sea an orange scar towards the horizon and its sinking self like a knifeblade drawn through skin. Wraps are handed around and dabbed at and swilled down with tepid vodka, which towards the end of

58

the bottle now sports a thinly bubbled head of different spittles. Ianto slaps the beat of the music out on the knees of his jeans and gazes out at the country they drive through up and on to the mountain road beyond the sprawling Penparcau estate climbing up the hillside and the Glan-yr-Afon industrial estate spreads out below them on the valley floor, dark buildings and cooling towers and a river silver and wormlike. The tall white windmills of the wind-farm star the far hills, losing their whirled and kaleidoscopic lustre now in the darkening sky. Green fields begin to bunch then expand from horizon to horizon dotted intermittently with small whitewashed cottages and barns and bothies and sheep, and bordered with fenceposts and barbed wire and streak-shadowed by the big black birds which soar low across them. Ianto sees a hare break cover and dart through long grass, a sudden snapping movement which he likes, the sleek slim runner whipquick in right angles so sharp they should be alien to any lifeform born without corners and edges and designed with setsquares and keyboards in some office. He smiles to remember recently on one of his interminable walks seeing in early morning mist two hares box in dew-tutus, their powerful back paws slapping the floor and he bunches his fists and begins to jab at the back of Griff's seat snorting breaths audibly through his nose.

—Having a box, are we, Iant? Go on then, mun, yew pound fuck out of that seat boy. Fucking give it some.

Ianto does and Griff's large head swings slowly around like a giant owl's.

—That's getting on me wick. Stop it now or I'll break yewer fuckin fingers, Ianto boy.

Danny and Llŷr do the 'woooo, get him' noises and Ianto laughs and Griff just grins speed-light and Marc turns the music up even louder and accelerates when they turn off the road on to a smaller less frequented byway, which leads them through trees and across a sheep-strewn field and around a low hill and over a small humped greystone bridge across a shallow fast river. Here another car flashes them and slows and edges up alongside, a worried face beneath a baseball cap craning through the driver's window. Marc turns the music down and winds down his window.

—What's up?

—You off to TalyBont?

—Yeh. What's the matter?

The other driver shakes his head sadly and jerks a thumb back over his shoulder.

—Fuckin roadblock like. Fuckin vanloads of Old Bill there stopping everyone, searching them an turning em back. Fuckin bastards. Our mates got arrested, all fuckin four of em. Didn't they?

He turns to look back into his car and three other heads in there all nod in unison.

—Fuckin cunts they are. Not doing anyone any fuckin harm like. D'you know another way through?

Marc nods. —Go back this way, like, bear left till yew hit the main road an follow the signs for Bont-goch. There'll be other cars there, I'm sure.

—Right. Thanks mate. Have a good one.

—Yew n all.

The cars edge past each other over the bridge and Marc eight-point-turns in the narrow lane and then they drive back over the bridge and around a low hill and across the sheep-strewn pasture and through trees and back on to the A-road. Other cars pass them, beeping and flying makeshift flags made from garments or bags out of the windows, with smiling eager faces pressed up against the back screens giving thumbs-up signs or waves or small esoteric finger-signals as of some code of some sect. A brightly painted Transit van lumbers past and a girl in the back lifts up her top and presses her breasts against the back window, the flesh compressed to the glass with the dark nipples like the pupils of eyes, the shocked and compound eyes of some abducted and transported creature. The men all cheer and Marc flashes his lights and honks his horn in appreciation.

—Like that Ianto, aye? Griff shifts in his seat to look over the headrest at Ianto. —When's-a last time yew saw a pair-a tits like that then, ey? Twenty-odd years ago when ey had to drag yew off yer mam was it?

He turns back laughing to face the front again. Ianto looks at the back of his head for a second or two then just looks away blank-eyed and untouched in any way at all, then suddenly they leave the forest they have been driving through for some moments and are in a muddied clearing in the trees with cars and vans and bikes and one old painted double-decker bus like a lone pike in a shoal of minnows parked chaotically and the shapes of people drifting between the vehicles and through the trees blue-tinged by the climbing moon towards and then above and past a fire burning in an oil drum illuminating the words THIS WAY in dripping black letters on a car bonnet propped up against a young pine. There are many people, scores of them, scrambling over automobiles and ducking under tree branches and piggybacking each other some running some walking all towards the fire and the sign. Attenuated figures drifting through the trees like sprites or phantoms.

—This must be it, aye.

—I reckon so.

Marc squeezes the car between a Mini and a birch tree and turns the engine off and the music dies and in the relative quiet they can hear the noise of the people, the babble and the laughter, and the dull thump of distant techno coming over the mountain and through the trees.

—One for the road, ey lads.

Griff takes a bag of powder out of his jacket pocket and dabs in it with a finger and licks it and rubs it around and over his gums, then passes the bag over the back seat to Danny.

—Good Christ, Griff, how much is in here? Fuckin sherbet dip, mun. Where's the lollipop like?

—Three ounces. Off Roger. Make a lot of dosh up yer, I can see. So if any of yew need to buy any more later like then I'm yer man. Yer's plenty to keep us going. An notice I said 'buy'.

The bag is passed from man to man and dabbed at by each one. Ianto uses two crooked fingers to scoop almost a gramme of the powder into his mouth, grimacing at the vile taste then palpating his cheeks to stimulate saliva and mixing it around in his mouth then swallowing the foul and acrid paste in one huge gulp, suppressing the gag reflex with one hand clamped across his lower face and frantic swallowing.

61

—Pill time as well. Do em in now an we'll be well up by-a time we get yer.

Marc passes small white pills around to each person excluding Ianto, who holds his hand out expectant. Marc stares down at the open waiting palm.

—What's all that about then, Ianto? What the fuck are yew after?

—An E.

—Oh aye. Paid for one, av yew?

Ianto doesn't reply.

—Iant, these cost fuckin money. I asked the other day didn't I. I said, if anyone wants a pill for TalyBont then put up-a cash an I'll get it sorted. Yew were there. Didn't I say that?

Nods and murmurs.

—Yew gave no money so yew get no pill. Simple as fuckin that, mun.

Ianto drops his hand and Danny slings an arm around his shoulder. —Ah don't get upset Ianto, mun. Yew'll be able to get a pill up yer, like, in-a rave. Yer'll be hundreds floating about. An anyway, yew've still got some whizz left, ant yer?

Ianto nods.

—Well, there yew are then.

Ianto nods again and then finds that he cannot stop nodding or indeed blinking because he has in fact ingested a large amount of amphetamine throughout the afternoon as well as various blends of alcohol and that scoop of Griff's speed he has just eaten has brought it all up to critical mass and as they leave the car and move through the trees and other parked cars and past the fire in the barrel and the sign and up and over the hill via the muddy track towards the music, growing louder, and the mad flashing lights in the sky, growing brighter, Ianto's heart begins to rattle and shake like a rock in a tumble-dryer and his hands and face are all twitchy and his scalp crawls and there is a lovely toothy tension in his mouth and to burn some of this wire-tight energy off he wants to run. Look for any lassitude within him and it will not be found, not now, not ever; never amongst the flame and light crackling through him, battling through him, although he knows it not. He just wants to run, and indeed he does run,

62

roaring, reedy arms above his head towards the growing music and the brightening multi-coloured lights.

—G'wahn, Ianto!

—*Get* the fuckers, boy!

—Go for it, mun!

He runs up and over the hill splashing through mud ruts and past and through walking groups of people who look at him bemused or yell encouragement and he crests the hill and there below him in a natural bowl between an encircling rim of high hills is the main body of the rave with people swarming insectile and hive-like around tents and fires, strobes shredding the scene and the music rocking the thick-trunked old trees and the moon and the stars above it all and the ramshackle mansion up on the valley rise bursting blue then red from its windows, dancing silhouettes moving behind the glass, and from each of the throbbing marquees the beats of different musics merge and mix into one single mad euphony and it is like a world separate yet within, host to another race different yet in some ways assimilated, gathered here via a wide network of recondite signals and codes comprehensible to its members alone to come and celebrate as they do their willed apartness secret and discrete. Like an alien species of nomenclature unknown among the world hiving then swarming to prove in a display of their twinned two navels that most others have only one. That their origins differ, that their conceptions oppose.

Ianto moves downslope towards the largest fire, across whose thrashing flames black shadows of humans and dogs leap and tumble. Groups stand in silhouette drinking from cans and bottles and passing around long spliffs, whose gleaming ends flit from face to face like luminous winged insects that feed on human spit. Glo-sticks dart and drift like angler fish and a member of the Eternal Cru sits in the mud with his back against a tree dealing wraps from the deep pockets of his Diesel anorak. A long-bearded man in a top hat and sporting a silver-topped cane treads his foppish proud-backed way through a fallen galaxy of empty beer cans. A small skinny man hunched over in a green baseball cap and square green shades executes some sort of intent chopping dance with the blunt blades of his hands as

63

he orbits a group of four squatting on the wet grass around an elaborate bong. Ianto waves to and grins at those who greet him, slapping backs and squeezing arms, and jerks into the large barn out of which the best music pulses and in here steam rises from the clustered dancing bodies up towards the high rafters, upon which other figures dance too, feet firmly planted on the thin beams, rhythmically swaying their arms and torsoes and heads, and one girl hangs upside down with her knees hooked over the rafter pumping her arms madly, her long hair falling in a curtain groundwards, her T-shirt slipped down to reveal the pronounced and stretched muscles of her stomach and her breasts spilling out of the tight white lace of her bra. Some in here remain wallbound drinking or smoking and watching and some dance with a wide-eyed determined drive towards exhaustion and some dance atop other's shoulders and one walks on his hands and others merely stand resting or observe. Bright clothes abound like aposematic coloration, warning potential predators of poison, peril. The DJ is a hunched dark featureless shape in an elevated grotto of yellow light at the far end of the barn, hurling out these deep and fervent sounds which throb in the earth and pulse in the walls of this old stone structure, which sway these massed people now this way now that, now slowing them down to an almost stately pace then instantly smashing them together and up again with beats born in bloodrun and breathing, in the exaggerated pumping of sexuality and the stamp of danced sacrifice or entreaty enacted on the cones of the surrounding volcanoes when they still smouldered, or on the skyscraping crests and flanks of the encircling mountains when parts of them were still soft to the attentions of wind and of rain like faces creased by the wailing and weeping of the planet, or on the bog-soft banks of the lakes and rivers beseeching harvest and bounty in the only way they knew how and which worked, sometimes.

Ianto feels arms around his neck and turns to face Gwenno grinning up at him and moving her hips with the lights minia-tured in her dark large eyes and bouncing back off her teeth and the bolt through her eyebrow and his heart accelerates still further. She yells something in his ear and he feels her breath

64

warm and smells it minty with a faint metallic underwhiff of MDMA, and he can't make out her words so he leans closer and she yells it again but all he can make out is the one word 'fine' which is enough and he encircles her naked waist with his hands and she dances away again, punching the air with her arms above her head and her long hair bouncing, and he sees the span of her belly smooth and honey-hued between the cropped top and the belt of her faded jeans hanging low on her prominent hips, the wide legs almost entirely covering apart from the toes her mud-splattered black and white trainers. Ianto tries to move towards her, a need in him both to stoke and feed from her gorgeous delirium but she is lost in the crowd and he sees the upturned face of Margaret Jones between shoulders, lost in pleasure and surprise as she watches a small sparrow-sized bird flit into the barn through one entrance and whir through the lights and the steam above the rippling close-packed heads of the dancers and out through another entrance into the darkness again. Imagines that, that small slice of light and noisy activity between the two immensities of blackness.

Ianto is lost, spinning. A roaring ponytailed Irishman steams by with a small dark bottle of amyl pressed to his nostril, his shouting face bright red. A small blonde girl with a Welsh dragon flag draped across her back floats by on someone's shoulders, drifting above the swarming heads like a strange fakir proving the falseness of our corporeal claims. The speed in Ianto is rampant, jackhammering his heart and bulging the veins at his neck and temples and he dances madly, twitching like some young bird attempting take-off or a puppet in the hands of a mad master, bent slightly forwards at the waist with his arms hacking the clogged air and his teeth like his fists clenched, the very image of one swiftly sluicing the rage resultant from some terminal acceptance. He sees nothing but lights and shapes and he smells nothing but fresh sweat and ganja smoke and the sweetness of trampled grass and all his muscles are alive beneath the giant organ of his skin, atingle, grasped in the ecstasy of the moment and only that, the eternal present with its tremendous release and relief and the expression of the enraptured realisation which can demand or even indeed be satiated by not one other method.

65

This is all Ianto requires, here, this is all he could need, just this perennial thumping second, the movement gravewards halted, and the sweat and the booming and all the motion outside his spinning sphere and if Ianto could stretch and reach and rip the moon from its moorings then he assuredly would. He dances like some laggard seeking to supercede the world's fury, its insanity, he dances as if in fevered denial of those times he has danced alone in the cold and the darkness with no music playing, as if to disprove how difficult it is to do that. He dances amongst these reaching bodies in the polish and refinement of that first primal prowl and pounce, more than football, more than war. A bodily victory speech, frantic and static lap of honour circumscribing only the body's orbit. Simple praise of itself.

He dances until thirst overtakes him and he cannot swallow, his spit is wool, so he ceases his movement suddenly no winding down just split-second cessation, one second a blur the next a person and leaves the barn in search of fluid. Parked outside the building is a small car with its hatchback up like a spread carapace revealing slabs of canned beers and soft drinks. Ianto buys a can of Challenge lager for £1.50 and shakes his wet head in answer to the man who asks him if he needs anything else and drinks half the lager in one warm gulp and takes it to sit under a dripping tree at the side of the path rapidly becoming a quagmire, then moves as he catches a whiff of the Portaloos nearby and finds a place beneath the low branches of another tree at the bottom of the bottom field, the hills rising above. He leans back against the ridged bark among the moths falling silently like petals, like snow, to escape the sonic seeking of the hungry bats above the trees and stands sipping at the lager, feeling the moisture dry on his face, his clothes hanging in heavy wet folds from his thin frame, his prominent bones. He smokes a cigarette and watches balloons trail their strings like tadpoles or spermatazoa across the moon's pale face, feels the music throb in the soft earth beneath his feet, through the worn soles of his trainers. People are having sex somewhere in the bushes behind him; the almost-pained groans of the woman sound to him like the cries of a sea-bird unseen and heard across the estuarial sand flats at night-time, almost yearning, beseeching. Were he able to he would tumesce at these sounds alone, but the amphetamine has temporarily robbed his penis of all resilience and all blood and he knows from past experience the futility of kneading and palpation resulting only in a sore wrist and skin rubbed raw, although the desire is there heightened irrepressibly to grab flesh and thrust and slide, exacerbated by the sulphate, which sensuous accentuation of a need containing within it the frustration and hindrance to the satisfaction of that same need can be instanced as some summation of the war which burns in Ianto's skull and chest whenever consciousness itself returns to him with each new day, be it in cottage or squat or cave or copse or hovel. He is tempted to squirm his hand into his jeans and pull and tug at his prick anyway because of the way it simply tingles, but he doesn't. Then he does; he slides his hand between denim and flesh and with the fingertips of his first two fingers tweaks the end of his knob, feels it small and sulphate-shrivelled and lacking in all incipience of growth or expansion and he runs his thumbtip over the rough ridge of scar tissue and he caresses that almost tenderly then withdraws his hand and sniffs at his fingers and with that hand takes the wrap of amphetamine from the inner pocket of his jacket and dabs at it twice then tips the remainder into his lager, swishing the can around to assist dissolution and then takes rapid pecking sips at it like a bird at seed. He smokes another damp cigarette, his jaw working now like some piston-powered machine, and he notices that the pleasured sounds in the bushes behind him have ceased and there is rustling and then a boy emerges his top half swallowed in a big baggy fleece, leading, by the hand, a long-haired girl crop-topped and hipstered and Ianto catches the light reflected off her teeth as she smiles and the metal in her eyebrow and he also gets a glimpse of snub nose as she walks just-fucked, holding hands with the boy, up and into the vast mad body proper of the rave and was it Gwenno? Was it her? Ianto thinks with a lurch that it might have been Gwenno, Gwenno he heard groaning in the bushes only a few feet behind his back. Gwenno not a body's length behind him surrendering to some stranger thrusting, insistent and she smiling. Eyes closed and lips parted.

67

He drains the can and tosses it away, then strides up the softly sloping wet meadow, attempting to trace the route of the maybe-Gwenno and her partner. Danny dashes out of the crowd to embrace him and slap his back and bellow something in his ear and Ianto responds distracted and perfunctory then ducks into the nearest marquee, where he is instantly assaulted by the deafening drum and bass, the body-shocking jerks of the irregular spiralling drum and the whining sliding movement of the bass, so deep and loud as to vibrate in the spongy soles of his soaked shoes and rattle the bones of his ankles. It is dark in this tent, very dark; gangling shapes vault and gibber through what weak light there is and looming still figures clustered around the sturdy central pole pass around small pipes which they entirely envelop with their hands as they suck at them. Quick glimpses of heavy jewellery and sweat gleaming on bared skin. Ianto stands and stares for a minute or two, but there is nothing for his eye to lock on to; each focal point seems to burst and re-gather in a manner unacquainted with each sudden shift in the tempo of the music and no two tableaux the same or even akin excepting the main players involved, the only constant is extreme transformation second by second by second, in an eyeblink a leaping overcoated figure has moved to the back of the marquee twenty yards away, where the overcoat becomes a bomber jacket and a large woolly hat is donned and then there is a woman in the time it takes to blink an eye, which Ianto is doing very very rapidly now, several times per second in fact, as he buckles under yet another powerful sulphate rush and the immediate world is coming at him in shredded tendrils sundered and unconnected, so he leaves that tent in one fluid movement turn and dash and trips over a guyrope and falls headlong in the mud. Lying there still and face-down and blaming the planet, the way it spins for ever. How he can never feel its whirl. Quickly there are hands in his armpits lifting him upright.

—You all right, man?

A friendly black face looks concerned into his. Ianto nods and spits mud.

—Fuckin lethal them things are, aren't they? Went flying over

68

one meself earlier. Should paint em white or tie ribbons on em
or something so we can see. Sure yer all right now, yeh?

—Yeh.

—Good.

He pats Ianto's back and disappears into the drum and bass
tent and Ianto rubs the mud off his hands on to his jeans and
uses the hem of his shirt to wipe his face clean and crunches
grit between his teeth and will not feel embarrassed. A passing
man in a woolly hat sees Ianto spit and offers him a bottle
of Volvic, which Ianto takes and drinks from gratefully and
greedily, then returns it and wipes his lips with the back of his
hand which comes away dark-striped and he moves towards a
squat stone outhouse-type building across the field outside which
very young people, say mid-teens, are gathered looking almost
terrified, white-skinned and stalk-eyed like the damned. Ianto
moves through them stopping once to stare unabashed at a very
young girl whose white and growing breasts are spilling out of
the top of a pale blue Wonderbra and she thrusts these out at
him, insulted and defiant hands on her hips, and Ianto grins
loose-lipped at her and opens his mouth to say something, but
is then bundled by a bouncing crowd of school-age people into
the gabba hut and is in half a second battered and left jellylike
by the insane thrashing ear-raping noise and the epileptic lights
and the MC screaming in the voice of a demon. Ianto shakes
his head and roars and plunges gleefully into this collective
fit, sweat looping through the lights and the heat instantly
resoaking his clothing and he has forgotten the maybe-Gwenno
or remembers her only half-lit and vague and scumbled as he
would perhaps a dream, but the hot fist still remains clenched
in his breast goading him to leap and seethe along within this
crazed demented noise and tempest, the people moving like
smithereens each one random and uncontrolled and haphazard
with no real purpose pre-mapped or pre-empted, none apart
from the brief but vital destruction of all that lies beyond the
encircling ring of lakes and mountains in the quiet houses under
the falling drizzle and yellow sodium of the streetlights. That's
all. Some of these people here, sixteen maybe seventeen, sat
down in this hut hours ago as the amps and decks were being

brought in and banged up on skag or temazepam or methadone or any other brain-hammering opiate derivative and they will remain here through the same unchanging hysterical shrieking frenzy without rest or respite until the dancers drift damaged and ghost-like away and the music winds down twenty, twenty-four hours ahead in the formless future. They sit there now nodding at the edges of the dance floor slick with liquid spilled, secreted, their backs propped up against the sweating stone walls, moving only to lean to the side and spew or slowly to lift their heavy slack unsteady heads and grin.

Ianto moves madly, bouncing and spinning and kicking and pumping his arms, injecting the chaos of this furnace place with the hot blast of his own fury, and he does this and does this and does this over and only ceases when the urge to piss is so great that his belly hurts and his thighs are damp with impatient pee and the need to drink scorches his throat. He can see blue morning sky through the open door of the hut. He leaves and stands there rocking in the daylight with the muscles in his legs screaming and his ears throbbing and a cliff-face of slag about to shift and slide in his humming head. The speed wars with the exhaustion within his body, the need to lie down, rest and sleep punched dumb by the amphetamine. He walks unsteady up the mud-swamp track to the Portaloos, one of which is engaged and the other of which is sizzling over with shit stinking so he pisses up against the side of it, groaning in relief, his knees trembling as his cloudy yellow urine meanders through the grass to join the wider and deeper tributary of the track.

—Aw Jesus. You dirty bastard.

A man has left the previously engaged toilet and is standing there in disapproval watching Ianto piss.

—Fucking disgusting that. Could you not have just waited? I was only a couple of minutes, man. Christ, have you no control? There're kiddies gonner be playing around here in a minute. God, have some respect for others, ey? Least you could've done is gone in the woods, like, if you were really desperate. Full view of everybody.

Ianto bites his lower lip and shakes off and shoves his dick back into his soaking jeans and walks over to the man, three strides, and punches him full in the face. He feels the connection in his shoulder and neck and the impact explodes in his bunched knuckles and the man falls back flat in the running midden of mud and piss, his nose a flattened burst of rapidly spreading redness and his eyes rolled back, showing nothing but slightly yellowed whites fine-laced with bloodshot veins. Ianto pulls his foot back to kick and probably kick again, but there are faces watching him from inside a parked car so he simply steps over the man as he would any other small obstacle and follows the track down and around to the bottom of the site by the small birdless pond, where a low khaki tent emanates soft music tinkling like rain off forest leaves and a wooden crate by the entrance has been painted with the white words: CHILL OUT/FOOD/FIRST AID. This is what Ianto needs.

And they have him, these days, these moments of misrule; possessed of them he is quick and entire in his thin, zinging skin, alive, real, on the planet. In them and of them he stirs on this earth, connected to others and himself also in a peril formed from his own forcing, spun from his zinging skin. Better this mess of a life than a life so pointless. Better this botch of a life than one so drab.

It is cool in the tent, and dark, with ambient music dripping pleasant and dreamy down the low canvas walls. There are smells of tea and coffee from the steaming silver urns like little volcanoes by the table laden with cellophaned cakes and sandwiches and fruit and bars of chocolate and manned by smiling middle-aged hippies, all thinning dreadlocks and tie-dye and washed-out combat gear. A mongrel dog sleeps beneath the table, his muzzle on his forepaws. Groups of people recuperating or regathering or simply exhausted sit at the white plastic garden tables or on the trampled grass and smoke and drink and talk in low voices or put their heads on their folded arms and sleep, their legs and hands jiggling with drugs and the somatic memory of the music now become biological, and it is calm in here and mellow and relieving, and Ianto likes it and approaches the counter to order coffee off a Noel Edmonds look-alike if Noel Edmonds had a multi-coloured matted beard down to his belt buckle and black beads in the only hair left on his head in tufts above his ears. This man pours Ianto's coffee in a floppy plastic cup and takes his seventy pence and gestures to the milk in a UHT carton and sugar in a bowl clotted with dark lumps on the table before him.

—You look as if you've been burning off some energy tonight then.

Ianto nods and sips his drink.

—Yeh, I bet you have. Good do this, innit? Came out to one here last summer I did, but it wasn't anywhere near as good as this one. Bangin tonight. About eight thousand here, all in all like, throughout the night. Eight bloody thousand. If they was charging entrance . . . Christ, they'd clean up, wouldn't they? Sitting on a fucking gold mine they are. Money in the bank, man. Course, they'll have broken even with the mark-up on the drinks an that like, but . . .

Ianto blows on and sips his coffee through puckered lips now beginning to crack white and flake with dryness.

—I'm away up to Barmouth in a few hours. The Sandancer. An all-nighter's kicking off there sometime late this afternoon. You going?

Ianto shrugs.

—Yeh, probably the right idea. Get some rest like, recharge your batteries. Bit of sleep and a bite to eat, that's all you need. Be raring to go after that like.

He begins to mop the table with a cloth and Ianto turns to find a place to sit, the coffee held to his lips, his face in steam, and he sees Griff gesturing him over to a table, at which Llŷr sits also with his eyes inflamed and his cheeks callow and sunken next to Ikey Pritchard in mud-crusted white trainers and black sweatpants and a sleeveless grey T-shirt which shows his tattoos, some sharply coloured and clear, others old and empurpled and starting to run, drilled into the flab stretched over the slabs of muscle which move and ripple, stacked in cables and thick sheets. There is a scar across Ikey's deltoid, a thumb-thick slash of silvery cicatrice between two rows of blobs three apiece, each the size of a ten-pence coin as if this wound had been staunched with a marquee-spike and docking-hawser. Ianto sits down opposite him.

—Ikey.

—Ianto, mun. How's me faverit fuckin half-wit then eh? The world's best inbred backwoods feeb psycho mong?

—I didn't see yew before.

—That's cos I wasn't yer, boy. Only just turned up see.

—We rang him, Llŷr says. —On-a phone like.

Griff leans over the table conspiratorial. —See, Ianto, we got Ikey up yer like cos we're gonna go over to-a big house in a bit and turn it over. Pocket a few things like. It's alright, I've checked it out, yer's only a few fuckin middle-class English poofs in yer, ey own it like, no fuckin probs dealin with them. University drop-outs like, made-a load-a fuckin dosh an bought a house out yer. That kind-a thing it is. Should see-a fuckin stuff those twats've got, mun; silver, paintings, wouldn't fuckin believe it, mun, aye. And I'd bet any fuckin money yer's jewellery around somewhere and wads-a cash as thick as yewer arm. Always fuckin is in those places.

—Probly a shitload-a fuckin drugs an all, Llŷr says. —Wouldn't surprise me, that, like. One of em was dealin some good hydroponic before, like, in-a techno tent . . .

Ikey splutters. —Hydroponic be fucked. No fuckin profit in that, mun. It's-a powders yew want, like. Step on em a few times, yewer laughin.

—So anyway, Ianto. Griff nudges Ianto's shoulder with his. —Yew in? Yew up for it then? Could use another man.

Ianto sips his coffee and lights a cigarette and looks absently around the tent. Llŷr sighs deeply and puts his head in his hands.

—I think we can take that as a yes.

—An where's that fuckin Roger cunt? Thought yew said yew were goin-a phone im as well?

—I did, Ikey. He's in hospital. Don't know what for like, but yer he is.

—Oh. Good enough excuse, I suppose.

Ianto sucks the smoke through a raw throat and down into raw lungs. Feeling scoured and grated and borderline hysterical, some fanged and flapping thing behind his eyes, in his face and banging head. Quick sips at the coffee help to calm him as does,

73

paradoxical and peculiar, the memory of the punch by the Port-a-loos, the satisfying thud and crunch the energy expended with a palpably clear result, the complaining man out cold in the mud, the bubbling blood. Ianto's three tablemates are hunched in a huddle whispering and planning and beyond them Ianto can see another group slack-faced with tiredness wearing red Welsh rugby shirts armpit-darkened with sweat and can hear their conversation exhaustion-slow yet earnest. Ianto the eavesdropper:

—I'm tellin yew, mun, its fuckin happening. It's gonna come. A nation once again. It's on its fuckin way boy, nothin fuckin surer.

—My arse.

—I'm tellin yew. I saw it on-a telly before I came out like. Fuckin devolution, boy. Plans're being made, for the election like. National fuckin assembly.

—Ah yeh, an how many punters yew reckon're going to turn out to vote then? Twenty, thirty percent of-a population? Remember 1979?

—No. I was six.

—Same thing'll happen. Apathy. Can't-be-fuckin-arsed-ness. That's what's wrong with this fuckin country, mun, the general fuckin apathy of its inhabitants. Nothing fuckin moves em. Nothing fuckin gets em off eyr arses. Telly an beer an-a takeaway curry an they're happy.

—Meibion.

—Well them maybe, yeh, an-a Free Wales Army like, but that's all. I mean, apart from them, who else? Who else has ever got up off eyr fat fuckin arses an done somethin about it all? Eight fuckin centuries of subjugation an who are ar heroes?

—Saunders Lewis.

—Yeh. Sion Aubrey Roberts.

—Nah, I'm talking modern fuckin times mun. Contemporary like. Yer's no one. Moan about it in pubs, that's all we fuckin do, or write the odd fuckin poem. Does fuck all. Tellin yew, it's a pitiful little nation this. A fuckin boil in-a ocean. I mean, the Irish kill each other, the Scots kill emselves, an us, well, all we do is kill time while we wait

74

for someone else to come along an do somethin for us. Tellin yew. It's –

—Well, y'see, that's exactly-a fuckin attitude that's fuckin well holding us back like. No fuckin backbone, mun. No balls like. I mean yer's a fuckin chance like, at last yer's a fuckin opportunity to really fuckin do something about ar fuckin situation an yer's cunts like yew doin nothin but moan about it. Last thing we need is more fuckin whingers. Should be fuckin expelled from-a country if yew don't vote, mun.

—I never said I wasn't going to, did I? All's I said is that I doubt many will. That's all. This fuckin apathy, mun, the Welsh disease it is.

Ianto stares down into the dregs of his coffee. He drops his cigarette butt into them and it hisses and dies and releases a small shoal of black ash flecks into the tepid brown lees like wasps leaving a hive. He agitates it and watches as the cork-patterned paper begins to peel away from the nicotined filter, splayed and fluffed like mould.

—Ianto. Yew fit then?

Griff nudges his ribs and they all stand and leave the tent into the bright morning. A version of 'Guantanamera' floats out of the techno tent and the gabba barn still rages, although most people have left the rave now, and of those that remain most sit in cars or under trees or in their own personal pup tents pitched in the bottom field between the parked cars, and of those left standing very few are capable yet of movement coherent enough to dance. One girl in a long white dress like an institutional robe sits up a tree in the high branches and howls like a dog at the clear sky, stops to laugh and then continues. A pair of Kickers lie empty in the mud looking oddly stunned. Ianto thinks of trying them on for size and taking them if they fit, but the momentum of Ikey and Griff and Llŷr will allow no hiatus as they walk up the hill unstoppable towards the big house whose windows look like benign mild eyes, some children playing on the swing in the flowered and fenced-off garden and one small boy with baby dreadlocks throwing a stick for a mongrel dog, who scampers happy and stupid to wherever the stick lands, be it in gravel or grass or mud or water.

75

—So then, Llŷr says, panting slightly. —The plan is . . .

—The plan is yer is no fuckin plan, Ikey says. —Just play it by ear, that's all we fuckin do. Ask to use-a bog or somethin an ransack the fuckin upstairs. Just take what we can like. Fine. An if it kicks off then that's fine as well. Only a bunch-a fuckin posho English tossers. Christ, piece-a fuckin piss, boy. What're yew so bleedin worried about?

—I'm not, it's just that I'd like to have things clear in me head, that's all. Plan of action like. I mean, what if –

Griff interrupts: —Llŷr, mun, yew've necked two Es an dabbed a gramme-a whizz an smoked endless spliffs an necked a bottle of vodka in-a last, wha, fifteen, sixteen hours. How-a fuck can *anything* be clear in yewer fuckin head now?

Llŷr grins. —Aye, suppose. But like, it's just, I mean what if-a filth get involved? I mean I do *not* fuckin fancy comin down in a fuckin cell, mun, no fuckin way. Done that before I yav an it's no fuckin fun, boy. A fuckin nightmare I've got absolutely no intention of repeatin if I can fuckin help it.

—Well fuck off then, Ikey snarls. —Yew shite it an yew'll fuck the whole bastard thing up for us all. Why can't yew be like Ianto yer? Look at him – not one bother on the twat, is there, mun, eh? Calm an collected. Clint fuckin Eastwood, mun, innit?

He slaps Ianto's back and Ianto stumbles but doesn't fall and they all laugh and then they enter the back garden of the house, a fishpond among ornamental shrubs and a creosoted wooden bench and terracotta animals, squirrel and frog and hedgehog, and a disassembled motorbike on jacks, and they all fall into single file behind Ikey, who strides up the path a man with sole purpose and into the kitchen through the open door, his shoulders scraping the jambs and his hair brushing the lintel. Four people sit at the large wooden table around a teapot and cafetière and crumbed, crusted plates and knives smeared with butter and jam. There are two women and two men, one man wearing an England football shirt and the other tanned and topless and the women both in chunky jumpers, multi-coloured. They look up at their intruders apprehensive, masking that with small smiles.

76

—Morning, lads, the football shirt says in an unplaceable accent, uninflected, generic. —Have a good night then yeh?

—Fuckin cracker, mun, aye, Ikey says as he pulls out a chair and sits at the table and the others find places to lean against, worktop or oven still warm from breakfast. Ianto leans against the sink, tableware sunk in cold greasy water and folds his arms across his chest.

—Can we help you fellers? one of the women says. Pretty, Ianto notices, with her long hair and her nose slightly upturned like Gwenno's.

—Ikey shrugs: —Not really, no. Just want to, like, show ar appreciation for the good night yew laid on for us all. Had a fine time din we ey, lads?

Griff and Llŷr nod and Ikey helps himself to a cup of tea from the pot and sips it surprisingly daintly, his little finger stuck out, the cup handle held delicate between forefinger and thumb. He blows on the tea even though it doesn't steam still and his dark eyes over the rim of the cup crinkled and amused survey the table and its four attenders.

—Well, that's very nice of you, the topless man says. —And we're glad you enjoyed yourselves. But, ah, we're just finishing breakfast as you can see and we're all extremely tired and are about to go to bed.

—Fucking knackered, footy-top says. —Been up all night.

One of the women speaks rapidly: —But because last night was such a success we'll probably be having another one next month or the month after and you boys are more than welcome to come. Providing we can swing it with the local constabulary, that is.

She rolls her eyes ceilingwards.

Ikey leans forwards, the eager pupil. —Yeh, I'm wondering about that. How *did* yew manage to pull off something this size without any police interference? I mean eyr right fuckin busybodies round yer ey ar, always stickin eyr fuckin snouts in, like. Ow did yew keep em away? I mean, not as if this was a quiet little do, was it?

Griff, leaning against the fridge-freezer, begins to thump his heel against the tall door: thud thud thud. Steady and rhythmical

77

and no hint of cessation. Footy-shirt looks at him and purses his lips and shakes his head, but Griff will not stop. Thud thud thud.

—Can you stop doing that, please?

Thud thud thud thud.

—Well, y'know, the topless man shrugs and grins in answer to Ikey's question. —A little gift in the right pocket can work wonders, can't it? God, we had to, erm, *persuade* certain members of the local council before they'd even let us move in here. Didn't want a bunch of dropouts in their parish. Amazing how quickly the right kind of donation in the right place can change minds, isn't it? Would've been even quicker as well like, but . . . we'd fallen on hard times. Had to do some tricky negotiating.

—So that's what you did? Yew bribed the councillors like?

Thud thud thud thud.

—Well yeah. Had to. We'd fallen in love with the place, but they were blocking our move. Ex-hippies, dropouts. Didn't want us here.

—Can't blame em, really, can yew?

Thud thud thud thud.

—Oh? Why's that?

—Bunch-a fuckin pricks on yer doorstep, I wouldn't fuckin want that either, mun. Bunch-a fuckin arseholes like yerselves.

—That's fucking rude.

—Stuck-up tossers like yewerselves, movin in yer cos yew've got-a fuckin money behind yew like when yer's cunts homeless down-a fuckin road in Aber an Mach. Young girls sleepin rough. Pure fuckin disgrace, that's what it is.

Thud thud thud thud.

—There's no need for that. Get out of our house.

—Yeh, go on, fuck off. Footy-top stands up. —Cheeky Welsh bastard.

Thud thud thud thud.

—Can you please stop your friend from making that noise?

—Go on, get out! Fuck off!

THUD THUD THUD THUD.

—Can I use yewer toilet, please?

All noise and movement ceases and everyone turns to look at

78

Ianto standing with his hand raised as if at school. Frozen tableau for a moment, Ianto hand-raised in the centre of the kitchen as if about to perform a magic trick awaited by all, then a mud-caked and blood-crusted figure stumbles in through the doorway, his eyes sunk in swellings black and purple, his nose a squashed, split sprout in the middle of his scabbed face and he looks around the kitchen from face to face each one then his eyes settle on Ianto and he points at him stiff-fingered and screeches:

—THAT'S HIM! THAT'S THE ONE! HE BROKE MY FUCKING NOSE!

And then instantly they are overcome by dark carnival and Ianto pounces on the late arrival like a cat and punches his split nose again twice in quick succession, his fist sinking in mush like punching a cowpat and Ikey is battering a head with a teapot the white football shirt rapidly turning red and Griff is dragging the topless man across the kitchen floor by his neck and stamping on his stretched abdomen and one woman ducks underneath the kitchen table and Llŷr grabs the other one and attempts to tear her jumper away, but she screams and scratches his face and he backs away with his hand over his eyes. She darts and snatches a knife from the sink, but as she turns Griff hits her and she reels away, lips split, teeth red-grouted. Ianto follows the man toppling backwards into the garden and before he hits the ground has kicked him twice in the ribs and he turns and flicks back into the kitchen, where Ikey is bent over a blood-soaked and comatose man ramming the spout of the dented tin teapot up his nostril, a muscled shove and a grunt then something gives with a crunch and more blood jumps. Llŷr is kicking a huddled woman screaming that she's blinded him and Griff is wrestling on the floor with the topless man, who has clamped a hand around Griff's balls, and Griff is screeching like a snared fox and Ianto grabs the first thing his hand touches and lifts it and smashes it over the man's head and the man looks up and around puzzled his face and hair speckled with biscuit crumbs from the burst packet of digestives which Ianto drops, then leans to drive his forehead into the man's upturned face and the man rolls away his face clenched in pain around a burst nose and Griff is curled up on the floor with his hands between his legs shouting for Ianto to boot the cunt in his bollax, which Ianto does twice and then

79

the ribs too, hearing a crack, and then in the back of the neck as well. Clamour and shouting, roaring and chaos. Caught in uproar and blood-whelmed this kitchen spins like a wheel. Ianto yanks out drawers and scatters their contents and Llŷr begins to grab parts of the fallen woman, who kicks and screams and scratches his face again and Llŷr falls backwards and Ikey overturns the table with one heave and drags out the balled woman from under there and grabs her head in both huge hands and with one blow against the thick table leg robs her of consciousness and she goes instantly limp in his arms and he lays her back almost gently on to the tiled floor, re-arranging her skirt back down into a below-the-knee decency level from where it has ridden up over her thighs. Griff is upright now, wet-faced, and is kicking the topless man who lies still and Llŷr goes for the woman yet again, who springs to her feet and darts out of the kitchen falling headlong over the lying man outside and then up again and running away with her hair streaming out behind her and Llŷr makes to chase her but Ikey drags him back in.

—We're not fuckin yer for that! Leave her! Screw the fucking house!

Ianto can hear their feet thumping up the stairs and Griff follows them and there is breaking of glass and the crash and wallop of falling furniture. The topless man drags himself groaning across the kitchen floor towards the telephone, which Ianto yanks from the wall and throws through the kitchen window and steps back over the battered crawling man and even oddly apologises as the toe of his trainer clips the back of his head. There is a blast furnace in Ianto, detonation following detonation, and he reels under their might and his head is whirling and his mouth is dry completely his teeth grinding and his face twitching as the ingested amphetamine begins yet another rush, catalysed by this sudden flurry of excitement, and he stands in the wrecked kitchen his hands writhing at his sides clenching and unclenching and he doesn't really know what to do, so he snatches the sugarbowl from the worktop and throws it on the floor. The scrolled silver spoon skitters away on the polished slate and ricochets off a box of matches and Ianto almost smiles as he takes them up and strikes one and puts the flame to the bottom of the small green curtain stiff with old cooking grease over the cobwebby window above the oven and the flame flickers tentative for a moment, just tasting, then joyously it seems it scurries up the curtain and black smoke billows and the flame burns blue and yellow and a little spider abseils from a thread on to the windowledge and lands and lies clenched for a moment then unfurls itself and scuttles away behind the cooker. The burning curtain begins to fall apart in almost liquid drops, oily, and the wallpaint begins to bubble and blister and then it too sprouts small saplings of fire and the ceiling above the blaze blackens and the heat quickly intensifies and Ianto turns away. The topless man is now sitting upright, his face held in his hands, and Ianto leaves at a run, leaping over the broken-nosed garden man and away from the decelerating rave and across the field and up and over a hill into a wood, where he crouches against the trunk of an old sycamore, panting and regaining his breath with drool on his chin and something undulating in his eyes like a large strong fish glimpsed in dark waters. There is some blood hardening on his hands and on his clothes and the air whistles through the fungal runnels of his nostrils and there are twigs in his tangled hair and a ringing in his ears and a trembling in his hands which he cannot suppress. Were he to stand it would be on unsupportive knees, so he sits and waits for his breathing to regulate itself and when it does he checks himself for injuries and can find none but can hear a siren somewhere growing louder so he stands and walks through the wrestling vegetation of the wood and out into a bright field, which suddenly darkens as the sky above begins to pulsate with stormlight, and he hasn't slept nor taken food for quite some time now and the hysteria is within him and he walks until the ground begins to rise beneath his screaming feet up on to the mountains, delirious, fevered and demented as if in some narcotic dream this rock-strider bloodied and ravaged, muttering hard-consonanted words to himself through teeth gritted and jawlocked and yellowed and mortared with a foul toxic froth. He strides on resolutely as if charged with that office alone among men, solitary in the world, ever higher into the physical hindrance of the gathering wind like rad-blast hands pushing him backwards, a furnace force without heat, through this unpeopled landscape and through the windfarm, where the strange giant white windmills spin high above his head producing a thrum which shimmers the air and ripples his skin, dwarfed Ianto through the forest of these long-legged machines atremble with power and quaking with the immeasurable might never-ending they have been erected solely to harness, to hold. Their singular pulsing moan hiding voices or only one voice, perhaps that of the unseen face that Ianto feels sometimes has been scrutinising his every move since the very second of his birth, holding him and everything he has ever done or will do in its vision and he could never escape even if he knew the means to, not that face bigger than the mountains or the sea, nor this voice now in the rotor's huge beating saying whoyouwhoyouwhoyou.

He stands for a moment and watches a female deer at a distance lope tiny through the giant stalks. Her white tuft of a tail bobbing behind a rise. A warplane rends the sky above the windmills, swarming silver spurs of hail bombletting out of the sonic boom and skyshred of the shock and throb of its passage, which adds to the horrored hollering already in Ianto's skull, and he walks again deeper into the swelling land to exhaust himself and bring on sleep, through the sloping graveyard where no date on the listing slabs or weathered Celtic crosses spans more than forty years, testament to the slow-poisoned rivers and earth here leached from the local lead mine, now long disused but still steadily sweating its sly venom. There is a small dark silent chapel here storm-strafed just below the snowline and Ianto seeks shelter in its doorway from the gathering tumult, curling up into himself on the small slate bench there and the stone walls around him ajudder with the ceaseless wind and the centuries of preaching witnessed, the hwyl and the howl, this land cowering under the ever-present threat of extinction from a long long limb which can simply reach out and snuff a civilisation between forefinger and thumb. Ianto pulls his jacket up over his head and huddles whimpering against the cold stone and the heavy riveted oaken door unbudgeable. Beset with visions of cowled and cloaked supplicants gliding above the snow in single file. With flame-haired flailing preachermen vomiting floods and frogs. Huddled into the dark moist corner unique and odd and deadly like a toadstool, a deathcap, those things that haunt and distress him with their stasis, their patience. With their failure or refusal to live by motion.

If Ianto sleeps in this small stone space he does not know it, since consciousness has become indistinguishable from dream and concrete objects have adopted the properties of rubber including his own limbs, and all he knows or is aware of is that he is walking again on unreliable legs stiff-jointed with the cold, still deeper into these everswelling mountains, a memory of flame propelling him and desire for he knows not what leading him on only a bung to stop this hole within him through which leak his waters vital and sustenant. There is a scream behind his gritted teeth and his loose lips and the still-active amphetamine casts shapes when he closes his eyes, colourful swirls and whorls and retina-pricking stars, many-coloured flashes of false bright light. He walks diagonal across a valley wall topped with tortured formations of wind-carved rock like reaching claws and wormed with sheep-runs, along which a few scrawny animals hobble on moistly blackened legs gnawed at and stumped with foulfoot. The wind wails up the valley side bringing the smell of vanilla from the gorse bloom and the moss-campion shudders around the lichen-pied rocks and Ianto steps over the carcass of a sheep, its face seething with maggots and saxifrage tendrilling its appearing bones, salt-white yet streaked slurry-black with the creeping necrosis which caused it to lose its footing on these high rocks and fall and buck broken-backed to rest, still-living pabulum for worm and for fly. Or perhaps harried off the mountain top to its broken death by a red kite, then ripped and hacked at by that same bird. Ianto follows the sheeptrack up and over the valley wall, where it joins a clear and shallow river, chortling over polished stones, and the drizzle has begun to fall again so he seeks shelter beneath the old low stone bridge there, troll-like Ianto crouched in the shadows, bedraggled, tattered and bramble-gashed across his slack face and bony hands. Encrusted and muckied Ianto crouches on a dry rock under the old stone bridge, the mossed and dripping arched underside only inches above his aching head, half in and half out of shadow he is, like some fleeting smoke-made wraith

83

dimension-slipping confounding the flat map of awareness. He wafers his scabbed and shivering hands between his trembling thighs and huddles shuddering against the wind. A small pinkish fish flits through the stones in the knee-deep water and he watches it and thinks of food. A red kite soars vigilant over the mountain peak and through the rumbling sky and he watches it and thinks of food. A lanky spider hangs still in its web above his head, sucked husks of insects tossed by the wind, and he watches it and remembers a hospital bed and him lying in it, small boy, his being centred on pain.

Over this bridge horses once thundered and sheep and cattle were herded for market, for slaughter. Once this bridge rang with the trudge and tears of the Cleared. It has been here for a long, long time. And under it things creep into Ianto's head, untouchable things, things with the substance of petal or of moth, but still they crawl and creep into his humming head. They gather whispering around the wind-bleached bones of dead animals and the long stalks of tick-haunted grass and over the snailshell-scattered and blood-drenched slabs of rock where predatory birds have fed and they float like seeds, like plucked feathers, or fur red-rooted on the strengthening wind and they enter the head of this trembling skinny person bedecked with scab and filth, hunched for shelter under the old stone bridge in this remote mountain pass, where people rarely walk now save farmers seeking lost lambs or hikers gone astray or peculiar prodigies like himself, who squats simply and chatters his teeth and waits for something to happen.

Which it does: some time later when the sky is filling with vast shadows Ianto is woken from some senseless trance which might as well be termed sleep by the sound of boots tramping over the bridge just inches above his skull. The footsteps thump and echo under the bridge and off the moss-slippery stones and Ianto raises his head to listen:

—Not far now, lads. Buck up. Couple of miles and we'll be at the lake. Although Group B will be there well before us unless you lot get your bloody skates on.

Tramp, tramp.

84

—Just down the end of this valley now. Not far. Hot food and a kip and we could all do with that, couldn't we?

The footsteps march on and Ianto can see a group of red-cagouled people led by a taller person with a stick and a more authoritative stride. They all have their hoods pulled up over their heads and small knapsacks on their backs and the taller leader appears to be checking his bearings between a compass held in his hand and the position of the dull sun very low in the sky and rapidly sinking further. Ianto watches them walk on, smiling slightly with a secret thrill that they had no knowledge of his lurking presence mere inches below their feet, and as he smirks and watches he sees the straggler, slighter than the others, lag further behind the main group and then suddenly dart and crouch behind a rock and squat waiting until the group are some distance away and barely discernible in the enveloping darkness and grey rain and then stand and give the wanker sign to the backs of the vanishing group. Ianto hears the person chuckle and then watches it walk towards him down the valley slope. It hops over a log and then slides on a patch of mud and splashes into the shallow stream and walks upstream jauntily under the bridge with Ianto, who just squats there staring, impassive, a shape chipped from chalk. The boy rubs his hands together and gives another little laugh and removes the hood of his red cagoule, then sees Ianto and yells and jumps so that the top of his head clunks against the arched underside of the bridge.

—JESUS CHRIST!

He rubs his head and looks at Ianto.

—Fuck me stiff! Near fuckin shat me trousers then!

He checks his hand for blood and finds none, but rubs it against his chest anyway.

—Who the fuck are you?

Ianto doesn't answer.

—Oh, you're from Group B. Must be, eh? Same idea as me then, yeh? Well, I don't blame yer. I've had enough of that Crossley wanker. Sooner do this Outward Bound than another two weeks of DC like, but not with him, Crossley, fuckin tosspot-and-a-half. Hope he breaks his fuckin neck on that bastard mountain.

85

His accent is Midlands English, almost. His hair is fair and his face is babyish, with a certain sneer to the mouth and hardness in the eyes and jaw. Ianto watches him select a dry rock and wipe it and sit down on it and remove his knapsack and take from it a packet of sandwiches, which he unwraps and proceeds to eat. Ianto's breath deepens and becomes heavier and his temples commence to pulse.

—Don't say much, do yer? How long have you been under here then?

There is a shred of lettuce on the boy's lip. Ianto watches it slither slug-like down on to his pimpled chin.

—And where's yer cagoule? Yer meant to keep it on at all times, y'know, so they can recognise you if yer get lost. Well, that's what they say anyway. I reckon it's so you won't do a runner. Crossley'll have yer bollax if he finds yer without it, tho.

He takes another bite of the sandwich. The wind howls and lifts his hair up off his forehead in one horn.

—Can't yer speak?

Ianto stares.

—Yer not dumb, are you?

Ianto stares.

—Say something, Christ. Giving me the fucking creeps you are.

Ianto's voice comes out over a dry and parched throat, strained and gruff and whining:

—I want yewer sandwiches.

—Oh, so yer *can* speak. I was beginning to think you were a fuckin ghost or something. Well, you can fuckin want. Where's yer own butties? I'm fuckin starvin, me. Haven't eaten for ages. Been walking all fuckin day. Six o' clock he got us up, Crossley. Nazi bastard.

—Give me yewer sandwiches.

—I've told yer, no. They're mine an I'm hungry. Fuck off.

Ianto rocks forwards slowly until he is on all fours in the water and begins to slow-creep snake-bellied over the submerged rocks towards the boy. Staring at him with hooded eyes.

—What's up? What're you doing?

86

He stares, one cheek bulging with food, Ianto's eyes drilling out of his filthy face getting bigger.

—Oh Christ.

The boy begins to repack his knapsack.

—You're a local. Might've fuckin guessed. Something fuckin weird about you sheepshaggers, I'm tellin yer. Fuckin banjo-players round here. Ere, you can have me butty.

He tosses the half-eaten sandwich at Ianto and it bounces off his shoulder and falls into the water and breaks up into bread and cheese and lettuce and cucumber, these parts drifting downstream bouncing off rocks and veering with the current. Ianto is close and still creeping to the boy now, who without looking at him is trying to crook his arm through the handle of his knapsack, and Ianto's fingers grope and fumble on the streambed over the stones and close with natural ease around a rock apple-sized which matches the individual contours of his hand precisely, as if aeons ago it cooled with the earth and was formed by this small river over millennia incomprehensible and waited here as cities fell and were built again for only Ianto's hand to clutch it and put it to this very coming purpose and employment and naught beside. The boy stands with his right arm tangled in his sack and his cagoule very red in the failing light and then he slowly turns his head to look down at the snakelike Ianto, his eyes wide and his lower lip atremble, and what he sees in Ianto's upturned face causes him to say softly:

—Oh fuck.

And Ianto reaches out and as if in obeisance to some terrible prescript the boy's leg jerks forwards into Ianto's grasp and he yanks and the boy slips back on to the rocks, the air thumped out of his lungs with a yelp. Ianto straddles his kicking legs and raises the rock and as the boy opens his mouth to shout Ianto slams it into that widening hole, feeling teeth crunch and give and come away and the sound of enamel against granite grating in his sleepless sore ears. The boy begins to thrash, his fingers scrabbling up towards Ianto's face. Ianto grabs an arm in his free hand and pins it to the streambed and hefts the rock again, it coming away from the smashed mouth trailing strands of spit and thick blood lumpy with tooth-chunks, and the mouth is

87

now a gurgling hole semi-liquid and Ianto slams the rock into it again and feels a cheekbone shatter and the mouth manages to scream, high-pitched and ululating like an alarm so Ianto plugs it with the rock bearing down with all his body weight on his palm forcing the rock deeper into the spurting hole below the bulging eyes until the jaw gives with a sharp crack and the sudden yielding of that resistance causes Ianto to slip directly on to the boy's wrecked face. The boy thrashing madly wriggles out from under Ianto and scrambles across the stream with his face horribly elongated and stone-mouthed and streaming and Ianto spins and lunges and grabs the boy's flailing ankle and yanks and the boy slams over face-down into the stream and Ianto is on him in a second and sitting atop the boy's head, holding his face under the water. Arms and legs flail and windmill and the torso contorts at the waist almost bending itself double, folding back along itself, and red bubbles rise from beneath the trapped head and drift downstream and burst in a patch of crimson foam and gradually the limbs still and Ianto might giggle a single time or two and once the boy is entirely unmoving he remains sitting on the broken head while he smokes a cigarette still miraculously dry, drawing the smoke deep into his wheezing lungs waiting for the pounding at his temples and the drumming of his heart to settle. He reaches for the fallen knapsack and takes from it everything edible – sandwiches, smoky bacon crisps, banana – and places the food on the boy's unmoving back and eats it like that, off the extraordinary trencher that the boy has become. He eats and then smokes another cigarette, the last in the packet, and washes himself off in the water setting a dark slick off drifting downstream colouring those rocks which protrude and crawls out from under the bridge into the fallen wet and wailing night and walks away over the valley wall, leaving the body and the crumbs of his repast like a unique and remarkable smorgasbord for the prowling host of hulking low-bowed shapes which slide out of the mountain darkness sure and silent, led by death-stench with their eyes moonlit intent and determined and their teeth and talons grinning glittering silver, white and grey, the spectrum of decay's terrible chemistry. Is this sacrificial, this ravening here under the old low stone bridge? Might the mountains need and

88

demand this, the unacknowledged harrowing of those that cling to their immense flanks like lice? Ianto would have no answer to offer as tatterdemalion vile and ragged he seeks sleep and shelter from the wind and rain in a shallow cave that beasts have used to partake of provender in, imparting their own rooty stench and the musk of their spoor and their torn leavings of snapped bone and feather and scale and fur, bird furcula like parentheses against the wet rock walls, propped merrythoughts of their reptile geneses. Amongst this dark detritus in this thin and secret ossuary Ianto curls and sleeps the weighty sleep of the utterly exhausted and wakes with the sun, one side of his face lumpy and mosquito-sucked after a vivid dream of rodents grown huge, rats and mice and squirrels rearing up to the sky-splitting height of the Blaenplwyf transmitter, their titanic and terrible teeth and eyes capped by cloud. A peculiar yearning quality to this odd vision although for what Ianto could never even approximate as he crawls from the cave frozen and insect-bit and creeps Mohawk-cautious across the unpopulated peaks, disarrayed with stain and spillage he is, towards Llŷr's cottage and some food and a hot bath and a bed which is neither shale nor rock on which he can fall and fold himself into sleep, free for once and perhaps at last from guilt or need or even (strange power in his stride now, alien lift to his limbs) shame.

IANTO IS EIGHT.

The pebbles and small hardened pellets of soil he is flicking aimless and desultory into the stagnant weed-choked water of the shallow irrigation ditch which borders the field swaying with young green corn disturb a slender yellow-bellied frog, which in two large and spread-legged hops is squatting by Ianto's scabbed and grass-stained knee and it looks up at him and burps. And then burps again, the small feet flippers, the golden-green sheen of its skin, throat distended like blown rubber with each croak. Leaper between worlds squatting here by his knee, this liminal life manifest in the biological characteristics, one in the dry earth crumble of its call and the other in the smooth fluidity of its flight as it leads Ianto scrambling up the bank of the ditch and into a tangled thicket of briars sprouted about some old fenceposts bundled and secured with rusted barbed wire and discarded here by some land worker some time ago. Down on all fours small Ianto follows the small frog into the twisted bracken, through and along a rough-tube tunnel trodden probably by fox or by badger, with winged insects long-bodied whirring and lanky spiders high-stepping fleeing before him and finds himself suddenly inside a scene which pulses regularly in his nightmares, this mausoleum silent-screaming here of small impaled beings, striped lizards and a stag beetle and a large grasshopper and a baby bird feathered and with haemorrhoid eyes and other frogs these ones stiffly splayed and cruciform, all these creatures skewered on long sharp thorns and barbed-wire spines rusted orange and flaky or jammed into the forks of twigs. On all fours and statue-still Ianto stares, taking it all in, sees a mouse twitch, its thumb-sized soft-fur body curled over the thorn which exits its gaping mouth, small tortured contortion, sees a skink, a shrew, a slug crumble wetly in dark rot. One long thorn exits a small round yellow eye burst and leaking ichor, a thin white knobbled thread of tiny spine cranes out of torn and greyed flesh, jointed chitin legs and wingcases are splayed and rigid with old agonies. All of this, this secret quiet seething carnage hidden in leaves and flowers, now detonating in Ianto's head as he backs rapidly away from this strange orchard, these

90

writhing vines with their peculiar fruit, sees as he flees a thorn-speared unrecognisable and unnameable bulge of ripped meat weakly dripping old blood on to the once-white snowdrops struggling to grow below and he understands it to be a human heart, his heart, torn and wrenched and spitted and still softly throbbing, polluting the striving flowers beneath with its leakage rank and reeking, the very epicentre of some apex, some pinnacle, yanked and staked and displayed amidst carrion. The centre of himself, of his race, hopeless, bleeding. Whimpering he backs quickly along the beast-carved tunnel, his hands and knees abristle with thorns and spines, and striped by the weak sunlight which itself is sliced and serrated here in this strange and terrible grotto, knowing this to be the foul pantry of some dragon or scaled and dripping scuttler said to inhabit one of the local lakes or some silent hooded fanged figure who appears here only during full moon and storm, his knifeblade and teeth atwinkle, and back out into the sunlight arse-first and Ianto is panting on his back a sickness in his belly, and lying there like that with his nightmares stoked for years to come he is scolded by some branch-perched bird with hoarse and hiccuping smacking sounds, the white underparts unbarred, head and nape the colour of ashes, a certain ferocity to the curve of its beak, this shrike like some thrush or jay gone demented, psychotic, a songbird whose tune is the screaming of souls. It pours scorn on the supine Ianto for some time, this small feathered thing, Ianto's chest heaving and struck with horror at its sounds, its fever. He watches the butcherbird squall with black tongue and blood-rimmed eyes hooded and reptilian, then watches it hop to the ground and sprint oddly like some winged lizard or dwarf-vulture into the thrash of vegetation and its demonic larder, and he is up and then running homewards stumbling over a ploughed field before he can hear the shred and tear of flesh and snap and crack of small bones even though such rapine booms in his breast and he can taste it in his mouth, old marrow, putrefaction, blood become black and the forbidden whey of wound and wart. And how the churned ground and the punctured lives are each business of one whole as if the entire world conspires in torture, as if the matters of men and the world they harrow are all about one pain, one death.

That night and for a thousand nights to come his dreams will fall on darkened wings and he will cry out into the blackness and his grandmother will come concerned and night-robed, but he will be away in talons and the world will blur beneath him and he will be left gasping, flailing, speared on the branch of a lightning-blasted blackthorn and bared to the storm and the cracking sky above, which can no longer, if indeed it ever could, harness his spreading horrors.

—YEH, I ALWAYS wondered like why he had to borrow kex an a shirt off me that time. Thought it was strange, I did. An he never told me what had happened to is own gear, like.

—An yew didn't think it was strange –

—What have I just said?

—Didn't think it was *peculiar*, like, that Ianto was burning his own clothes an stuff in yewer fire? Fucks sakes, Llŷr, did yew not think there was somethin up, there, likes? Somethin amiss?

—Well, fuck, alls I knew was that when I got back home like yer was Ianto near fuckin bollocko wrapped in a blanket before a blazin fire. Twat'd climbed in through a kitchen window.

—An yew didn't even think to ask im what had happened to is jeans an jumper, like? Why he was burnin them? Didn't think that was unusual at all?

—Course I fuckin did, mun. I asked im as well, but he just shrugged. Yew know what he was like. Couldn't get a fuckin word out of im sometimes. I asked im loads-a times, like, I even told im that I wouldn't lend im any of my stuff until he told me what had happened to is own, but he'd just shrug an fuckin stare off into space. Yew *know* what he was like. Christ alfuckinmighty, Griff, it wasn't my fuckin fault what that cunt did. *I'm* not fuckin responsible for is actions.

—Not sayin yew are, mun.

—An anyway, if I hadn't've lent im me anorak then we wouldn't've had any proof that it was him, would we? Wouldn't've found it in that fuckin mine, like, with them bodies. So yew can fuckin well thank me.

—Fuck off. Tell me yewer takin-a piss.

—All's I'm sayin is that it wasn't my fuckin fault.

—Not fuckin sayin it was.

—Well what the fuck *are* yew sayin then?

—I'm sayin that I reckon yew should've been more, what's-a

93

fuckin word, vigilant. Should've looked out for things a bit more like. Kept yewer fuckin eyes open.

—Yeh, but that's easy to say after the fact like, innit? What, yew think I went home an thought: oh fuck, Ianto yer might be a serial killer, I'd better keep me eye on him? Bollax. I mean, don't fuckin forget like that I'd only just got back from a mad fuckin rave an only just escaped from a fire. Alls I wanted to do was have a bath an a kip, that's all. I was fuckin exhausted. Duw, tell yew-a truth, I couldn't've really given a fuck about Ianto sittin starkers in me house. Wouldn't've looked twice if he was wearin women's fuckin underwear, mun. I was knackered. Off me fuckin head. Yew would've been-a fuckin same, mun, don't say yew wouldn't.

—He's right, Griff. None of us could-a known. Yewer bein unfair on the boy.

—Yeh! I mean, yew know what it's like, mun, yew've bin there before. No sleep for two days, no food, yewer still speedin in yewer head but all yewer body wants is rest . . . yewer in that state an yer's Ianto fuckin bollocko in yewer house like, what the fuck d'yew do? Yew give-a fucker somethin to weat an crawl off into bed. *That's* what yew do. That's all yew fuckin *can* do, innit? Alls yew can think about is sleep.

—An a good wank.

—Yew, maybe, Marc, aye. Thinkin of Ianto nuddy put yew in mind-a that, did it?

—Oh yeh. Always had the hots for Ianto, I did. Fuck off. No, alls I'm sayin is that that's what I want when I'm crashin, like, when I'm comin down; a good long wank an a kip. Nowt wrong with that, is yer?

—I still fuckin reckon tho that yew all had yewer heads up yewer arses. A little bit of fuckin awareness like, that's all was fuckin needed. Just some fuckin . . .

—Oh! Says fuckin *yew*! Jesus, Griff, I don't see yew including yerfuckinself in this, this fuckin, collective fuckin ignorance shit. Where-a fuck are *yew* in all this like?

—I NEVER FUCKIN LIVED WITH THE CUNT, DID I? Hardly ever even saw the fucker, me. Once-a twice every two months like, an that was fuckin it. That's all. But I'm fuckin tellin yew, If I

94

had've fuckin shared a house with the bastard then I would've fuckin sussed that somethin was up. Tellin yew. Too fuckin right I would've. In a fuckin dreamland, yew, all-a fuckin yew. Heads up yewer arses. Open yewer eyes, this is-a fuckin real world. Fuck's sake.

—Yeh, but yew could hardly ever speak to the man! Yew *know* what he was like, how he could be. Hardly ever said two words in-a course of a day. Fuckin mute or somethin like. Dumb. What was the longest conversation yew ever had with im then? Go on, tell me that. See! An why's that? Because the cunt hardly ever fuckin spoke, that's fuckin why. How'm I supposed to know *anythin* about someone who, one, I hardly ever fuckin see, an two, hardly fuckin speak to when I *do* see em? I mean, I'm not a fuckin mindreader or anythin. Fuck. What d'yew fuckin expect? How the fuck was *I* supposed to know what the fuck was goin on, what that twat did out in-a fuckin mountains? Ey? Jesus, don't fuckin blame me. Sort yewerself out.

—Griff . . .

—Take it easy, mun . . .

—I mean, Llŷr's right, Griff, in a way. I mean, it's like, y'know, his silence was just part an parcel of the way Ianto was. His fuckin, his mystery or whatever yew want-a call it.

—Pervertedness.

—Yeh, sound, call it that if yew want to, like. But the fact stands that he was, well, quiet, to say the fuckin least. Never saw im react to anythin, like. Just his general stoic attitude.

—Here we go. More bullshit about to come from Danny.

—Fuck off, Marc. Prick. We're trying to work out what fuckin happened here. Why four people fuckin died.

—Three.

—Four if yew include Ianto isself. Four fuckin people battered to death in case yew've fuckin forgotten like. Or aren't arsed, which with yew is probably the more fuckin likely scenario. Four innocent people.

—Ha! Ianto? Innocent? Don't make me fuckin laugh, mun.

—Splittin fuckin hairs now, yew are. Innocence int the fuckin point, mun –

95

—Well why use the fuckin word, then? That's what yew said, 'innocent'. Not me.

—An nor is fuckin blame. What we're talkin about like is how none of us noticed anything, until-a end of course, like, how Ianto could, like, y'know, be ar mate an do-a things he did without any of us suspecting a fuckin thing. Without any of us bein any the fuckin wiser.

—Well, I *suspected*, like . . .

—No yew didn't.

—Well, what I mean is, is that, when I found out like, when we *all* found out, it dint come as no surprise. No fuckin shock to me at all mun.

—Yeh but yew didn't actually *suspect*, like, did yew? Not when it was all going on like, not when Ianto was alive. Yew didn't have a fuckin clue, then, mun, none of us did.

—It's as Llŷr says, tho, innit? Ianto hardly ever talked, like, an nor did he really spend that much time with any of us. Always on is own, like, wanny? It was just his, like, his . . . what was that word yew used before, Danny, about Ianto?

—Stoic.

—Aye, that's it. Ianto's stoicness made it difficult for us all like.

—Yeh. It was just-a way he was, wannit. He just, like, seemed to absorb fuckin everythin, didn't he? Just like this fuckin, this quiet sponge he was. Just sittin there, like. Could never tell what he was thinkin about. It's like the way he was with drugs, or drink; he'd just absorb it all. Anythin yew put in front of him, like, straight down his fuckin neck. Drink any drink, do any drug, without, really, any noticeable effect either.

—Yeh. Apart from he'd sometimes fall asleep.

—Aye. Or murder some poor fucker halfway up Cader Idris.

—Only three times he did that. Well twice, really. On two occasions, like. An of course we didn't know it at the time, did we?

—No, which is what this whole bastard conversation is about. Christ. Come full circle, yew have. Back to square fuckin one. Might as well talk to-a bleedin wall.

96

—An anyway, who's to say that it was-a drugs which made Ianto, like, hunt people, kill them? I don't reckon it was. Because if so then these mountains would be fuckin *full* of dead bodies, wouldn't they? Cos Ianto was off is head nearly all-a time. I mean, yer'd be more corpses than fuckin daisies, wouldn't there?

—Yeh.

—Which proves that what the police said was shit. They –

—We all know the Bill talk wank, mun, it's a given fact. Learnin nothin new yer, like.

—Yeh. Knew ey spouted a biggest load-a bollax on earth before any of this ever fuckin happened. Don't talk to me about-a busies, mun.

—Too fuckin right.

—Yeh. I mean, a only real sign that Ianto was wrecked was not that he'd take isself off on a killin spree, like, as the busies seemed to think, it was that either he'd crash out or, or, remember, he'd do almost any fuckin thing yew asked him to do. Remember that? No matter how embarrassin or dangerous it was.

—Yeh!

—Remember!

—Christ aye. That time he crapped on the roundabout in Machynlleth.

—He did *what?*

—Yeh. Straight up. Did a shit in-a middle of the roundabout as yewer goin in to Mach. Five o'clock in-a evening, like, dead busy roads. And this wasn't a proper roundabout, like, y'know, not like a big one with trees an bushes an stuff. This was just like a little white hump in the middle of the road. Clear as fuckin day, mun, all these cars an buses goin past, yer's fuckin Ianto curlin one out. Kex down, squattin over a great big red steamer. Laughed me fuckin head off I did. Nearly shat me *own* kex I was fuckin laughin so bastard much. Should-a seen it, mun, yer's Ianto, squattin, strainin, Jesus . . . funniest thing I ever fuckin saw, mun.

—Was he pissed, like?

—Pissed? Christ aye, off is fuckin face, mun. Wouldn't-a done it otherwise, see.

97

—Sounds just fuckin like im, that. Only way to tell if he was lashed or not was to ask him to do somethin mad. I mean yer'd be no slurrin of is speech or anythin, like, wouldn't fall over. He'd just do any mad fuckin thing yew told im to. He should-a been on one of those telly programmes, y'know the ones where knobhead members of-a public drive Mini-Mokes over a ravine or something? 'Don't Ever Do This At Home' or whatever the fuck it's called? Yeh? He'd-a been fuckin well up for somethin like that, Ianto would. Christ yes.

—Yeh. Get im pissed, give im one-a the All Blacks to try an shag, yer yew go, yer's your programme. Pay to see that I would.

—Ianto would've paid to fuckin *do* it, mun, pissed or no.

—Yeh. Would've fuckin loved it, like.

—Yeh. He *was* a bit of a dirty get, wanny?

—A 'bit'! A fuckin 'bit', he says! Christ, remember who yewer fuckin talkin about yer, mun. Remember what he did.

—Yeh.

—D'yew think he died a virgin? D'yew think he ever had a shag like?

—Fucks. Not with anyone alive, no. An certainly not with anyone human. I mean, what girl in-a right mind would ever have opened em for that ugly fucker? Half-wit. Smelly. Fuckin perverted. Jesus, what a catch.

—Was into Gwenno, tho, wanny?

—I shagged Gwenno.

—We know yew did, Marc. How could we not? Yew remind us every fuckin day, like. Shut the fuck up about it. Poor girl's probably still havin psychiatric treatment for it now, like.

—Yeh. Post-traumatic stress disorder. In with all-a war veterans, shakin like a leaf.

—Fuck off. Jealous.

—Of *yew*? Yewer arse.

—Ey, that was the night that Ianto got is knob out, wannit? Anyone remember that? Up at Llŷr's?

—Oh fuck aye. Ad a bleedin wank in front of us all, dinny? Gwenno an er mates, fuckin everyone there. Didn't give a fuck like, just whapped it out, started thrappin. Didn't know whether to laugh or bastard cry. End of is knob all chewed up like that, Jesus.

—Aw yeh. Did anyone ever find out what happened? To is knob, like? Why it was all mangled like that?

—Shudder to fuckin think, mun. Stickin it where it wasn't wanted.

—Caught in is zip or somethin.

—Some sheep playin hard to get. Snapped out at the end of is nudger.

—Yeh. Fuck knows where he'd bin stickin that thing of is. Oo Jesus . . . sends a shiver down me spine just thinkin about it, that does. Aw Christ.

—Didn't seem particularly embarrassed about it, tho, did he?

—Should've been.

—Just out with it an on with it he was. Pissed bastard.

—Dirty twat.

—An Gwenno an er mates screamin . . .

—Oh aye, yeh. *I* remember Gwenno screamin, I do.

—Oh for fuck's sake, Marc. Shut the fuck up, ey?

—I reckon he kind of fell in love with Gwenno that night, I do. Ianto, like. Don't yew reckon? That's where it all began, I reckon. That night up at Llŷr's.

—Ianto? *That* fucker? Love? Didn't fuckin have it in im, mun. No fuckin way. Incapable, that cunt. Must-a been like.

—Well, see, that's what I've been tryin to say all along. About Ianto like. That, y'know, on the one hand like he could, likes, fall in love with Gwenno and on the other . . .

—He could be a fuckin killer. Rapist. Fuckin . . .

—No, I mean, that he could . . . I don't know, maybe one drove im to the other, I dunno. But what I'm tryin to say is like that he, Ianto like, wasn't, first an foremost, a murderer. There were other things inside im as well. Circumstances, like, y'know. The world he was in.

—World he was in be fucked. We're all in a same fuckin one, mun, or have yew never fuckin thought of that? D'yew see *me* batterin some fuckin schoolboy to death with a rock? D'yew see *me* rapin some poor fuckin hiker? No, yew don't,

99

an I'll tell yew why, it's cos I'm not a sick, dirty *cunt* like that bastard was. Very few of us are in this world, thank fuck, an we all live in-a same fuckin one. So yewer talkin out yer arse.

—Again.

—No, fuck, I don't mean *this* world, the one around us, the one we live on. I mean *Ianto's* world, y'know, the one that he himself was in, his own little world. The world of his, his fuckin *life* and his upbringing. *That* world. The smaller world around him that he grew up in. We all have one. An unfortunately for Ianto, his was a fuckin mess.

—Jesus. Should've been a fuckin social worker yew, Danny. Wishy-washy fuckin liberal like.

—Yeh. It's all bollax, mun, an yew fuckin know it.

—No, I just think that it goes to prove the fuckin mass of contradictions that we all are. That we have a nice side an a bad side. Yew know, good an evil, yin an yang. Darkness an light. I mean I'm simplifying things, like, but that's so thick cunts like Marc can get some idea of what I'm talkin about.

—Fuck off.

—Don't yew agree, tho? I mean don't yew think that we're all a mass of contradictions, that we're all capable of doing a horrible thing one day an a good one the next? That that, an nothin else really, is what makes us fuckin human?

—No. Contradictions, like, maybe, but to that extent? What Ianto did? Fuck *no.*

—Alright, so yew think Ianto killed those three people?

—Fuckin *know* he did, boy. Proven.

—But yew don't think that he was in love with Gwenno?

—No fuckin way, no. Love be fucked. He just wanted to shag her, that's all.

—Like *I* did, yew mean?

—Aw fuck off, Marc. Just fuck right off.

—So what's yewer point, Danny?

—Dunno. Forgotten it now. Doesn't really matter anyway.

THE STORM BEGINS around midnight out in Cardigan Bay, equidistant between mainland Wales and the Irish Republic. It boils black-blue above the darkly humping silver-scrolled waves and picks up power and tosses a trawler like a toy and sucks up salt water in a tight spout and heads Waleswards, rocking and tossing the sea, which angers underneath it as if affronted, and breaks up a small student party on the pebbly beach and spins water and gulls and litter through the emptying streets of the coastal towns and steals the hats off pub-returners and skirls through the deserted university and into the uplands, howling around the sharp-cornered cathedral bulk of the National Library and rocks caravans and crumples a tent in the holiday village and judders the rugby posts in their concrete stanchions and is not in any way broken or weakened by the mountain ramparts, but instead appears to be enraged further by their buttressing and screams over their bare rock and owl-scoured crests and howls down into the cwm, seeming deliberately to seek out the small whitewashed shack with the orange-glowing windows in the coppice of twisted leafless trees, and yanks the smoke away from the blackened chimney-pot in pellucid spermy twists and hurls rain like gravel against the windows loose in their rotting frames. The cottage trembles before this onslaught, but years of withstanding such bombardments have eroded shallow slashes in its whitewash and exposed grey stonework and serrated the lip of the chimney, turning it almost sawtoothed, and smoothed its corners and buckled its guttering and wafered its sliding slates, and there is no valid reason to suspect that this new storm now will be any more destructive than what has come seething and wailing before or will have any more discernible effect or outcome than merely to augment the erosion, catastrophic in mountain-time or sky-time or storm-time but negligible and barely even noticeable in the daily rise and fall of our own.

Inside the cottage, the large fire in the grate, built on

coal scraps and foraged wood and a broken kitchen chair, the laddered back of which is still skeletally visible in the flames like a child's ribcage, and with the charred pot of mushroom tea most of which has been drunk throughout the evening warming on the tiled hearth before it, illuminates the relaxed and recumbent grinning figures reposing on floor and in chairs orbited by empty or emptying cans and bottles and some plates smeared with sauce and grease and small brown bottles of prescription pills and record sleeves and magazines scattered with torn-off cigarette filters and matchsticks and tobacco curls, general spliff debris. Stuffy in here with the fire's dry heat and the sweet smoke hanging in foggy strata. Like a whimsical lord, Griff reclines in the bulky armchair by the fire sipping on a can of Tennent's through his lolling smile, Llŷr cross-legged at his feet head nodding chin on chest, diazepam-drowsy. Perched on a wooden crate fixed-grinned Danny builds another spliff, skewering a large lump of resin on the tines of a twisted fork and holding it above the fire to render it friable. His trainers were once mostly white and are now split at the seams at the side knuckles of his big toes, where bunions will bulge in later life, and his jeans are grass-greened at the knee from keeping goal earlier that day and he giggles to himself as at some private amusement, building the spliff painstakingly and thoroughly distributing the crumbled resin evenly along its length and snugly fitting the roach and twisting the loose paper at the end, one bleared eye on utility and the other on aesthetics. On the sagging settee against the far wall which abuts the tiny kitchen Gwenno and Jane and Fran sit in bright and loud triune sharing their own joint and drinking from bottles of lemon Hooch a crate of which chills behind them in the cold space beneath the sink, no need for electric refrigeration. On the carpet at their feet, one pair bare and painted-nailed and mucky-soled, another clad in scuffed boots and the other outsized in fat-soled trainers, sit Marc and Ianto one at each end of the sofa like earthenware hearth dogs, Marc widely grinning as colours spin around him and perspective dribbles through space under the mugs of mushroom tea he has drunk. The thumb and forefinger of his right hand bracelet Fran's ankle every twenty minutes or so until she kicks her foot free and tells him to fuck off and he apologises and then waits to do it again and then does it again, and Ianto sitting quiet for now drinking a glass of whisky and humming to himself and feeling the heat on his left shoulder from Gwenno's knee only a couple of inches away and whenever he thinks he can do it unnoticeably he steals glances up at her face, the framing auburn, almost maroon hair and the thick red lips and the large green eyes and the slightly turned-up nose, which he describes secretly to himself as 'pixie', this adjective picked up from somewhere but specifically where he knows not or has long forgotten. The wind screams, moans, then screams again around this small house and whips the flames in the fireplace and rain batters the windowpanes which quake in their frames, the ragged curtains swaying, and these sounds almost drown out the compilation tape playing in the corner, 60 Foot Dolls giving way to Catatonia, which Griff being the nearest leans to turn up because he likes the song and because he can't hear it clearly or loudly enough above the wind roaring against the rattling window just behind his head, a draught chilling a palm-sized patch on the back of his cropped skull which would ache and irritate him and cause him to move were his senses not dulled and were it not for the agreeable feeling of being overseer or precentor, which the location of this old heavy comfortable armchair at the head of the room adjacent to its source of heat and light confers upon him.

'I Am the Mob'.

Griff nudges Llŷr's yielding and relaxed back with his knee.

—Ey, Llŷr . . . Cerys Matthews. Yew fuckin *would*, wouldn't yew? *I* would. Too fuckin right, mun. In a fuckin second.

Llŷr raises his head slowly eyes closed and makes a small sound in his throat, then his head drops again on a neck made it seems from jelly or stripped of spine. Griff looks at him and tuts in disgust.

—Wasted cunt . . . Ey, Danny; Cerys Matthews. Would yer?

Danny's voice comes out strained and croaky as he holds smoke in his lungs.

—If I had to, like, yeh. If there was . . . He exhales in a

103

whoosh. —If there was just me an her at the end of a party or somethin like an All Saints an Siân Lloyd had all gone home. *Then* I would, aye.

—Siân Lloyd? Fuck off. Fuck right off, son. Siân Lloyd? Reminds me of me old headmistress. Wouldn't fuckin touch that with yours, boy.

—Yew wouldn't be able to cos I'd be using it meself.

Danny takes another toke on the spliff and then passes it over to Griff, who accepts it and draws deep on it and then points with the lit end across the room at Gwenno like some strange weatherman indicating a pocket of high pressure.

—Yew. Gwenno.

She breaks off mid-laugh.

—What?

—Yew look a bit like Cerys Matthews, yew do. Remind me of her likes.

—Cerys Matthews? Oh do I? Well that's nice to hear. Considering she can't sing for shit an she looks like my fuckin dad. What a bastard compliment.

She rolls her eyes at the ceiling.

—If I look like her then yew look like . . . She thinks and then grins. —Danny de Vito.

Fran and Jane laugh loudly and Marc and Ianto splutter and Griff gives them both an evil look and they shut up.

—She's right! Fran yells. —Danny de Vito, *that's* who it is. The fuckin spit. Always wondered who it is yew remind me of. Danny de fuckin Vito. Could be fuckin twins, aye.

—Fuck off. Danny de Vito yewer arse. But I'll tell yew what . . .

Griff fumbles at the flies of his jeans.

—. . . my *knob* looks like Danny de Vito. Fat an round with a shiny dome, see?

He pulls it out over the waistband of his jeans and the girls shriek and laugh. He waggles it and pulls the foreskin back and speaks squeakily through his clenched teeth like a ventriloquist:

—Hello. My name's Danny de Vito an I'm a crap Hollywood actor. I'm fat and round and shiny like a Welshman's penis.

—Aw Christ! Put the fuckin thing away!

Jane flaps her hands, her eyes scrunched shut.

—Dirty bastard, Griff! Put it away, mun! Yewer makin me sick!

Griff waggles it again then stuffs it back into his trousers and rebuttons his flies. He passes the spliff back to Danny with the same hand he handled his dick with and Danny automatically sucks at it and then wrinkles his face in distaste. He scrutinises the roach end and picks something off it which he flicks away and hands the joint back to Griff.

—Fuckin pube on this, mun. Fuckin pubic hair. I'm not suckin on anythin which as been within a fuckin mile of yewer naked knob. Ere, yew can have the bastard thing back.

Griff shrugs and sucks on the spliff then thinks for a moment.

—Ey, Danny.

—What?

—Is there a famous person who looks like *your* baldy lad, would yew say? Who'd yew say yewer knob looks like, if anyone?

—Like Carl Cox in a polo-neck jumper. Life fuckin size, mun.

—Good one. Llŷr?

No answer. Llŷr is sleeping upright. Griff continues:

—Fuckin Tom Thumb I'd say. Marc?

—Dunno. But me balls look like John Malkovich an Sean Connery standin side-by-side. Seen from above, like.

—Good one again. Ianto?

Ianto just shrugs.

—Get it out then, mun. Let's have a look.

Ianto covers his crotch with both of his hands.

—I can't, it's . . .

—It's what? Dropped off? Too small? Ach Ianto, mun, don't be shy. Get yewer knob out for-a people, boy.

—Later.

—No, not later, *now*. Do as I fuckin well say, boy.

—Aw leave him alone, Griff. Cruel bastard. Gwenno leans and puts a protective arm around Ianto's neck and Ianto blushes pink and grins. —He don't have to show us if he doesn't want to, do yew, Iant?

105

She pecks his cheek and sits back again and the grin on Ianto's hot face is like a clean wound.

—What about yew girlies then? C'mon, let's see which look-alikies yewer all hiding from us. Get yewer minges out then.

Marc says: —I can tell yew without seeing them: Michael Douglas with a splitting headache.

—Aw Jesus, mun!

—Aye. Griff nods soberly. —Or all three of em next to each other, like. Fuckin photograph of a First World War battlefield that would be. All-a slimy wet trenches.

—Yeh! Marc laughs. —With men's feet stickin out of em!

Jane and Fran howl and hold each other and Marc laughs again, too loud. Gwenno doesn't smile.

—Fuckin dirty bastards yew two, aye. Is that all yew ever fuckin think about?

—Yeh, Jane says. —That's how yew amuse yewerselves, is it? By thinking about other people's genitals like?

Griff shrugs, all innocent. —Well, yeh. Of course.

—Sad, sad men. Can yew not think about anythin else, then? Incapable, is it?

—Well no, I mean, I *can* think about other things, yeh, course I can, but I *prefer* to think about yewer sexual organs. It gets me . . . He narrows his eyes and licks his lips theatrically and whispers: —*excited*, with an exaggerated shudder of his shoulders.

Jane and Gwenno laugh and Fran makes a noise of amused disgust. Ianto laughs too, a bucktoothed yuk as is his fashion and realises that he is still protectively cupping his crotch with his hands quite tightly, in fact tight enough to ignite a spark of pain in his testicles, but he feels safer that way and leaves his left hand in that place and with his right raises his glass to his mouth and remains like that sipping until he has drunk a half-pint tumbler of neat cheap Scotch, which on top of all the other alcohol he has already drunk, the beer and the cider and the mushroom tea two cups and the dabs of amphetamine and the never-ending passed-around spliffs, affords its own particular kind of fortification or if not that then at least a capacity to manufacture indifference and in that frame he can let his left hand rest easy on his bent left knee and not care now about his crotch covered only with cloth. Spirit intoxication is now coming upon him in a surge as it does and not in the steady sequential increase of inebriation caused by lighter drinks. Lager, say, or wine. Were one capable it can be focused on a specific few moments: there I was sober, here I am drunk, but of course the mental clarity required to do this is shattered itself and muddied and muddled by the immersion of the desire to do so in the obscurant cloudiness and grainy fizz somewhere behind the eyes, which undeniable and unfightable is the point. Ianto knows this, in some working organ gurgling inside him somewhere and tubed to another which in turn is ganglioned, yet again he knows this, which is why he can let himself lean familiar against Gwenno's black-jeaned leg and smile and look up at her face.

The smoky air takes on that slight electrical crackle and shadowless hue which can always be breathed in a roomful of people rocking on the rim of drunkenness. A Manic Street Preachers song comes on, 'Australia', and Fran stands to dance, unsteady, her arse swaying in her shiny hipsters her midriff bared white a ring in her navel and Marc stares unashamedly pleased and salacious at those parts of her and she either does not notice or does not care. Drinking the Hooch, her head thrown back so that her light brown hair touches her belt loops, her eyes closed. Griff and Danny also watch her appreciative and the sleeping Llŷr lists slowly sideways further and further until he is kept upright only by Griff's lower leg.

—Jesus. Will yew look at this *twat*.

Griff jerks his leg and Llŷr falls to the floor with a thud.

—He's still breathing, inny?

Griff says nothing. Danny repeats his question:

—Llŷr's still breathing, inny, Griff? Better check he's still alive, mun.

Griff inclines his ear towards the supine Llŷr and hears nothing above the music and the storm outside, but nods his head and drinks from his can and says: —Yeh.

—Good. Only it was diazepam that did for Gareth last

month, wannit. Or the month before, whenever it was. Can't remember.

—Nah. Methadone that was, not diazepam. Bad fuckin stuff that methy. This twat yer's only on-a diazzies, no fucker ever died from a diazzy overdose mun. Methadone, aye, but not diazepam. Mickey Mouse downer, diazepam.

—That's not all he's on, tho, is it? Polished off a whole bottle-a Bell's before like, I saw him. Or almost a whole bottle anyway.

—Ach, he'll be alright. Just leave im sleep. Look at Janey now.

Danny follows Griff's eyes to see Jane dancing with Fran, both of them more active now swinging each other around, Jane falling backwards in a heap pulling Fran down on top of her and Gwenno diving on to them both yelling, all three creased in drunken laughter, and Marc and Ianto looking on amused, aroused. Griff watches them for a moment grinning and then addresses Ianto:

—Ey, nice jacket, Iant. Nice new kex as well. New, is it? Where'd yew get them then? Seen Llŷr wearin some exactly-a same. Where'd yew get them?

—Llŷr's cupboard.

—Oh aye? An what happened to yewer old ones en? That bloody brown shirt yew always wear? Run off on its own, aye?

Ianto says nothing and turns again in his new blue anorak to watch Gwenno try to disentangle herself from the twist of bodies on the floor, bent over, her arse in her jeans smooth-globed a foot or so before his open face. Marc moves to assist her.

An especially powerful gust thumps the window and it jerks as if about to shatter. The impact can be sensed and felt in the floor, in the thick stone walls, in the fire suddenly fanning in the grate and the soles of their feet.

—Christ, hear that? Danny asks. —Fuckin hurricane, mun. Hate to be out in that, I would.

—Ah yeh. Griff nods his head sagely. —Be fuckin crazy out yer now. Fuckin wild.

And it is: the outlying leafless trees thrash madly as if struggling to uproot themselves and run and the very mountains themselves seem to shake in the storm's fury. The dark rectangular entrance to the disused silver mine over the hill is a toothless howling mouth and as if playing on a demented harp the wind screams through the circle of standing stones which sprout above the mine and have sprouted there for these three thousand years and more, ancient arcane megaliths scratched and scored with twisted petroglyphs, these markings and the stones themselves of intent unknown and of purpose long lost now fervidly strummed by the storm into a hundred tortured voices. In the sheltered lee of a lichen-pocked and still sturdy drystone wall a ewe groaningly gives birth, its complaint snatched away, the lamb stillborn, with a further vestigial leg hanging withered from its caked shoulder, caesium-warped from Chernobyl fallout. Like many these past fifteen years have been and will be again. The secret poison seething in the grass and the soil and the water that falls deceptively clear on to these reaching hills. The very moon and stars above seem to shudder in their fixings before the storm's wrath, its ceaseless battering of the landscape entire seemingly focused on the small cottage only, the walls and roof atremble, its hysterical force and roaring pitch like the incomprehensible expression of some ancient grievance in rage and ransack appeased not one fleck by the consolatory grace such a fury embodies, ignorant of the elegance a passion carries irregardless of its aftermath in ash or in smoke or in its singular rivered leavings of blood.

Danny stands on legs unsteady and draws back the tattered curtain to look out through the racing water on the pane at the crack of grey light washing the sky low over the storm-strafed mountain. Dawn here, in this weather; grey appearing, greyness spreading, the moon drawing the blackness below the planet's curvature and giving way to the grey and insipid silver sun. Climbing grey sky to come.

—Anything interesting?

—Nah. Danny shakes his head and sits back down again. —Hills, rocks, sky . . . seen it all before, mun. Mad storm, like. Glad I'm not out in the fucker.

—Snug in yer tho, aye?

—Yeh.

—Built-in entertainment as well, look.

Griff nods over at the far wall, where an angry Fran is fiercely poking a protesting Marc in the chest. Jane is supporting her at her left shoulder like some guardian spirit and Ianto and Gwenno merely stand and look on wordless.

—Dirty fuckin bastard yew are. Dirty fuckin pervert. Grabbin my fuckin tits.

—I never, I –

—That's fuckin *rape*, Jane shouts. —Fuckin molestation. Could av yew fuckin done for this, boy.

—Rape be fucked! I did nowt! It was a fuckin accident!

—Oh, was it then? Yewer hands just happened to, like, *fall* on me tits then, did they? Fran yells in Marc's face. —Just kind of ended up yer, like? Up me fuckin shirt like?

—Yeh! That's all that happened! I couldn't bastard help it! Christ, think I'd feel yew up by fuckin *choice*? Jesus, woman. Not *that* fuckin desperate.

Fran's poking sends Marc back against the cold stone wall so he cannot retreat any further. He shakes his head vigorously and spreads his arms, a gesture of outraged innocence.

—Honest, mun, I did fuck all! It was an accident, I swear! I was just tryin-a help yew up like cos yew'd fallen over, that's all!

—Oh aye, yeh. Good way of helping someone up, that, grabbing eyr knockers like. Is that what yew do in-a street? Bet yew can't wait for winter an the icy roads, yew.

Marc looks helplessly over at Griff.

—Griff, tell um, mun. I did fuck all.

—Yeh, Griff, go on, tell im, says Fran. —Tell im we'll take a kitchen knife to is maggot fuckin dick if he dozen learn to keep is little fuckin hands to isself.

Griff shrugs. —Nothin I can do, mun. What're yew lookin at me for? Fuckin referee now, am I?

Jane and Fran each grab a handful of Marc's hair and hiss in his ears, one to each mouth. Marc grabs their arms and shakes his head protesting and Danny gets up to separate them from each other.

110

—Ey, c'mon now, that's enough. This is gonner come to blows like.

—Too fuckin right it is. Fran's face is angry red. —Grabbin me bastard tits. I'll rip-a bleedin bollax off the dirty twat I will.

—Marc, yew comen sit yer. Griff, recumbent in the armchair, points with a cigarette at the upturned wooden crate Danny has just vacated, a folded jumper on it for a cushion double-dinged with the imprint of Danny's arsecheeks and Danny pushes Marc over in that direction. —Yew two can sit back down on-a couch.

The women do, scowling. Ianto and Gwenno also sit back down again and Gwenno asks Fran is she's OK and Ianto just watches without words or expression.

Marc takes the crate. —I did fuck all, mun. All's I did was –

—Aw shut-a fuck up, Marc, yeh? Just fuckin leave it, mun. Stop causing trouble.

—I wasn't.

—What?

—I said I wasn't.

—Well, that's what it fuckin looked like from where I'm sittin.

—Yeh, but yew didn't see.

—The girls wouldn't get so fuckin worked up over nothing, now, would they? Must-a done *some*thing.

—Yeh, but it was an accident. I was just tryin-a help um up, that's all. Weren't *my* fuckin fault if I accidentally grabbed old of her tit, like. Not that yer's much to fuckin grab anyway.

—Oi!

Jane springs up from the settee, but Gwenno and Danny settle her back down again.

—Just ignore him, Janey. Chopsy cunt, that's all he is. Don't let um wind yew up. That's what he wants. Just ignore him.

Danny turns to face Marc.

—And *yew*. Just shut yewer fuckin gob, alright? Funny ow somethin like this always seems to fuckin happen when yewer around, dunnit? We're just havin a chill, few spliffs, an yew start causing fuckin grief. Stop it fuckin right now or me an Griff'll throw yew out in-a fuckin storm.

III

—Oh will yew? Like to see yew fuckin try, Danny.

—Aw Christ Marc, mun. That's enough. Griff makes placatory gestures with hands. —Take a few of Llŷr's diazzies, will yer. Calm yerself down like.

—What, an end up like *him?*

Marc nods down at Llŷr, curled and snoring in the mildewy corner.

Danny gathers clean cups and glasses, seven of them, one each excluding the comatose Llŷr. —Now we'll all share-a couple-a spliffs an av a nice cup-a mushie tea. Calm us all down likes. Keep us mellowed. Swhat we all need, like, innit? Don't yew reckon?

He pours tea and passes the cups and glasses around.

—Who's rolling up? Marc an Fran, do one each an en give em to each other. Peace offerings like. Makes sense, dunnit?

They grumble and sip their tea and commence to make reefers. The atmosphere begins to brighten like the sky outside only at a quicker pace and Danny pokes and feeds the fire, coaxing it up into a blaze again, the orange glow playing off and highlighting cheeks and chins and foreheads and the smooth reflective surfaces of glass and crockery and laminate. When the spliffs are built Marc and Fran exchange them each to the other.

—Sorry, Marc says.

—Aye, well yew should be.

—It *was* unintentional, tho.

—Yeh, right.

They light up and sit back and smoke. The fire snaps and crackles and the wind wails outside and down the chimney. Llŷr snores like a distant chainsaw, rising and falling, rising and falling, steady and slow and deep like the soft movement of his drug-heavy chest. Ianto giggles once and others turn to look at him and he coughs and is quiet for a moment but then giggles again and this time he draws no eyes, no attention. The marijuana and the mushrooms slowly relax, gently soothe. Tense faces crumple creaseless and happyloose.

—Good tea, this, Gwenno murmurs. —Don't as a rule like mushies much like, but this is alright. Not too trippy like.

Ianto giggles again.

—Aye, eyr good this year, Danny says. —Me n Griff n Llŷr picked em, didn't we, Griff? Not loads like, I mean this tea's not that strong. But yeh, eyr alright. Not too trippy like. Which yew've just said, haven't yew?

—I have, yeh.

—I have, yeh, Ianto quickly repeats then giggles to himself again his left hand cupping his lower face concealing mouth and chin and jaw.

—Well my God. Griff shuffles on his arse until he's perched on the edge of the armchair. —I do believe that young Ianto yer's just made a joke. Not a very funny one like, but a joke nonethebastardless. Crack open the champagne. Be a long fuckin time before we hear *that* again.

—*That* again, Ianto says and laughs further, watery tea trickling down his chin. Under the drugs everything is beginning to amuse him or rather amuse him more; his general daily demeanour appears to be one of drooling humour to those around him. A drifting unfocused and wordless amusement they acknowledge Ianto embodies. As if he and he alone comprehends completely a vast and abstruse joke. As if he and he only is the private undeclared perpetrator of an original prank on the world entire.

—Jesus Christ. Another. God help us. Griff shakes his head and rolls his eyes. He is smiling.

Gwenno bemused is watching Ianto laugh. Her eyes study his face and then slip to his neck and shoulder area where Llŷr's jumper, too big for him, has moved down somewhat below his prominent collarbone. Her eyes focus there and the small smile leaves her face.

—Ew God, Ianto, that's a hellish bastard boil yew've got there. Size of a bloody cherry.

She cranes forward to study Ianto's shoulderblade and he ceases laughing and tries to turn his head to look at her, her face so close to his skin, but she gently with a spread palm holds his head still and slightly bent at the neck.

—No, don't move, let me see . . .

She leans and looks closer and touches softly with a fingertip. Just a gentle stroke, prod.

113

—Aw Christ. This is no boil. Yew've got a bastard tick, mun.

Ianto jerks galvanically away from her, but instantly Marc and Griff and Danny are on him and he is on the floor and they are holding him down.

—Stop fuckin struggling, Ianto! We've got to burn-a fucker out or he'll burrow in further an set up fuckin home inside yew. Don't want that, eh?

Ianto squirms, but Griff sits on his legs and Marc holds his arms and Gwenno and Fran and Jane stand above looking down like some covenants at secret ritual, like some slight, bright attenders on a bloodletting. Ianto bellows into the dirty carpet and Danny pulls the neck of his jumper up and away and down from his scapula-area revealing an expanse of blue-white plucked-chicken skin in which like a small dark oasis throbs a single bead of dark colour, garnet scutum of the sucking mini-beast ruby and reflective with plundered blood.

—Jesus. Look at that.

—Big fucker, him, inny?

—Aw Christ. That's horrible. Jane shakes her head and looks away then looks back again both hands up to her face shielding it up to the eyes, which remain wide and staring above the fenced fingers.

—That's a fuckin sheep tick, Marc says. —Been feeding for ages, it looks like. Almost about to fuckin burst.

Griff leans down to talk into the trapped Ianto's reddening ear. —Hear that, Ianto? A sheep tick, Marc says. How'd yew get a fuckin *sheep* tick on yew, I wonder. As if we don't all bastard know what yew get up to on those long fuckin walks of yours.

Ianto squirms and kicks.

—How do we get it off? Gwenno asks, her expression a mix both fascinated and appalled. —What do we do?

—Got to *burn* this fucker off, Marc says with obvious enjoyment. —Only way to do it, see, got to *burn* the bastard out. I've seen ese before, on me uncle's farm, like. Horrible little fuckers, aye. If yew pull em, see, then-a head comes off an stays in an keeps on burrowing until it rots away and then yew've got problems; infection, septicaemia, fuckin anything. Seen sheep die from it, like, I yav. Don't know about humans like but's best not to take-a risk, innit? Who's got a lit fag? Or a match?

Ianto twists his head out from under Griff's knee. His face bright and flushed and sweaty.

—Fuckin let me up! I'll sit quiet, like, yew don't have to hold me fuckin down!

—Ah but how can we be sure? I mean it's a delicate fuckin operation this mun. Needs ar full attention likes.

—*I* don't want-a bastard in yer either, do I?

—Oo I dunno. Might av got attached to im, like.

—Fuckin gerroff!

—Little bastard's certainly attached to *yew*.

Ianto thrashes like a snared shark. Marc looks up at Griff.

—What d'yew reckon?

—Aye, leave im be. He'll sit still sure enough.

They lever themselves up off him carefully and he sits upright panting, red.

—Yew bastards. No fuckin need for that. Near fuckin smothered me, fuck. Twats. He purses his lips and rubs the back of his neck. —What's it like? Big one is ee, aye?

—Fuckin *huge*, mun. Biggest *I've* ever seen anyway, and I've seen thousands of um. Marc holds his thumb and forefinger about an inch apart and squints through the gap. —That big, I'd say. Full up with yewer blood, mun, ee is. Gorged itself like. We'd best get im off yew before yew pass out from blood loss like.

—Lie flat down on yewer belly, Ianto, Griff says. —Make it easier.

Compliant Ianto lies spreadeagled his head chin-propped like a creature couchant, staring at the fire in which Danny is holding a kindling twig. Ianto feels his jumper being pulled up and away to bare his upper back by whom he knows not and he glances behind him and sees it is Gwenno and he gasps in his throat and feels his heart thud and a small swelling in his groin pressing into the carpet beneath him. Her physical closeness, the smell of her skin. The soap she uses. He wishes that he could see the feeding

115

tick but of course he cannot yet he can hear the oaths and murmurs half in appraisal, half in disgust and can form a picture in his mind all serrated mandibles and compound eyes and pincers gripping and vice-like. He is secretly, strangely happy even when he sees Danny withdraw the burning twig and blow on the end and advance towards him, the twig glowing and pulsating red like some small cattle-brand. A rat-brand, say, something like that. And they stand and crouch around Ianto as they would in stern counsel, assessing the suitability of the scrawny sacrifice supine below and asking whether this wasted white flesh is sufficient to quell wrath rain-bringing and storm-forming fury. Which it isn't and could never be.

—Yer, I'd best do it. Marc takes the splint from Danny and holds it delicately in his fingertips, the hot end pointing at the ceiling. —I've done it before, see, I know what to do. Get to make sure yew get the head out, like. That's-a most important bit, getting the bastard head out. Vital that is.

—Jesus. Fran whispers as if in awe. —Look at it. It's horrible. Never seen one before, cept in pictures like. It's fuckin amazing.

In a hush they crane their heads towards the bean-sized sucking animal. Extended with blood the scutum is stretched transparent-thin, all natural patterning lost in this extension and the hindpart radial grooves, the sex-telling festoons bulging out and over the stubby clawed legs like the adipose ankles of a severely overweight man. Sunk in Ianto's skin and just visible beneath the blood-drained outer dermal layer as if frozen in cloudy ice is the capitulum with the prominent mouthparts, the pair of chelicerae curving in like tusks to the twinned skin-pricking digits and the central hyposteme, like the beak of some blood-sucking squid, serried with tiny recurved teeth and the pair of fat and stumpy palps hiding and protecting between them the terminal-pitted humidity-detecting organ with which the creature stalks its hosts, blueprint for foreign arteries hot with blood drawn and stored in this microscopic nodule athrob with antique thirst. Mud-born being, tiny vampire, its kind fevering the dreams of cave-sleepers and corn-walkers and dog-keepers. Little life-thief rooting itself in skin and from there psyche,

116

waddling bloodsucker joining that host of horribles which seethe beyond the light of waking, in restless wait for the hands that hanker and the heads that yearn. Offspring of ooze, small slobbering issue of forest-floor rot brought to roost on Ianto's skinny back in this storm-shook shack gorging itself to bursting point as if it has sought and indeed found a hunger and a need as unslakeable as its own, as unassuageable as its own. Mixing the two bloods. Making them only one.

—Christ. That is. Fucking. Disgusting.

—Certainly is, Gwenno, Marc says cheerily. —Vile wee bastards these are, aye. Saw a sheep once, its whole fuckin head covered in um. Fuckin covered. On its tongue, its eyes, its lips. In its fuckin ears, mun. Everywhere yer was skin was one-a these little fuckers. Fuckin horrible it was. Tellin yew. Worst thing I've ever seen.

—Bloodsucking little fucker. Danny points to it with a finger. —See how distended it is? How much blood it's sucked like?

A shudder ripples Ianto's back. —Well get-a cunt off, then! Don't just fuckin stand yer talking about it, mun, get-a fucker *off*!

Griff laughs and ruffles Ianto's greasy hair. —Boy's right, for once. Get on with it, Marc, an burn-a little fucker out before that stick gets too cold.

—Might be already. Let's see . . .

Marc pokes with the twig and the tick's bulging body ripples away from the heat as if some small tide is working within its blood-stuffed frame, then the hot and sharp end of the stick breaks through the stretched-thin skin in a tiny puff of smoke and a tiny barely heard hiss and the freed blood trickles down Ianto's back and the insect, its legs scrabbling and its jaws chomping, tries to drag its burst sack of a body away from the danger, burrowing frantically further into Ianto's twitching flesh and Marc presses hard with the spill and Ianto yells and his back stiffens and arches and the blood on his scapula deltas and rivulets, the remarkable sprightliness of this ruby substance when freed from its proscribed routes. Marc presses still harder and Ianto turns his head to gnash his chipped and yellowed teeth at him and Griff exerts more pressure on Ianto's outstretched

117

arms and Marc withdraws the stick, its end smoking around what looks like a popped grape and he studies it closely and sees the jaws clamped tight around the ashy wood and he holds it up above his head like a conductor's baton to catch the light and they all stand circled staring up at it Ianto too now upright and awkwardly reaching with his right arm over his left shoulder to rub at the spot sore and smoking, staring upwards, wincing with the others at the burst and dying bloodsucker as if in awed obeisance to a tiny god whose corporeal embodiment seems to enfeeble its might. They watch the clawed and stubby legs scrabble and kick, see its deflated sack of a body trickle one last bead of dark blood.

—There's the little twat. Marc lowers the stick in front of his face to talk to the dying insect. —Got yew, yew little fucker. No more fuckin vampire games for yew now, eh? Horrible little get.

He crosses the room and tosses the stick into the fire, where it flares instantly into flame.

—Yew alright, Ianto?

Ianto continues to rub at his back and doesn't answer and Gwenno answers for him:

—Course he is. Big brave lad yew, Ianto, aye. Didn't hurt, did it?

She rubs at Ianto's back and he turns his head to smile at her his eyes twinkling in the firelight. They all retake their seats.

—Well. Bit of excitement there, wannit?

Griff nods. —Aye, that's-a night's entertainment likes. Good fuckin show, Ianto. Should've charged admission yew should.

Ianto just grins at Gwenno.

Danny begins to skin up again on a record sleeve balanced like a bridge across the twin pontoons of his knees. —Well! Time for another spliff, I reckon, after all that activity. Need one, like, to calm meself down.

—Again.

—Again, yeh. Never a dull moment in yer, is there?

Llŷr sits up in the corner like a statue suddenly animate. His hair in his face and his face swollen and bleary, his voice slow and strained:

118

—What's going on? What's happening?

—Aw Jesus, Griff says. —Yew've missed it all, mun. Ianto had a tick. Go back to fuckin sleep, boy.

Llŷr lies back down and does.

—Christ . . . wasted twat, Griff says again. —Loves his fuckin downers, Llŷr does. Moggies, temazzies, methadone. He'll do um all that cunt will. Long's he can blot out-a world like, he'll fuckin do um.

He shakes his head sadly.

Danny licks Rizlas and glues them together. —That's fine by me, mun. Don't have to listen to is bigoted fuckin bullshit if ee's crashed out, do we? I mean he's full of it, Llŷr. As bad as-a fuckin Sais, mun.

—Nah, that's goin a bit far. No one's as bad as-a Sais.

Danny smiles and breaks open a cigarette and twists the flakes of tobacco into the papers. —Makes yew think, tho, dunnit.

—What does?

—That tick.

—About what, like?

—Well, like, about evolution an stuff. About life. About how things are formed in-a world, y'know, about, like, how they get to be what they are. It's like: what fuckin good do they do? What's-a fuckin *point* of um? Why are they yer? I mean, even fuckin flies, now, even those shitty little bastards serve a purpose; their maggots eat up all-a dead things, the carrion like. They clean-a place up. I mean I read somewhere once, like, that if yer were no dung beetles then the whole of Africa would be about three feet deep in shite. A whole bleedin continent, like, three feet deep in shite. Imagine that. But ticks, like, an leeches, those kinds-a things . . . I mean what's-a fuckin point? All's ey do is cause problems. Eyr good for fuckin fuck all, mun. Fuck all. So I mean why-a fuck are they yer? What fuckin good do they do?

Griff shrugs. —Fuck knows. Eyr just yer, that's all. Evil little fuckers, like.

—Yeh, but that's the thing, see . . .

Griff sighs and rolls his eyes: —Here we go.

Danny heats resin and crumbles it into the tobacco and rolls and licks and seals the spliff and puts it in his mouth and lights it with a match struck on the stones of the hearth. He knows that Griff isn't the kind of person to discuss such things with, but he is both stoned and drunk and his brain is firing and he cannot stop himself talking nor fight the irreducibility of his own lively mind, that common human denominator.

—I mean, like, why is it, are they evil? Eyr not evil. Just a part of nature like, of evolution. I mean nothing natural can ever be truly evil. It's just-a way eyr formed, mun. Evil is when yew know-a difference between right an wrong an yew still commit the wrongness for yewer own personal pleasure or gain. Yew know, like when yew cause others to suffer cos eyr suffering'll benefit yew. That's evil, like.

He passes the spliff over to Griff, who takes it and draws on it deeply.

—So yewer sayin, then, that only people can ever be evil?

—Yeh, I'd say so.

—Fuck, I'll go along with that, mun. Maggie fuckin Thatcher, yer's one. Satan's fuckin wife, mun.

—Yeh, I mean take that tick, now, all's he wanted to do was suck Ianto's blood in order to stay alive. That's all he knows, like: suck blood or die. Ideas of right an wrong or good n bad don't even come into it, like, it's just, like, nature, a fuckin force of nature. Simple as that. I mean, listen to-a storm outside . . .

And as if on cue the crack of thunder can be discerned as of some great rent, some scissure forming. Some brutal breach being hacked in the sheltering sky.

—. . . read-a paper tomorrow, likes, an I bet yew there'll be several dead from tonight from falling slates or drowning or trees an telegraph poles falling on eyr cars an houses, all just cos of-a storm. The storm does nothin but destroy, that's, like, all it wants-a do is knock things over an cause chaos an maybe even kill. But it's not evil. How the fuck can it be? It's just natural. It knows nothin else. It can't choose. I remember when I was a kiddie, up at-a chapel, like, the fuckin vicar used to go on an on about how this world was made by a God who was all love an peace an understanding an that He wanted no harm to come to us, His favoured an bestest creation. An that we are

120

all His children an He loves us all equally an without bounds an that if we loved Him back then when we died we'd go to Heaven an be with Him an all ar dead relatives an live in eternal happiness for ever. An I remember thinkin, I mean I was seven, eight years old an I remember thinkin: what bollax. Complete fuckin shite. I mean if God loves us an cares for us then why does He make such things as phthisis an leeches an wasps? Germs an poisonous toadstools? Why does He send storms to blow ar houses away? I mean one lad at the school died of a viper bite, seven fuckin years old an he dies of a fuckin viper bite. Why did God create-a snake to kill that kiddie? Is that looking out for him, to let him get bit by the adder? Fuck no. That's what I remember thinking. An I asked him once, the vicar like, about all this an he said that it was because of original sin; that because fuckin Adam disobeyed God then He made iss fuckin world a hard an nasty one full of danger an evil, as a punishment like for Adam's fuckin, whatsit fuckin called, transgression. Which then means, of course, that evil has fuckin well won. Dunnit? I mean if a force for good creates evil then evil wins. It's just pure fuckin logic, mun. It's, like, the worst evil is committed by those who genuinely believe that eyr workin for-a greater good. The Nazis, for example. The fuckin Tories.

He reaches out for the spliff and Griff takes a last quick drag and hands it back. Griff's eyes are narrowed and his mouth is slack and he is regarding Danny through these slits.

—It's like, it's like, it's almost as if that supposedly all-powerful force doesn't even know that it's lost, like it can't even see the immense fuckin joke played on it or the huge fuckin mistake that it's made. It's fucked up. It's fucking thick. It's like a test; we've been given this sense of right an wrong or good an evil like an then we're put in a world where all-a bastard time it seems that evil is rewarded. Material gains, profits like, ey *always* fuckin come from evil. Be bad, an you'll have a comfortable life. That's the temptation, see, not-a fuckin knowledge from eatin-a apple . . . it's-a fuckin cruelty in this world that will get yew what yew want. Or desire. So if we can stay away from that, like, then ar reward will be in-a next fuckin world. Stay fuckin daft an poor an you'll be rewarded in Heaven seems to

121

be-a message. Spouted by people who are given great big fuckin houses to live in an positions of prominent power within-a local communities.

He shakes his head and trails off and stares into the fire, smoke leaking from his nostrils dragon-like. Griff waits for a few seconds for Danny to continue, but when he doesn't he asks with an edge to his voice:

—So fuckin what, like? What's yewer fuckin point?

—My point . . .

—Yeh. What's yewer fuckin point? Why ar yew talkin about all iss shit?

—Well, my point, it's like, my point is that this system of punishment an reward in this world or the next is meaningless because . . . erm . . . yeh, well, y'see, if yew set up a dual system like good versus evil, which is part an parcel like of this whole punishment an reward thing, then yew can't declare yewerself as wholly on the side of one because yew've also made-a other one. It's opposite, like. Yew see what I mean? So yew must've had part of that, or the sense of it at least, within yew to begin with otherwise yew never would've even been able to make it or recognise it, likes. See what I mean? I mean yew can't have one without the other, yeh, I'd go along with that; I mean, like, yew wouldn't know what loneliness was unless yew knew what it felt like to av company. Yew can't have one without-a other is what I'm talkin about, like. Yer's no light without darkness an vice versa. Yeh, I understand all that. No problems yer, like. But why then, I mean where's a fuckin reasoning in like holding yewerself up as a paragon of one if yewer also responsible for making the other? And I mean really fuckin *making*, like, in-a sense that it wasn't even there before yew came along. Yew fuckin built it like, yew put it in-a world. It would never have even fuckin existed without yew. It all stands to reason. Which means that the fuckin clergymen av got it all wrong; God int this force for good, pure good or love or peace or anythin like that. *Fuck* no. Bollax. What He *is* is the fuckin *world*, mun, this vast fuckin, this randomness. Yew don't know what's waiting for yew over-a next rise, sunshine or storm. Or behind-a next rock, a butterfly or a viper. A only fuckin thing yew can do is accept its madness, resign yewerself to-a fact that tomorrow no fuck in-a next fuckin *hour* yew could be fuckin dead or responsible for-a death of someone else, some other poor fucker.

He draws deeply on the spliff and stares at the flapping flames in the fireplace. Looking at nothing but this burning he says:

—I mean yer ar things in-a world it would be fuckin stupid to name. Even if we could ... Stupid to even fuckin *try* an name them is what I mean. I don't mean fuckin politics or anythin like that – fuck all that stuff. I'm talking about things *above* all that stuff, above an outside of the, like, human world ... Things which make the fuckin world turn. Things which we know fuck all about but eyr all around us. In-a rocks, like. In-a fuckin trees an-a rain. We're walkin on very fuckin thin ice, mun. Very fuckin thin ice.

With a small smile Griff says: —What the fuck ar yew talkin about, mun? 'Very fuckin thin ice?' What-a fuck does all that mean then?

—Easy: that we're all on ar fuckin own. We're just fuckin here, that's all. An someday we fuckin won't be, an what happens then? Eh? What the fuck happens then?

Griff just shrugs. —Wormshit, mun. That's all.

Danny mutters something further about forces of nature and about the futility of seeking to name. About the flimsiness of what we see, what we hear, even what we do. Maybe even what we are. About perhaps the reverberations of an ancient evil heard in a modern political curse, and then something about forces of nature again.

Griff raises his left arse cheek and farts.

—An what if yewer of the opinion that it's all a load of fuckin shite?

Danny laughs. —Well then, yewer a force of nature also. Like that storm. Which, I must say, seems to be goin on inside yewer fuckin kex at the moment as well as outside.

Griff leans forwards and sniffs then grimaces and wafts his hands around at chest level.

—Fuck's sakes, mun. Mings. Must be that fuckin curry sauce I yad before, aye. Giz that spliff yer.

Danny hands it over and Griff sucks on it and rests his head

123

against the back of the chair and stares up at the cracked and webby raftered ceiling as if searching for an answer there or if not that then at least some clue. Something among the dangling dusty loops and hanging sacks of spiders and sucked husks of flies that could be interpreted as indication or pointer or signal, not even promise. Finding nothing, he exhales and regards Danny again.

—So that's it, then, is it? That's yewer philosophy?

—What?

—That the world's a mad place an we can't do anythin about it an that we should just accept it as it is? That's it? Jesus. Could write a fuckin book about that yew could boy, aye.

—Christ, mun, av yew not listened to a fuckin word I've said? I never said that at all.

—Yew fuckin did. I yerd yew.

—No I didn't. What I said was that, yeh, the world *is* a mad place, aye, but yew don't have to accept it like that. I mean yew *do* in a sense because it's much fuckin bigger than we ar an nothin we ever do could ever change it, but yew do what yew have to to make it a saner, easier fuckin place for yewerself to live in. It's an insane fuckin mayhem we're all born into, likes, an we all have to do whatever it is that gives us peace. Well, that's the second step; a first is fuckin *finding* the twat. An that's the universal human longing, likes, that's maybe what we're all yearning for. That's maybe why we're all so fucked up. Why everything's in such a bastard mess. Soon as we're born we start searchin for this thing, this fuckin whatever it is that'll make everything just a little bit easier until we die. An because we can't even *name* what we're looking for, can never even approach any understanding of what it even fuckin *might* be . . .

Griff sits wordless. Staring at Danny as still as a graven image and Danny continues:

—. . . then yer's not really much fuckin hope, is there? He grins. —That's why chapel fills yewer head with this fuckin ridiculous idea of eternal reward, like, heavenly bliss. I mean it doesn't want yew to appreciate-a full fuckin hardness, *bleak*ness of-a situation. The vicars don't want eyr flock fuckin toppin emselves, do they? I mean God, heaven, sin, retribution, all iss bleedin stuff, it's all about a, a yearning, a need; it's about somethin that we all want, somethin for us all to believe in, a fuckin afterlife or somethin or maybe just some kind of fuckin meaning to *this* one. I dunno. Just, like, something to live for. Otherwise we're all fucked. The whole human world is fucked.

Griff takes a last sip on the spliff and leans to flick the roach into the fire. —Nah. Fuckin rubbish, mun. When yewer dead yewer dead an that's it. Wormshit, as I said. That's all yer is to it. Jesus, how-a fuck did yew get on to this shite when we started off talkin about fuckin ticks?

Danny smiles and shrugs and lifts the record sleeve on to his knees again and pulls Rizlas out of their packet on to it, begins to glue them together. —Dunno. Tryin-a make sense of such things is fuckin futile. Best just-a keep quiet about the whole fuckin thing really.

—Wouldn't disagree with that, mun. Would not disagree at all.

Griff refills his glass with neat cheap whisky and then pours the last few drops into Danny's.

—Ta.

—Not much bevvy left, I don't think. Apart from-a fuckin kiddie-booze in-a kitchen like. Might av to go on to Llŷr's homebrew in a minute.

—Oof, Jesus. Go bastard blind drinkin that stuff, mun.

—Aye, it's rotgut fuckin stuff sure enough. Moonshine, likes. He makes it out of fuckin potato peelings an fuckin grass. He've got a still in the shed.

—I know. I've seen it.

—Sooner that than nowt, tho.

—Oh yeh. But yer might be some. He takes a swig of his Scotch and belches. —Some cider left in-a fridge. Janey brought some, I think.

Griff looks over to the far wall, where Marc is telling some story in a low voice and Jane and Fran and Gwenno and Ianto are listening to him. Ianto is seated on the floor and is looking up at Gwenno's turned-away face.

—Oi! Janey! Griff shouts. —That cider yew brought still in-a fridge is it?

125

She nods.

—Well go an fetch it for us aye? Yer's a good girl.

Jane looks incredulous —Get it yewer fuckin self mun, Christ. What did yewer last slave die of?

She turns back to Marc and Griff laughs to himself and takes a drink of his whisky and screws up his face at the cheap sour taste. He has drunk a lot of it throughout the evening and night and it seems to have coated his tongue and the back of his throat with fur. He coughs to clear it and asks Danny whether he read in the local paper last week about the discovered body.

—What body?

—Some young lad. Schoolboy. Under a bridge out Bontgoch way. He'd been fuckin battered to death with a rock. It was on-a telly an everything.

Danny nods. —Oh yeh. I yerd about that. He wasn't from a school, tho, was he? Borstal boy I yerd, like.

—Well, schoolboy age. Fifteen or sixteen, likes.

—Yeh.

—Well how does he fit in with yewer ideas, like? How does-a death of a fuckin schoolkid fit in with it all?

Danny shrugs. —Difficult to assess specific events, like. Individual cases. I mean we don't know-a history behind it, like, what's gone on, I mean he was in a fuckin borstal for Godsakes, all kinds-a things go on in those places, like. He might've been inside for rape or anything, we just don't know. Could've been a fuckin murderer isself, like. All's we know is that he was found under a bridge in-a hills battered to death with a rock by person or persons unknown. Could've been revenge, anything. Yew don't know anything else about how, or why, he died.

—Oh, an that makes it all OK, then, does it? It's alright that a schoolboy's died? Been murdered?

—Did I say it was? Did I say anything of the fuckin sort? Are yew fuckin wilfully mishearing me like or ar yew fuckin tryin-a wind me up or what?

—I just want to know how all iss fits in with yewer ideas like, that's all. Because ey sounded like bullshit to me, mun, an I want to know how a young boy getting beaten to fuckin

126

death fits in with yewer view of-a world cos I for-a fuckin life-a me can't see how-a fuck it does.

Concentrating on rolling the spliff in his fingertips at face height, Danny purses his lips and raises his eyebrows and shakes his head.

—I'm not gonner get drawn into this, Griff. I'm not going to answer. For one I know fuck all about-a lad or what the fuck happened to him or why it happened, an for two I don't know what yewer talking about. My 'view of the world'? I wasn't aware that I'd expressed one. An for three yewer just fuckin tryin-a wind me up. Yewer gettin all tetchy for no reason that I can see. Lay off-a fuckin whisky, mun. It turns yew into an arsehole.

—*What* did yew fuckin just call me?

Griff is on the edge of his chair forwards-leaning, his barrel neck harped with straining sinew and craned. All Danny can see is his face, it fills his field of vision, the clenched jaw and the brow furrowed and the dark eyes swallowed in slits. Danny waves a placatory hand at it.

—Griff, fuck, it's me, mun, Danny. Calm down, likes. I didn't mean to call yew an arsehole, mun, what I meant was that-a whisky *turns* yew into one, like. Which is a bit of a shame cos yewer not one usually. An I didn't mean to say 'arsehole', that's too strong a word. I didn't mean that. It just came out. A weed an-a bevvy, yew know. Sorry.

—Well, what the fuck *did* yew mean, then? Eh?

—I dunno, 'tetchy' or something. Y'know . . . it's just, like, yew can wind people up at times. That's all. Nowt wrong with it, like, I'm not sayin yer is. I'm just sayin that it can get a bit . . . a bit, like, yew know. Exasperating is the word. Exasperating. That's all.

Some of the colour leaks from Griff's face and his scrunched forehead relaxes, smooths. He is still staring hard at Danny and is about to say something else, but Fran yells from across the room:

—Silence! Yer's too much fuckin silence! Put some bastard music on someone before I fall asleep!

Griff gives one last look at Danny then swings his head towards Fran.

—What d'yew want on?

—Anything! Anything! Just stop iss fuckin hush, mun! I'm beginnin to hear meself think!.

Marc agrees: —Yeah, Griff. Somethin lively. We're all beginnin to flag, like, put some good dance on or somethin. Somethin-a perk us up like.

Jane looks at him wide-eyed. —Flag are we? Speak for yewer fuckin self, mun. Fuckin lightweight.

Griff stands and takes his camouflage jacket from the back of the chair and puts it on. —I'll tell yew what; *yew* put-a sounds on, an me an Danny'll go an fetch us some more to drink. Some-a Llŷr's moonshine like. *That* ul perk yew up, Christ. Too fuckin right. C'mon, Danny.

—What, go out in this? We'll get fuckin blown away, mun. Fuckin tornado out yer, like.

—Aw get yewer fuckin coat on boy. Shed's only ten fuckin yards away, don't be such a fuckin puff.

There is a genuine sneer on Griff's face and Danny sighs and stands and shrugs into his fleece. Griff picks up empty bottles from the floor and hands two to Danny and pockets a pair himself.

—We'll need these. Right, if we're not back in quarter of an hour send out a search party.

—Yeh, Danny says. —An make sure yew search-a fuckin treetops like cos that's where we'll end up in this fuckin wind. End up in bastard Barmouth or somewhere.

—Ey, an stay away from Ikey's stash, Marc says, all serious. Both Danny and Griff turn to look at him.

—What?

—I said stay away from Ikey's stash, mun. He hides his Es an stuff in a bag under the roots of that fallen tree, y'know by-a disused silver mine, like? So stay away from em. Ikey'll fuckin murder yew if yew dip into it, like.

Griff and Danny look at each other then shake their heads. Griff mutters: —Prick. Danny hands the half-smoked spliff to Ianto, Griff yanks the front door open and a roar of almost-triumph sucks them out into the mad loud slowly brightening night and then slams the door behind them. In the howling

128

wind beyond the old stone walls those left behind can hear Griff roaring wordlessly and Danny yelling one long and drawn-out word: —Fuuuuuuuuuuuuuuuuuckk!

—Mad bastards.

—Where've they gone? Fran asks.

Marc replies: —To get more booze.

—What, in fuckin *town?* That's eight fuckin miles away! They'll be gone till tomorrer!

—No, yew clueless cow. Llŷr's shed. He've got a still in yer. Makes his own hooch like out of old veggies and fruit. Mad fuckin stuff it is an all. Makes that whisky seem like fuckin Vimto.

—Good. An don't call me a clueless cow, yew dickless tosser.

Marc ignores her: —Ey, Ianto, d'yew remember the last time we had a night on Llŷr's homebrew? Remember it, like?

Ianto grins and nods, but he doesn't.

Gwenno looks inquisitive from Ianto to Marc. —Why? What happened?

—Aw it was fuckin crazy. Marc shakes his head almost it seems in wonder. —Ianto yer took all is fuckin kit off, an I mean *all.* Stark bollocko naked he was, runnin off into-a mountains. We found him in that old silver mine like all fuckin covered in mud an shite an what was it yew were doing, Ianto? D'yew remember?

Ianto just grins again and does not answer and Gwenno must coax Marc.

—What was it? What was he doing?

Marc shakes his head. —Can't tell yew. Too harsh for delicate ears, like.

—Well I'll ask-a man isself then. She turns to face Ianto and his cheeks begin almost instantly to redden. —What were yew doing in-a silver mine, Ianto? Tell me. I'd love to know.

Ianto draws on the spliff and leaks smoke through his fixed grin. He remembers nothing and knows only that eyes and attention are on him and that he must greet them with a grin.

—Polluting isself, Marc says. —That's what he was doing.

Interfering with imself like. Helping himself along as it were. Giving it six-nil on the old spam lance.

—No.

—Afraid so, aye.

—He never was.

—Afraid so. Llŷr's hooch turned im into a right old lusty sailor, didn't it, Ianto? A right studly boy he was, oh dearie me, yes.

Gwenno turns back to look at Ianto again, whose expression remains unchanged. The slightly glassy, vapid grin. She smiles at him and ruffles his hair.

—Ah, look at the grin on im. It's all a big joke to yew innit, boy, she says with affection. —Best way to be, I reckon. Laugh it all off, in that right, Ianto, eh?

The room explodes into music loud pounding for Jane and Fran have selected a techno tape and are dancing fast in the corner of the room, the comatose Llŷr on the floor between them like a large humanskin handbag. He doesn't move. Disturbed by the noise two woodlice and a lanky spider scuttle away up the wall above his head like three thoughts leaving him. The feet of Jane naked and those of Fran in trainers clean and fat-soled slap the floor around his head and shoulders and still he doesn't move.

Marc yells above the ruckus: —Christ! Turn it fuckin down a bit! Doin me bastard head in!

Jane shakes her head her brown hair flying. —NO fuckin WAY! Yew aren't fuckin sleepin tonight, boy!

Marc stands scowling and crosses the room around them and steps over Llŷr and squats and turns the music down, not a lot but noticeably. Fran turns on him:

—Fuck's sake Marc! I was enjoying that yew twat!

—Turn it back fuckin up, mun!

—Nope. Why d'yew need it so fuckin loud? I mean listen to it, it's still loud enough to dance to innit? It's just that we want-a have a fuckin natter like an can't fuckin hear our *own* voices never mind each others' with that fuckin blastin out. That's fair enough, innit? It's still fairly loud.

They pull frowny faces at him and he crosses the room to retake his place on the sagging settee and there is a smugness in his bearing which Jane and Fran do not like, but grumbling they sit on the floor by the fire and Fran pokes it back up into a blaze again and Jane begins to build a spliff and soon they are smoking and dancing whilst sitting, with their snaking hands and tossing heads and twisting torsoes. Their hair is in their faces and their arms are outstretched, hands describing sinuous flowing movements like eels or water itself perhaps or perhaps nothing more tangible than a notion of what form this music might take if by drug or dream or mere effort of will it could physically be seen. Loops and swirls and arabesques.

—Are *we* getting some-a that spliff then, Ianto?

Ianto takes a final pull and passes it on, the last soggy inch of smouldering nicotine-yellow cardboard. Gwenno takes it and looks at it distastefully and passes it on to Marc, who too does not draw on it but stubs it out instead in a saucer brimming with the little yellow sunbursts of spent filters and the clustered holes of roach-ends like tiny mouths howling or the apertures of eyes. Ash scattered in grey powder or small silver ferns or fragile friable cylinders.

—Didn't leave much on that Ianto, aye? Fuckin potpig yew.

—No.

—Too fuckin right, mun. Fran! Fran!

She stops dancing and turns to look.

—What?

—Pass that spliff yer, woman.

—Yewer arse. Make yewer bastard own.

She starts dancing again.

—Jesus. Selfish cow. Last bit-a toke yew get off me, mun, I'll tell yew that for nowt.

She ignores him. Just dances.

—Who's got-a weed then? Gwenno is it?

Gwenno shakes her head. —Na. Smoked me last before, like. Brought a teenth up yer with me an it's all fuckin gone. Smoked away.

—Fuck. An yer's no fuckin point askin *yew*, Ianto, is there?

Ianto shakes his head also.

—No, that'll be right. A day yew buy yewer own drugs

131

is-a day I fuckin die, mun, I'm tellin yer. Never seen yew with-a stash, fuckin never. Fuckin freeloadin bastard yew are, aye. Scavvin twat.

He stares hard at Ianto and Ianto just grins back at him, his pupils shrunk down into pin-pricks in the swollen red fleshy surrounds and his mouth wet and loose-lipped and hanging slightly open. Marc continues to stare at him and Ianto will not break eye contact and Gwenno watches the two faces eyes left then right as if spectating tennis and then Marc sighs and reaches into the kangaroo-pouch pocket of his hooded top and withdraws Rizlas and a small chunk of dark resin cellophane wrapped.

—Ah well. Suppose I'll just have to smoke me own then, won't I?

—Jesus. Gwenno shakes her head in disbelief. —Yew sneaky get.

The front door bursts open in a sudden wail of wind and there is abrupt shock as the external world and all its noise and icy frenzy pounces into the room for two seconds as red-faced Griff and Danny return, slamming the door behind them the wind screaming in disappointment and thwart. They cross the room with bottles of cloudy liquid, sediment settling in them like dandruff, like two questers returned from a place uncharted with specimens curious and not come by battle-free. The storm has slapped their cheeks red and wrenched their hair up into spikes and they stand before the fire nostrils flared and rubbing their hands together with a dry windblown raspy sound and puffing air out through their storm-raw cheeks.

—Christ! Fuckin *mad* out yer it is! Wild!

—Fuckin harsh conditions out yer, mun. Tellin yew. Don't know how Llŷr's shed's managing to stay upright. Honest. Be a heap-a fucking firewood before morning, that.

Marc looks up from the spliff he is working on. —Bit breezy is it, lads? Wee bit fresh, like?

—Seen that film *Twister*? Danny says. —Well that's a fuckin *draught* compared to that, mun. A mere fart. Jesus. Never fuckin known a wind that strong.

—Giz a drink, then, Fran says from the floor.

132

—In a minute, yeh. Just let us get some fuckin warmth back in us first, like.

—Need to wait for-a sediment to settle anyway, Griff says.

—Can't drink-a fuckin sediment, like, yew'd be over in Bronglais puking yewer ring up. Poison, see. Specially this batch, don't know what Llŷr's made it with like but yer's fuckin twigs in yer, all kinds-a manky stuff. Look like human fuckin bones.

Danny nods. —Wouldn't fuckin surprise me if they were. Not with that fucker. Him an his gun.

They look down at the slumbering sedated figure and Jane's face softens. —Ah no. Look at him. He looks so peaceful like that, dunny.

—Don't yew fuckin believe it, Danny splutters. —It's a delusion. I mean I for bastard one wouldn't like to see-a dreams he's havin right now. He thinks about it for a moment and then shudders. —Oo fuck no. Hieronymous fuckin Bosch, aye.

—Who? Bosch? Don't ey make power tools?

—Aye, they do, Griff, yeh.

Griff looks puzzled. Danny removes his jacket and sits cross-legged on the floor by the fire. —Who's got a spliff on-a go then?

Fran hands him hers half-smoked.

—Diolch.

She smiles into his face. —Croeso.

Griff takes his jacket off too and takes the floor alongside.

—Toke on that after yew, Danny boy.

—Oi! Fran pokes his meaty shoulder. —It's *my* weed! Ask *me*! Cheeky get!

—Duw, Fran, we're just havin a smoke. Spliffs get passed round like. Make abastardnother one, aye.

—Try tellin that to Marc, Gwenno interjects from across the room.

—Oh aye. Griff sneers. —Been up to is tight-arsed tricks again as he? Fuckin typical. Tight as a gnat's twat yew are, Marc, d'yew know that? Tight as a fuckin gnat's twat. Blood from a stone, yew an yewer fuckin gear like. Wouldn't give the steam off yewer turds as a Christmas present yew.

133

Marc holds his spliff up for all to see. —Oh, an what the fuck's this, then? A spliff, innit? An made with all my own fuckin ingredients. Skins *and* baccy. An a fuck sight stronger than those Silk fuckin Cuts yew fuckers have been passin round all night, I'll tell yew fuckin that.

—Well let's av a test of it then. Pass it yer.

Griff reaches out for it and Marc takes a last deep drag and rises and hands it over to Griff like the relaying of a baton. Griff sucks on it and smacks his lips and looks pensive for a moment then nods.

—Aye, not bad that. Cheers, Marc.

He sucks on it again and makes no motions to return it and Marc tuts and mutters and begins to make another. Danny snorts laughter and raises a bottle of homebrew to the light and checks it for clarity, then gathers cups and empty glasses around him and divides the drink equally into them, a wild-headed druid dispensing elixir with flame at his shoulder and his face set thoughtful as in some grave undertaking of a great import. The liquid glugs syrup-thick into the containers and even the sound of its agitation the slosh and gulp emanate potency and potential peril. The heaviness of its movements as if fraught with alcohol content. A faint petroleum whiff taints the air. When the receptacles each contain an approximate equal amount Danny hands them soberly around one to each like some revered apportioner disbursing a nostrum, some mad but convincing mediciner making good a promise to cure pain and ill. Hands reach out and take glasses and cups from him, hold them up to catch firelight for eyes to study and scrutinise.

—Now, Danny addresses them all like a teacher. —If this is as strong as the stuff Llŷr usually makes then it's goin to be *fuckin* strong. So go easy with it, like. Just sips. I mean I've seen it send certain people crazy before, out of eyr fuckin heads, like. In that right then, Ianto?

Ianto grins and nods.

—So: have a care. Just sips. Iechyd da.

Soft sounds of slurping and swallowing and then a sudden rough explosion of coughing and hacking, people bent over holding their throats faces screwed up and eyes leaking tears

134

and lips cornered with sour froth. Griff grits his teeth and roars and then daintily takes another sip, sucks it over his teeth and sloshes it around in his cheeks like a demented wine-bibber.

There is yelling:

—Christ! It fuckin *burns*!

—What the fuck *is* this stuff? Me fuckin throat's on fire!

—Jesus!

—Water! Give me some fuckin water!

—It tastes like bastard diesel!

—What the fuck is it made from?

—Kerosene and stagnant pond water. That's what it tastes like, anyway.

Danny takes another sip and shakes his head vigorously as he swallows. —Ah, yew get used to it. Ah yeh, it tastes like the foul piss of Satan at first like, but after a while it's alright. Becomes bearable at least. An just wait till it fuckin hits yer; *mad* stuff, I'm tellin yer. Like a fuckin speedball or somethin, honest.

Griff takes another sip and says pleasantly: —Well *I* think it's alright. A bit like Special Brew, only not quite as sweet.

Ianto holds out an empty glass. —More.

Danny, incredulous: —*More?* Jesus, Ianto, go fuckin easy, mun! Strong fuckin stuff this y'know. Needs a bit-a respect like.

Ianto jiggles his glass and Danny refills it and Griff looks on admiringly.

—That's our Ianto. Takes moren a few swigs-a moonshine to lay *yew* out, dunnit, boy?

—Yes.

Ianto sits back and sips at his drink. Gwenno regards him.

—Jesus, Ianto, how can yew? Fuckin disgusting stuff this is. Tastes like, I dunno, fuckin *oil* or somethin. Horrible.

Fran's nose is wrinkled in distaste. —I'm going to mix mine. Dilute it with somethin like.

She fetches a big plastic bottle of cheap cider from the kitchen and pours some into her glass on top of the homebrew and it fizzes and sizzles like acid. When it calms down she raises the glass to her face and laps at it.

135

—That's not too bad. Quite pleasant, really. Takes-a vile taste away like.

She takes a larger swig and nods approvingly and then Jane reaches for the cider bottle and dilutes her drink too and then passes the cider around each of them making a cocktail with it and the moonshine and only Griff rejects the cider bottle and takes the spirit neat. Ianto gulping the homebrew already loose-limbed and rubbery, his lips and chin agleam with spittle and his laughter becoming more frequent and shrill and at nothing discernible.

The storm continues to punch the cottage with a fist of air the size of a stable at the end of a swing that begins on the horizon, no abatement of ferocity or signs of cessation or hiatus or even enervation of intent, if indeed intent it could be supposed to possess. The irregular horizon mountain-toothed and thorn-backed in the fading of the false dawn re-bleeding black around the mountain spines, its brief and lying light swirled and paisleyed now and again with the deep darkness, which will not be harnessed although the stars have lost their guiding brightness and the low sky behind their scattered clusters appears barred with grey, vast slashes of a lighter dimness, as of the mirroring of a forest petrified and earthbound the trees long gone rigid, limbless and frozen to stone. Blown clouds burst feebly with the moon's dulled nickel slowly sliding, beginning now its ageless descent, although as yet there is no sun nor hint nor tinge of one yet still the moon slips as if all illumination is about to end, all higher guidance to halt. No shape darts through this flat black sky not owl nor bat, only the invisible wind and the reek it brings from the low-lying estuary, no tide now to mask and rinse its denuded rank mud and the pockets within it of decay and ancient gas. The clumps of seaweed rotting on the foreshore. The leprous white and mushy kayak of the dead seal lain there this week long. The dingle and the coastal cliffs tremble under the storm and the wide glacial valley waits like a chalice held up to cup the falling moon, just one drop of curdled milk.

Inside the cottage, the drink and drugs accumulated topped off with the levelling strength of Llŷr's homebrew have begun to take effect and Jane is leaning back against a wall her face slack as if boneless and her chest jerking with damp hiccups and Fran is trying to dance but falling on to Griff, who with big hands on her thighs keeps her upright. Marc is talking slurringly to Gwenno, who is finding it difficult to discern his words below the roaring in her ears and the techno thump and Ianto stops jerking and dancing like a storm-thrashed scarecrow and retakes his seat to listen in on what Marc is saying to Gwenno and Danny is watching all this and sipping at his homebrew, his lips slightly curled in mild amusement although at nothing in particular, simply the whole scene, the movement, the noise. It is one of those brief flurries that occur between the long stretches of talking and imbibing when a group of people are in one room together getting drunk and have been doing that for some hours. One of those quick intervals of motion and sound that intersperse the lengths of relative stasis, the gulping and the sucking and like all the others its fragile flame will burn itself out shortly. It stems from a complex need, the varied and rarefied fulfilment of which will not at this moment feed or sustain and it will eat its own oxygen soon, there only being tonight a small supply, and steadily it does and Danny watches as people wind down very much like clockwork toys exhausting their fuel and sit again and drink and smoke and stare into the middle distance or at the fire lively in the charred hearth and do not for a minute or two talk nor even acknowledge in any way each other's presence or indeed give any indication that they are anything other than utterly alone.

—Jesus. Danny shakes his head it seems sadly and blows smoke at the floor. Talking to Griff but without looking directly at him he says in a small voice: —Jew know something? It's at times like this that I really fuckin miss the skag. I yaven't had a toot for three fuckin years now nearly, but at times like this I could really bastard well use one. Just-a smooth things out like. Just one little toot.

—Fucking *bollax*, mun. Griff is glaring at Danny, his eyes wet slate. —Don't yew *ever* fuckin say that, boy. Don't yew *ever* fuckin say that yew miss-a fuckin brown. I fuckin remember yew shamblin down Great Darkgate Street tryin-a pawn yewer

137

own mother's fuckin weddin ring an yewer fuckin father not two months in the ground. Fuckin shit-stains all over-a back of yewer kex.

—Yeh, well I'm not sayin that I'm not ashamed of that or anythin like. I mean, all's I –

—An I fuckin remember yew down Plas Crug with spew down-a front of yewer fuckin shirt screamin at-a passers-by cos ey wouldn't lend yew any fuckin money. Cold turkeyin like. D'yew remember all that, Danny? Remember how fuckin lucky yew were not to get custodial when yew mugged that fuckin pensioner? Oh aye, big brave fuckin boy. Remember all that? So don't fuckin say that yew ever miss the fuckin brown cos that means that yew miss all that shite as well cos that's what goes with it. Yew fuckin well know that one leads to-a other. Don't yew?

—Suppose.

—Yeh, suppose, aye. Listen, yewer not a fuckin *ex*-junkie, mun, yewer a fuckin junkie who's just not using at the mo. No such fuckin thing as an *ex*-junkie, mun, an yew fuckin know it. Never fuckin forget it either cos if yew do then yewer in deep bastard shit an I'm not gunner be around to elp pull yew out this time. Fuck no. Yew can fuckin well sink.

—Alright, Griff, Christ. I was just fuckin saying. Duw, a few fuckin years ago I would've walked-a ten miles into town in this fuckin weather just-a get meself a toot. Now tho I just fuckin say it without doin anythin about it. That's all I do, just fuckin *say* it mun, nowt else. That's a big fucking improvement. Fuck, I mean, if I *really* fuckin wanted some brown I'd go out an get myself some fuckin brown, wouldn't I? Jesus.

—Fuck off, Danny. Junkies, yewer all-a fuckin same. Saying, just fuckin *saying* like that yew'd like just one fuckin toot is-a first fuckin step on-a road to bein a sad fucked-up fuckin smackhead again an rippin off yewer mates an yewer own fuckin family an muggin old soldiers for eyr fuckin pension. Yew know that as well's fuckin I do, mun, so don't fuckin pretend yew don't.

—Aren't yer times when *yew'd* like a wee bit-a skag? When *yew* could just do with that warm glow like?

—Yeh, course.

138

—Yeh, an what d'yew do then?

—I go out an score meself a bag of brown, mun. Find meself a nice quiet place to just drift off. But see, I'm not a fuckin junkie. Never fuckin have been, never fuckin will be. Don't have the mentality. But with yew, tho, with *yew*, the heroin is stronger than yewerself. Yew have no control over it and yew cannot stop it from controlling yew. Yew are completely fuckin powerless before it, like. Junkie's mentality, innit. Fuck, yew should know all this. Didn't they teach yew fuck-all in Bronglais rehab?

Griff takes out papers and tobacco and rolls himself a cigarette, this time weed-free. As if proving some obscure point. He offers the tobacco to Danny, who shakes his head and holds up the half-smoked Lambert & Butler in his right hand for Griff to see.

—I know all that, Griff, all-a that's true, like, but . . . well, if something is such a big part of yewer life for so fuckin long like then yew can't help but fuckin miss it when it's gone, can yew? It's like my mam; I mean, I miss her as well, like, in-a same way that I miss-a heroin. She was yer for so long, like. It'd be like yew suddenly stoppin drinking, or smoking, or even fuckin eating. I mean yew'd miss it wouldn't yew? It's like that, that feeling of calmness I was talkin about before. Brown used to help me find that. Wouldn't yew miss that?

Griff shrugs. —Maybe. Suppose, like, yeh. But I'm no fuckin junkie, mun. I'd fuckin die if I didn't eat, wouldn't I? That's not-a same fucking thing at all.

—No, but what I'm saying is that yew can't miss what yew've never had. Yew can only long for what was once yer an isn't any more.

—Bollax, mun. Fuckin bollax. Griff blasts smoke out ceilingwards. —Look at fuckin Ianto yer, for example. It's like, I'd say that he's a virgin. Never popped is cherry like, that poor cunt, never dipped is wick. But don't yew think he wants to av sex, like? Don't yew think he ever gets horny?

Danny shrugs.

—No? Well then let's fuckin ask im, shall we? Find out likes.

He shouts across the room:

139

—Oi, Ianto! Need yew to help us sort somethin out yer, mun.

Ianto looks drunkenly over on a nodding head.

—Danny yer's saying that yew can never want for what yew've never had, but I'm sayin that's shite an that yew, yewer good fucked-up self, wants a shag even tho yew've never had one in yewer entire life. So tell us then, butt; is that true? Yewer virgin string still intact, is it? I'll bet yew it is. Bet yew anything it is. Duw, if it's not, then I'll let yew shag *me*, mun.

Ianto tries to smile on his bobbing head. Extremely drunk now, his vision adrift in broth and aware only of grinning faces looking at him, burbled words directed at him. Some form of comprehension crawls to him slowly and weakly out of the walls and over the strewn floor.

—What?

—I'm sayin mun that I reckon yewer a virgin. In fact we all do. We all yer reckon that –

—Don't be cruel, Griff. This int fuckin fair, mun.

Danny is ignored.

—We reckon that yew've never had a shag in yewer entire life. That yewer still, a fuckin virgin, mun. The big V. Carnal relations like with yewer right bastard hand only, mun. It's trew, innit? Great big girly virgin yew are, aye. Wouldn't know what to do with a fanny if it was put on a plate an handed to yew, mun. No fuckin way. Would not know what to do with it at all.

Griff shakes his head sombre and sad. As if there is no hope whatsoever. Ianto opens his mouth but no sound drops.

—Couldn't fuckin live with that, I couldn't. Never havin known what it's like to make love with a woman like. Never knowin that pleasure. What it's like to av someone want yewer body. Fuckin shame that would be. I'd have to fuckin top meself I would, see, do-a decent thing likes. Put meself out-a my own bastard misery. Fuckin mercy killing like.

Gwenno protests: —This isn't fuckin fair. Stop bein so fuckin nasty to him, Griff. He can't help it. Stop having a go at him. Fuckin cruel bastard.

—Ah, see that, Ianto? Gwenno stickin up for yew like. Fancies yew, she does.

—Fuck off, Griff.

—It's fuckin trew, mun, she told me, before likes. Said she fancies yew an would let yew fuck her cos she reckons that yew'd be good in bed, a right fuckin shag like, but I said nah, likes, poor old Ianto knows fuck all about women an what to do with em cos he's a fuckin virgin. Never even *seen* a minge in his whole fuckin life, never mind *fucked* one.

—Don't listen to im, Ianto. He's talking bollax. Just ignore the fucker.

Ianto tries to rise from his seat to do who can guess at what, but the attempt is pathetic and he flops back bonelessly into the broken-springed settee. Marc is watching him with a large leering grin and Gwenno is glaring at Griff and Danny is staring at the floor and Fran is laughing beneath her hand and Jane like Llŷr is asleep. The storm still howls and the fire still smoulders around glowing coals and sticks like charred bones or talismans, amulets to effect harm and revenge. To level at someone and will wastage. Skin eruptions, maybe.

—I I I I I I ... mmmmmm not ....

—Just ignore him, Ianto. Yew don't have to defend yourself from that bastard. Yew don't have to say fuckin anything.

—Quiet, Gwenno, I can't hear what-a boy's tryin to say. Let im speak now.

Griff leans forwards in his chair, right hand cupped around his right ear. —What's that, Ianto? What're yew tryin-a say, mun? Speak up now cos I can't hear a fuckin word yewer sayin.

—Not ... a ... a fuckin virrrrgginnnnn ...

—What's that? Yewer not a virgin yew say? Oh, aren't yew. Well fuckin prove it then. Go on, mun, fuckin well prove it to us. That's-a only way for us to believe yew like cos we all apart from Gwenno, who must be fuckin mad or in bastard love, reckon that yew've never been with a woman in all yewer sad life. In fact, I'd go bastard further; I'd say that yew can't even come. Yeh, I would, I'd even go so far as to say that yewer unable to even spurt like any other fuckin normal man. Never even had a wank, have yer? At least not to fuckin completion likes.

—Fuckkkk ... offfff ...

—Ianto, just fuckin ignore him, mun. He's actin the twat. Don't encourage him. He's just tryin-a wind yew up, mun.

—Go on then, Ianto mun, fuckin prove it. Prove yew can shoot yewer bolt an yew never know, Gwenno yer might even go to bed with yew. Let yew fuckin do her, like. Suck yewer knob. Wank yew off. Like that, would yew? Course yew fuckin would, mun, any normal feller would. Sexy as fuck Gwenno is like. Look at-a fuckin tits on her, mun.

The disgust, the anger on Gwenno's face: —Yew arsehole! Shut the fuck up!

Marc giggles and Griff continues, light in his eyes: —Go on, mun. Have yewerself a wank. Show her yew can come, like, show her yew've got what it takes to please a woman. Go on, mun, now's yewer fuckin chance. Get yewer old man out.

With underwater movements Ianto begins to fumble at his fly. Gwenno looks horrified:

—Aw Ianto, mun . . . fuckin don't, boy . . . yew don't have to do this . . .

Marc cranes forwards eager and amused to get an unobstructed view: —Yeh, Ianto, go on mun! Show us yew can do it! Get yewer lad out for the people!

Ianto's eyes are closing in collapse and his face is drooping floorwards, but he fumbles still and jerks his zip down and reaches inside and gropes and twists and prises his own prick out and tugs at it three times and before Marc and Griff and Fran cease their cheering he is asleep as if this exposure has at last robbed him of all lingering sobriety and adrenalin and he can for the moment do or move no more. Like a mannequin obscene he reclines comatose with spread legs, all exposed; like some lusty puppet unemployed.

Big grin of Griff's face. —Well. There it is.

—Fair old size, mind, Fran says.

—Aye but yer's something wrong with it. Marc's grin falters. —Comen av a look at it . . . it's all, like, fuckin chewed up or something . . .

Gwenno takes an appalled peep and then quickly averts her eyes again and they all even Danny shuffle over to crowd around Ianto for a second time that night and encircle him again in grim ministry, stern convention like revenants awed around some icon martyred and damaged, eyes downcast and voices hushed as if in respect or perhaps even fear:

—My fuck, Griff whispers. —What the fuck's happened to is lad? Looks like he've been circumcised with a fuckin chainsaw or something. Good fuckin God.

—Poor bugger. Must've had some kind of accident, likes, Danny observes.

—Aye, tried-a give isself a blowjob like. Bent isself double, bit off moren he could chew. Marc laughs, but is not followed.

—He grew up on a smallholding, didn't he. Must've had some kind of accident, I suppose, Danny repeats. —Caught isself in some kind of machinery or somethin. Got imself all fuckin mangled up, like.

—Aye, well, he've got a smallholding *now*, that's for fuckin sure.

—Oh shut yewer fuckin gob, Marc. Gwenno, still seated, looks up at the grim faces over her and the comatose Ianto at her side. She sees heavy-lidded eyes and loose cheeks and stubble and the thick cosmetic on Fran's face caked in some parts and run in others and the smug amusement playing around Marc's lower face, these grey and wasted visages thrown into shadow by the throbbing glow from the hearth behind them and they appear to her like figures from fever seen once more in recovered strength and now neither feared nor threatening but merely disdained for their previous violation, their presumption, their eager and febrile exploitation of weakness. Unlike theirs, Gwenno's voice is strident, strong, deliberately raised:

—Well, I hope yew bunch of bastards are all pleased with yewerselves. Think it's a good fuckin laugh to humiliate someone in this way aye? Gives yew all a cheap fuckin thrill does it? Christ, yew should all be fuckin ashamed of yerselves. Poor fuckin Ianto. Yew couldn't be happy until yew'd made im look a twat, could yew? No. Well I'll fuckin tell yew; *yewer* the fuckin twats. Too fuckin right. All-a yew. Twats. Playground fuckin bullies yew are. Need to all fuckin grow up like yew do. So fuckin worried about yewer own little dicks that yew av ter laugh at someone else's is it? Is that what it is? Fucking grow up.

143

Griff puffs out his chest indignant and insulted. Danny objects:
—Not me, Gwenno. I had fuck all to do with this.

Fran nods and Marc smirks.

—Still over yer avin a good fuckin gawp tho, arn yew?

—Yeh, but only cos I wanted-a see what was wrong with Ianto's knob, like. I mean Marc said it was all chewed up like an I wanted-a see. Just curious like. I mean I wasn't . . .

—Well whatever's wrong with it it's nobody's bastard business but Ianto's. It's got fuck all to do with anybody else.

Expressionless and gentle Gwenno takes Ianto's slack and damaged penis between her left forefinger and thumb and carefully tucks it back inside his jeans. She takes the fly button in that hand and pulls upwards to tauten the crotch area and then with the other hand she draws the zip up slowly, taking pains not to catch any skin, most of it already cicatriced. Then she takes the hairy tartan blanket from over the back of the settee, poor antimacassar, and unfolds it and arranges it over Ianto so that only his turned-in shoes and sleeping head are visible. She flaps her hands at the standing people, dismissive.

—Right, that's it, show's over. No more dicks to see yer. Go back to yewer seats. Go on, go on. Shoo.

—Bet yew fuckin enjoyed that. Like men's dicks, do yew?

—No moren yew do, Griff. Quite fuckin insistent about Ianto gettin his out, weren't yew?

Griff smirks and returns to his armchair and Danny smiles at Gwenno and moves away stumbling, followed by Fran in similar fashion and Marc sits back on the sofa close to Gwenno their thighs touching and she does not look at him but neither does she shrink away from him, which pleasantly surprises him somewhat as he expected her to. Emboldened and encouraged by this he leans against her, his mouth close to her ear, its clean whorl:

—That was nice, that, what yew did. Caring, like. Considerate. Like that in a woman, I do, a bit of heart, likes. Bit of, y'know, humanity. Sticking up for-a underdog, like, shows yewer not afraid to stick up for yewerself. Shows yew've got a bit-a soul, like. Bit-a strength.

Gwenno smiles wry and shakes her head slightly. —Jesus. So fuckin obvious. Could yew not have come up with something a little bit more original, like? And fuckin hypocritical as well, it goes without bastard saying.

Marc says nothing. Gwenno goes on:

—Last week, Friday I think it was, I was out at K2, necked an E, had a great fuckin time. The Ian Rush tournament was on an the Wales International Under-21 team had had a practice match that day an some-a them were in-a club like. One-a them, I think he plays for fuckin Ipswich or somethin, he wouldn't fuckin leave me alone, all night like he was all over me, buyin me champagne an stuff. Gorgeous lookin as well he was, great fuckin body on im. Had his Porsche outside as well, his own personal fuckin driver waiting for him so's he could av a drink like. Asked me back to his hotel.

—Oh yeh? An what did yew do?

—I knocked him back. I just wasn't in-a mood like. I'd had a great fuckin pill, dancin me tits off, avin a great fuckin time, that was all I wanted to do. So I knocked im back, said thanks but no thanks, y'know, not tonight. But the next day, see, comin down likes, we all went back to Iestyn's house to get lashed and Twmi was yer, yew know Twmi? Ugly fucker with a shaven head?

Marc nods.

—Yeh well he was yer an I ended up in bed with him. Let him fuck me brains out, like. I was horny, see. I wanted a shag. I'd danced for fourteen fuckin hours nearly and just wanted a shag. I mean Twmi, ugly fucker, fat, skint, but I fucked him an not the rich good-looking football player cos that's what I wanted at-a time. That's what I was in-a mood for, see.

She glances at Marc and he nods again.

—I'm telling yew this because I'm probably going to shag yew as well in a minute, but I don't want yew to think that I really fancy yew or anythin like that cos I don't. It's just sex. That's what I want right now. Sex. I'm randy as fuck an I want a shag an yew'll do.

Marc coughs. —Oh. Erm, fine by me, like . . . erm . . .

—Alright?

—Yeh. No problems yer, mun.

—Yeh, so no fuckin followin me around tomorrow or ringing

me up on-a phone or anyfuckinthing like that. I fuckin hate all that stuff.

—Fine, yeh. Don't fuckin flatter yewerself, woman.

—Good. As long as it's clear, likes.

—Crystal.

—Good.

—Fine.

She picks her glass up off the floor toxic cocktail of cheap cider and spirit made from whatever Llŷr plucked from the soil and drains its dregs and swallows it around clenched and hissing teeth.

—One thing, tho, Marc says.

—What?

—Could yew, erm, wash yewer hand? Only yew touched Ianto's dick see an I don't want yew to, y'know, touch mine or any part-a me like with-a same hand. Not being paranoid or anythin likes, it's just that, y'know . . . might put me off a bit like . . .

Gwenno shakes her head. —No.

—No?

—No.

—No what?

—I won't wash my hand.

—Why?

—Cos yewer going to. With yewer tongue.

—Fuck off.

Gwenno turns her head to look at Marc squarely for the first time during this conversation and he tries to focus through pissed and swimming eyes on her face, its symmetry and its colour, the set of it in the frame of hair the colour of cayenne pepper or old blood the thick fringe of which she tosses back out of her face so that she can see him better. So that he might see her. She holds her slim right hand before him and level with his mouth, thumb and index finger poised as if to pinch.

—I'm not joking, no. If yew don't suck these fingers yer clean I'm not going to go to bed with yew now or at any other time in-a future. Yew'll *never* get to fuck me. I mean it.

Marc looks hard at her face and then at her waiting fingers and

146

then away at the fire and then back to her face again and with eyes open and unreadable he takes her digits into his mouth and fancies he can taste sweat and something slightly cheesy, but he sucks her finger and then her thumb and she watches him smiling slightly an expression of what, disgust, amusement, difficult to read. He runs his tongue over one and then the other, nail and knuckle and cuticle, a slight whimpering in his throat. Gwenno slowly withdraws her long finger through the O of his sucking lips and he finds himself craning his neck to chase her escaping hand unable to stop himself doing this, although his face burns red and there is a small birdlike noise in his throat which he will hate himself for making tomorrow when the hot memory of making it will writhe at him through the fog of his hangover. Gwenno wiggles her wet fingers a foot or so in front of his face and he lunges at them mouth open like some hungry fish, but she holds him back with her left hand on his chest and gives a small low laugh.

—God. Blokes.

She stands and sways and then when she is steady she reaches and takes his hand and pulls him upright.

—Right, c'mon then. Fuck me until I fall asleep or beg yew to stop, whichever comes first.

He nods and she leads him away into the bedroom. Closes the door with a snick. At which small sound Griff from his seat by the dying fire raises his nodding head and registers the absence of Marc and Gwenno and then gimaces at the sight opposite him of Fran astride Danny straddling his legs with hers and holding his face in her hands and sucking deeply at his mouth.

—Aw Jesus, mun! Can yew two not find a bit-a privacy to do that so's we don't all have to fuckin watch yew at it? Don't want to see that, mun, Christ.

Danny peers at him from around Fran's shoulder.

—Bedroom occupied is it?

—Yeh. Fuckin Marc an Gwenno.

—Right.

Danny carefully levers Fran off him and as she watches he takes a sheet from the small press in the alcove by the hearth and pulls the couch away from the far wall and tucks one edge

147

of the sheet over the back of the settee and in behind the snoring Ianto to make a kind of semi-tent. He beckons Fran over and she goes to him.

—There. Our own little cave, eh?

They both crouch and crawl into it and Griff watches and soon he can hear groans muffled by gritted teeth or covering hands. Squeaks of springs from the bedroom, Gwenno's rising beseechings, wordless, yearning. He rises unsteadily and moves over to the wall, against which Jane sleeps stepping over Llŷr on the way and rests his back against this wall then slides down it until he is sitting alongside Jane, who does not move. With one hand the palm almost engulfing her entire head he turns her face his way and presses his mouth to hers and she could be a figure made of soft rubber or plastic, all muscles relaxed and hinges loose. His tongue explores her lips and butts and buffets her teeth, but they will not yield, so he holds her face between his spanned hand and with one squeeze he opens her mouth and worms his tongue in that heated place, but the teeth clack closed again hard around his twisting tongue and he yells and withdraws and spits into his palm to check for blood.

—Fuck.

There is no blood. He wipes his palm on his khaki cargo kex then takes to nuzzling Jane's lolling face as he slides his hand over her tight T-shirt, the slight pot belly and her heavy breasts.

—Aw Jane, Janey . . . waited a long fuckin time for this I yav . . .

She will not respond. He desists and sits back on his haunches and looks at her then reaches out suddenly and grabs her shoulder and shakes her hard once and then again her whole body shaking like a rag doll until she exhibits some form of consciousness, a tightening of the eyes and a groan and her epiglottis bobbing frantically as she swallows.

—Jane, wake up . . . wake up, mun . . . everyone else's gone to bed . . . let's fucking, like, let's us two pair off eh? What d'yew say? Always fuckin fancied yew I yav. From since I first saw yew likes . . .

Her eyes snap open. Griff smiles into them his best seductive smile and lets his face fall towards hers lips open to kiss, but then

148

her whole torso jerks and bucks and a hot jet of orange vomit shoots into his lap. He backs kicking away and the spew splatters along his trousers, soaking them, steaming, a pungent vivid slick in which his trainers flop and flounder as if beached.

—Aw for fuck's *sakes!* Yew stupid fuckin *bitch!*

Hunched over Jane groans a stalactite of chunky spittle linking her face to the floor between her legs. Vile icicle, stinking string. Her body bucks again and she retches this time pukelessly, then she wipes her mouth with her forearm and falls back against the wall again smacking her lips. She is snoring within three seconds.

Griff rises, dripping steam snaking from his drenched legs. He takes each leg of his trousers almost daintily between thumb and middle finger of each hand and pulls them away into jodhpur shapes with a faint slurping sound from his hot sticky skin and looks down at himself in disgust.

—Oh fucking bloody hell . . . daft bleedin cow aye . . . what am I supposed to fuckin do now?

He walks bandy-legged to the cold kitchen, stealing one glance only into the makeshift tent behind the couch where white skin slides on white skin, and he stands in the darkness with the humming fridge and takes a plastic blue spatula from the draining board and tries to flick and scoop and shovel the vomit from his legs into the overflowing flip-top bin the flap of which is wedged tight against an almost solid stuffed bulge of crusts and ash and empty cans and bottles. The sick splatters everywhere except the bin, over the floor and the sink and the cupboard doors and even at times up into his face so he throws the spatula aside and kicks off his shoes and peels the reeking trousers over his clammy legs and then his socks too and balls them up into one fuming slimy bundle and dumps that into the sink on top of the unwashed plates and beakers and cutlery. He tries to clean himself with a damp and mildewed rag found stiff and crusted over the spigot and made wet with cold water from the hot tap, but to do this he must stand on one white and blocky leg to wash the other and unbalanced like that he topples sideways and slams treelike on to the linoleum, his head cracking against the pedal of the wheel-less and seatless bicycle frame wedged between bin and oven. He lies there for some time unmoving, bleeding, then he drags himself vertical by handle rim and chairback and hobbles barelegged back into the front room almost entirely dark now that the fire has almost died and filled with the rising and falling audible breathing of five sleepers in tones diverse and discordant. By what weak light there is off the barely pulsing embers he on all fours rummages through the debris on the cooling hearth, the teapot and fag ends and spent matches and small coins and crockery, until he finds the small brown bottle that contains Llŷr's diazepam. He opens it and tips four pills into his palm then spades them into his mouth and washes them down with a swig from the nearest can to hand, a gulp of stale lager and ashes, hellish. Half-naked he curls up into a dark corner growing cold and with teeth chattering and limbs trembling is drug-dragged into a deep and dreamless unconsciousness.

There is a stirring in a corner. Groans and stretching, joints popping and a pale-faced shape rises in the gloom and speaks gruffly with Llŷr's voice:

—Where is everyone? Is anyone there? Aw fuck . . . what's happened? Has everyone gone home? Aw Jesus . . . how long have I been out?

There is no answer.

—Fuckin downers . . . did I miss anything?

There is no answer. The shape redescends silently and will not rise again for some hours, indeed for some hours there will be no voice at all or motion whatsoever in that room with its dying fire and its snared air breathed stale and sour over and over again and its stained walls and smeared glass in its rotten wood frames beleaguered by storm.

Which slowly, gradually, finally begins to die. The sky stills and turns grey and the sun rises to shine a tarnished silver through one hazy cloud which spreads skywide and will not drift or billow. The mountains resettle and the lakes lap quietly and the dingle slopes smoothly to the estuarial mudflats dotted and picked over by oystercatchers and turnstones and small fat phalaropes and curlews with their high curving cries and snipes which run for a little bit like that then stop. Which run for a little bit again then stop. The seal festers on and the standing stones and their hacked arcana gleam secretly atop their tumulus and ticks emerge to wait on stalks for thin and throbbing skin to pass. A sheep nuzzles its stillborn, deformed lamb, moaning over its remarkable small corpse. The cottage itself sinks and resettles in its beams and its footings, another frenzy withstood, another screaming storm seen to its uneventful death and the old wood and stone of the small house hand-axed out of the surrounding mountains in pure rain and stenchless wind and the sun each dawn reborn in blood-prayer seems to snicker as it sinks back into the hard lava and rock of its shallow foundations, earned purr at another passion passed, spent and futile and untrophied.

IANTO IS NINE.

He has been sitting like this for some time, here amongst the thorned stalks and deeply green large leaves almost prehistoric and the spindly-limbed insects whirring around his head through the sunbeams slanting through bush branches into the small sun-washed clearing where the two white people are at each other. His heart thuds. The contrasting skins, the one taut and smooth and the other hard and hairy and apelike hulking over and above the woman on all fours, her face pressed into the grass, her pale wrinkled soles tucked between the man's straining and trembling legs harpstring sinews on his kneebacks and with each thrust the cheeks of his bony arse opening and closing as if fishlike gulping air and Ianto can see it all, the secret pulsing hole and the madly moving testicles and the member swallowed in that moist and mythical bivalve. Back muscles tense and ripple with each rough thrust. The woman screams and then reaches out for the red rucksack nearby and drags it to her and bites down hard on its strap. The man cranes over her and with one long gibbon-like arm presses her face into the earth and her toes point and she wriggles herself back against him. Ianto just stares, his chest booming. There is an almost painful burgeoning between his squatting legs which seems to match the pained throes of the couple in the clearing and indeed who could say that such writhings here, such jerkings in this quiet forest amid the massive and ancient trees, do not resemble some form of anguish, some suffering, not least to this spying nine-year-old whose biology now pulls him this way and that way like a curse? Like misfortune, even like some mishap? He has heard talk and stories of this, this thing that people do, has seen sheep and cattle and rabbits do it but nothing in words whispered or braggart or in his following imaginings or dreams or in muddied field mountings has prepared him for the sounds and the straining, and what he sees seems to him either a grotesque parody of the told legend or simply terrible in its awful authenticity, its ache of urgency, another element of the horror that awaits him on the other side of his quickening years and in which he must like all others live. Saliva rushes into his throat as the man's *thrusts increase in pace pounding and peremptory and he can see the man's face now, the teeth and eyes clenched the cheeks tautened, and the violence in its set. The woman's painted feet drum on the earth. Her hands grip the grass. Ianto feels a dizzying rush avalanche somewhere in his body and his lower area throbs and burns and his hands fall down there and he can feel the transformation terrifying of softness to hardness as if bone has escaped or broken through as if skin has become steel incomprehensible and uncontrollable, this unknown activity in his flesh and their cries rise together as if in mounting panic. His eyes close to tight slits and his little fists beat his head and the whole forest seems to tremble and he knows as he has known a thousand times before that without some heroic application of his own small will the sky above will split and rend and through will spill fire, chaos, a river of blood in scarlet waterfall, everything south of order. He knows this will happen. He knows it now as he knows it each night awake in bed in the small cottage listening to the hectic muttering of his grandmother's nightmares and the wind torturing the gables and the rain lashing the thatch. Nothing could be more sure to him and nothing more unsure, more unknown than his small soft body's big and hard abrupt reaction to the sight of this secret grappling couple, their wrestling a reaction to their isolation in these thick trees and their towering, their darkened pathways and bulk of bush, glittering cobweb and spongiform fungus. Two voices cry out simultaneously in excruciating release the man head back spitting curses at the sky and Ianto's vision turns crimson and he drags a bramble branch from the tangle at his feet not feeling the thorns rip his skin and then he is in the clearing and is thrashing the man's back with this branch his tears hot on his face and the taste of his own blood on his teeth.*

– What the fucking hell!

The man rolls away from the woman and the woman rolls over, the two of them leg-splayed. Ianto sees the clusters of long hairs moistly matted and all the wet folds and frills. The purple bulges and the pink tips. Ridges red as if rubbed raw.

The woman looks at him flush-faced and laughs.

– Oh, it's just a young lad. What's wrong then, little man? Why are you attacking us then?

– Didn't like what we were doing, aye? The man asks. There are flecks of foam in his short wiry beard and he too wears his hair long like

153

the woman. —*Don't worry. I wasn't hurting her. Everybody does it. You'll be doing it yourself in a few years' time.*

The woman takes a coat from the pile of clothes at her side and covers her nakedness. The man doesn't, but he does close his legs. Ianto stands and stares trembling as if in fury and there is something terrible to him about their affability, their oneness with every giant he meets, the strange protective and kindred thread which seems to link them to him. How well humanity hides its horrors. How well it masks its madness. As Ianto watches a slug of white slime begins to creep towards him along the man's shockingly naked, shockingly hairy thigh.

— I'm sorry if we upset you, my little friend. What were you spying on us for? No, wait, don't be afraid. Look, we're not hurt or anything. We weren't harming each other. It's just what grown-ups do, we . . . where are you going? It's all right, don't be scared, we . . . there's no need to run away!

They start to laugh. Ianto drops the bramble branch and turns and runs and the forest darkness swallows him up.

—NAH, LISTEN, *I'll* tell yew who Ianto was in love with.

—Who?

—An it wasn't Gwenno.

—Who then?

—Yeh, go on, Danny, who? Tell us, mun. I can't wait to see what daft fuckin theory yew're goin-a come out with next.

—Roger.

—Roger? Roger *Price?*

—Ianto, in love with Roger? What in-a name of *fuck* are yew bleedin talkin about, mun?

—Roger my arse.

—No, no, I can see Danny's point, mun . . . see what he means like . . . not a fuckin *sexual* love or anything like that, fuck no, but . . .

—Ianto an Roger givin it to each other up the shitter. Jesus.

—Yeh. Suckin each other off . . .

—Arousin fuckin image is it then, Marc?

—. . . it was eyr closeness . . . or no, not even that. It was eyr . . .

—Similarities.

—That's it, Danny, yeh, eyr similarities. Like brothers or somethin.

—Or not even anythin that specific really. It was just like, y'know, that they seemed sort of, likes, to be part of-a same species. I mean not like the rest of us, like.

—What kind-a shite is this? The human fuckin race, mun! *That's* the fuckin species!

—Yeh, but different like, somehow. Like a sub-species. Like ey weren't quite-a same as most other people, but they were the same as each other. That was eyr closeness. Like say a penguin an a eagle; I mean eyr both dead different like, but fundamentally eyr the same. Both birds, see. Both-a same species.

—This is-a biggest load-a bollax . . .

155

—Well, *yew* fuckin explain it then. Go on. Ianto an Roger, I mean they spent a fuck of a lot of time together, dinney? Ianto was with Roger more than he was with anybody else, wanney? So why?

—Easy, mun. Cos ey were both fuckin psychos, that's why. Simple as that, like.

—Which is fuckin exactly what I've been tryin-a say, innit? Christ, does anyone ever listen to a blind word I fuckin say?

—No.

—Alright then: Explain to me why Ianto was so fucked up after Roger carked it like. I mean, ee went off is fuckin trolley by all accounts. How come?

—Yeh. The police reckoned that that was when ee done is second like, after Roger died like. Those two hikers, Ianto murdered em after ee found out that Roger'd been killed. That's what the busies reckoned anyway.

—Altho how they managed to work that one out is fuckin beyond me, mun.

—Most things are, Marc.

—Yewer arse.

—Specially my arse, yeh.

—Well, *I* don't fuckin well know. I mean yewer fuckin askin me to explain-a workings of a psychopathical mind. How-a fuck do *I* know, mun? It was just like, I dunno . . . I mean, Roger was Ianto's mate. Maybe it was just another sick an twisted excuse. Y'know, like: oh fuck my mate's been killed so I'm gonner go out an murder some poor innocent fucker that never even met im to avenge is fuckin death. Or just-a make meself feel a bit fuckin better. I don't fuckin know. Ianto was a nutter. Roger died an ee lost-a fuckin plot. Sick bastard that ee was. I can't explain why like, but it had fuck all to do with any fuckin kind of fuckin *love.*

—I agree.

—Oh yew do fuckin surprise me, Marc.

—No, it's true, I mean think about it, mun; I mean we're not just fuckin talkin about murder yer are we . . . it wasn't just fuckin murder that Ianto committed likes . . .

—Yew don't know that for certain.

156

—Aw c'mon, mun, she ad her fuckin kex around er ankles. *And* er top pulled up. An a coppers said yer was bruising, rips in er skin an stuff like, fuckin *inside*. Which, they said, occurred fuckin *after* death. Post mortem like. So I don't for a fuckin life-a me see how Roger bein killed can lead to fuckin that. I don't see-a fuckin link at all. Yer's not one fuckin shred of logic, mun.

—Aye, but that's just it, innit? That's what I'm sayin likes. I mean we're not talkin about a logical person yer, are we, a logical mind. I mean no type of love is logical if yew think about it like.

—Aw Jesus Christ.

—Will yew get off this fuckin shit about love, Danny? It means fuck all, mun. Yewer talkin complete crap. Yewer tryin to explain things that can't be fuckin explained. Yewer tryin to relate them to yewer own experience an makin a pig's arse of everything.

—Am I fuck. I mean *I've* never fuckin killed anyone, av I? It's fuckin years since I've ever even punched anyone. It's got fuck all to do with what *I've* experienced, mun. It's beyond me like. I can't fuckin understand it.

—Yeh, so stop bleedin tryin to then.

—Tryin to what?

—Understand it. Yew've just said yewerself that yew can't understand it so why are yew lookin for reasons? Just admit like that yew'll never understand what went on and just accept it. I mean fuck knows what was goin on in that fucker's head. *Fuck* knows.

—Sickness. Perversion, that's what it was.

—I . . .

—Jesus, Danny, don't tell me that yewer goin to agree with Marc? That's a fuckin first if ever I've seen one. Wait an I'll get me tape recorder out.

—Well, it's not that I'm agreeing with im as such like . . .

—Yes yew are. Admit it.

—It's just that I'm, like, beginnin to think . . .

—Beginnin to think what? That yewer full of shite? At long fuckin last, mun. Finally yew've come to yewer fuckin senses, like.

157

—Fuck off. At least I'm fuckin *trying*, mun, *trying* to work things out like. At least I'm doin that. I mean Ianto wasn't born a killer. He didn't come out of-a womb with-a urge to kill people he didn't even know. I mean somethin must've happened to turn im that way, mustn't it. An that somethin could've really happened to any fuckin one of us.

—Shite.

—Not fuckin me, mun.

—I mean, likes, we're all blank canvases when we're born like an Ianto, well, straightafuckinway he was born into a shitty world, wasn't he? No dad, discarded by his alkie mam. An it's not as if he was a bright lad either, not as if he was born with-a mental capacity to understand is situation, to deal with it like. His fuckin cards were marked right from the off.

—Must-a been is old man's tinker spunk. Defective I reckon.

—It's just pure fuckin cruel. I mean born with half a brain into no life to speak of. Obviously he was unable to think or work things out the way most other people do like. His thought processes would take a wrong turnin somewhere, they'd veer off an get lost. I mean it's like normal people's go from A to B, his would go from fuckin A to six or somethin. A route that we could never, ever follow.

—Jesus bloody Christ. Av yew all yerd this cunt? What are yew fuckin goin on about, mun? Av yew fuckin yerd yewerself? Sound like that fuckin police psychologist twat, yew do. Both up yewer own arses like.

—No, go on, Danny. Tell us what yewer tryin-a say.

—Well, maybe, likes, in a way that we could never fathom, Roger's death somehow like brought Ianto closer to the very fuckin *idea* of death. D'yew see what I mean? Like he wanted-a see it first hand, like, wanted to try an understand it better. Somethin like that. Maybe, cos ee was all fuckin upset like, maybe he thought somethin along-a lines of wantin to prove to isself that death wasn't that bad so he wouldn't be so fucked up about Roger not bein yer any more. D'yew know what I mean?

—I don't agree. Because Ianto ad done it before, hadn't he?

That schoolboy. It's pure an fuckin simple, mun; he was pissed off an upset so he murdered some poor fucker to make isself feel better. That's all yer was to it. Psycho.

—Crackers.

—Yeh, psycho like, it has to be said, Roger imself. I know he was yewer mate an all that, Griff, an I'm not sayin anythin against-a boy like, but . . . well, fuck, I mean Roger had it in im imself, didn't he?

—Meanin what, like?

—Meanin that, well, y'know, that Roger was a bit of a psycho imself, wasn't he? That if is circumstances had of been-a same as Ianto's when he was growin up like then maybe he would've turned out-a same. Or maybe not quite as bad . . .

—Maybe fuckin *any* of us would, mun.

—Yeh, but Roger was-a more likely, I'd say. I mean he was nearly fuckin already there, wanney? He just had that small bit of self-restraint that Ianto didn't have. Just enough to stop, like, violence becomin murder. I mean, beatin some poor bastard up is one thing. Fuckin toppin em is another.

—Yeh, but maybe Ianto didn't mean to kill anyone. I mean we don't know. Maybe they were just accidents.

—Bollax. Pure fuckin bollax. He hit that schoolboy with a rock until his fuckin skull caved in. That's no fuckin accident, mun.

—Borstal boy. Not schoolboy.

—Splittin fuckin hairs. Whatever-a fuck ee was, Ianto beat is head to a pulp with a fuckin rock. An he killed-a others, them two hikers like, one of em a fuckin *woman*, with what did-a busies reckon it was?

—A fence post.

—A fence post, aye. An yew say it was an accident? Accident be fucked. He wanted them dead, that bastard did. Fuckin *dead*.

—Yeh. He wanted to create misery. Fuckin definitely.

—Yeh, cos ee was tired of bein in misery imself.

—Which is no sort of fuckin excuse. None at bastard all.

—I'm not sayin it fuckin is, mun. But it is a fuckin *reason*, innit, ey? I mean I'm not tryin to excuse what Ianto did

159

at all, but I am tryin to work out why he did it. That's all, like.

—Why fuckin bother tho, mun? Just fuckin accept it. Just fuckin accept-a fact that yer are things in-a world that yew'll *never* fuckin be able to understand. No one will. Police psychologists can fuckin waffle on till eyr blue in-a fuckin face an none-a us'll be any-a fuckin wiser. They'll think they are, but they won't be. Not really.

—No but like, Ianto was a mate, wanney? Before, likes, I mean. I mean we hung around with him, we drank with im, everything. And none of us ever fuckin suspected that he was capable of doin what he did, not for a fuckin minute like, so it's important that we try an work it out because maybe if we had've thought along these lines before then all those people would still be alive. Ianto isself included.

—D'yew know who yew sound like now, Danny? That copper. Member that fat fucker with-a blond hair? Little fuckin Hitler. Squeaky-voiced cunt: 'I can't believe yew didn't know anything. I can't believe that yew boys weren't in on it. He was your friend, after all.' Fuckin little gobshite he was aye.

—Yeh. Missed-a whole fuckin point, dinny?

—Which was?

—That Ianto was nobody's fuckin mate. Not really. None-a us ever *really* knew the twat, did we?

—Well maybe Roger did, see, that's what I've been tryin to say all along. Maybe he –

—Aw Christ. Yer we fuckin go again.

—Aye. Here we fuckin go again.

—An Roger's brown bastard bread anyway so what the fuck does it matter? Pointless to even talk about it.

—It's all in-a past, mun, it's fuckin gone. Roger's dead like Ianto. An all-a poor people that sick fucker killed. Best just to forget about it.

—Yeh. Let it fuckin go.

THEY'D ARRANGED TO meet in the pub over the Trefechan bridge at midday so Ianto slept in the squat in order to be on time, in the hall in a sleeping bag shiny with dirt, and was in fact an hour early and Roger was an hour late so he found Ianto alone in a corner by the fish tank, angel fish and guppies flowing from his ears like his dreams made visible. Six empty bottles on the table before him and an ashtray choked with the wet and pointed stubs of handrolled cigarettes and beer mats torn into several small mounds. Roger buys drinks at the bar, a pint of Wrexham lager for himself and a bottle of Brains Dark for Ianto and takes them over to the table and Ianto looks up at him, his pasty face breaking into a wide and damp grin although he is mildly disturbed at Roger's curly hair, the customary crop grown out, and the marasmus declared in Roger's tight skin and prominent cheekbones and wristbones probably chemical-generated.

—Alright, butt? Been yer long then?

Ianto gestures vaguely at the table and the detritus of his wait.

—That long, aye? I know, mun, I know, I'm late. Couldn't be fuckin helped likes. An yer's why.

Roger glances around the pub as he delves into the inside pocket of his dirty camouflage jacket and takes out two small white pills and surreptitiously picks away from them twists of clinging lint and dried shreds of tobacco.

—Had to hang around Jester's waiting for fuckin Jed to show up, din I? Worth-a fuckin wait, tho, mun, too bastard right. This is fuckin bangin E. Already had an arf, shared one with tha Scouse twat Colm like, an I'm coming up like a bastard. Fuckin great stuff aye. Fuckin tellin yew, mun. Yer, open yewer gob.

Ianto doesn't need to as it's already hanging open, slight sheen on his chin, and Roger flicks a pill into that round ever-wet hole.

—Now chew it. I know it tastes fuckin yack like, but's a quicker hit. Faster into-a bloodstream, see.

He flicks the other pill up into his own mouth and they both sit there chewing silently like ruminating ruminants, their noses and eyes wrinkled up in distaste. Simultaneously they swallow then reach for and raise and gulp from their drinks and wipe their mouths with the backs of their hands and burp and sit back in their seats, all movements mirrored one to the other like twins linked by some strange and strong umbilicus. Like puppets in the hands of the same master. Roger takes cigarettes from his pocket and offers one to Ianto and they both light up and inhale deeply and blow blue smoke ceilingwards.

—So, then, anyway. How's yewerself? Ant seen yew for a while like. Ow's it all goin?

—Alright.

—Where'd yew sleep last night then, a squat was it?

Ianto nods.

—No trouble?

Ianto shakes his head.

—Good to fuckin hear it, mun. I've told yew, haven't I: any fuckin trouble off those scroungin fuckin gypo cunts an yew come straight to me. Straight to fuckin me. Love a fuckin reason to sort out those mingin twats I would. Fuckin *love* one, mun. Roy had his flat turned over last week like an I'm fuckin sure it was one-a those crusties, fuckin sure of it, mun. Never been bastard surer. Ey, yew dint see anythin yer last night, did yew? No new video or telly or CD player or anythin like that? Mountain bike or anythin?

Ianto shakes his head again. —I wasn't really lookin, Rog, see. Just sleepin likes.

—Aye, suppose . . . might have to pay a visit up yer later likes. Just-a check things out. See what's goin on, like. Know what I mean?

He elbows Ianto as Ianto is in mid-drink and the bottle wobbles and beer spurts up Ianto's nose and he coughs and splutters and Roger laughs.

—Gob or shnoz, mun, slong as yew get it down yewer fuckin

neck is all that fuckin matters. Drink up an I'll get us another. *Plenty* fuckin more where that came from, mun.

He takes a thick roll of banknotes from his pocket and waves it in front of Ianto's face.

—Duw. Where'd yew get all that then?

—Never yew fuckin mind, mun. What yew don't know no cunt can beat out-a yew, in that right?

He passes it back and forth under Ianto's nose.

—Smell it, mun? See what it smells like? Fuckin freedom, mun, freedom is what that smells like. A few days of lovely fuckin freedom. Dun it smell sweet? Fuckin love that smell I do. Fuckin *love* it, mun.

He smells it himself, an exaggeratedly deep gulp, and exhales as if in ecstasy.

—Now what yew avin? Same again is it? Dark Brains? How very fuckin apt.

He fetches more drinks from the bar and when he returns he tells Ianto how he came by such a large amount of money, a confusing and convoluted tale involving drugs and a stolen car and many threats of violence and people short-changed or ripped off or both and promises made with absolutely no prospect of their being honoured. When he has finished Ianto's jaw is working to grind his teeth audibly and he is sniffing and scratching his head and swallowing rapidly and there is a smile creeping up on to his face like a growth and a peculiar coruscation in his eyes.

—Fuck, mun . . . that fuckin pill . . .

—Comin up, are yew? Told yew, boy, it's bangin fuckin stuff. Fast-actin an all. Just fuckin ride it, mun. Go with-a flow.

And it is a fleet and pleasing flow that takes them away into a heaven chemical and temporary and one possessed of a remarkable alchemy, an ability to transmogrify a passable situation into one of near perfection. An adequacy to an idyll. It spits and crackles in Ianto's skin and he could want for absolutely nothing other than to be here in this pub on an overcast early weekday afternoon drinking with Roger with bright small fish adrift behind his head and the rich taste of the beer and the smell of the cawl simmering in the small kitchen and the customers

163

talking and laughing below the jukebox music, some cheesy chart dance. Even the wallpaper, its pattern and its colour suit the situation immaculately and all is unimprovable, it is given and pristine. Ianto could not be happier, here, now, could never wish for anything more. He begins to writhe in his seat. Roger watches him and grins.

—Told yew, din I. Tidy fuckin E, mun, innit.

—Yeh.

—Yew alright?

—Yeh.

—Only yewer wrigglin like a fuckin worm, mun.

—Just feel-a need to move, mun, that's all.

—Yeh, a know what yew mean. Tell yew what, let's go an play a few games-a pool, eh? Won't fuckin gouch out if we're doin somethin like. Come on.

Roger stands and Ianto follows him out of the small lounge and along the cold corridor past the bleach-reeking toilets and past the fruit machine bleeping and flashing, which snares Ianto's eye and he stands and stares at that bright motion until Roger returns tutting and takes him away by the arm up the few steps and into the smoky public bar. Old men sit and sip pints and watch the rugby on the TV screen above the wooden gantry and dogs sleep under tables, heads on paws. Trawlermen from the nearby harbour stand at the bar and glitter with scales and salt at cap and cuff and boot and stink of fish guts and brine and broken crabs and chase pints of dark beer with large whiskies. Exposed skin on handbacks and faces and necks raw, flayed. There are some small stacks of coins along the wooden rim of the pool table but nobody actually on the table so Roger feeds it money and yanks the handle to release the balls. At their thud and small thunder two studenty types at the bar turn to look.

—We were next on there. That's our money, look.

Roger arranges the balls in the triangle. —Yewer alright, boys. We won't be long, see, just a single frame like. It's to decide who buys-a next round, see.

They turn away displeased and grumbling and Roger bares his teeth at their backs and Ianto chalks a cue and stands there passing it from hand to hand with some force, liking the sensation, the sharp smack of smooth and burnished wood on his slick and yielding palm. He likes the smells and the sounds of the pub and when Roger breaks he likes the mad and random burst of the balls, the yellow and red bounce and spin, the colours gleaming beneath the low bulb, and the lone white chasing the lone black along the side cushion, the spots of reflected light on the balls' curves like sunshine on sea. The nap of the green felt like cropped grass and indeed yes he thinks this could indeed be a small field and the balls a herd of some bizarre cattle grazing and the pockets like –

—Oi, bollockchops. Yew gunner av a shot then or ar yew just gunner stand yer gawpin all fuckin day?

Ianto grins at Roger and leans over the table and goes for the most obvious option, a yellow teetering on the lip of the far corner pocket. He clips it in and hears it rumble through the table's inner warren as he stands and watches the white ball trickle on backspin to a stop at a perfect position to pot another. He shakes his head slightly, awed at his own skill.

Roger pushes him out of the way.

—Foul ball. Two shots ter me.

—Ey? What the fuck for, mun? That was never a bastard foul.

—Fraid it was, Ianto boy. I'm yellow, see. Potted a yellow on-a break likes. Got to learn to pay attention, yew av. Think fuckin Ronnie O'Sullivan stands yer gawpin with is gob angin open? Pilled up fucker yew, mun.

He smiles at Ianto and takes his shot and misses and then takes the second of his free double and misses that too. Ianto pockets a red then another and screws back to line himself up for a third which he misses and Roger takes over and flukes a yellow in off the black and then fouls as he pockets another with the white ball following in with. Ianto wastes his two shots and Roger takes over again and the game progresses poorly this way, the two of them giggling and grinning and grinding their teeth and bouncing impatiently on the balls of their feet as they wait their turn until the balls are all sunk apart from the black, which will not go down for eight, nine shots until in frustration Ianto simply whacks it and it ricochets and slows and trickles and clunks into the middle pocket somehow like a turd and Ianto raises his cue over his head in triumph.

—Yew jammy fuckin twat. Flukey fuckin bastard.

Roger feeds the table coins and one of the student types comes over to stand at his bent back.

—It's our turn now, mate. That's our money there. We're in the middle of a tournament.

Roger nudges him to one side with his hunched shoulder so he can reach the released balls.

—A bit-a space yer if yew don't mind please.

He tosses a crumpled fiver on the baize.

—Get-a bevvies in, Ianto, while I rack um up.

Ianto takes the money up to the bar and Roger triangles the balls whistling and ignoring utterly the weak protests at his shoulder. The complainer might as well not be there, might as well not exist. He returns red-faced to his companion at the bar when Roger turns his back on him to chalk his cue. Another game is played which Roger wins so they must then play a third as a decider which Roger wins again largely on the insistence that Ianto fouled, then they vacate the table and repair to a corner, where they drink more beers and talk more and drum on their knees with flat hands and bask and relax in chemical glow and the instant and immediate busy pub world turned golden and flawless. Ianto caresses a mongrel dog which comes to sniff at his ankles and Roger converses with a dreadlocked young white man he addresses as Weasel, who sits at their table and after exchanging small talk for a minute or two approaches the real reason for his joining them:

—Roger, I'm, erm, I'm lookin for a toot, like. Been clean for fuckin months now an I'm just after a little toot, likes, y'know, just to chill. Yewer not carrying, are yew? Just a tenner bag like if yew can do that, I'm not wantin-a get back into-a scene or anythin, like, fuck no. It's just I fancy mongin out for an arvo, like, that's all. Been mad fuckin busy all week, like, an I just need a rest, know what I mean?

He looks at Roger pleadingly. Roger shakes his head.

—Carn elp yew yer, Weeze, he says. He sounds almost pleased. —I yant touched-a stuff for months meself, like. But

166

I'll tell yew who's got some hellish good brown, tho; Black Jerry. Yew tried im? He've got fuckin stacks of-a stuff, mun. Good fuckin gear as well. Call up at is gaff, like, he'll be able to sort yew out.

—Out in Llanbadarn aye?

—That's-a place. He'll sort yew out, mun. Dim probs.

Weasel nods and leaves the pub on steps quick and urgent and Roger watches him twitch past the window then splutters into his cupped hands. Enquiring, Ianto looks sideways at him.

—What's so funny, like?

—Him, mun, Weasel . . . Black Jerry hates that fucker. Reckons it was im who found is stash two weeks ago an nicked it, like. See, Jerry got dead para last month, likes, an fitted an infra-red camera up a tree where he hides his gear, like, an says he've got film of Weasel diggin it all up an avin it away. Says he's gunner take a blade to im-a next time ee sees im, like. Which'll be in about what, half a fuckin hour. Love to be yer to see that, I would. Too fuckin right, boy.

—Is it, is it true, like?

—What?

—That Weasel did that? Nicked Black Jerry's stuff?

Roger shrugs. —Fuck knows. Jerry reckons so, like. Says he've got im on camera so I suppose it must be. Altho avin said that I've seen film from Jerry's camera an yew carn make out head nor tail of fuckin anythin. It's all just a big fuckin grey blur, like. Could be anythin. Cheap camera, see. Fire damage or somethin. Picture's a load-a fuckin shite, mun. Might as well-a filmed a fuckin window in a washin machine cos that's all it fuckin looks like.

—So it might not-a been Weasel then?

Roger shrugs again. —Really couldn't fuckin tell yew, mun. Not that I care, likes; it's just a good fuckin larf, mun, innit? He tips his glass to his mouth and drains it. —C'mon, mun, drink up. Let's move on. Sledgin a bit in yer I yam like.

Ianto gulps what remains of his drink and they leave the pub together and stand for a moment squinting on the pavement allowing their senses to adjust to the bombardment of light, bright light which it seems to Ianto he can feel on his skin

167

like a pelt of warm fur and taste in his throat like honey, and he closes his eyes and hums low then a dark cloud is blown over the sun like a veil and they head off across the Trefechan bridge stopping halfway across to lean over the old stone balustrades and look down on the river below and its waterfowl, a few ducks and seagulls drifting with the current slowly towards the open sea. Roger pushes thick and white cottony saliva out through his pursed lips to hang and sway and then break and fall splat on to the sluggish water, where a drake stabs at it once and then again then swallows and mutters to itself. A seagull hops up out of the water to perch on the moss-soft and slimy sewer pipe and preen, Ianto admiring the cruel hook of its yellow beak and the reptilian torpor of its dark eyes. Roger points a pistol at it made out of his thumb and forefinger and cocks his thumb and shoots with a noise which reminds Ianto of playing Cowboys and Indians in the hills as a boy. They head on. Ianto's limbs are loose and relaxed and he feels that his movements are all fluid and easy and that the slight swagger in his stride now is not chemically induced but is simply his natural carriage and he could imagine for himself no other gait or locomotion.

They turn down on to Alexander Road, past the tall grey tabernacle open for today to host a jumble sale and they talk about going in there but decide against it because of the gaggle of old ladies filing through the heavy oaken doors and walk further on instead for a drink in the Mill. They play more pool, two games, and win one each and stand by the jukebox drinking, both of them shifting from foot to foot and taking small swift sips at their pints and scratching and twitching their faces, gurning under the mixture of ephedrine and caffeine and MDEA and amphetamine and unknown substances which was sold to Roger as Ecstasy but is still far stronger and of far more appreciable effect than nearly all stimulants peddled under that name, although without the general empathic consequence of a dose of straight MDMA their sight is necessarily turned inwards and their sensual riot ends at the tingling tips of their tongues and fingers and is played out only on the backs of their own flickering eyelids.

Ianto's eyes are bouncing around the empty pub. Roger, more

at ease, leans his arse back against a table and lights a cigarette with languor and lets smoke dribble down towards the sticky maroon carpet.

—Tell yew what we're gunner do, Ianto, he says. —Yew know Mad Cyril's? Up by Y Cŵps like? Well yew know all-a junk ee sells; marital fuckin aids an stuff like. We'll take a wander up yer an see what he've got. I'll buy a biggest fuckin plastic knob yew've ever fuckin seen in yewer life. Av a laugh likes.

Ianto looks sideways at him. —What for?

—What for? For a fuckin larf, mun, what d'yew think? That's all. What more fuckin reason d'yew need to do fuckin anythin? No point doin fuckin anythin unless it's a fuckin larf, is yer? Jesus, Ianto. A lot to fuckin learn yew av, boy. Just go with-a fuckin flow, mun. Just fuckin ride it, like.

They finish their drinks and go back outside again into the falling light and walk past the twenty-four-hour garage, where a van honks its horn at them and a figure inside it waves and they wave back even though they do not recognise their hailer and walk on level with the Lord Beechings, where the smell of beer and smoke and the thump of music is too much to resist so they order vodka and Cokes in there and drink them quickly standing at the bar then leave and pass the Cambrian Arms twenty yards further on and stop and raise their heads to sniff the air like predators scenting prey and grin at each other and walk back and into that pub and order more vodkas, this time neat with lots of ice, and stand against the bar sipping, looking. A man approaches them, an acquainted face seen amongst the local crusties and rough sleepers, even though his dress is conservative, jacket and jeans and white trainers and he wears his greying hair short.

—Hi, guys.

They nod noncommittally. Ianto has seen this man perform-ing unbalanced tai-chi on the beach of a morning and badly singing blues on the promenade of a summer's day; Roger has on sufferance and in the past endured his self-obsessed ramblings and has vowed never to do so again and now neither he nor Ianto are in the mood for this man's overbearing attention-seeking nor even for the way his top lip disappears when he smiles.

—What're you two up to today then eh?

169

They don't answer.

—Just chilling, yeah? Yeah, me too. Quiet drink like. Just having a day's break from scribbling, y'know.

Roger looks at Ianto and raises his eyebrows: here we fucking go again.

—Yeah, you've got to take the odd couple of days off, y'see, let your fuckin brain rest, like. Gets on top of you after a while, writing away . . . He chuckles and shakes his head. —You end up, sort of, not really appreciating anything, just thinking about things in terms of description, how they'd look on the page. Gets too much. Both a gift and a curse it is, yeah, too fucking right. Both a gift and a bloody curse. Don't ever do it, lads. Anybody asks me for advice on how to get started as a writer and that's exactly what I tell them: don't. Do something else. Takes a special kind of person to put up with the demands and some people would be absolutely destroyed.

He grimaces as if in pain and sips at his drink. —I'm sure Amis and Auster would agree with me, would both say exactly the fucking same. Takes too much out of you. Don't do it. Don't create unless you'd feel you'd die if you didn't.

Ianto and Roger look at him impassive, like they'd look at a sheet of glass painted black and unreflective. Roger sucks at his drink and crunches ice.

—Oh aye?

The man nods. —Oh yeah. It's as I say, both a blessing and a curse. There are times when you've got to bring your brain back down to earth again, stop, like, fucking dwelling on the higher things. Have to live in the world sometimes like. That's when stuff like this comes in handy.

He bends and delves into the Spar bag at his side and takes out a glossy magazine which he smooths on the bar: *Asian Babes*. He flips it open to the centre pages and Ianto grinning darts forwards to look and the dark-skinned barmaid hair black and straight and shining rolls her eyes and begins to dry glasses.

—Aw, for fuck's sake, man. Have a bit-a fuckin respect, eh? Roger takes the magazine off the bar, out of the man's hands. —Girlie yer dun wanner see that, do yew, love?

The barmaid shrugs and does not meet his eyes.

170

—Course yew fuckin don't. Fuckin obscene, mun. He rolls the magazine into a tight cylinder and points it close in the man's face. —Yew a writer then?

—Yes. Not published yet, like, but . . .

—Well what the fuck d'yew need *this* for then? Roger shakes the rolled magazine like a percussive instrument. A tambourine or something. —Carn yew write yewer own porn? Duw, yew've got a fuckin imagination, haven't yew? Couldn't write otherwise, likes. Well put it towards creating some wanking material for yewerself an stop fuckin embarrassin women in bastard public.

He drains his drink and slides the magazine into his hip pocket.

—I'm afraid I'm going to have to confiscate this. Yew obviously carn be trusted with it.

—You'll bloody well give me that back. That cost three pounds fuckin fifty!

—No, no, I'm sorry, but yewer obviously not mature or responsible enough to be in possession of such material. You can have it back when you're old enough to use it in a responsible manner. I'm afraid you'll have to use yewer imagination from now on. Come on, Ianto.

The man snatches at Roger's jacket as he passes, but Roger nimbly sidesteps his swipe and says quietly with a light in his eyes:

—Don't. Just fuckin don't. Alright? One warning only. Yewer lucky I'm E'd up to my eyeballs yew are, mun.

The man looks into Roger's face and then looks away again. Ianto giggles and stands by Roger, who loudly addresses the barmaid:

—See this twat? He points at the man. —I'd fuckin watch im, if I was yew. Fuckin pervert like he is. Just one fuckin look at that magazine as made im blosh all over yewer fuckin bar.

Ianto giggles louder and they leave the pub and laughing wait with the crowd at the zebra crossing until they can cross between the parted cars. They move around the beige bulk of B-Wise and on to the thin strip of waste ground between the walls of that and the railway yard and there amongst the broken glass and dock leaves and nettles and empty wrappers rustling in the breeze they observe gleaming images of skin and hair and holes held open moist. At close-ups of erectile tissue and far faces positioned below rumps and flanks. Ianto begins to murmur as the pages flip and pretty soon to pant. Roger looks at him askance.

—Jesus, Ianto. This fuckin turnin yew on, then, is it? This fuckin thing? Duw, yewer as bad as him, mun, that prick in-a Cambrian. It's just a fuckin magazine, boy. Just fuckin pictures, like.

Ianto looks at him concerned, chewing his cheeks and his eyes less bright. A suggestion of wobble in his lower lip. Roger sighs and puts his arm around his shoulder.

—Aw don't get upset Ianto, mun. I'm not avin a go at yew, like, it's just . . . well, likes, yer's a time an a place for porno, mun, an this isn't it. Yew *knows* it int. On yewer own, like, yeh, in yewer room or something if yewer feelin orny, that's alright, but in public, mun . . . a public's a place for lookin at *real* fuckin women, boy, not just fuckin *pictures* of um. It's like in-a pub, just then; that binty behind-a bar was fit as fuck, mun. A right fuckin shagger n all – yew could see it in er eyes like. Now wouldn't yew sooner look at *er* likes instead-a a fuckin stewpid picture of someone who just looks like er?

Ianto nods, his eyes flicking between Roger's face and the image he holds in his hands of tanned and lifted breasts.

—Aye, course yew fuckin would, mun. Yewer not like im, ar yew, that thick fuckin *rude* cunt in-a pub?

Ianto shakes his head.

—Nah, course yewer not. Got a fuckin brain underneath it all, aven't yew, boy? He pokes Ianto's skull with a rigid forefinger. —Fuck knows ow it works, like, but's a brain in yer all-a fuckin same. Don't need this, do we? He flaps the magazine like a broken-backed bird. —This shite yer? Couple-a shaggers like us? Too right we fuckin don't. *Real* fuckin women for us two, mun, innit? *Real* tarts likes, oh yeh.

He stands and moves over to the wall which borders the train platform and raises himself up on tiptoes to peer over it. He grins over his shoulder at Ianto and beckons him over.

—Watch this.

172

Ianto peers over the wall alongside Roger, a pair of Kilroys, and sees people milling, tensed pensioners and impatient parents and their restless children and two couples emotionally hugging. He watches as Roger tosses the magazine among them, sees it smack and slide off a blue rinse and flop to the floor and land open at a pink and parted, giant shining close-up. Gynaecological camera angle. He hears a shriek and pale faces swing his way and then he is laughing and running after Roger over the uneven strip of wasteland and past the graffiti'd back wall of B-Wise and into the bus station, where they come to rest on a bench by the blue-burping exhaust of an idling double-decker, grinning and panting with their heads hung.

—Jesus, Ianto pants. —That was so fuckin funny. Caused a, a few fuckin *heart* attacks yer, din we?

Roger gives three quick small nods. —Fair few fuckin hard-ons as well, I reckon. He breathes deeply and smiles. —Fuck me, that was funny.

They sit and grin and regain their breath, which is easy since they weren't actually out of breath anyway not having run very far, and with the exponentially increased energy that the chemicals are giving them then they move on down Thespian Street, passing an Indian woman in full shalwar-kameez with several children in tow similarly dressed. Ianto gawps and Roger sneers and they both watch the family pass. One small child glances up at their faces and then looks away again very quickly. Ianto tries to nudge Roger into the Weston Vaults, but Roger shakes his head.

—Can't mun. Barred. Yew knows that, don't yew? Or av yew forgotten what happened in yer last time, like?

Through a thick fog Ianto recalls Roger arguing with the barman two weeks or so ago over something, a refusal to serve perhaps, recalls then Roger chewing up a pint glass and spitting shards and spittle and blood over the bar right into the barman's face. Remembers also sitting bored in the hospital while Roger had his lips and tongue and cheeks stitched back together again. He grins up at Roger and gets a smile back.

—Remember now, aye?

—Yeh.

173

—Yeh. Funny as fuck, aye. Roger shakes his head at the memory and smiles then bulges his inner cheek with his tongue. —Dead fuckin sore as well tho. Twenty-seven fuckin stitches, mun, aye. He runs his tongue around his mouth and lips, feeling the sensitive ridges, not quite healed.

They turn on to the main road past the Weston Vaults and almost literally bump into a tall blond man, who stands above them with the twitchy hands and sweaty forehead and frantic chewing of amphetamine ingestion. Roger appears to know him:

—Malcolm, yew twat! What's-a fuckin news en, boy?

Malcolm spreads his arms and replies in a voice of high Essex inflection:

—Ya see it awl, Roger mate. Skint, speedin . . .

Roger leans in towards Malcolm, speaks lower, conspiratorial: —Yew've not got any left, av yew? Only I could do with a toot, like.

—Nah. Ad it faw breakfast, mate, din I? Awl gone. Up me shnoz.

—Ah well. I believe yer. Thousands fuckin wouldn't like. Ey, yew don't know where we can get hold of any more E, do yew? Ianto yer's fuckin dyin-a get loved up, in yew, boy?

Ianto giggles and dribbles slightly and his head bobs loosely on his neck. He is not really hearing this conversation, distracted as he is with the high humming in his head and the bright patterning on Malcolm's jumper. Led by Roger as he has been led by the movements and imperatives of others seen or unseen touched or untouchable since he was born he will move when Roger moves and stop when Roger stops and make some noise in his throat when addressed. In streets and within buildings he can do only this: it is when he is apart from the noisy human traffic that he can feel other whisperings in and from his heart, hear other murmurings from souls both carbonaceous and siliceous and at those times when he feels he'll die if he doesn't do their hidden biddings.

Malcolm shrugs exaggeratedly, his shoulders rising to touch his earlobes. —Ya could try Jed. Or Jerry's. Scottish Iain did av some, some stars I fink they were, but he's fucked off somewhere, fuck knows where, like. No one's seen im fer ages.

—Al maybe av a call up at Jed's then, I reckon. Got somethin to get tho first, an we, Ianto? After a great big fuckin dildo we are, likes. Mad Cyril still sellin um, is he?

Malcolm shrugs again. —Couldn't tell ya, mate. Got no cawl fer them meself, like.

—Ah no, yew still usin them cucumbers then ey! Roger pokes Malcolm's stomach. —An-a fuckin carrots an-a parsnips and Paulie's fuckin lad when he feels like it aye!

Ianto splutters with laughter. Malcolm watches him impassively then looks up at the helicopter flying high overhead, its high clatter then back down at Roger and he says nothing but he does smile.

—Orright, see yew then, boy, Roger says. —I'll be in touch. Next week yeh? Big rave out at Dolybont. Be there.

—Yeh. Be lucky.

Malcolm moves on, some small relief evident in the resettling of his shoulders and back and neck, and Roger and Ianto walk up past the charity shop and the newly relocated Andy's Records, a burst of Chemical Brothers as they pass, that song with the video that Ianto likes, the dancing policemen in their yellow slickers. Roger mutters:

—Stuck-up southern English cunt.

Ianto giggles but stops suddenly and looks worried. —Why?

—He just is, that's all, Roger replies. Then thinks for a moment and says, softer: —No, ee's alright, really, and will say no more until they enter Mad Cyril's shop, dark grotto festooned with hanging T-shirts and lengths of material all colours and a thousand eyes of watchfaces, clockfaces and the myriad glint of accessories, rings and necklaces and lighters and buckles for belts and clips both money and roach pewter and nickel and silver. Draped bootlaces like worms and potpipes some smooth stone, some wood elaborately carved, and bottles of poppers arrayed in trays upright like attentive snails and small sculpted dragons and warlocks on glass shelves, shallow bowls patterned with Celtic knots and woolly hats and socks and underwear all patterned green and white with the dragon emblazoned red and rampant.

175

Fecund bazaar this, spiced with patchouli and sandalwood and tobacco and the airclog of scorched metal from the lathe in the corner the wood floor beneath it stubbled with fallen filings. Cavern crammed with useless treasure which is the best kind as is known by the proud junk-monger behind the counter standing fat and tattooed, arms folded across his keg chest, his face wide and watchful and lost in a tangled mass of red beard, snarled copper wire. Trash-chandler, Mad Cyril:

—Afternoon, boys. What can I help yew two with then?

Roger approaches the counter and leans his palms on the glass top. Cyril looks down displeased at Roger's hands then back up at his face while Ianto's gaze darts like a stickleback around the shop, over the adorned walls, the varied shelves, the heavily garlanded ceiling.

—Erm, we know this girl like see, an it's er birthday, an we're after a, like, jokey present for her. Bit of a goer she is likes see so we thought that, as a *joke*, like, y'know, we'd get er a fuckin big dildo. Make er larf, like. Biggest yew've got in-a shop.

Cyril nods and reaches down under his counter and takes out a large tray on which are arrayed in their plastic-windowed boxes plastic pricks of various colours and sizes.

—These'll make er eyes water.

—Oh no, she's not gunner *yewse* it like, it's just . . . altho she probly will, knowin her.

Roger leans to look, Ianto peering over his shoulder. Small white torpedoes, conical plastic cucumbers featureless and others quite convincing replicas of the real thing, flanged and veined and abulge. Some with detachable heads in the likeness of finger and thumb or small mace or sickle or miniature clenched fists and some detachable heads actually in the shape of detachable heads complete with little faces like diminutive sarcophagi. Roger points to a large lurid pink penis, unadorned and blatant, simply a big pink plastic prick.

—That one by yer.

Cyril nods again and Roger removes his choice from the display and Cyril replaces the tray out of sight and rings the purchase into his old-fashioned non-computerised till.

—Nineteen ninety five.

176

Roger hands over a twenty pound note and takes his single coin change.

—I've got somethin for yew lads, if yewer interested. Male equivalent, like.

Roger's head tips sideways. —Eh?

—Placcy fannies like. Even a couple of blow-up dollies if yewer interested. Close yewer eyes an yew'll never be able to tell-a difference. Like a look?

—Oh Jesus, no, don't get em out yer. Ianto yer'd be on em in a flash, wouldn't yew, Iant?

Ianto nods and giggles.

—Some other time, mun.

—Alright then, boys. Hope she enjoys it.

—I'm sure she will.

They leave the shop and run amused like children with a new toy down the alleyway adjacent to the chipper opposite Y Cŵps pub. Roger removes the dildo from the box and throws the packaging away. A woman's face in feigned ecstasy. In large letters 'HER NEW BEST FRIEND'.

—Amazin fuckin things these, aren't they, Iant . . . Tell yew what they look like; like-a rubber bullets we used to use in Belfast when I was in-a army. Same size an everythin. Oh aye, we'd av all-a Paddy slags causin riots so's they'd be able-a pick up a new fuckin dildo. Fuckin women, ey fuckin *love* these things, y'know. Ah yeh. A good fuckin knobbin without all-a complications likes. At's what most of em are after. Mark my fuckin words, mun.

He holds it up between them.

—Bet yew wish yew ad one this big, eh? Wouldn't need a girlfriend then, mun, would yew, cos yew could shag yewer own fuckin self then, couldn't yew? Yeh, like THIS!

He lunges for Ianto and spins him with one hand against the damp and mossy brick wall and begins to jab roughly at his arse with the dildo. Ianto howls and slaps at his backside as if he's trying to repel a snapping dog.

—Gerroff me, mun, yew twat! Gerroff my arse!

—Ah keep still, Ianto boy, yew know yew fuckin love it . . .

Ianto spins and Roger's last jab stabs the blunt head of the tool into Ianto's groin. Ianto lets out an 'oof' and bends double.

—Now look what yew've done . . . burst me fuckin bollax now yew av . . .

—Don't talk soft, mun. Hardly fuckin touched yew. Nowt yer to burst anyways if yew ask me, like.

Roger stuffs the dildo down his jeans, where it swells and bulges against his leg. He stands there hands-on-hips and thrusts his pelvis out.

—How's it look then? Fuckin Led Zeppelin aye. This'll av-a girlies lickin eyr lips, eh.

Ianto straightens up and points smiling at Roger's crotch.

—Looks fuckin great dunnit, mun. Roger turns to one side and then the other, appraising his bulge from different angles. —Yeh. Fuckin porn star aye. All's I need is-a tash an-a 'fro. Let's goan av a bevvy in-a Cŵps.

They go giggling over the road into the pub, Roger walking stiff-legged and pelvis-forward like a man unaccustomed to prostheses. He orders at the bar and then turns around to survey the small and dingy pub, his elbows back against the bartop, his hips out-thrust. The only other customers are an old man in the corner reading *Y Faner Goch* and two young women sitting directly opposite Roger and one of these notices the unfeasible protuberance in his jeans and her face drops shocked and she leans to whisper something in her friend's ear and she looks too and they both splutter into their cupped hands and fall against each other laughing, incredulous.

Roger grins, enjoying their amusement.

—Alright then, ladies? Nice out today innit?

They laugh further and Roger and Ianto take their pints over to join them, Roger making a show of sitting down on the stool, adjusting himself and groaning bandy-legged, hefting the weight in his trousers with his hand. The women crack up.

—Are yew OK? one of them asks. —Nothing wrong with yew then is there? Nothing, like, erm . . . deformed, or anythin?

Roger shakes his head mock-innocent, wide-eyed. —No. Course not. Why'd yew ask?

—Oh, no reason.

—Altho actually, now that yew come to mention it, yer *is* somethin I need to see-a doctor about, yeh . . . He leans in towards the centre of the table, towards the women, and Ianto mimics his movement. —It's a bit embarrassing like, a bit, erm, delicate, but I've been suffering lately from what can only really be called . . . willy shrinkage.

Uproar.

—Ah yeh, yer's no other word for it like. Willy shrinkage, that's what it is. Puren fuckin simple. Only last week I had a right bleedin whopper an today I wake up with this little tiddler yer. Don't know what's appenin to me, likes. Got me worried it as.

One of the girls stops laughing. —Well, I'll tell yew what, I'm trainin to be a nurse, see. I might be able to tell yew what yewer problem is. But I'll have to av-a good long look at it, like.

Roger looks around, over his left shoulder, his right shoulder. —What, here? In-a pub?

—Well, yeh. Why not like? Terrible disease, that is. No time to waste like, see. Urgent bloody treatment, that's what's required. Go on, get im out an let's av a look. Don't be shy. I'm a nurse, I've seen it all before, mun.

Roger again looks around the pub then shrugs and delves with one hand into his jeans and Ianto laughs and the women yell as he removes the big dildo and places it upright in the centre of the table. It quivers vertical with the shuddering of their outraged laughter, the low bar lights catching the smoothly sculpted dome of its pretend prepuce.

—Yer he is, in all is glory. What's wrong with im, nurse? What's-a diagnosis then?

The woman stops laughing and reaches out and picks it up in her hand. Red nail varnish and Ianto inhales sharply.

—It's come bastard *off*, that's what's wrong with it, boy.

She holds and examines it and Ianto stares until Roger nudges him beneath the table and his face flushes red and he raises his drink to his mouth.

—Where'd yew get this, then?

—It's a present, like. For one of ar friends.

—Oh aye? Male or female?

—Female. Only as a joke, like, y'know. Just-a maker laugh an that, innit, Ianto?

Ianto nods and takes another drink. The girl replaces the dildo on the table this time lying flat, horizontal like a cerise turd.

—Wouldn't make *me* laugh, that. Insulted to fuck I'd be.

—Yew were pissing yewerself larfin just now, woman! Don't tell me yew weren't!

She shrugs. —Yeh, but . . . as a pressie, like, for me birthday, that'd bloody piss me off, that would. I mean . . .

The other girl licks her lips ostentatiously and stage-whispers throatily: —Oh I dunno . . . I think *I* could find a use for it . . .

—Aye, I bet yew could! Ianto says without smiling and the girl looks sharply at him and he hides behind his Guinness again. She turns to Roger.

—What's wrong with yewer mate, then? Don't say much, does he?

—Ah, don't yew worry about Ianto yer. Roger throws an arm around his friend's shoulder and pulls him to him. —He's harmless, in yew, boy? Just a bit, erm, *shy*, that's all. Shy, Ianto, that's right, innit? Shy an a wee bit strange. Sums yew up that dunnit, mun?

He rubs a knuckle into the crown of Ianto's head then lets him go. Red-cheeked and ruffle-haired Ianto sits and takes quick sips from his pint, never fully lowering the glass from his face, sometimes even nibbling the rim with his lips. He makes eye-contact with no one neither Roger nor the women but nevertheless one of them eyes him, slightly worried, as she might a snarling dog. She shuffles in her seat sideways on to him as if seeking to expose as little of herself as possible to him and if Ianto notices this he makes no reaction, no shift in his hunched posture nor change in his nervous sipping nor indeed slight alteration to his expression impassive and fixed.

—So then. Roger places his glass on the table and slaps his knees. —What are yew two doin out so early in-a day? Bit too soon to start a sesh innit?

—I told yew, we're nurses. Just come off shift like we have. No time's too soon to start drinking if yew've just been on

180

yewer bastard feet twelve hours cleanin up shit an sick an blood an wipin arses.

—Yeh, says the other. —Stitchin faces together after they've been glassed, like.

—Yewer *both* nurses then?

They nod.

—I thought yew said only one-a yew was?

—No, yew thought wrong.

—We both are.

—Oh. That's alright then. Yew like a drink, yew nurses, don't yew? Like to party like aye. What is it yewer drinkin now?

—Nothing thanks.

—We're fine as we are.

Roger stands. —No, I insist. Won't hear of it. I'm fuckin loaded I am see. Got to spend it somehow, ant I?

They grudgingly order Jack Daniels and Cokes and Roger moves over towards the bar then stops halfway and returns and hands a ten pound note to Ianto.

—Tell yew what, Ianto, yew goan get em in. And get another for yewerself while yewer up yer aye.

Ianto takes the money and goes up to the bar. Roger retakes his seat. One of the women passes the dildo over the table to him.

—Here, put that away, mun. Joke's worn off now like.

Roger shrugs and takes it and slides it into the inside pocket of his jacket and it bulges like a gun in a shoulder holster. The intensity of the initial chemical rush has dissipated now but it has left in its wake a warm contented glow and Roger's bearing in his seat and his movements and general body language are parts of a wide ease and expansiveness and soft yielding pleasure. Slumping with his legs apart and his shoulders loosened into his chest, lips and eyelids and facial muscles softened by the alcohol, which is beginning to supercede the chemical cocktail, he wants to do and indeed does nothing but smile sloppily and calmly at the two women opposite him, seeing in their faces not the well-worked fatigue in and around their eyes and chins nor the hospital dryness of their hair and the solution-scaled skin on their hands and necks, but merely their physical proximity

181

and their overall shape and the way their epiglotti move when they swallow drink or inhale smoke. One of them drums her nails on the table top and he watches the tendons in the back of her hand ripple like the strummed strings of an instrument. She watches him watching.

—Yew alright there, boy?

He slowly nods once.

—Sure?

—Pos . . . it . . . ive, he drawls. —Why? Shouldn't I be?

—Na, no reason. Just look like yewer about to fall asleep, that's all.

—Asleep? Me? Oh good Christ no. No fuckin chance of that. No fuckin chance of that at all.

She glances at her friend as if to say that that might be a pity. Ianto returns with the shorts and places them carefully on the table, then returns to the bar and brings back the pints, Guinness for him and Wrexham for Roger. He sets them clumsily down and the Guinness slops over.

—Aw Jesus, Ianto, mun. That's near half a bastard pint yew've wasted yer, mun. Good job it wasn't fuckin mine, I'll tell yew that.

Ianto sits and coughs and stares into his glass, sees the creamy foam like an aerial photograph of tundra. The chemicals and the alcohol have somehow curdled within him, clotted, turned pleasure into a creeping paranoia and the tingling in his extremities which was earlier so agreeable has now become something like cramp and the previous sensual sense of his own physicality as being open and candid and receptive has fermented now into an awareness of desperate exposure and susceptibility to danger and harm or if not that then at least aspersive judgement. He wants to say something, anything, to arrest this decline and knows that the right words are floating through his field of vision like little flying creatures, thrips or gnats, but he cannot catch them and knows he will look ridiculous if he tries. The only other viable option is to gulp at his beer, which he does.

Roger suddenly shifts in his seat, sits up straighter. —Yeh, so, anyway, right, after these bevvies yer we're gunner move on somewhere more, er, upmarket likes. That new wine bar up by-a market hall? Try yer I reckon. Looks dead fuckin posh it does. An special promotion all iss week, any treble spirit for a quid. What's it like? D'yew know?

The women shake their heads.

—Na.

—Well yer's space an yer's money for another two. Get yew two steamin fuckin drunk I will.

Again they shake their heads: —Looks a bit bloody snobby to me, like. Full-a fuckin suits an Pimms drinkers.

—Aye, yeh, yer right. We'll go on to-a Angel instead then. Drink up.

They do, but do not accept Roger's offer. Shrugging into her overcoat one of them says: —Ta an all that like but, really, we're too bloody tired. Twelve-hour shifts like, knackered we are. Just want-a go home an get some sleep, right, Eleri?

Eleri nods agreement. —Oh yeh. Asleep on me bastard feet I am.

—Oh. Alright. Comin out later tho are yew?

—Might be. Don't know where yet tho. Ta for the drink.

—Yeh. Tara.

Ianto and Roger do not reply and the nurses leave an Roger takes a great swig of his lager and says, quietly: —Slags.

Ianto sniggers and agrees. —Bints.

—Don't fuckin need them, do we, Ianto? Pair-a studs like us? Fuck no. Don't know what eyr fuckin missin, boy, do they?

Ianto shakes his head.

—Too fuckin right, mun. Tell yew what, I'm gettin a bit sick of all ese fuckin pubs like. Full-a fuckin arse'oles they are, mun. What we're gunner do is go to the offy, get a bottle an take it on-a beach an get bastard well lashed. E's gunner be wearing off soon like an I wanner be pissed out my brains when it do. What d'yew reckon? Get pissed, call up at Colm's or Marc's later or someone's. Get more fuckin pissed. Go out an pick up a couple-a tarts, likes. Sound good to yew, aye?

Ianto nods on a neck turned unsupportive.

—C'mon then. Get yewer drink down yewer throat, boy. Yer's *serious* fuckin drinkin to be done.

They leave the pub and go from gloom to glow passing

183

between worlds like they always do, under lintels between jambs over steps these drifting figures desultory in whom designations can be calibrated in mere minutes. From shadow to light and back again, from secret to stridulent this world to them is a clamour of polarities, catalepsy and blur, these states sought and discarded then sought again in restlessness perennial and inexhaustible. From the burning of their waking to the somatic insistence of their sleep each single second to them is a galaxy replete both with devouring furnace and still ice vacuum, a unique warring fever forever fed by the fuel of their inability ever to settle, ever accept and their screaming need to search and quest and sometimes find then always kick away again, kick away, chilled by the moon and scorched by the sun.

Roger leads Ianto into the Spar on the corner and jumps the tutting queue to the counter.

—Bottle of whisky.

The young girl assistant takes a bottle of Spar own-brand blended from the shelf behind her and begins to wrap it.

—Erm, what's that?

—Bottle of whisky, like you said.

—Yeh, exactly, *whisky*, not povo headfuck cheap piss like that. What, do I look like a bleedin jakey, do I? Give us that bottle of Bushmills yer. No, not that one, the other one. The Black Label. The twenty-quid-a-bottle one. Yeh.

She turns and replaces the cheap bottle and takes down the Bushmills. Roger shakes his head and mutters:

—Fuckin Spar piss . . . as if . . . must think I'm a fuckin alkie gunner drink it in-a bleedin bus station . . . Jesus Christ . . .

She begins to wrap the whisky.

—No, woman, don't yew wrap it. Just give it yer.

She does and Roger tosses a twenty pound note at her and Ianto snorts amused and they both leave the shop and open the whisky and take alternate belts at it as they pass the town hall bright white in the sunlight and walk through the refurbished public shelter, newly roofless so that the homeless have one less place to sleep away from the rain, away from the tourists and on to the promenade some students in Sharp shirts kicking a football to each other and a group of crusties drinking cider

184

on a bench and past the Glengower hotel people outside in T-shirts and shades even though the sun is beginning to sink now and a cold wind is blowing in off the bay, and down on to the pebbly beach and they find a small sheltered recess in the tall wall of Constitution Hill and sit in it out of the breeze's bite and the encroaching shadows although they will be on them soon. Darkness creeping up the shingle towards them. Ianto takes a deep pull at the whisky bottle and gags and coughs.

—Jesus, go easy, mun. Fuckin good booze this is, see. Should be fuckin savoured, likes.

Roger sips at the whisky and smacks his lips, looking out to sea. A yacht tacks slowly in towards the harbour. Ianto wipes his watering eyes with the sleeves of his jumper and rolls and lights a cigarette.

—Yew alright, Iant?

—Yes.

—E all gone now then has it?

—Yes.

—Yeh, fuckin mine an all. Good while ey lasted like but fuck, ey didn't last bastard long, did they?

Ianto shakes his head.

—Ah well. Fuck it. It's been a fuck of a long time since I ad a good, decent pill. Have to lower yewer fuckin standards nowadays, mun. Tellin yew.

He passes the bottle to Ianto and digs inside his jacket and pulls out the dildo and grins at it in his hands. In the fading sunlight it looks fleshy and purulent as if real, severed and crudely embalmed.

—Them girls . . . Ianto says almost gingerly. —They, er, they dint like that much, did they?

Roger's small smile drops and he holds the dildo by its end between thumb and fingers upright and pointing at the sky, and as he talks he holds it like that, almost delicately towards the early stars like some odd antiquarian expounding on a rare artefact of some value and interest:

—I'll tell yew about girls, Ianto. See, they, they all want fuckin *this*. He nods at the dildo. —I don't mean this exact fuckin thing yer, an I don't mean cockies in general like, but they don't want-a real fuckin thing. No way. An yew know why? Cos ey can't be doin with all-a complications like, all-a fuckin other stuff, all ey want is-a sex an someone to be with an tell em they look lovely all-a fuckin time an that they ant got a fat arse an saggy tits an fuckin stretchmarks on eyr bellies. Ey can't fuckin handle-a horrible bits-a life like, ey want fuckin everythin to be simple an false an fuckin, fuckin *plastic*. Fuckin robots, mun, that's what they want. Fuckin robots with big knobs. Tellin yew boy, yew've got to fuckin watch out for them cos ey'll fuckin turn yew into a bastard robot like if ey get half a fuckin chance. An yew see um on-a telly an in-a streets like, lookin down eyr fuckin noses at yer, dressed in ese tight tops an little skirts lookin at yew like yewer a piece-a shit on eyr fuckin shoes an before ey even fuckin look at yew yew've got to fuckin crawl to um, suck eyr arse'oles, lick eyr fuckin shoes, tell um eyr a best fuckin thing on-a bastard planet. It's not fuckin right, mun. Ey'd av yew eatin eyr fuckin shit off-a pavement before yew bastard well know it an then, right, *then*, then they'd turn around an tell yew that ey don't wanner fuckin know yew an yew can't come anywhere near um cos yew've made a fuckin arse of yewerself an yew've got no self-respect. An it was fuckin *them* who made yew do it! Slags. Tellin yew, mun, eyr evil fuckin creatures ey are. An I've never met one, not fuckin *one*, who int like that. Eyr all-a fuckin same. Money, big cars, big knobs, that's all eyr fuckin interested in. An eyr all-a bleedin same.

He spits on the sand and crushed shells. —Women, ey. Can't live with um, can't fuckin kill um. What a cunt.

He looks out at sea for a moment then turns to Ianto and ruffles his tangled hair.

—Ah, yewer a good lad, Ianto, yew. One of-a very fuckin best, aye.

Ianto beams and Roger stands and draws his arm right back over his shoulder and hurls the plastic penis into the air, novelty gift for the ocean. It spins and cartwheels through the sunlight like a boomerang and skims off the crest of one breaking wave then bobs in the swell like some surfacing holothurian and then begins slowly to sink, the thicker battery end submerging first and pulling it into the vertical and the crude helmet pointing

186

upwards like a missile straight at the bruising sky like the reaching limb of some drowning monoped then it is gone and there are only bubbles and then there are not even bubbles only the glassy surface coruscating of the calm reflective sea.

—Yer we go, Roger says. —Some big fuckin fishy'll eat that thinkin it's a great big worm like an he'll get caught an some posho cunt'll buy him in a restaurant. Av a fuckin heart attack when they cut im open, Ianto, aye.

Ianto throws his head back and laughs loud at the thought, Roger watching him amused. The chemicals have almost effectively left Ianto now and he is falling, swooning into a happy drunkenness and indeed he could be said to be happy here on this beach with the whisky in his veins and the gulls calling plaintive and the distant sounds of voices and engines and music from the prom and Roger standing above him with the sliding sunlight masking his face, turning him halo-headed like a visitor from some far and other world. So happy in fact is Ianto that he begins to sing a song taught to him by his grandmother as she would hang out the washing, small old lady stooping and standing, the wet wash snapping in the wind and her white curls rising, little Ianto sitting on the scrubby grass behind her watching the trundling beetles and hearing her voice high in the mountains and querulous. He could if asked pinpoint the specific moment and Roger having heard this song many times before stands watching and smiling and joins in on the word 'big':

Nobody loves me, everybody hates me
I'm going to go and eat worms
BIG fat juicy ones
Long thin slimy ones
Ones that squiggle and squirm
Yum! Bite their heads off
Oo! Suck the juice out
Throw the skins awaaaaay
Nobody knows how much I thrive
On worms three times a daaaay!

Ianto sits smiling with his arms wrapped around his drawn-up

187

knees looking up at Roger as if awaiting approval. Which he gets:

—Good fuckin tune that, Ianto. Too fuckin right. Yew like that song, doan yew?

—Yeh.

—Aye, I remember yew singin that when we were kids like. When I used to come up visitin from Merthyr. Remember?

Ianto smiles, nodding. Roger looks out to sea and appears to think deeply for a moment then looks back down at Ianto.

—Drunk, are yew? Lashed is it.

—Yeh.

—Me 'n all. Let's goan get drunker. Glen, I reckon. Yer's a fuckin bouncer in yer I wanner av a quick word with anyway.

He holds out a hand and Ianto takes it and he helps him upright and they leave the beach together, crunching over the pebbles in the slowly setting scarlet-spilling sun towards the nearest lights and music and people and booze on tap. Towards something that is not this.

Ianto runs through the rain-lashed streets sloping harbourwards and over the hiss and sizzle of the rain and the steady thump of his pounding feet his breath can be discerned, his panting panicked and desperate. As if fleeing some terror he bounces off a lamp-post and spins but does not fall and continues to run past a hunched couple walking home with steaming parcels of Chinese takeaway under their arms like guests bearing gifts, and as he passes they catch a glimpse of his pallid face through the falling water his eyes wide and haunted his nostrils flared and teeth bared his hair slapping across his gleaming white forehead in matted and sodden ropes. They look quickly back over their shoulders to see what might be chasing the fevered runner but see nothing, only the swimming lights from windows and the steep upsurging road like a strip of wet leather, all blurred behind the grey rain and when they turn back again Ianto is nowhere to be seen, he has ducked down the gunnel piss-reeking and rain-sweating and is bounding up the Hanging Steps three at a time, his drenched trainers slipping on the wet slate slabs and his rapid breathing amplified in the enclosed space into some

188

stentorian thing from nightmare, and indeed he himself could be a figure from fever gaunt and grasping gangling leaper up this dark and narrow stinking stairwell down which condemned men were once led to the waiting gibbet on the beach, the lapping greedy sea their last sight on this earth and Ianto could be one of the executed returning, retracing his final steps the horrors of the grave and whatever awful agent of accountability may wait there gnashing at his soaked shoulder, his leaping heels. He takes the final few steps in one enormous splayed bound and lands on his worn heels, which jerk away from under him and the crack of his skull on the shining slate echoes off the stone walls like a gunshot. He sits and whimpers in the wet and rubs the back of his head then springs upright again and sprints, his saturated clothes clinging to his bony body to the end of the dripping terrace and hammers madly on the door of the house where Gwenno lives:

—Gwennnnnnnnnnnooo! GWENNNNNNNNOO!

A second-floor window rattles up on its sash and Fran's face peers out.

—Who is it? What d'yew want!

Ianto steps back and looks up, his cheeks slick with tears, with rain. —I want Gwenno! Get Gwenno to me now!

He lurches forwards and pounds on the door again screaming Gwenno's name and the door opens inwards and he collapses over the threshold into Gwenno's arms like a half-drowned faun and through the snot that clogs his nostrils he can smell the washing powder in her outsized grey woolly jumper.

—Gwenno . . . aw Gwenno . . .

Gwenno holds his thin and trembling frame to her and feels her clothes begin to absorb the clammy seeping moisture of him.

—Ianto . . . what's the matter with yew then, bach? This about Roger then is it?

He nods into her collarbone. —Roger . . . Roger . . . he's fuckin *dead*, mun . . . he's fuckin *dead* . . .

She strokes the small swamp of his hair and makes gentle hushing noises at the top of his skull. —Sshh now . . . I know, bach . . . I know he's dead . . . sshh now . . . sshh . . .

189

Fran appears at the top of the stairs.

—Oh. I see he's yerd about Roger, then.

Gwenno nods and gestures her away with a toss of her head and soothes and strokes Ianto as he sobs into her bosom and when he is calmer she takes him into the back kitchen and seats him at the table and as she pulls away from him he lunges for her with hands like claws, his facial features obliterated in anguish, lost in creases and crumples like balled newspaper.

—It's OK, bach, I'm not going away. I'm just getting us both a drink, look.

She pours cheap Spar Scotch into two cups, twice the measure for Ianto as for her and hands him his, which he takes in both hands and gulps at, and she places a chair close by him and sits in it. Wet from Ianto's head, the rain and his heavy tears spots the table top and his whole upper body is racked by his sobs, each sob raking through his sunken chest and out of his folded face with the sound of distant rockets and extreme physical jolts as if someone beneath the table is ramming a fence post into his sternum at two-second intervals. Gwenno takes his shaking hand and strokes the back of it softly with her thumb and waits for his deep weeping to subside. He pulls the frayed sleeve of his jumper over his hand and wipes his face with it sniffling.

—Poor Roger . . . he's dead . . . Roger's fuckin *dead* . . .

—I know he is, bach, I know he is. Who told yew? How did yew find out?

—In-a pub.

—Who told yew?

—Don't know . . . some tall feller in specs. Is it . . . is it true?

She nods. Green snot gurgles out of Ianto's red nose and he sniffs it back up.

—He got into a fight in Carmarthen. Tried to take too many of um on by all accounts and he . . . well . . . She shrugs, sadly.

—What . . . Carmarthen . . .

—I don't know what he was doing up yer. Gone to see some friends or somethin, I dunno.

Ianto crumples again in tears and she puts an arm around his

190

shoulders, which quake under her hand, fragile and prominent like the bones of a bird. She lets him cry for a few minutes then she stands.

—It's alright, I'm only going upstairs for a minute to get some blankets an stuff. I'll make yew up a bed on-a couch, like.

He takes a morose sip at his whisky and Gwenno leaves the kitchen and pads upstairs and knocks on the door to Fran's room and enters. Fran is lying on her bed in a towelling dressing gown smoking a long spliff with a full ashtray on her belly and ambient music drips from the walls and ceiling.

—Ianto gone then, as he?

—No. I told im he could stay yer like, downstairs on-a couch. Don't mind do yew?

Fran makes an ambiguous face. —All upset about Roger was he?

—In bits, yeh.

—Good fuckin riddance, I say.

—Yeh, so do I, but don't tell Ianto that. In fuckin bits ee is.

—It was just a matter of time anyway if yew ask me.

—What was?

—Roger's fuckin death, likes. Sooner or later he was gunner get in-a face of a wrong person. Looks like he've done it now, dunnit, an I can't say I'm bothered particularly; I mean, yer was always somethin fuckin creepy about that boy, tell yew-a truth like. Always somethin . . . y'know. Fuckin *odd*.

—Yeh, well, just let Ianto kip yer the one night. He's heartbroken, poor bugger.

—Alright. But I'm lockin me fuckin door tonight, I'll tell yew that. Don't trust im one bit.

—Fair enough. If it makes yew feel safer like. An do us a favour.

Fran raises her eyebrows.

—Giz a couple-a those temazzies yew got yesterday. He'll keep me up all bastard night likes if I don't knock im out.

Fran points with the smouldering end of the spliff to a small brown bottle on her cluttered dressing table and Gwenno thanks her and takes two of the tablets and leaves and hears Fran slide the lock on her door shut. She takes a thick heavy blanket

191

from the airing cupboard on the landing and returns to the kitchen, where Ianto has his arms wrapped around himself and is rocking and shivering uncontrollably, his teeth actually chattering. Gwenno, never having seen teeth actually chatter before, watches him.

—Aw bach. Gunner catch-a death of bleedin cold yew are, aye. Take yewer wet jumper off an wrap this around yew. Take these first, tho. They'll make yew feel much better.

She hands him the two caplets and without even looking at them he swallows them with a gulp of whisky and removes his blue hooded anorak and the sodden jumper underneath that, beneath which he wears nothing. Gwenno wraps the blanket around his pale and scrawny frame the colour and texture of fishbelly, an angry red rash of pus-headed spots across his shoulders through which some long black coarse hairs sprout like spider legs as they do too around the screw-like brown nipples on his otherwise bare chest. The box of his ribcage threatens to erupt through the tight white skin and if there is a single muscle in his torso or arms Gwenno cannot see it.

—Come into the front room, Ianto. I'll put-a fire on for yew. Don't worry, I won't leave yew. Not until yewer asleep. It's alright, don't worry about a thing. Yer, we can take-a whisky.

She leads him by the hand, him shuffling along obediently behind her into the small and messy front room where whilst she is distracted lighting the gas fire he removes his trainers and jeans and covers himself cowering with the blanket on the couch. He takes a gulp of the scotch straight from the bottle. The occasional sob jolts his head and torso, but his grief is now largely evident only in the red tunnels of his eyes and the trembling of his lower lip and the bulb of his nose rubbed red raw. The rest of his face has now simply settled, softened under his loss as the human facial features will do, time and time over, acclimatised as they become to the heat of bereavement, their plain melting into woe natural and unartificed.

Gwenno turns from the sputtering blue flames and tucks the blanket around him. The ends of her hair, blood-coloured, caress his face and he breathes in deeply the lingering scent of her shampoo, almost apples. He reaches for her involuntarily and slowly, but the telephone rings in the corner of the room by the television, and she answers it turned away from him and he listens to her and watches her back, the shapes in her leggings and the flawless skin of her bare feet one of them bent back vertical on the toetips revealing the innocently crinkled sole, which hits his eyes like a soft explosion.

—Hello? . . . oh, hello . . . no, I . . . yeh, I've heard about Roger, yeh . . . fuckin shame, yeh . . . Ianto's yer, he's all upset like so I'm . . . no, I'm goin to bed soon . . . I'm tired, see. Yeh . . . erm, an what fuckin business is that of yours, then? . . . No, Marc, look, I'll see yew around likes. I'll be out somewhere this weekend, yeh. Stop, look, stop ringing me so much. It's . . . Yeh yeh, I know how cool I am . . . great shag, yeh . . . best ever, aye . . . I know all that stuff . . . It's . . . no, I, no . . . Marc, I've told yew before that I don't want to, haven't I? How many times . . . I'm . . . ah fuck this, I'm going to bed.

She hangs up and returns to sit cross-legged on the floor at Ianto's side. She is a blur to him now, soft-focus and shapeless, as the drugs and the drink claim him and he falls into the meltdown, the collapse in chemical and in drink which he loves, has always loved, for its swooning familiarity with his soul. This levelling like a reckoning, like a brief extinction. Like a dropped nothing more true, more real to Ianto than the bang and glare and splatter of ordinary life.

Gwenno ushers him into sleep with the soothing platitudes she thinks accurately he would like to hear and says absolutely nothing of the devastating rapacity she saw in Roger, his preying on the weak like so many others and the strong sense in him of things gone irremediably awry and irrevocable for whatever reasons and nor does she talk of the strange light in Roger's eyes and his grating staccato laugh and the clench of his face when he would look at her sometimes and the grenade inside him smouldering nor of the unshakeable inkling she has that Roger may be better off dead. That his end was a natural terminus to the sharp trajectory of his life. That the parabola he described through the sky and casting shadow should come back to earth in this way, in blood in impact in shock and the world robbed of all mercy.

She sits with Ianto until he is snoring and then she quietly leaves, turning the fire off and closing the door behind her. When Ianto wakes, a noise escaping his encrusted lips a small whimper as of someone waking to a massive, recalled botch and wanting more numbness, it is dawn outside, faint grey light through the curtain cracks and the twittering of birds and the spatter and hiss of rain and he lies still, staring at the ceiling for a moment then he weeps for a while then he crawls out from under the blanket shivering in the cold room as he dresses with his head full of what feels like wet wool. He walks into the kitchen and picks his jumper and anorak up off the floor and puts them on still wet, clinging clammy to his skin like a hide of seaweed and he coughs up thin bile and thick mucus into the sink which he swills away with water from the cold tap which he also rinses his face under and drinks from. He stands unsteady in the icy, gloomy kitchen looking around and sees a pile of coins on the worktop by the crusted sandwich toaster, several pounds, and he pockets this and then returns to the front room where he finishes off the inch or two of whisky left in the bottle, gagging as he does so. Then he mounts the stairs as quietly as he possibly can, his breath roaring in his ears, and tries the handle on Gwenno's bedroom door but it is locked so he descends the stairs quietly again on trembling tiptoe and leaves the house and walks through the falling grey rain to the bus stop opposite the goods entrance to Somerfield, where trucks fart and grumble as they unload like great and patient beasts.

He waits a while watching at his feet a sopping pancake of dog shit with a frill of sucking slugs for the next bus to arrive and when it does he is like something dredged from the harbour long sodden in silt and brine, a being discarnate of mud and stagnant water waiting whitely in the wet. His skin appears so waterlogged it seems that a poking finger would sink in knuckle-deep. The bus hisses to a halt by him and the doors sigh open.

—Duw, get on quick, boy, before yew catch pneumonia. Yewer wet bloody through.

Ianto steps on.

—Corris.

—Single or return?

—Single.

—Off to work then, aye?

—Yeh.

The tongue of ticket unfurls rasping and Ianto tears it off and pays the driver and moves down the empty bus to sit on the back seat above the engine for the warmth. Clammy moisture runnels his face and he shakes his head and droplets fly and he stares through the rain-streaked dirty window at the passing town, very few passengers boarding at this early hour only overalled factory workers and stiff-clothed farmhands and a few enthusiastic hikers whom Ianto appraises silently, looking them up and down assessing strengths and weaknesses, then rejects. Through the Penparcau estate the bus moves and out again of this warren, passing the huge billboards there from the large banks designed to attract the potential student custom arriving from southern England; the boons on offer, a huge £20 note bigger than some of the rooms Ianto has slept in, bigger than the living rooms of the houses on this estate. Out on to the mountain road and Ianto sees the small huddled villages and seeping sheep and the grey-bellied sky over it all and the meandering river the colour of strong coffee and the vast expanse of Borth bog, steam rising, it stretching to the blurred horizon over the far estuary, where the mountains swell above the broken white line of Aberdyfi, a weak shaft of sunlight spilling across their grey and distant crests. Machynlleth is a small flurry of opening shops and busy workers and wet traffic seen through rain-slick glass; headlights burning through the drizzle and the streetlights still bowed and blushing, somehow dreamlike and unreal as if it is the hours of night yet, but the sky has not darkened nor will it. Ianto is carried over the swollen river straining its banks and he sees mountains rising rising, small whitewashed cottages chimney-smoking and mist and more green mountains rising, these parts of his own small country ancient and arcane this hard demanding land he was born on and into its small roads and sheeptracks leading maybe to marvel and secrecies revealed. Umbilicus unseen never to be snapped the brutal beauty of this place has battered itself into his blood, his brains.

He alights at Corris and crosses the road to look down at and on to the valley-bottom village, wet roofs, puffing chimneys penetrating the low mist like the backs of breaching sea-creatures. There is no noise, only the perennial hiss and whisper of the rain and the sizzle of a rare passing car. He moves on up the road past the craft centre, its hexagonal buildings clustered like giant hives, and past a tinker's encampment on a muddy verge at the roadside, two thin horses cropping grass and bony dogs curled wetly around the weak smoke of a small cooking fire and a bash made from tarpaulin and crates and rope some dark faces just visible in the flap, and they call out to Ianto in their own strange tongue and he stops and stares dripping for a moment this thin figure in the rain and they call to him again sibilant, guttural, but he cannot and does not answer and would not answer if he could and if there is some flicker within him some recognition of blood shared some cognition of consanguinity he gives no sign except to walk away.

He leaves the road and takes a path which leads up into the mountains, going deeper. Going further. Higher into these lumps of rock like separate planets in themselves. He keeps to the path little more than a sheeptrack turning to midden now for a mile or two climbing climbing skywards and then he leaves that too and clambers up mud and grass and scree, bedraggled mountain man dragging himself up towards the heavens on fingers ripped and bleeding soaked to the cold bone and caked from the knees down in mud like some peculiar centaur, some horrid hybrid of flesh and filth. Panting he reaches the mountain top, the bare branches of two trees over a nearby crest as if some giant stag lurks there for him, and fully exposed to the wind which slaps his lank hair against his face he pulls the hood of his blue anorak up over his head and walks like that, like some oblate, some monk, across the scraped and skytorn mountains opening up into a waun over the thin and desiccated grass and hard spurs of rock and through the infrequent ruins of farmsteads and cottages their tenants long fled leaving the rooves to rot and crumble and the walls to fall and these leavings dot this ravaged place, a settlement, a civilisation entire decimated not by bomb from air or land nor by any flame from man's hand but by the immeasurable barrage of time itself, its patient picking and pulling, and the slow drift and shift of the mountains and the artillery wet and electric from the never-brightening sky. He sees a still intact chimney stack rising out of weed-choked rubble and he huddles for shelter in its hearth, the flue above him blocked by the abandoned nest of some bird, twigs tangled and stuffed into that narrow aperture, and the cessation of water drumming on his head is relief enough to draw from him a sigh. He wafers his hands between his thighs and leans back squatting against the cold stones still blackened with soot and he imagines the scene here before desertion and decay, the fire's warm and honeyed glow, tea and dropscones on the grate the wind and rain battering the window pane and he little Ianto safe, protected, much as he was in childhood sitting with his grandmother by the flickering flames, Radio Ceredigion burbling in the background, plates of teisen lap and jammy bara and condensed milk and sugar boiling to toffee in the fireplace and his grandmother close, the curdled milk and lavender soap smell of her, the kindness of her arms harm-scaring. Clearly and completely he remembers this and then he remembers Roger too ruffling his hair, passing him pills and pouring him drinks, one time jumping to head-butt a tall man who laughed at Ianto and his face now is wet again this time not with rain but with waters still more common, even up here in the clouds these waters still more common. He pulls his hood further up over his head and ties the toggled drawstring tight beneath his chin. He wants a cigarette but guesses they will be unlightable now, but he takes them out and is surprised at how dry they have kept in the inside pocket of this jacket he took from Llŷr's cottage after his first frenzied adventure. He lights one without too much of a struggle. Tiny puffs of smoke escape this free-standing chimney, rising up through the empty nest and out through the flue like a weak memory or mockery of what once was. Like a cruel nod towards what could never be again.

The rain slackens to a drizzle. Ianto flicks the end of his cigarette out into it and leaves his poor shelter and walks on further, ever deeper into the mountains which seem to swell and harden at his approach as if affronted. Cresting one wind-razored rise another rise, rise upon rise, this place taking him forever upwards, the world opens out below him in a colossal spread and he can see the distant dull nickel of Bala lake to the north between two cloud-capped humps and to the south Tal-y-llyn is another grey escarpment in the rain under the faded sky, the towns Bala and Abergynolwyn respectively clustered at their furthest shores like sedge or bulrush on smaller waters and closer to him at dizzying depth he can see the grey stone and mist of Dolgellau, its tight and twisted streets looking huddled, embattled and besieged, the characteristic air of mountain towns. He stands and surveys this immense space and feels inside him in his lungs in his blood that it is his. That it is one vastness before which his mind will not shrink or recoil; that this unknown will not affright him as it might others. That it is possessed of a voice and a codicil and that he is its only knower. A warplane rends the sky above this land and for a small second only he gets it whole, all of it complete, everything so stupid and everything so tragic. So endlessly strange. So immeasurably sad.

He walks on. On a slight descending incline now he walks on through trees and across the top of a disused quarry, the blasted craters below him great gouges in the earth, some bleached bones among the stones on their floors, and he crosses a stream at its shallowest point some small silvery sewin hovering in the shadows in the deeper water beneath the bank and the bright blue dart and plunge of a kingfisher, beautiful shimmering bird. Ianto watches this bird at its work ankle-deep in the icy water his feet turning numb and sees the wriggling minnow disappear down the gulping gullet and he nods at the bird unsmiling as one would at an acquaintance with whom one has fallen out of favour and he steps out of the stream on to a bank strewn with torn fur, broken bone, leftovers of fox or otter and the dark clotted spraints of a predator and he follows the trail along the riverbank for some way, stopping only to pick and gnaw at a sprig of wild watercress, welcoming its bitter bite. He follows the trail through a wood and on to a rutted tarmac path wide enough for Forestry Commission vehicles and he follows this to the bottom of the Pumlumon valley, where the

Hyddgen plaque stands, monument to a battle in 1401 when men led by Owain Glyndŵr slaughtered 200 Saesneg regulars and Flemish mercenaries, leaving the bodies to be mutilated by local peasant wives dismembered and gutted and defenestrated and excoriated some of these parts reputedly eaten or thrown into trees and streams, vile fruit, vile fish, the ground here fertile still with this spilled blood and mulched flesh and fuming bones. Occasionally through the mud rise coins, knives, hacked medallions of steel. Bits of rib, chunks of skull. And it is here that he sees them standing before the plaque and reading the potted history thereon, their red cagoules slick with rain, sees them with the lurching intent that the buzzard must feel when the rabbit breaks cover below and before they can see him in turn he has ducked behind the trunk of a fir tree and with the tang of turpentine in his nostrils he is straining to catch their words, his own breath a bellows in his head:

—1401 . . . this must have been during the Glendower rebellion, then . . . it's full of such battles, this place . . . absolutely full of them . . .

—Yes, I can feel them, the woman says. —I can feel the, the *pain* in this place. Lots of sorrow here.

The man points over to the far side of the valley. —Owen's troops would've been dug in over there. A smaller group would have engaged the English and Flemish forces here then feigned a retreat and led them straight into an ambush. It must've been a rout. A massacre.

The woman nods. —Yes, it was . . . I can feel it somehow. The ground seems to, to ache. It's an exceptionally powerful place, isn't it?

—Absolutely.

—We must show John and Emma this place. We must bring them up here, they'd love it. Maybe next Sunday, if John can get the time off . . . bring a picnic . . .

They look in silence at the wide valley, its thick ranks of trees and its slim and rushing river and its green, its steam. They are fairly young, carrying rucksacks, and jeans tucked into grey woolly socks tucked into expensive hiking boots in turn, the man bearded and baseball-capped and the woman with

199

hair tied back in a ponytail which is probably, when dry and not colourless with drizzle, blonde. Ianto peers at them through pine needles his throat dry and his heart racing, and when they move on down the valley he stays behind them with them in his sight creeping low and quiet through the trees like some sprite on mischief, mayhem bent. Some woodland imp armoured in mire darting from tree to concealing tree, forest-flitter silent across the soft floor creating no more noise than the whispering rain.

Ianto's eyes are like those of a cat at a hamster cage, focused with an intensity breakable not by thunderbolt nor earthquake, an iron unanimity of purpose to his senses. He looks only at the moving backs of the hikers, his hands and his feet utterly unaided by sight taking him smoothly through the trees over bracken, under branches and through fallen trunks as if his body has no more substance than air. Should they happen to glance over their shoulders into the forest at their backs the walkers would see nothing untoward, no creeping wreaker, no avenger intent on reckoning, only perhaps a small shift of shadow in the thick woods a barely remarkable trick of light and shade unimportant and unworrying. They are heading Ianto knows towards the end of the valley towards the disused silver mine within walking distance of the house of his childhood and the circle of standing stones which must be on their itinerary and he will follow them that far if he must and further: when they return to their homes this evening Ianto will dart at their backs through the door with them like a shadow, like a gust of wind. He will lie supine beneath their bed, eyes boring into their backs through ticking and through spring. He will stand in wait behind the shower curtain, his hands curled into claws. His teeth bared in a grin.

The forest ends abruptly and the ground begins to swell bare of trees into a hillock. Ianto waits behind the rotting trunk of a fallen tree until his quarry is out of sight, then he jogs up the road after it and crests a rise and sees it, the two people, further up the sloping track above and ahead of him and he waits until they are out of sight and then sprints after them again. Waiting yet again, panting, he sees a bundle of rusty-wire-wrapped fence posts at the side of the track awaiting some worker and he untangles one from the rusty barbs and briars and drags it out and examines it; arm-width, leg-length, made from some hard and solid wood still creamy from the lathe at the pointed end and hammer-flat and edge-frayed at the other. He holds it up in front of his face and strokes it with one hand tenderly like a lover. Says softly to it:

—*There* yew are . . . been lookin for yew, I yav . . . found yew now tho, eh . . .

Holding it at port arms like a rifle he follows the muddy path in the walkers' direction and tops the hill in time to see them disappear into the dark doorway of the silver mine and he runs around the mound of that old tunnel into the circle of standing stones, where he hides himself behind one his face against the wet and gleaming annealed rock its ancient coldness that he himself is intimate with is indeed host to chilling his skin, seeming to kick against his face as if electrically charged. The stone of him pressed to the stone, stone against stone, two stones touching. The wind whistles through these circled megaliths alien both in their age and indivinable adornments, the carved markings hacked offerings to a god now dead or sleeping or the fumblings of a creature seeking to grasp the notion of written communication. Millennia of wind and rain and frost in their Ordovician stone already old they were when the sky itself was young and refined in the hell of original creation spun from flame and dust from gas, from magma these elements soft and ferocious hardening into invincible slabs dug and wrenched by unknown hands and dragged to this place on this tumulus and erected for reason unknown and slashed and patterned for reason unknown, centuries sliding off them like rain. All worlds in them they are perhaps monuments to a monumental need. The central lodestone has been used by a merlin and perhaps other raptors as a plucking block to strip their prey and is strewn now with wilting in the wet small bones and ripped feather and fur. Lichened with black patches of old blood.

Ianto peeps with one narrowed eye around the edge of his protecting stone once carved sharp, now eroded smooth, and he sees the hikers enter the circle on delicate and reverent steps. They stop and look around and the man spreads his arms wide

201

and the woman clasps her hands clenched to her chest as if in prayer.

—Oh my God . . . such power . . . there are so many spirits here, this place is the centre of everything, it –

—Sshhh, says the man, placing his hand gently on her shoulder. —Don't speak for the moment. Just exist in this place now. Feel its ancient power. Let it wash over you.

Imprinted into the stone in Ianto's eye beneath the skin of running water and quite apart from those old glyphs of man's hand there are fossilised tracks made by beings long extinct, the writhing runnel of a worm and the stippled tracks of a trilobite converging upon that vermiform trace and a gouged and flurried meeting of the two and then the worm track terminates and there is only the trilobite's trace, first and original predator father. Ianto sees these marks in his twitching eye and knows not what they are but knows fully what they signify. And if that is all he knows then it is more than enough.

The man and woman are now standing back to back linking arms around the central lodestone their faces tipped up into the rain. They appear to be emitting a low hum. Ianto steps out from behind the rock, the fence post held under his arm like a lance, and he strides towards them, the pallid skin of his face tight around the miniature infernos of his eyes, steam rising from his head and his shoulders as if he is an absconder fresh from hell. The man and the woman see him and break hands with a start and the woman stares unsmiling and the man tries a grin, a greeting, tentative and unsure. He raises a hand palm outwards:

—Hello, I'm sorry, we, ah . . .

Ianto stops his stride and stands in front of the man staring into his eyes and he shifts the fence post over his shoulder holding it two-handed like a baseballer and grunts once and swings it full strength. It swings, smashes into the man's face and slams his head back against the stone, double-thud impact, thud and crunch. As if merely surprised, the man yells: —Oh!, and raises his hands to his face, the blood already clotting in his wiry beard and Ianto hits him again, this time directly on the top of the head as hard as he possibly can so many years of meagreness in his swing and the man rocks, his eyes rolling back and Ianto repeats this action jumping, actually leaving the ground for added leverage, and the man falls to his knees muttering and gurgling and Ianto hits him yet again in a low roundhouse a tooth in the wood of the fence post and blood splattering against the dark stone immediately disappearing absorbed, slurped up by the thirsty porous rock and with bleeding ears and nose and mouth the man topples face-first, sighing into the mud. Ianto hits him again twice with the fence post and then stamps twice on the back of his head, driving his face deeper into the sludge and his legs cease kicking. He looks up for the woman and sees her backing away from him, her hands flapping weakly at the air in front of her her mouth gulping like a goldfish her face a synopsis of horror, and she turns and runs the rucksack bouncing on her back her ponytail bobbing, and Ianto drops his weapon and leaps the fallen man, gangling, urgent, and is at her heels and can hear her inhaling deeply a prelude to a scream and he is on her before she has left the stone circle, has rugby-tackled her and slammed her into one of the still stone sentinels, her skull cracking off its hardness. He straddles her back the breath coming out of him in whoops and gusts and out of her in a high whistle and he pulls her head back on her neck and slams it hard into the stone and then repeats this action and then a third time each crack of impact successively softer and her tensed body beneath him between his knees relaxes, suddenly limp. Ianto feels the heat of her in his groin. He stands and grabs her ankles and hauls her back towards the lodestone, leaving dragmarks in the mud like the trace of some sluggish reptile, and she begins to twitch at the hands and feet a rapid trembling in all four extremities and Ianto looks around for the man and sees him at several yards distance pulling himself along slowly on his hands and knees leaving a trail of thick maroon blood the rain drumming off his rucksack and cagoule. Ianto drops the woman's ankles and retrieves the fence post splintered and blood-streaked with two slightly yellowed teeth in it like staples and moves over to the man chuckling to himself almost avuncular as if observing the amusing antics of an infant crawling and exploring:

—And where d'yew think yewer going then?

The man grunts, burps blood and drags himself over the churned earth.

—What're yew looking for, then? Ey? What is it yewer after?

The man looks back over his shoulder up at Ianto, his face a pumping red mask. He just looks up as if offering this target already ravaged and Ianto looks down and sees a chip of tooth surfing on a spurt of blood leave the man's burst lips and catch in his clogged beard with the other mess already matted there. Sees the eyes trying to focus adrift in their reddening whites and the mouth opens and gurgles and the tongue writhes like a slug on the quivering chin, and Ianto draws a foot back and places a mighty kick under that chin and the remaining teeth clack together and the tongue tip rolls over and off the beard to flick and curl in the mud and blood and the man's eyes roll back all white again and he rolls over groaning, supine, his torso raised slightly on the rucksack, the head flopping back boneless, the neck and the throat pulled taut. Like some sacrifice to the ever-wet sky. Ianto curses and hops on one leg and grabs the toes of his right foot with his left hand, sucking air in over his teeth.

—Broke me fuckin toe now, I yav! See what I've fuckin done!

He hops three times then replaces his foot on the soggy ground gingerly, stands that leg on tiptoe to test. A small quag red-bubbling swells around his caked trainer. He hears a noise, a high keening as of some vocal creature striving to form words or lamenting an awful loss, and he looks up and around and sees the woman pull herself up the lodestone to her feet, her arms wrapped around the rock in a desperate hug as if seeking protection, her new blood joining the old already spilled on the stone in some terrible red palimpsest and Ianto limps over to her, her damaged face turned to the downpour, the grey sky, and he grabs her ponytail in a fist and pulls her head back until she chokes and slams her face into the stone again and then again until she remains upright only by dint of Ianto's supporting shaking arm and he bends to peer into her face and can discern no real feature only protruberances

204

beneath the red slime which could be either bone or swellings, he knows not, and he releases her and she slithers to the floor in an almost spreading movement like a sack half-filled with fluid. Bubbles in the sump of mud and blood around her head form briefly and then pop and Ianto tries to stand on her back to drive her further into the liquefying earth and his feet slip on her slick anorak and the Goretex of her rucksack and the little midden of her head and Ianto performs this ungainly dance like some puppet on long strings controlled by a mad master enthroned in the black-bulging clouds, arms spread for balance like wings vestigial and featherless. He bends to use his hands to punch and pummel and hears a growling noise and he jerks upright again and there's the man trying to stand, his face in the mud and his arse skywards. His arms appear to be without utility and he seems to be seeking to push himself upright using his knees and forehead only. Ianto tuts and steps off the broken woman and moves over to the dropped fence post. Muttering to himself:

—I've had just about enough of this, I yav. Fuckin ridiculous this. Fuckin daft. Time-a stop this fuckin nonsense once an fer bastard all.

He bends and lifts the fence post, slippery in his hands, so he wipes his palms on the legs of his jeans and the fence post on the sleeve of his anorak and strides over to the man, whose upturned flanks sway unsteady. Ianto stands and positions the flat end of the post above the back of the man's head and like some infernal smithy he raises it to full stretch and brings it down hard on the back of the skull, the dull thunk of impact dampened by the drenched air and sky overhead and vile marsh underfoot. The man's bent body goes rigid, the back bowing at such an angle it seems it must surely snap, and the fingers spread stiff and Ianto repeats the action and the feet kick and scrabble frantic in the mud and grumbling noises happen inside the man's mired jeans. Ianto repeats the action again, groaning with exertion, and all movement in the man abruptly ceases and Ianto steps away and his victim topples sideways silently to lie foetally on the swelling sodden ground. The man's whole head a morass, Ianto squats to brush away filth and feel for the soft spot of the temple, finds it and stands and places the pointed end of the fence post against that fontanelle. He pauses for a moment to let the power fill him, to throb in his limbs and flash in his eyes and scorch away all the sick chance and circumstance that has brought him here to this very place now with death held in his filthy hands and it seems to him that he has at his mercy the very agent of his misery, the arbiter of his misfortune, the architect of his own unluck, and he breathes and exhales deeply as if in tremendous relief and tips his blood-streaked face up into the falling water and opens his mouth to taste. Feels it tickle and cleanse his skin. Feels it rinse his eyes. Then he shakes his head vigorously and slicks his sodden hair back over his skull and he places both of his hands on the top flat end of the fence post and raises himself up on tiptoes and with the whole weight of his scrawny body channelled through and into his shoulders and arms he bears down on the post and feels it sink slowly into the man's temple and the man's feet immediately begin to scrape and flounder in the mud as if he is running sleepily in the throes of nightmare and Ianto feels hard resistance to his downward momentum and grits his teeth hard and strains, his voice leaving him in a kind of clenched roar and he hears a cracking a series sharp and hollow like distant small-arms fire and the man's kicking grows in urgency and his hands reach to slap blindly at the wood in his head and the fencepost breaks through the bone barrier suddenly and seems to be sucked downwards into the earth through bone, through flesh, and Ianto looks down and is shocked at the facility with which the man's physiognomy disintegrates, the eyes leaving their orbits in twin geysers of ichor and plopping into the mud to squint cross-eye upwards and the whole cranium shifting the rippling movement beneath the clotted hair and beard and the skull abruptly collapsing flat on one side and that ear bubbling pink porridge and the lower jaw sliding prognathously out and up and over the nose, which itself sinks or is sucked back into the imploding face, all this in a small red maelstrom. Ianto springs away as if electrocuted from the fence post, which remains upright juddering, and slips back on to his arse into the mud and panting stares at what he has done to the man's head and marvels that the feet are still kicking, but as he looks and wonders they cease and lie still.

He feels piss escape into his jeans and momentarily warm the sodden bog beneath his legs. His heart hammers in his breast and all he can hear is the boom of it in his ears and his stomach heaves and his mouth fills with saliva and he lets his chin drop on to his chest and he spews into his own lap, steam rising from his piss and his vomit to wreathe his clenched face. He raises his hands up in front of his eyes and stares at them noting every crack and mound and ripple beneath the runny filth and turns them this way and that way to examine and his nails are rimmed with mud, with blood, and he turns them again palms inwards. Sees the nicotine stains on his fingers and the pulsing veins in his wrists and the electric trembling of his tendons. He sees the rhythmic bump of his pulse strong, as if augmented now by that which he has stolen and the knowledge that he now has something extra to deal with, something huge and something hideous, some thief of peace memory every minute of every day until he too will die, robs his body of all sensation and his humming head of all thought. Skinny obliterator Ianto sitting in his own sour muck. Drenched annihilator, bedraggled and examining his hands.

There is movement in his eye and he looks and sees the woman slowly writhing in the mud like a drugged serpent. She too appears to have lost the power of her limbs and can move only her trunk and this is bucking and bowing in caterpillar rhythm the rucksack on her back like a poor shell and Ianto groans and stands dripping and squelches over to stand above her and look down. He looks hopelessy around the stone circle as if for assistance, as if pleading counsel from their ancient posture, their ancient matter and then looks back down at the slowly spasming wreck at his feet.

—Aw please die, bach . . . please stop moving . . . it's too late, cariad, yew have to die . . . yew must . . . aw why won't yew just fuckin die?

She slithers and undulates in the mud, the back of her head twisting from side to side and Ianto squats and almost gently places his right palm in her matted hair and leans forwards pressing her face into the quagmire the earth has become, muttering the word 'please' over and over and exerting pressure

207

relentless until she stops moving and all air leaves her body with a wet sigh. Ianto remains squatting stroking the back of her head for a few minutes then he springs vertical as if startled and muttering to himself, just sounds, no known word distinguishable, he takes up the woman's feet and grunting drags her out of the stone circle and down the slight incline, where she slips forwards in the slime and nudges Ianto sideways with her momentum and he sits and watches the body face-down slide in the mud to the bottom of the small hill, the old silver mine, the tumulus that it was and now again is. He moves gingerly down to the corpse and takes up its feet again and drags it over to the entrance to the disused mineshaft and hauls it in there and lets it go and it turns languidly in the knee-high stagnant water to stare sightlessly dirt-eyed up at the sweating tunnel roof, and Ianto looks down at what he has done to the face and he makes a mewling sound in his throat. The leathery flutter of bats' wings sounds in the darkness deeper into the tunnel and Ianto leaves that place and pulls himself with his hands up the hill become now a slanting torrent of mucilage and mud and he re-enters the stone circle like a wild-eyed man of slime, where three big black birds are tugging at the wrecked head of the man. Ianto claps his hands and two of them lift and wheel away trailing things in their beaks and the third flaps up to perch on the flat end of the fence post upright around the seething head and as Ianto looks it cranes its sleek head skywards and swallows something in one great gulp. It spreads its large and blue-black wings and stares at Ianto and opens its beak to scream croakily at him and Ianto sees the pearly pink inside of its gullet. He spreads his arms as if mirroring the bird in imitation deficient and hisses at the raven, which shifts from foot to clawed foot atop the fence post and screeches at him again and he darts forwards a few steps hissing through his teeth and flapping his thin arms and the bird turns and wheels away almost lazy, indolent, its powerful pitch-coloured wings rippling at the shoulder more in the manner of ray than bird. He watches it land and settle on one of the standing stones and he flaps at it again, but it will not move from that stone. Get gone, Mórrígán, mistress of massacre great queen of slaughter, all war and rapine in this your sable shape. On wings of ink you lay claim to carnage, steal sight and cast no illumination in your dark turn.

Ignoring this bird's envious eye Ianto approaches the dead and havoc-headed man and reaches out to pluck the post from the earth, but quickly drops his hands to his sides again as if afraid. He breathes deeply to steel himself then grasps the post and with an abrupt twist wrenches it free and it slurps and slobbers and comes up trailing a sticky string of purple mucus and Ianto retches dry, hunched over clutching his stomach, then when that reaction passes he wedges the post between the rucksack and the dead man's back refusing to even glance at the head and picks up the man's feet and drags him too out of the stone circle leaving a trail of slime and leakage which the black birds descend on again once Ianto and his awful freight are out of sight. At the top of the incline semi-fluid now Ianto lets go of the corpse and nudges it once with his foot and it slews sideways for a few yards then stops and Ianto must nudge it again this time with more force and it slides smoothly to the bottom like an obscene puck made in mayhem and Ianto follows it and takes up its feet again and drags it into the mineshaft and drops it into the murky water. Bubbles burst around it and emit a foul-smelling gas and it turns once and bobs against the woman twice, three times, persistently, like a bored child seeking attention from its mother. Panting and exhausted Ianto sits down on a relatively dry rock although the wetness of his seat would make no difference at all, saturated as he is, with his feet in the water and smokes a cigarette, his eyes growing catlike accustomed to the gloom and his heartbeat returning to normal, his nerves relaxing, the roaring in his head dying down and he regards the broken figures at his feet with a measure both awful and affable, paternal and odd as if somehow approving of these twisted creations of his and only his although he will not look at the red devastation of the man's head nor the woman's black and battered swollen features, but appraises instead the wet cling of her clothes tight to her thighs and torso. And as he watches he sees her feet begin to kick again and he assesses this movement until he is certain that it is volitive of her and independent of the water's buoyancy the hands now shuddering too and he drops his cigarette into the water and

209

wades over to the woman, silt clouding his lower legs, and with one foot pushes her beneath the surface and holds her there, feeling her tremble against the sole of his trainer one of her hands even weakly scrabbling up his leg and out of the water to flutter against his knee and when that mothlike movement ceases and the bubbles have stopped rising from her head he removes his foot and watches impassive as the body rises slowly to the surface and he bends to check for death with his hand against her heart the swell of the dead breast beneath his palm. There is a noise like a squeaky brake in the back of his throat as he yanks the zip of the woman's red cagoule down and opens it and rolls her drenched jumper up over her pale belly bloodless and in a cream bra the breasts the colour of the bleached grey sky outside. Ianto tugs at the clasp of the bra and it snaps and the breasts spill one to each armpit bereft now of the resilience of life, the sturdy support of blood and breath. This revealed shape only ever seen by him on paper and once in a forest clearing unclear in memory and it not at all like he's always imagined or seen, the silver snail-trail stretch marks and the rolls of fat. Whining through clenched teeth Ianto mauls this yielding torso the body shifting in the water under his attentions its partner bobbing against the backs of Ianto's bent knees and he tugs at the nipples hard and when he releases them they do not retain their original shape, the melanin stolen from this carcass along with everything else, the pointless plunder now nowhere but carried in Ianto's heart. He supports the corpse with his left arm under its back and leans and takes a nipple into his dry mouth and with his right hand fumbles at the buttons of the jeans and yanks them open and he stands to draw the wet denim down the legs the skin bloodless white and the knees frowning, the garment now bunched at the stiffening ankles. He stares at the dark patch of hair waving in the water like weed and stabs at it clumsily with rigid fingers and feels something fibrous like twin tendons glued together but underneath that some softness, some peach-like thing, on his fingertips like the fur of a leveret or like moss. Or like feathers. Smelly it is though with the voidance of violence and he turns the body over to stare at the buttocks almost blue now with settled sunken blood the water tinkling off them and then he rolls the body face up again and stands over it supporting himself with one arm palm flat against the greasy tunnel wall and the other pulling his prick out through his fly and pumping it vigorously, his grunts and groans echoing off the tunnel walls. He pulls until he spurts semen on to the dead flesh then he zips himself back up again and will not look at this his last inflicted indignity and he turns his back on the bobbing bodies the unnatural glow of their lifeless skin and splashes water up over himself and swills his face and removes his blood-soaked blue anorak and discards it over his shoulder. It drifts in the murky water like a jellyfish. He bends and heaves and pukes bile and remains bent double like that for a minute or two with his face in his hands, sobs jolting his back then he stands and without a backward glance at his trace, his record, he leaves the mineshaft into the colourless air and the never-ending rain, two awoken bats flapping frantically out behind him like souls from hell.

To his left over the hill and across the field past the lightning-blasted tree lies the house in which he spent his childhood, but he will not move towards the shame that awaits him there and instead he walks in the opposite direction, hunched, soused shape trudging through the grey rain. Mucoid being wringing wet. Wraith born in swamp of deluge and of drench. He follows a sheeptrack around a mountain, Dolgellau sprawling out beneath him, and he crests that mountain and enters for shelter a small copse of pine trees. He squats beneath the lowest branches of a fir, the rain hissing in his ears, and stays like that until he notices smoke rising through the trees some small distance away, little clouds of it puffing up out of a hollow. Leaving his poor shelter he walks squelching towards that signal and down into the hollow and sees a small whitewashed cottage there like an illustration for a fairy tale, orange firelight flickering in its quartered windows, a satellite dish bolted to the gable end like some giant fungus. He approaches it through the tall thin trees, his clothes hanging soaked off his skinny frame, stinking with spilled blood and bad water and piss and vomit splashed up on to his chest, and his hair clotted and reeking and his eyes hot and hollow with the horror he has seen, has caused, a thick scab of blood not his cracking on his lips and chin like a phantom from

211

delirium he is hobgoblin from hallucination risen thus adorned from the very forest floor and he drifts, the wet ruin of him, through the trees and up to the cottage and knocks with a split knuckle on the heavy riveted oaken door. There is no answer so he knocks again louder and shuffles his feet on the slate slabs he stands on and the door slowly opens and a small wrinkled old lady blinks up at him through the thick lenses of her spectacles a small gummy smile on her pale lips and if she is startled or perturbed in any way by her strange and dishevelled visitor she gives no sign. She has pale blue eyes and a small croak of a voice as of a warm wind rustling rushes:

—Ia? Ga'i eich helpu chi, machgan i?

Ianto blinks down at her and does not know what to say standing uninvited on her doorstep bedecked in blood and ordure in a sour puddle of his own and others' sloughed filth and so she repeats her question:

—Ga'i eich helpu chi? Chi'n edrych ar goll.

He swallows and finds his voice and it carries no more weight than hers:

—I'm, erm, I'm sorry to bother yew. I'm lost. I'm cold and I'm lost and I've, erm, I've had, like, an accident.

She smiles up at him looking only at his face and then she stands aside.

—Dewch i mewn.

He steps into the warmth of the small house illuminated only by the frisky firelight. The whitewashed walls, the heavy furniture. The sweet smell of baking from the kitchen and the tick of a clock and the snap of the fire in the grate. The old woman moves in front of him like an elf and gestures with a wizened hand at a small slate bench in the inglenook hearth.

—Eistedda.

Ianto sits on this bench leaving footprints of blood on the stone of the grate like the record of a penitent and the flame's warmth is like a blessing, a caress on the skin of his scarlet-sequinned face, even though it casts his shadow on the white-washed wall behind him gangling and attenuated like a vision of his lesser fetch, his dark and mocking other. He feels the bones of his cheeks and chin expand and throb gently as the sunken

212

coldness is drawn out of them, can feel a calmness wrap him like a cloak from the strong stone walls of this hidden house and the gentle beldam standing before him, her flaxen head level with his now that he is sitting. Her small eyes in nests of wrinkles, she looks him over now, the appalling condition of him, and still the small serene smile does not flee her face. She asks for a third time:

—Ga'i eich helpu chi?

Ianto shakes his head. —I can't understand what yewer saying. English? Saesneg?

She shakes hers too: —Dim Saesneg. Cymraeg yn unig.

He doesn't know how to reply, what to say. She looks him over again then says softly to herself:

—Te. Te, a dŵr gwresog.

She shuffles off to the kitchen in her fleece-lined slippers with her hands clasped in front of her and when she returns she is carrying a blackened kettle which she places on the fire and then she fetches from the kitchen a tin bowl and a mug with milk and a teabag in it and then she returns to the kitchen and comes back with a plate of flat currant scones, which she gives to Ianto and he thanks her and bites into one and chews it thoughtfully and then wolfs the remainder of that one and then the others. Snapping and chewing and gulping he is like a fox, like a goshawk, like a pike, ravening for everything beyond what this world can offer or ever in an aeon supply. She sits in the armchair opposite him and does not take her benign eyes off him as in the fire's warmth he begins to steam like a man of flame just doused. When the kettle boils she wraps a teatowel around her hand and lifts it off the flames and pours some water into the mug and the rest into the bowl and dunks the teabag into the mug and squeezes it between her fingers and hands the tea to Ianto. He sips it and she watches him and he cannot help but smile back at her. The filth on his face cracking as he does.

—Thank you. This tea an them cakes. I, I . . .

She nods. —Iawn.

—I, I . . .

—Iawn.

When he has finished the tea she takes the same teatowel

from the pocket of her cardigan and dips it into the bowl of hot water and wrings it out and approaches Ianto. She takes his chin between thumb and forefinger and tips his head to the left to catch the light from the fire. Her fingertips on his skin delicate and satinate as if his face is held by a flower.

—Chi wedi'u anafu.

She scrubs his face with the hot cloth, cutting through the caked dirt and grime, the thick dregs of his doings and he sighs as the water purifies the mixen that is his face. She scrubs his chin and neck and then rinses and wrings the towel in the bowl and washes his ears and cheeks, her hand on his chin gentle and leathery, and teases the twists of muck from around his eyes and cleans his nose each side of it with smooth and long downstrokes. Three times she does this, three times she washes his face until the water in the bowl has become a thin gruel of molten muck reddy-brown in which float bent blades of grass and clumps of hair and scraps of skin not his. She stands back and studies his now exposed facial features.

—Chi'n gwaedu heb anaf. She shakes her head slightly as if baffled and repeats: —Chi'n gwaedu heb anaf.

She shuffles away into the kitchen and Ianto strokes the clean skin of his face and when she returns she hands him something warm wrapped in a chequered cloth. Ianto opens it and sees inside several of the flat cakes he has just eaten. He looks up at her, understanding that he is being dismissed.

—Bendith Duw.

—OK, I, I . . .

—Iawn. Bendith Duw, machgan i.

He stands and thanks her and she sees him to the door and opens it and he steps outside and she blesses him again and closes the door and he walks away through the dripping woods and out on to the sheeptrack and up on to the mountain again, his face already darkening in streaks from the dirt that the rain is swilling out of his hair. He sits on a spur of rock exposed to the downpour and eats the cakes and looks out over the wide valley, the floor and the mountains and the huddled dark town under vast anvil-shaped clouds, distant hills like a recumbent green giant beaten supine, far valley walls like legs spread, bent at the knees the landscape a titan laid low or ravished a colossal green scream awaiting a throat to voice it and in his body he knows it, in his head he hears it. He finishes the cakes then bundles the cloth and pockets it and begins to whine in the back of his throat a desperate mewling and he falls to his knees in the mud on top of the mountain and scoops up a handul of drenched dirt out of the saturated grass and rubs it in his hair and his face spoiling it again and he forces another fistful into his mouth immediately spewing it back out along with bile and tepid tea and half-digested chunks of dough and peel and raisins. He topples slowly forwards on his knees, his feet leaving the ground, until he is bent like a bridge supported only by knees and by brow and he claws and tears at the ancient earth and growls into the very fertile rain-clogged soil some disjointed noises, entreaties beseechings nonwords and nonsense:

—*NNNNNNN* yew fuckin bastard, *why* yew fuckin bastard never I've never yew fuckin *nnnnnnn*, fuck, yew, I, cunt, *nnn* yew fuckin fuck fuck fuck *why* yew fuckin all I've ever fuckin wanted is yew fuckin bastard fuck yew cunt yew fuckin lissen yew fuckin never yew fuckin *NNNNNN* me yew fuckin fuckin . . .

He raises himself up on his knees his arms outstretched his head bent back to the darkening sky like some sodden supplicant and desperately infatuate with he knows not what he looks up at the first stars swimming in the grey and watery dusk, which a warplane suddenly and without warning splits, and Ianto lets out a noise beneath its roar a howl sprouting out of that pain estranged from blood and bone bouncing off mountain and vast valley basin up starwards, where all Ianto has known or will know, his remarkable deeds, the testimonial of his passing, one footprint of blood like the step of a pilgrim will be born and born and reborn over among those far fires emanating no felt heat and very little light which nevertheless can snuff in an eyeblink all fevered dreaming of this soil and all its partnered follies, expanding, contracting like living lungs along with and under and indeed slave to the fickle benedictions of the foremost frantic star. And that people pass away, Ianto knows, but not so the world that has them in it until that too, big as it is, shall

215

fizzle or shall drown. Yet who is he to deny or disbelieve that the minds of the dead may yet live on, all loss and puzzle, in some other less mountainous realm maybe some place less drenched or aflame or even more so? Who can state that each leaf throbs on a sap not distilled in other former veins? That the hills we climb and that the birds we see do not ascend or study us too?

Ianto knows not where he is, knows not the way back to whatever darkened corner he must perforce this coming night call home. Kneeling atop the mountain like that in the rain and mud and blood and screaming with the articles of war roaring above his head he surges skywards like some stele self-erected, already crumbling and useless in all but the fact of its very construction, like his mere footprints the cryptic expression of a singular need, a delible remnant of his breath, further red relic of his tread. Just a wee bit pigeon-toed.

IANTO IS NINE and a half.

Belly to ground he commando-crawls on elbows and knees to the very edge of the cliff, peers down from this promontory coarse-grassed and pink-thrifted at the boiling sea below, which wild waters appear to exult at the sight of him and hurl and break themselves repeatedly against the dark rocks protruding like carious teeth, like rotten fangs in an open mouth waiting to swallow Ianto should he fall. He raises his head and gazes horizonwards, sees the far islands in the mist, magical and dreamlike landscapes of Ynys Enlli and the Llŷn and the distant rises of Ynys Môn beyond and above that peninsula and further still the blurred blue suggestions of the mountains of Wicklow. Lands from dream and phantasm peopled by warlock and dragon. This could be anywhere. The spaces are immeasurable.

He peers down the precipitous cliff face dropping sheer below him at the protruding perpendicular ledge roughly halfway down, a shelf scattered with bleached and broken bones and caked with a carpet of guano and blackened blood, which signs denote an old nesting site here in this location safe from the pigeon-fancier's gun or the egger's odd obsession or the insidious poisons of organochlorines and DDT. As he watches, the blue birds grey-banded with the rolling-shouldered gait of parrots or thugs walk to the edge of the ledge and stamp their baggy-trousered legs and spread their striped wings, displaying their remarkable coloration which gives them their local name of y gwalch glas, the blue hawk, the same word used here for rogue and for bandit. He watches the tiercel scream at the sea and flex its powerful shoulders and launch itself off the shelf into the azure air and flap frantically to achieve height, somehow ungainly and graceless, its wings appearing truncated as if designed for a smaller bird. His eyes follow it up and then further up until it is just a dot in the sky cloudless and cerulean. The female watches her mate climb then drops away from the nesting site and swoops down to soar-skim the scrolled waves, her flight cross-tracking and interlocking, describing around a bobbing, crying gull a large eternity symbol like some small deity, some worshipable flyer declaiming its unique and

217

supernatural properties. Her flight patterns shrink successively tighter, spinning an invisible web around the seabird, smaller and smaller still, until with a cry it runs for a few yards on flat pink feet across the surface of the water its wings spread and takes to the air, circling above the female peregrine and complaining and well aware what is about to come to pass. Ianto squints up at the hovering male a half-mile or more above him in the high blue, sees it break its hover abruptly and flap still higher then bank suddenly into a dive, a Stuka swoop, its wings in tight to its sides streamlined and lethal and conical like artillery launched from heaven. As if drawn there by laser, some inexorable computerised mapping, the tiercel descends in a whistling stillness in which even the sea seems awestruck and at shocking speed towards the oblivious gull and gulps great gulfs of blue sky in its eye-searing stoop, young Ianto watching breathless its unstoppable descent and he sees the impact before he feels in his bones the sonic thump of that contact and hears the scream amid the white burst of feathers. The tiercel wheels away from the crippled gull some dripping thing clutched in its claws and the seabird spins brokenly seawards regaining its power of flight a metre above water climbing then hit from beneath by the female, the silver flash and spin and the scything slashing talon. The gull screams and drops again caught in mid-stoop a mere foot above the waves by the male falcon in a neck-breaking grab and borne limp, brokenly aloft, head and wings drooping, back to the nest, passed from claw to clutching claw in mid-air as the predator birds share the burden. Wheeling and screaming between two blues the raptors revelling in murder. No aerial dance this; rather a torture, balletic and brutal, the birds settling on the ledge with their carcass cargo and the blood-nubbed drifting feather confetti the chunk-tearing plunging beaks the belly ripped open and the small guts yanked out in slippery steaming streamers, the inevitability of the weaker bird's death, torn agony end.

And world of marvel this that holds such prizes, the birds and the boy watching, agog, agape, struck dumb. Such rare wonders, such hidden gifts. The miracle in the claw and the enraptured rending, and this boy with something in him of the rarely glimpsed and the prodigious and the unique expression of that enigma as yet ahead and unformed and even he cannot guess at the shape it will assume, cannot know how it will hatch in what species and in what livery but hatch and fly it must.

Ianto is finding it difficult to breathe. These sky-shredding hunters, these absolute birds, avians utter, entire have in their beauty brutal and cruel clogged his young lungs. Perfect and quintessential airborne killers that live in and for vast tracts of space, measureless horizons, they have swooped and snatched and butchered through his world, his being. Wide-eyed he watches them rip, sees the blood shoot, sees the female bend and yank and sunder and rise with the head of the gull the yellow beak hanging open the black tongue lolling and drop it over the side into the crashing sea, which claims this offering with a hiss and a roar. She turns and raises her tail and drops a mute after the head into the thundering waves. Red-masked the partnered predators scream triumphant at each other over the torn and tattered corpse and then up at the sky itself and also the seething sea below, wings spread blue-grey and black-barred to cast shadow and catch sunbeam, stamping their hard-clawed carnival on this spindrift and lichened secret bethel of viscera, high and salty temple of bone. All Ianto can do is watch and wonder and wait to exhale again.

—D'yew wanner know what I think?

—Not particularly, Danny, no.

—What, Danny? What d'yew think then?

—I reckon that yer was some sort of abuse, back in is past, like. Yer fuckin must've been. Some, y'know, fuckin sexual stuff, likes. Kiddie fiddling. That's what happened to im, that's what made im what he was. *I* reckon, anyway.

—That's it, is it? That's yewer fuckin, like, remarkable insight, is it? Jesus Christ.

—Danny, that's been said already about ten bastard times. We've already fuckin established like that Ianto'd been abused or summin. Or at least that we *think* ee was. Have yew not been lissenin?

—Yeh, an anyway, who was around to abuse im? His granny? It's only male members of-a family who do stuff like that, and –

—Not always it's not.

—Alright then, it's *usually*, nine times out-a bastard ten like, male family members oo carry out the abuse. Women, females ardly ever do. An who was yer around to abuse Ianto? Not his grandmother. Surely yewer not suggestin that, mun. Not that sweet ole biddy.

—No fuckin way, mun.

—Well, it doesn't have to be a family member, does it? I mean, fuck, yer's no fuckin laws that says it has to be, is yer? An some women *do* abuse, altho I'm not fuckin suggestin for one fuckin moment that Ianto's mam-cu did. But, like, take Gladys Trevithick, for one. Case in fuckin point, mun.

—Aye, but she's an exception. That evil ole fuckin slapper int the norm. It's very fuckin rare that women do such things, *very* fuckin rare.

—Or, or it could've been a friend of-a family or somethin like, couldn't it? I mean –

—What friends?

—What fuckin *family*?

—Or, I dunno, just some stranger. That happens as well, y'know. I mean, none-a us ever found out what happened to is knob, did we? Why it was all half-chewed lookin like. An I remember him bein in hospital for ages, when we were kids like. Never did find out what for. No one'd fuckin tell me.

—Born like that, I reckon. His dick I mean likes. Some deformity or summin.

—Or maybe even just some accident with a piece-a farm machinery or somethin. Accidents happen all-a fuckin time on farms, especially to little kiddies like.

—Yeh, but it was moren that, tho, wannit? I mean it was just-a way he was, mun, is whole fuckin demeanour. The creepy way he was with women. Always like leering at em, he was, fuckin right up in eyr faces gawpin at eyr tits an stuff. I mean, I know most blokes do that kind-a stuff like, but with Ianto yer seemed to be somethin extra to it, a deeper dimension like. Almost fuckin predatory or summin. Women seemed to be scared of im. As if they could fuckin sense it like.

—Gwenno wasn't scared of im. Not until the very end, like, I don't think.

—She wasn't scared of *me*, either. Oh no way. Not fuckin scared of me at all, mun.

—Aw, fer fuck's sakes, Marc. Give it a fuckin rest now eh. Gettin right on me fuckin tits now yew are, boy.

—Well, whatever happened to im it was no fuckin excuse. No fuckin excuse whatsoever. Fuckin pervert that lad was, puren fuckin simple. Yer's no reasons, yer's no fuckin excuse in-a whole wide bastard world for what he done.

—No, but yew don't know what happened, do yew?

—To who? To Ianto? No, an I don't fuckin need to know either. Don't even *want* to fuckin know to tell yew-a trewth. Too fuckin easy to blame some cunt else if yew ask me, to say ah yeh I'm like I am cos-a this, cos-a him or fuckin her. It's just a fuckin cop-out, mun. Yew've got to take personal responsibility for yewer actions some fuckin time, like.

—Oh! Says *yew*!

221

—*Yeh* says fuckin me. I've never killed no fucker. Given several chopsy cunts a smack or two like when they've fuckin asked for it like, aye . . .

—Moren a smack, Griff.

—. . . but I've never fuckin killed no fucker. And especially not like fuckin that, fuckin schoolboy, fuckin *woman*. Cold bastard blood likes. Coward. Pervert. The people *I've* ever damaged have all fuckin asked for it in-a first place and have been grown fuckin men like. *And* have been able to walk away afterwards. Or at least when eyv come out-a the hospital, like. Never been part of anyone's death, me, no.

—Bollax.

—Fuck off. What're yew fuckin talkin about mun?

—What do *yew* think we're fuckin talkin about? Ianto, that's what. What about im? An-a fuckin way *he* died then?

—Ah yeh, but that's different.

—How is it? How the fuck is it different then, Griff?

—Cos that was him, like, that was fuckin Ianto. Way of-a fuckin world, mun, innit? Killer gets killed, that's just-a way things are. Dog eat bastard dog see. Don't have to fuckin like it likes, but it's-a fuckin way things are and have always been as well. If yew ask me I think it's a tidy situation, eye for an eye like. Says so in-a Bible, dunnit? It's always been that way. An anyway, it wasn't fuckin me who fired-a fatal shot, like, was it? And fuck, we were *all* fuckin involved, not just me. I dint see any-a yew cunts standin aside when-a kickin was goin on or runnin to phone-a busies or anythin, so just fuckin lissen to what yewer fuckin sayin, mun.

—No, but . . . well, it was-a whole frenzy of the situation like, wannit? The heat of the moment. Fuckin mob rule or whatever yew wanner call it. It was the sight of those bodies all, like, battered an fuckin rotten an Ianto's fuckin anorak lyin yer an Ianto imself screamin . . . maybe it was-a mushies as well or somethin. I don't know. But just seein those corpses like all fuckin smashed in an decayin an-a woman's kex round er ankles an fuckin Ianto all skinny an twitchy like ee was, it all just fuckin . . . I remember him, Ianto, lookin to me like a fuckin devil. Like fuckin Satan imself. That's what he seemed to be, to me at-a time like, fuckin Satan imself. That's what I thought he was. An if I joined in in is murder it was only because I was so fuckin scared. At the time, like, I mean.

—My arse. Scared? Yer was a big fuckin grin on yewer face boy if I remember rightly. An I do. Yew were fuckin enjoyin it, mun, don't tell me yew fuckin weren't.

—Yeh.

—That's fuckin *exactly* what I'm gunner tell yew, that I wasn't fuckin enjoyin it one tiny bastard bit. It was fuckin horrific. It made me sick an it gives me fuckin nightmares even now, mun. Three fuckin years on, like.

—That's because yew don't want to recognise yewer own dark side. Yew'd sooner believe that it doesn't exist rather than accept-a fact that yew can be an animal as well, like-a rest of us. Like-a whole-a the fuckin human race, mun. Yewer nothing special, Danny, nothin different. Yewer just a fuckin ape underneath it all, just like-a rest of us.

—Yew've missed my point entirely, Marc. Which is only to be expected seein as how yewer thick as shit.

—Touched a nerve yer, av I?

—Fuck off.

—Well tell us, then, mun. Tell us again what yewer witterin fuckin on about.

—Well Jesus Christ, Griff, Ianto was a mate. I liked im. We all did. An yer we all fuckin were jumpin up an down on-a poor cunt's head. An I didn't fuckin enjoy it, no, course I fuckin didn't. It made me spew up if yew remember. Still avin nightmares about it now I yam.

—So why did yew join in then? Why dint yew run away or even try to protect Ianto from us? I mean seein as how yewer so fuckin fond of murderers an rapists like.

—Aw fuckin hell. Lissen to yewerself, Marc, just fuckin lissen to yewerself. Sound like a twat yew do, mun, aye.

—Doesn't answer my question, tho, mun.

—I, I joined in because of what I've just said. The heat of-a moment, the mushies . . . I was off my fuckin head. Trippin, like. Properly. An seein them bodies, it was like bein in a fuckin horror film or something, I thought I'd been taken down to hell.

223

I just went mad, like we fuckin *all* did. Temporary insanity like, wasn't that what our brief called it? Fuckin spot-on yer he was. I mean, I dint know how to react cos nothin even remotely like it had ever happened to me before, so I just went along with what all-a yew were doing. Which was . . .

—Killin fuckin Ianto.

—Oh I get it. It's all our fuckin fault then, is it? We're to fuckin blame like?

—I never fuckin said that, Llŷr. An yew, Marc, are yew bein deliberately fuckin stupid or does it just come naturally like? I didn't know what I was doing, ow many times do I have to fuckin say it? An I don't think any of us did, either.

—Well, *I'm* not fuckin sorry for anything. Got fuck all to apologise for, mun.

—I never said yew did.

—Fuckin probation? Suspended fuckin sentence? Should-a given me a fuckin *medal*, mun.

—An we would've got time in Swansea fuckin nick like Ikey, if it wasn't for that lawyer.

—Yeh. Justice my fuckin arsehole.

—Ikey'll be out soon, won't he?

—Yeh. No bother for im anyway, he've done time before. Out he'll come with money in is back bin an bigger muscles, that's all. Like a fuckin holiday to im nick is, see. It's easy. The four years I did for dealin-a E that time were a piece-a bleedin piss. Tellin yew boy. Just spent all fuckin day stoned out-me brains like. No problem. An anyway, d'yew think Ikey'll be losing any fuckin sleep over what we did to Ianto? Fuck no.

—Yeh but that's because he's –

—Because he's fuckin nothing. Because Ianto had it comin to im, mun, that's all yer is to it. It was just a matter-a time, that's all. An yew wanner know summin? If toppin fuckin Ianto meant that we saved-a lives of other kiddies an women that that fuckin pervert would-a gone on to kill, then I'm fuckin glad, *glad*, that we did what we did. Too fuckin right. No two ways about it, mun, I'm fuckin glad. I'd do-a whole thing over again if I fuckin had to, like. No bastard remorse, no fuckin guilt. None. Wouldn't think twice, me. An yew say yew have nightmares about it, yeh, well I say I have . . . pleasant fuckin memories. Sweet fuckin dreams, cos I think of is victims, see. Of-a poor fuckin people he murdered. Yewer far too fuckin liberal, Danny mun. Yew should think of-a schoolboy an-a woman rottin away in that fuckin hole in-a ground. An about all-a other people we stopped im from murderin. An rapin.

—Yeh, but –

—No bastard buts about it, mun. Yew should be pleased with yewerself an sorry not for helpin to kill Ianto but for all those innocent people he would've gone on to kill had we let im live an that's all yer is to it.

—Yeh. Yewer right, Griff.

—I know I am, Marc. Fuckin end *of.*

HE SEES THEM, Ianto does, the police helicopters sputtering high overhead, combing the forests and the mountains, and the uniformed figures, their luminous yellow waistcoats gleaming in the trees and on the storm-stripped spurs of rock like insects scavenging for foodscraps after some titanic picnic. He sees the ragged groups of local men with old dogs and older shotguns sallying forth drunk with drink and contravention from the hill village pubs, sees them back in those same pubs bedraggled and frustrated some hours later and hears their low talk of missing persons, of a young boy's battered body found beneath an old stone bridge. Of a young couple gone missing, disappeared into the mountain fastness, two flames of life snuffed in the colossal rises and sky-puncturing crags and perpetual downpour as if simply swallowed by that terrain and not as yet spat or shat out again. He hears their whispered surmises of lunatics escaped, of nationalist outrages unprecedentedly extreme, of a hill half-wit gone feral and psychotic as he sits alone by the fruit machine and sips at his pint. On the local news he sees facial images, one a scowling mugshot and the other two tanned smilers on a sweaty sunburned holiday and he recalls those features swelling, spurting, breaking apart, bursting and collapsing and pleading through blood. He hears talk in a chip shop of devolution fever, of millennial psychosis. Of drug-crazed teenagers, of community care. He hears suppositions of secret muggings in off-licences and squats and galleries, there among the garish glass and tin and the hanging smoke and scorched foil and needles beaded with bad blood. In street markets the guessings at motive and reason and method, verbal stumblings as in the attempted capture of a terrible dream days distant, still dreadful. He sees policemen going from door to door with questions and clipboards like census-takers. Outside early-morning chapels he hears the bellowings about Lucifer returned, about punishment and apocalypse, about the first skirmish of an imminent armageddon, and he stands in the graveyards with his hands plunged deep in his pockets and he raises his eyes skywards to scope for birds soaring or perching on steeples.

Ianto hears and sees everything. And also he remembers; sometimes when he lies supine on the spongy dry ryegrass with sheep's bit and woundwort probing his ears and tickling his cheeks, the drugs leaving his system shredded and exhausted, the clouds above drifting like torn wedding veils through his field of vision rent by the warplanes which shriek on manoeuvres and tear but do not open that sky, which contains and will never yield all that flexes outside ourselves, flexes always, never-ending, or when he lies sleepless and solitary on a borrowed bed in squat or shelter staring up at ceiling-goblins made from water-damp and dusty bunting of web swinging slightly in the humid updraught of his breath and his pulse racing as here comes the horror he remembers, Ianto does, he recalls it all. There is nothing he can do at these times to stop it coming back.

IANTO IS TEN.

The sun is going down, is turning the lake blood red, is casting its fires upon the waters. The little boy sits on the bank and watches the still waters burn and sees the feeding bats flit and dart for insects across the red lake. Their small forms squeaking out of the watery flames like souls turned to smuts.

He likes to sit here at dusk, Ianto does, likes to watch the bats hunting and the tiny deaths and likes to see the first white owls rise like ghosts from the charred ruins of the big house across the lake. Once he saw an otter slip smoothly from this water and climb the bank with a fish wriggling in its tomcat mouth and slide like oil into a burrow. Once he saw a heron highstep and stab and swallow an eel whole. He does this as often as he can, sits silently at this lakeside watching the sun sink across it and it turning to blaze, knowing that in the small house over the hill behind him his grandmother will be adding onions to the cawl and slicing bread thick at the set table.

A kind of peace in his strange young heart. Or if not that then a stillness. A calming down. An icy bite to the pure air now as the sun sinks and the sky darkens. The horizon burning above the mountain

227

tops, those flames reflected in the calm lake, the sun falling again from the sky but Ianto knows it will return, will always come again.

He hears twigs snap behind him and turns to look over his shoulder, sees a hiker bearded and ponytailed in a red cagoule and tight shorts, his bare legs thin and hairy and white knees knobbled and red. He smiles at Ianto, a movement colourless and mechanical in his straggly beard, and swings his rucksack off and places it on the damp earth. He breathes in deeply and sits down cross-legged at Ianto's side. Ianto smells him immediately; patchouli oil and sweat and something else. Peeping out of the breast pockets of his cagoule are an Ordnance Survey map, Landranger series, and two dog-eared books: Buddhist Scripture and A Pocket Guide to Celtic Britain.

—*Hello there, young man. Don't mind if I sit here, do you?*

His accent is clipped, southern English, imperious. Ianto shakes his head and looks back at the lake, but cannot stop himself from casting sideways glances at this man, the hook of his nose, the prominence of his epiglottis in the lower wisps of his beard. The shine in his eyes and the way the tip of his tongue flickers pinkly in the surrounding hair like a newborn bird in a tangled nest.

The man groans and rubs his face in his hands.

—*A long day, a long day . . . done a lot of walking today. Must've covered twenty miles at least. Calf muscles fit to burst. Feel that.*

He stretches one thin leg out to tense the muscles and looks at Ianto, but Ianto does not touch.

—*Go on, feel it. Hard as steel.*

Ianto does not touch and the man snorts and tucks his leg back beneath him. He rummages in his rucksack and takes out a paper bag of mint imperials, which he offers to Ianto and Ianto takes one and puts it in his mouth. The man watches him intently, watches him suck.

—*Live local, do you?*

Small edge to his voice and Ianto doesn't know why. The man is staring at him so hard that he feels he must answer and does:

—*Yes.*

—*Oh good, you can talk. Whereabouts?*

—*What?*

—*I said: Whereabouts. Do you. Live?*

Ianto sucks the mint. —*Just over the hill. With my mam-cu.*

—*With your what?*

228

—*Mam-cu.*

—*'Mamky'? What's a bloody 'mamky'? Can you not talk bloody English? What on earth is a 'mamky'?*

—*Grandmother.*

—*Oh well, why didn't you bloody well say that then? Expect every visitor to your little province to know your bloody language, do you?*

Ianto doesn't answer. His mouth has gone suddenly dry and the mint in it now feels like a ball of hair.

—*Is there only your, what is it, 'mamky' in this house? No other adults?*

Ianto shakes his head.

—*No father or bigger brothers?*

Another shake.

—*And how far away is this house of yours?*

Ianto does not reply.

—*Oi. The man prods Ianto's ribs with a rigid finger. —I'm talking to you. Look at me when I'm talking to you.*

He takes Ianto's chin between his thumb and forefinger and swings his head not gently to face him.

—*That's better. Now answer my question: How far away. Is the house where you live?*

Ianto does not, cannot, answer and the man sighs in exasperation.

—*Stupid, bloody stupid, he mutters under his breath. —Let's try it this way; how long would it take you to walk home from here?*

No answer will come. Ianto's lower lip trembles and the world around him, the setting sun and the mountains and the fiery lake seems to have shrunk and tightened like plastic pulled across his face. He doesn't want this man here. He wishes he would go away. He feels as if he has done something terribly wrong and this man has been sent to punish him, but he does not know what it is. The man's fingers on his chin feel rough and foreign and intrusive, yet intrusive with some strong rights of trespass, some ineffable legal backing. He swallows the mint painfully down a seared and arid throat and croaks three words:

—*I don't know.*

Unsmiling the man mimics Ianto, whining high-pitched, exaggerated squeak:

—*'Don't know. Don't know.'*

And higher then, squealing, a manic parrot:

229

—'Don't know! DON'T KNOW! DON'T KNOW!'

And suddenly quiet again. The man lets go of Ianto's face and throws his hands up in defeat.

—I give up. Stupid. You're all bloody stupid. All that inbreeding has rotted your brains.

He glances backwards over each shoulder then out across the lake, then he turns back to Ianto.

—All right then, tell me this; if you were to walk back home now, which route would you take? You can answer me that, can't you? I mean you DO know your way home at least?

Ianto nods.

—Well then, that's something, isn't it? So tell me the way.

He begins to stroke the back of Ianto's head, gently, smoothing the unwashed and burr-lumpy hair down over the skull. Ianto jerks as if shocked and the man inhales sharply at that reaction and continues the stroking for a few moments more, staring intently at Ianto's turned-away face and then he sighs and drops his hand back into his lap as if disappointed, let down.

—Don't you like me doing that? Stroking your head? It doesn't, ah, it doesn't feel nice?

Ianto sniffles only in reply. The man tuts and shakes his head as if in some disgust then repeats his original question in a harder, much harder, tone:

—Tell me the way to where you live. How would you get there.

Ianto swallows nothing but cottonspit. He speaks through a mouth filled with dust:

—I'd, I'd go through the woods. Around the hill. Over the next hill. Over the old mine. Past the burned tree. And that's where I live, there. With my . . . erm . . .

—So it's quite a way, then?

Ianto nods. The man smiles. Shadows cast across his face, his eyes in black pits and black crescents beneath his cheekbones.

—You see? That wasn't hard now, was it? Do anything if you put your mind to it. And that deserves another little reward, I think. Yes, I can tell that you're a good boy really. A NICE boy. I meet many nice boys like you up here in the mountains, I do. Oh yes. Good, nice young lads like yourself.

230

He again takes out the bag of mints and offers it to Ianto, who shakes his head.

—Go on, have one. Take a couple.

—No thank you, I –

—Nonsense, I insist. Good boys deserve sweets. Have a mint.

This man's eyes are like lamps, the bright headlights of the ATVs that Ianto sees from his bedroom window at night-time during lambing season. Bone-white beams on the mountain peaks cutting across the stars.

The Englishman rattles the bag in his cupped palm, staring at Ianto with his gimlet eyes. His hand slowly lifts and then is on the back of Ianto's head again, touching, stroking soft and persistent. Such threat to Ianto in a touch so delicate. Twirling a tress of hair around a stiff finger. Twirling ever tighter until Ianto's scalp begins to sting. Ianto slowly and unsurely raises his trembling fingers and dips them in the bag and as he does so the man snaps his hand tight around Ianto's fingers and Ianto yells and jerks away and the man laughs. Staring laughing at Ianto as he tucks his hand into his armpit as if protecting it. Ianto starts to cry and the man snorts and once again removes his hand from Ianto's head.

—Big baby . . . scared you, did I? Gave you a fright? Aw diddums . . . big boys shouldn't cry. Only little girls cry.

Ianto sniffles and wipes his nose on his sleeve. Plundered he feels of personality and locomotion, eviscerated, stripped bare. All those powers he is beginning at this age to feel he possesses now looted by this strange Englishman with the dry tangled beard and the eyes like awls. He feels like he wants to vomit, like he wants to shit. Feels like he is losing all substance and sense of himself as a displacement of air, like if he stood he would throw no shadow. A boy made of gas.

But stand he does. On legs that wobble and threaten to buckle he finds himself standing above the man on earth that feels like jelly. The man looks up at him, his eyes trailing up Ianto's bare and mucky legs and up over his ragged shorts with the fraying hem and then up over his holed jumper and then up into his face.

—And where do you think you're going?

—I've got to go home cos my tea'll be ready. It's –

—You'll do nothing of the sort. Sit back down.

—I can't, I'll be late, I –

231

—DO AS I SAY!

The man's arm strikes out like a snake, the fang-fingers grabbing the waistband of Ianto's shorts and yanking him roughly to the ground. Ianto feels his entire body go limp in surrender and smells damp soil in his nostrils and then sweat as his face is pushed hard into the man's crotch. The man's hand like a vice on the back of his neck raising Ianto's head a few inches so with the other he can fumble at the fly of his shorts.

—You disobedient little bastard . . . little Taffy bastard, aren't you? You'll do as I bloody well say, you disobedient little bugger. Don't like my hand on your head, eh? Don't like me touching you, is that it? Find me repulsive, do you, like all the other little shits? DON'T LIKE ME FUCKING TOUCHING YOU YOU RUDE LITTLE PIECE OF SHIT!

The spongy end of a hard penis presses against Ianto's face. Smells of a dairy early in the morning, of forgotten milk left to sour on the windowsill in the sun. Ianto shakes his head vigorously and clamps his mouth closed and tries to draw his head back, but the man grabs his skull in both hands and shoves it back into his crotch and holds it there. The static head atop the thrashing body. Roaring in Ianto's ears, a rod of heat pressed to his cheek, dry hairs itching his chin like sunbaked grass.

—Suck it . . . go on, suck it, you filthy little bastard . . .

The man's hips begin to thrust. The hard hot rod begins to pump and scrape against Ianto's clenched face.

—Oof Christ . . . you love this, don't you, you dirty little Taffy bastard . . . luring me up here . . . turning me on . . . how fucking DARE *you . . . how fucking* DARE *you reject me, you little fucking . . .*

One hand holding, the other hand begins to explore Ianto's head, slapping the skull, probing the ears, pinching the hot wet skin of the cheeks. One finger tasting of salt and iron worms its way between Ianto's compressed lips and rubs itself back and forth against the locked fence of his teeth.

—Well, this is all you deserve . . . dirty little sheepshagger . . . cock-teasing little cunt . . .

The pumping accelerates urgent, fervid. The hot rod now slips and slides in a small slick of its own leakage across Ianto's face and the finger stabs repeatedly into Ianto's inner cheek, but his teeth will not yield.

—I bet you LIKE *shagging sheep, don't you? Dirty little . . . course*

you do . . . you're all fucking at it up here, you are, oh yes . . . perverts, the whole damn lot of you . . . the whole poxy little country . . . oof . . . aw fuck yes . . .

Ianto opens his mouth to gulp air and scream, but he inhales a mouthful of coarse hair and gags into the man's lap and the finger darts in to press down on Ianto's tongue, slide across it like a worm and Ianto closes his mouth tight around that finger so that nothing else can follow it in.

—Yes, that's it . . . look at you . . . dirty little sheepshagger . . . you fucking love this, don't you . . . you love me doing this to you . . . filthy little Welsh SLUT!

The voice breaks on the last word and the pumping becomes frantic and his cries high and urgent and the pressure on Ianto's head becomes more insistent and Ianto cannot breathe. The man shrieks piercing like a bird, some grebe or goose, and scalding glue squirts across Ianto's face. There in the dusk's quiet inferno and the hunting bats and the phantom moon rising over the mountain like an eye prying and cataracted. The finger pumps in and out of Ianto's mouth and as the thrusting hips subside and still Ianto closes his teeth tight around that intruding digit and bites down hard, feels the crunch of bone and tastes salty copper blood.

—Oh you fucking little bastard! YOU FUCKING LITTLE UNGRATE-FUL BASTARD!

A fist brought down hard on Ianto's nape springs his mouth open and the man withdraws his bitten finger. He yanks Ianto upright on to his knees and Ianto takes in great whoops of air, his face red and wet and polluted shiny with sweat and sperm and the lips spotted with blood, but the man will not look at that face, only at his damaged finger. His voice is sad, disappointed:

—Oh how could you . . . after what we've just done. You wicked little bastard . . . just like all the others . . . you're all the fucking same . . .

He places the bleeding finger in his own mouth and sucks it, his eyes staring thoughtful across the lake. Ianto watches him through watery prisms, feeling no rage, only a stunned acceptance of the weakness in his body and the costume it seems he must don. Like a stage prop only inanimate and backgrounded to be shifted and moved by figures larger

233

and more legitimate than his own. A piece to be shifted and shunted possessed of no volition or will.

The man removes his finger from his mouth and holds it upright and spittle-glistening in front of his face. He turns it this way and that way to study its damage and then he grunts and is in an instant astride Ianto, Ianto on the ground and a knee in his throat holding him to the earth and hands ripping Ianto's too-large shorts down over his bony hips, his thighs which stiffen shocked at the sudden cold. Bright white in the dusk his exposed and hairless skin his genitals shrinking back into his body as if seeking to escape, to hide.

—Right you little bastard. Let's see how YOU like it then.

Coughing and choking under the pressing knee in his throat, Ianto feels wet warmth envelop his penis. Almost strangely pleasant this soft cave of moist warmth in the cold evening air. Then the suction peculiar then the hard teeth nibbling exploring and softly biting up the length as if searching and then clamping around the long foreskin a chunk of meatus caught too in that light bite then pressure. More pressure, then shocking searing pain as the teeth clench and meet and wrench and tear and the man's head jerks the flesh away and spits it lakewards and the centre of Ianto's being is aflame. Like a white hot nail hammered into his urethra pain complete and overwhelming his whole body rigid around that screaming core.

The knee leaves his throat and Ianto cannot scream, although he tries to, only wheeze and gurgle around his bruised larynx. The man stares down at him expressionless then grabs the neck of Ianto's jumper and draws his head up to roar into his face only two inches away, his hot and horrid breath blood in his beard and shreds of Ianto's flesh in his teeth and Ianto's sodden face spattered with spittle and dots of his own stolen blood:

—LIKE THAT, DID YOU! YOUR OWN FUCKING FAULT! SEE WHAT YOU MADE ME DO! LITTLE TAFFY BASTARD! SHEEPSHAGGER! SEE WHAT YOU MADE ME FUCKING DO! ALL I WANTED TO DO WAS STROKE YOUR STUPID LITTLE FUCKING HEAD!

Ianto finds his voice then and can scream, but his face is plunged into the soft earth to stifle any expression of his agony and he feels himself moving dragged down the bank with mud clogging his mouth and then he is lifted and for one moment weightless, airborne, small broken body suspended between mountains above a lake of flame. Mid-air swastika

234

shape ruined and ransacked this strange strafed pattern in the darkening sky, the burning water below. Then he is immersed in colossal shock and total cold, a mind-wide silence only a distant booming in his ears and immovable he drifts downwards spreadeagled then slowly begins to rise again chasing the bubbles of his own fleeing breath and the instant he breaks surface he is a mad thrasher, screaming, arms and legs windmilling until his feet touch floor and he drags himself up on to the bank on all fours out of the glowing lake like a being forged in some enormous molten flame for a purpose beyond his grasp or imagining, spewing brackish water and half-digested chunks of apple scrumped some hours earlier when the world was the same, was all he knew or could ever want despite of its horrors, not changed and sullied utterly like now. When it was in all its madness enough. Small boy puking, broken on the bank like the bankrupt reality of the dragon said in the schoolyard to live in the lake, like the proof of the parody that dreaming is. Like the shattered physicality of the black and bridgeless breach that yawns between want and given. Or like the malformed foetus born of bat and fire in which will grow who knows what torrid vengeance, what stricken reckoning, what terrible redress.

He vomits until there is nothing left in him to eject then lies supine for some moments as the bats flit and peep over his wrecked and shaking form and the earth cold and ancient seeps into his pores, his wounds. Then he stands on boneless legs cupping his ruined groin with his hands, holding the pain tight as if shielding it from robbery, as if ascertaining that it remains his. How he reaches home he will never remember, but he will time and time over recall his grandmother's horror as she takes in the drench of him, the bleeding of him, her panic and her old encompassing arms his wet face pressed to her flour-smelling apron, her cries and her keening. He will also recall the ambulance journey and the bright antiseptic corridors of the hospital his first time in one not excepting his birth and the worried doctors with the furrowed foreheads and the gently but insistently solicitous policemen to whom he will speak no words, not one. He will recall recovery slow and silent, his grandmother at his bedside.

HE REMEMBERS ALL this, Ianto does. Clearly and completely he remembers this. His own blood in the matted beard of the

235

grotesque circumciser, his plunge through space into water aflame, a fall which will never end: in his head he will be forever plummeting through that sunset between mountains, over water. Of these things and of others he will tell nothing because there is no need. He never much liked talking anyway, Ianto didn't. Not really.

IANTO IS TEN-AND-A-HALF.

All he will do is lie in his hospital bed and say not one word and let them do to him what they seem to feel must be done; wash him, feed him, stitch him, talk to him, inject him, stroke his brow with hands that smell of liniment. Sleeping or awake the borderline between those states blurred and smudged with the painkillers and the trauma, sleeping or awake either one the peregrines soar and swoop and savage in and around his heart and head and somewhere within him living things are impaled on rusted metal thorns, wriggling and twitching and pleading in strange high tones for a never-coming clemency. The taste of mint in his throat. Teeth glinting through a clotted beard and a burning tree talking in a tongue of snap and sizzle. Deadweight of a lamb drawing him earthwards, his little fingers in its lifeless face flicking in the ruined ooze of its brain. All of these things and more in sleeping and in waking, but he will not talk of them although he hears others talk, of 'wounds consistent with human dentition' and 'psychoneurotic aphemia' and 'motor aphasia' and 'possible brain damage' and 'tremendous shock-trauma'. Words from an alien dialect descriptive of him and of the fever and greed of human need and all its extended fallout. As people talk or as policemen or his ever-haggard grandmother sit at his bedside and watch him, watch him, he rolls his head to look sideways at the wide web on the other side of the window-glass rocked in the breeze out there, the small fat arachnid at its hub, waiting with a patience great and astounding for whatever hapless drifter happenstance of air-current may bring to its tarrying trap. Not once does he see it feed but his recovery is hastened by the spider itself, its patience, the annihilation imminent in its soft thorax throbbing and spread suspended legs. This insect his restorative, its hunger in his healing.

And he will wait like the spider for whatever the wind will bring. For however long it takes. He will wait like the spider unaccompanied except by an urge for murder for whatever the wind will bring to him, and for however long it takes. The burning in his middle.

237

—MURDER WAS-A CHARGE, wannit. Premeditated murder likes.

—Yeh.

—I mean murder! For fuck's sakes! How they could ever have thought they'd be able to get us on that one, mun . . . fuckin beyond, mun, aye . . .

—Yeh, well. Not renowned for eyr fuckin subtlety, are they, those fuckers. Whatever they think they might just be able to fuckin pin on yew they'll fuckin do it. Or try to, at least. It's just fuckin promotion for those cunts, mun, ey don't give a fuck about yew as a human being like, it's just what yew might've done to break-a law, that's all it fuckin is to them. That's all yew are to them, mun, a criminal. A perp. Nothin else, that's it. Bastards.

—Ikey got time, tho, dinny . . .

—Three years, aye.

—Yeh, but that was really just for bein Ikey, mun. Fuck-all to do with Ianto, likes. I think it was just a case of one thing too many, y'know, too many final straws.

—Only three years, tho. Not too bad, really.

—An he pulled-a trigger as well, dinny? I mean Ikey was-a one who actually, like, delivered-a killin blow. I reckon that was what swung it in-a end, like.

—An because he've had convictions for violence before likes.

—Yeh.

—Aye but so have all of us, mun. Sept for Danny.

—No, I have. GBH when I was sixteen, seventeen. Twice. At Anfield.

—None of us anywhere near as much as Ikey, mun. His go back twenty fuckin years, boy.

—Three years, tho . . . that's no time at all; not so much a sentence as a couple-a words like. Tellin yew, nick is fuckin easy, mun. Get stoned all day, lie on yewer bunk readin porn

. . . piece-a fuckin piss, boy. Ikey'll be havin a fuckin whale of a time in yer, mun, no fuckin worries.

—It was eight at first, tho, wannit? Eight years like, commuted to three on appeal. Public fuckin uproar, mun. Crown Prosecution Service shat emselves.

—Extenuating circumstances likes.

—Still far too fuckin long if yew ask me. Should-a got a fuckin medal, mun, for what we did.

—Yeh, public fuckin service like, that's what we did. Murder my fuckin arse'ole.

—Kept-a streets safe.

—Well, the mountains moren-a streets like. An they've *never* been bastard safe.

—Nah, it was only a matter-a time before Ianto took to-a streets, mun, fuckin tellin yew. Fuckin Yorkshire Ripper, Fred West, Dennis fuckin Nielsen; fuckin cunt would've been up yer with those perverts, mun, too fuckin right. Mark my bleedin words.

—Yeh.

—Remember that twat of a judge?

—Christ aye. Fuckin ponce he was, mun, wanny?

—'Ay hev nevah in all may yahs seen a case of satch vio-lence end deprav-it-ehhh . . . thet this should hap-pen in ah civi-lised countreh hin this day end age beggahs may be-lief . . .' Fuckin knob-end he was, aye. Knew fuck all, mun. Hadn't a bastard clew.

—Yeh. Fuckin typical, tho, wanny; typical of all-a sheltered upper-class cunts who sit in judgement on us scum. Fuckin clewless, mun, all of um. Without fuckin exception. A whole bastard system needs revision. A whole thing's fucked up big style.

—Ianto should-a murdered some-a *those* fuckers, in my opinion likes. Stead-a fuckin innocent schoolkids an women.

—Least that judge let us off, tho. Most-a them wouldn't uv.

—Apart from Ikey.

—Well, he suspended ar sentences, like. Not really lettin us off, is it?

—Fuck all else he could do, boy. I mean, imagine-a uproar like

239

if he had've given us custodial. Fuckin chaos, mun, it would've been. The whole fuckin country was behind us, on ar side, like.

—Yeh. Remember-a demonstration outside-a courthouse? All them placards . . . the people chanting . . .

—An-a TV cameras an stuff. Felt fuckin great it did, all that support, likes.

—Imagine, tho . . . I mean, d'yew think we'd still be yer, free likes, if Ianto hadn't've been Ianto? If he'd've been, likes, the son of a high-rankin copper or lawyer or fuckin councillor or somethin? Regardless of what he'd done, likes, murder or rape or anythin, I doubt very fuckin much that we'd all be sittin yer now gettin wrecked an talkin if Ianto had've been, like, higher up on-a social scale. It was just cos he was homeless, a tramp like, that we weren't fuckin imprisoned. Another beggar off-a streets, that's what *those* twats thought, mun.

—Fuckin right there, Danny, yew are. A student or somethin, one of-a rich kids like an we'd all be inside now. Oh yeh.

—Wouldn't bother me, mun. Time's fuckin easy. Told yew.

—How long did yew do then, Griff?

—Four years. Six-year sentence, like, for dealin E an I was out in just under four with a pair-a fuckin biceps like an some very fuckin lucrative contacts. Met some-a me best customers in Swansea nick, I did. Picked up some valuable fuckin info n all. Tellin yew, nick's a best fuckin place for it, mun. It's like goin to college.

—Yeh, well, the decision was a right one, I say.

—What? Yew cunt, six fuckin years for dealin E? For givin people what they want?

—Nah, not *yew*, Griff, I'm talkin about *us*, mun. Us an Ianto. The suspended sentences like.

—Oh. Fuckin lucky there, Llŷr, I was just about to fuckin lamp yew one I was. No harm done, like. But yewer still talkin shite tho. No fuckin punishment at all would-a been-a right decision, mun. Pat on-a bastard back more like.

—Yeh. An we weren't the fuckin killers were we? I mean-a *real* killers like. The murderers.

—No.

240

—Ianto was. Ianto was the only killer, the murderer, really. Strictly speakin likes.

—Do yew, erm, do yew, likes, ever sort of miss im?

—Who? Ikey?

—No. Ianto.

—Ianto? Miss *that* cunt? Fuck off. He was a murderer, Danny, a bastard pervert. How can yew miss someone like that? How can yew even *say* such a thing, mun?

—Yeh. I mean all-a times he was with us at parties an stuff, sittin round drinkin he had-a blood of innocents on his hands. Schoolboy's blood, women's blood. All them times yew were havin a laugh with im he was plannin his next fuckin murder. Jesus, how-a fuck can yew miss someone like that? Yew must be sick in-a bleedin head n all, mun. Jesus.

—I never said that I *do* miss im, did I? I just asked. All's I said was –

—That's what yew were fuckin gettin at, tho. That's what yew *really* wanted to say.

—No it wasn't. What I was buildin up to ask was if any of yew are, like, at all sorry about what happened, that's all. Wasn't goin to say I missed Ianto in-a bleedin slightest. Fuck's sakes, Marc, let people fuckin speak before yew jump to-a wrong fuckin conclusions, eh?

—We've been through all this shite before, haven't we? Loads-a times.

—What?

—Eh?

—Been through what?

—The fuckin, the 'sorry' aspect.

—Well, are yew?

—What? Sorry?

—Yeh.

—*Fuck* no. I'd do the exact same thing all over again if I had to. Course I fuckin would. I think evryone else'll agree with me as well.

—Yeh. She was only a young fuckin woman, that one, in-a mine like. And Ianto had killed her and fuckin, he'd *interfered* with her, probably even *after* she was dead. So no, of course I'm

241

not fuckin sorry. I'm fuckin *glad*. World's a better place without sick fuckers like that.

—Yeh. I mean, how can anyone allow a pervert like that to live, likes? Bleedin sicko he was. Who knows what would've happened if we hadn't've stopped it then? Who knows what that sick bastard would've gone on to do?

—Aye. Psychopath, see. Yew never know what those fuckers are goin to do next, mun. No reason to em, see. No fuckin logic, likes. Jesus, it could've been one of *us* he took a fuckin rock to next. Or someone like Gwenno, with a knife or an axe or whatever he took a fuckin fancy to. Out of control, see. Psychopath, no other bloody word for it mun. Pure bleedin psychopath.

—Aw Christ . . . imagine him with that woman like . . . after he'd bashed her brains in he must've dragged her into that mine and pulled er clothes off like an –

—Aw, Marc, for fucks sake! Dirty twat! Don't be fuckin disgusting!

—Well, that's what-a busies reckoned like, they reckoned that he –

—Yeh yeh, mun, we know what they said. We all read-a fuckin reports, we were all in court as well. Yer's no need to go bleedin on about it like. Sick as *he* was yew are, mun, Christ.

—Yewer arse. I wouldn't've done what I did, wouldn't've, like, got so fuckin angry with Ianto if I had've been as fucked up as him, would I? Would've fuckin joined him if I was like him, mun. Would've done-a same fuckin things, like. Any idiot can see that.

—Takes a rare fuckin kind of person to do those things tho, mun. Yer's not many of us capable.

—Thank fuck.

—Yeh.

—So that's it, then, we're agreed: yer's nowt for any of us to be sorry about?

—We've been through all this, Danny. Again an again. Gettin fuckin on me wick it is.

—I know, yeh, but I just want to get it straight in me head. It's like –

242

—Danny, yewer *stoned*, mun. How can anythin be straight in yewer head at this moment in time? We've been smokin for fuckin hours, mun. Liam Herlihy's fuckin superskunk as well.

—The only thing to be sorry about is that, as a result of it all, Gwenno's not yer with us. She was great, Gwenno was. I liked Gwenno.

—So did I. An she liked me n all.

—Oh shut the fuck up, Marc. Annoyin little tosser.

—It was sad, wannit, what happened to Gwenno. The treatment an all that, like. The psychiatric treatment.

—Yeh. Post-traumatic stress disorder they called it. What people in wars suffer from like. Must've really fucked her up, I reckon.

—Saddest fuckin thing was her movin to England.

—Yeh. Whereabouts was it again?

—Dunno. Somewhere down south. Surrey, Sussex . . . one-a those places.

—Fuck. That *is* sad.

—Yeh. She must've been *really* fucked up by it all to move down yer likes. God.

—Needed to forget, see? Had to put a tidy distance between herself an where it all happened like. Only way to get over it, mun.

—Yeh, but . . . fuckin *Surrey*? Christ, mun. She must've gone bastard insane.

—Maybe she did.

—Yeh. I miss her, I do. I liked Gwenno.

—I . . .

—Shut it, Marc. Don't say a fuckin word.

—Yeh, Marc, just shut-a fuck up, mun. She went off her bleedin head an all yew can do is go on about how yew shagged er once. Which she told me was a crap experience anyway.

—It's all over, mun. Move on like, innit.

—Yer's one thing I can't stop thinkin about, tho . . .

—Oh aye? An what's that, Danny?

—Ah no, don't fuckin ask him. He'll come out with some bleedin mystical crap or something. Some fuckin social worker bollax.

243

—No, go on, Danny. Tell us, mun.

—Well . . . it's like, I mean, we're all sittin yer talkin about Ianto, like, aren't we?

—Yeh, so?

—An we've done this loads-a times before an we'll probly do it loads-a times again, in-a future like. Won't we?

—So fuckin what?

—Well, like, it's like I can't help thinkin that even tho Ianto's dead, we're all still talkin about him. An not just us, either; I mean, his name still crops up in-a papers sometimes an I'm not just talkin about-a local ones, I mean-a national ones as well. Even on-a bastard telly sometimes. An it seems to me like that he's kind of, like, still fuckin alive in some ways, he's still livin on. Even tho he's dead. An that when *we* die an become fuckin wormshit or dust in-a wind or whatever then people'll still be talkin about Ianto, he'll still be kind of here an remembered when the only fuckin proof that *we* ever bleedin existed will be ar names engraved on ar bastard tombstones. So I'm thinkin like, that, well, despite all the sick shit he got up to, hasn't Ianto fuckin succeeded in some ways? I mean, he's gonner be remembered. He already *is* remembered. He lived a crazy fuckin life. An int that what we all want, really, like, deep down inside? To live a crazy life? To be remembered, remarked upon? To live ar lives in such a way that we'll be remembered an talked about, ar names known long after we die? Int that what we all fuckin live for? What we all try to achieve? I mean, fuck, how can we ever stand it, to be ordinary. How can we ever fuckin bear it, not to be remarkable, likes, not to be fuckin . . . marvellous. It's all fuckin shite mun. The whole bleedin world is.

—. . . Jesus Christ.

—Fucks sake, Danny. That weed yewer smokin must be fuckin strong.

—Have yew yerd this shite, Griff?

—I fuckin well av, Marc, aye. An I'll tell yew one fuckin thing, Danny; yew ever come out with bollax like that again an I'll fuckin well murder yew myself. I fuckin well will, mun. I'm not fuckin jokin yer. I mean it; I'll put yew to fuckin death myself if I ever hear yew comin out with shite like that again.

244

THEY MOVE UP the dingle in an irregular horizontal, a rough phalanx picking and eating psilocybin mushrooms as they climb, bending to pluck at intervals each one to their own, like courting birds or labourers of this harsh land. It is a rare rainless day up here and the heath of tangled brown desiccated vegetation crackles underfoot like frosted grass, their heads bent, eyes downcast like supplicants to this brittle flooring to search for the extruding thin-stemmed brown nipples of the prized fungus. They have been doing this for quite some hours and on occasion one or another of them can be heard to giggle.

Llŷr is carrying his rifle at port arms like some ragged auxiliary and he slips it under his long canvas coat as a police helicopter whups overhead. He watches it pass above and then over the estuary, the sun bounced back off its rotors and when it is some distance away, small in the sky, he puts the rifle to his shoulder and takes aim at the flying machine.

—Christ no, Llŷr, don't, Fran says worried, mushroom stalks on her lips like parasitic worms. —Don't be bloody stupid.

Llŷr just makes a gunshot sound with his lips and grins at her.

—Wouldn't do fuck all anyway, Ikey says. —Not with *that* fuckin popgun like. Might as well use a bastard pea-shooter.

—Yewer arse. Llŷr looks insulted, offended. Holds the gun protectively to his chest. —Browning fuckin twelve this is, mun. Powerful fuckin weapon.

—Browning twelve, eh? Griff sidles over towards them, compressing a mass of mushrooms in his large hand into one swallowable lump. —Aren't they dead valuable? Int that worth something, then?

Llŷr hugs his gun tighter. —Worth more to me than any fuckin collector or Cash Converter, mun. It was me grandad's, this was, see. In-a war like. En*trusted* it to me he did an no fucker else.

Jane shakes her head. —Shouldn't've bloody taken it. Dangerous fuckin things they are.

245

Llŷr smiles bemused. —Well that's kind of-a whole fuckin point, Jane, see. I mean what good would a gun be if it wasn't dangerous?

—Aye. It'd just be a stick. Griff nods and looks to Ikey for confirmation, but Ikey is leering at Llŷr's gun as he might at pornography.

—It's old now, tho, Llŷr continues. —Started to lose its bore a bit now, started to shoot a bit to-a left, like, so yew have to compensate.

—What, yew mean like aim *further* to-a left than yew normally would? Ikey asks, his eyes not leaving the gun.

—To-a right, Ike, to-a right. If it pulls to-a left then yew aim to-a right, don't yew? Otherwise yewer gonner miss by fuckin miles.

—Ah.

Llŷr again raises the rifle to his shoulder and sights along the barrel, this time at a partridge flying and peeping overhead on stubby and frantic wings. He tracks it with the gun, swinging from the waist to follow it: —Oh aye, fuckin dead shot with this I yam, fuckin dead shot. Clint fuckin Eastwood, mun. Takin robins out-a the trees at thirty feet when I was seven, me. Me an my grandad like. Used to say I had a 'sniper's eye'.

He lowers the gun and winks at Fran.

—Long as yew can look after my stash, Ikey says, —that's all I'm worried about. Any fuckers rooting around up yer an I wanner see yew take some fuckin kneecaps off. That's my ticket to better times up yer, mun, that is. My summer in fuckin Ibiza. No cunt fucks around with that.

Danny and Marc and Gwenno and Ianto stand looking out over the estuary far below. The immense space before them seems to ripple and shimmer and flow, the sun-scaled water and the white dune swells beyond and the hazy blue rises of the mountains beyond them. It all seems to wobble before them like a mirage and to drift and split and run towards the horizon, but when they blink and shake their heads and look back again it is as before, solid and massive and awesome. Utterly unbudgeable, no millennia will scratch it.

—Amazing fuckin colours, Gwenno says softly. —Amazing fuckin . . . *space* . . . the light, like . . .

Danny nods in agreement stoned-solemn and Marc giggles and takes two steps closer to Gwenno. She glances at him and her lips tighten and she puts her arm around Ianto.

—Yew alright then, Ianto?

He swallows and nods.

—Only yew seem a bit quiet today, like. Worried about somethin. Yew sure yewer OK now? Yer's nothin botherin yew?

He shakes his head and looks over his shoulder at the rise of the dingle, green rise smoothly up to the cloudless blue and what he knows waits up there, but he will say no words. His throat is dry and his pulse is racing and his heart trips and thumps in his chest like a brick in a cement mixer, but he will say no words, no words.

—It's just-a fuckin mushies, innit, Marc leers. —Can't fuckin handle them can yew, Ianto?

—Bollax, Danny says. —He've eaten five to every one-a yours, an yew, Ianto? It's *yew* that carn take um, Marc. Yewer-a only bloody amateur up yer, likes.

Ikey and Griff and Llŷr and Fran and Jane walk past them upwards and in single file.

—Yew coming? Jane asks.

—Aye, or are yew gonner stand yer all fuckin day an admire-a pretty view? There is something resembling a snarl on Ikey's face. He is unusual in that any drug natural or synthetic possessed of sedative or soporific or calming qualities for others only works in him like gasoline on embers. He is or will be relaxed only in unconsciousness or death.

Like a small and shabby platoon they climb the sloping dingle, some of them sweating and panting with exertion, others pulling themselves upwards with their hands. Llŷr holds his rifle by the barrel and uses it like a staff and Ikey tuts and shakes his head at this disrespect and simply surges upwards in huge ground-gulping strides, his face agleam with perspiration. At the top of the dingle he holds his hand out towards Fran for her to take and she does and he drags her to him, pressing her to his chest with his arm her small frame engulfed in his.

—Oof, watch yourself yer, Ikey says. —Nearly got yewerself impaled yer, girlie.

Fran laughs.

The others breast the rise and most collapse wheezing on to the dry grass, lying spreadeagled and damp with dew, wet with sweat. Red-faced, whooshing air up skywards, their chests heaving like bellows. Ianto stares down the dingle at the distant roof of Llŷr's cottage like a crossword grid, some slates missing and Jane's tight T-shirt is glued to her skin and she pulls it away from her body with a soft slurping sound and then sighs in pleasure as the cool air licks her skin, and seeing this Griff rolls over on to his belly to peer down her top and Marc looks for Gwenno and sees her and attempts to move to stand beside her, but Llŷr intercepts.

—Yer, Ianto, watch this.

He raises the gun to his shoulder yet again and sights along it at a soaring buzzard. Ianto watches him dead-eyed.

—Don't be such a twat, Gwenno says. —Leave-a bird alone, mun. He's just out lookin for his tea. Done fuck all to yew. Leave him alone.

Llŷr lowers his rifle and grins. —I'd shoot-a fucker normally like, but I don't wanner see Ianto yer cry, likes. An he would as well, wouldn't yew, mun? Blub like a fuckin babby yew would, aye.

No sound from Ianto nor change of expression impassive, unreadable on his face. Llŷr pokes his tongue out at him and ruffles his hair and moves on to catch up with Ikey and they all follow him, some groaning at the resumption of activity although the ground here now is relatively level, and soon they are talking and giggling again and remarking on the colours of flowers and sky. Someone says loudly in a strange, strained voice that none of the others recognise: —I'm seein all kinds of weird things up yer, and those within earshot laugh in reply and look around for a speaker but cannot discern one.

—An what kind-a things would they be, then? Danny asks no one in particular, although if the direction of his gaze gives any indication of the direction of his question, then he asks it of the horizon. —Hills, like, an grass? Flowers? Mountains? Oh fuck aye I'm seein plenty-a them as well, mun. A few people, too, an some clouds. Fuck knows how *they* got up yer like.

They move onwards grouped loosely around the small sheep-gnawed hillock in the far lee of which squats the house of Ianto's childhood. There are some large cars and motorbikes parked in the driveway of this newly extended dwelling. The garden is empty of people, but there is the tinny sound of football commentary and the background crowd roar coming from one of the windows.

—Who's playin today, then? Llŷr asks.

Danny shrugs. —Some fuckin England friendly I think. Chile or someone like that.

—Ah well. Come on yew South Americans in that case, Griff says. —I'll never say another word against yew Spic fuckers if yew beat-a fuckin Sais.

—Ey, Ianto, yer's yewer chance. Llŷr holds his gun out towards Ianto as if offering its use. —Go on, mun, have a few shots. See how many of-a cunts yew can pick off eh? Do a fuckin Hungerford, mun, yer's yewer chance. Take it.

Grinning Ianto reaches out to take the weapon, but Danny darts between him and Llŷr and slaps Ianto's hand away.

—Jesus, Llŷr, how fuckin stewpid are yew, mun?

Llŷr just smiles.

—Yew know how Ianto feels about this fuckin place, boy, yer's no need to fuckin wind him up. Fuckin temptin him like. Yew silly bleedin twat. What-a yew tryin-a stir up fuckin trouble for eh? Christ, we're just fuckin chillin, mun, just havin a fuckin mellow one. Get a grip.

Ikey appears.

—What's goin on yer?

—Nothin much. Danny flaps his hands at Llŷr. —Just that silly bastard actin-a cunt. Told him not to bring that fuckin gun of his I did, Duw. Fuckin knob-end. Fuckin head-the-ball yew are, Llŷr.

Llŷr just smiles once more and Ianto looks disappointed, his lower lip jutting, but he does drop his hand away from the rifle. Danny stumbles across a small cluster of mushrooms like little

249

attentive coolies and wordlessly they all drop to all fours and grab at the ground and gobble from their hands like jackals, like pack beasts at a kill, until the fungi are eaten and then they all rise as one still wordlessly, dirt on their chins and lips grey spores on their grinning teeth, and move on. Ianto has a sense in him of some giant looming spirit sitting atop the mountain before him and scrutinising him and only him, his movements and his panic mounting and maybe that presence is the mountain itself cognisant of his deeds and his reaching and the starless darkness inside his heart maybe made blacker in him than in most others or maybe not. He feels that the mountain may at any moment grind and gape open to suck him in and swallow him and a quiet horror thumps in his skull and this feeling will not pass, even when Gwenno drops away from Marc's side and falls back to link her arm through his this feeling will not pass nor dissipate.

—Bit fuckin touchy-feely today then, arn yew? Griff looks puzzled. —Bloody Ianto don't know what to do, do yew, boy?

Ianto shakes his head quite vigorously, although it is in reponse to some other question silent and heard only by him alone, and Griff snorts and shakes his head also. They move past the charred and twisted tree a tangled nest in its warped limbs and Ianto looks up at it and whimpers in his throat and Gwenno looks at him concerned. He smells again ozone in his nostrils, hears the crazed screeching of the carrion bird, black-beaked blinder and feels again the downward pressure, twenty-year-old muscle memory, on his arm his entire body from the dead lamb. Panic rises from his groin to his throat sizzling in his face about to spit from his mouth, but he swallows it back, gulping rapidly as if suppressing a gag reflex, until it is gone or is at least temporarily quitened. The mellowness of the mushrooms in him, the torpor of the fungi has become something quite else, has curdled in the fevered brewery of him and is fermenting at searing speed. He feels the heat, judders with each bubble ballooning and bursting. Can both taste and smell the foul and heavy sediment produced, it sinking to settle in his stomach and give off its sharp poisons in a hiss.

—How far now? Fran asks. —Bloody knackered I am. Want-a sit down.

The dark oblong of the doorway to the old mine rises up over the groundswell like the unobtrusive entrance to an underworld and Ianto's eyes widen and again there is some noise in his throat very like a whimpering. Gwenno nudges him gently, but receives no response, and the doorway grows in his vision, stretches like pitch, spreads like bitumen.

—We're yer, more or less, Ikey says in answer to Fran. —Might as well have a seat aye. I'll go an fetch me stash.

They all sink to the ground with relief and Ianto watches Ikey walk towards the dark doorway and stands suddenly not knowing what he is going to do, run maybe, but Ikey veers away from that awful portal towards the fallen tree by it and squats and reaches under the shed-sized tentacled football like a giant Medusa head or some horrible terrestrial squid and gropes around under there and then extracts a plastic bag. He stands grinning, holding the bag up for all to see, and then returns back up the rise towards them and Ianto sits back down again.

—That it, is it? Marc asks.

—Yeh. Me stash. Ikey sits on the grass among them and begins to undo the knot that keeps the bag closed and water-tight.

—Dodgy fuckin place to keep it, mun. Whyn't yew hide it in that old mineshaft yer?

Ikey snorts. —Fuckin dangerous in yer, boy. Unsound like. Fuckin place could collapse or flood at any moment like, bury me fuckin livelihood under tons-a bastard rubble.

He delves and extracts from the bag a Tupperware sandwich box and takes out of that another, smaller plastic bag, this one transparent and ziplocked, in which small white pills are clustered like captured hail. He cups this bag in two huge hands and smiles down at it, caressing it with his thumbs. —Yer we are . . . one hundred an twenty five white doves. One hundred an twenty five little fuckin beauties. Ese are my fuckin summer holiday, ese are; two weeks on Ibiza in this yer bag, mun. My ticket-a better fuckin times like.

Jane holds her hand out. —Let's av one, then.

Danny and Fran and Marc copy her beseeching movement and Ikey looks at them incredulous.

—Got money then, av yew? Ten pounds each like?

251

—Back in town I yav, Fran says. —Not on me like.

—Yeh. I'll box yew off later. Marc twitches his fingers impatiently.

Ikey puts the small bag of pills in the breast pocket of his brown-checked shirt and buttons it closed and pats it. A breeze tumbles the larger bag away over the hill. —Well, yew'll get yewer pills when yew give me-a money. Simple as fuckin that.

—Aw Ikey, mun! Yew know we'll settle up, like! Be fuckin daft not to, wouldn't we?

—Yew fuckin *know* yew would, Marc, aye. Mate or no, I'd snap yewer bleedin arm like a bastard twig if yew ever tried-a rip me off. Fuckin ruthless in business that's me, mun, aye. Got to be, see.

—Yeh, an I know that full well. Which is why I'll be sure to pay yew, later, likes. Just ant got-a readies on me at the mo likes. C'mon Ikey, mun. Yew know I'm good for it.

Ikey shakes his head. —I'm takin no risks. Been ripped off too many fuckin times I yav. Say I give yew a pill now. Say yew don't pay me. I come after yew an break yewer bleedin arms, what then? Yew've got two broken arms an I'm *still* a fuckin tenner short. He shakes his head again and repeats: —Oh no. I'm takin no bleedin risks.

He lies on his back with his arms crossed and supporting his head. His shirt rides up to expose a few inches of his hairy slab of a belly. —I'm takin no risks, he says for a third time. —Just wait till later, likes. Anyway, why-a yew all so fuckin desperate for a pill? Duw, yew must be full-a fuckin mushies, likes, all-a yew. Mushies not fuckin good enough for yew then?

Jane shakes her head. —They're fuckin hittin me wrong today like . . . I'm gettin, like, thoughts . . . wish I'd never bastard eaten um now. She holds up a hand in front of her pale face and stares at it, twisting it on her wrist.

Fran shuffles over to her on the cheeks of her arse to sit close. The same strange voice as before declaims the same strange statement: —I'm seein all kinds of weird things up yer I yam, but this time it elicits no laughter, no response except a mild collective shudder and a tacit group decision to ignore it. A cloud drifts across the sun and a shadow rushes down the valley like a flash flood of thin ink and the temperature takes a slight but noticeable drop. Below the rise on which they sit a flock of some small colourful birds rises from the peat bog as if spooked and flies chirruping away over the moorland, the purple heather and the duller green encroaching rye grass. A wind passes over the people, rippling hair and clothes and moans low for a moment like an emanation of pain and then is gone.

Gwenno snuggles in tighter to Ianto.

—Why d'yew keep lookin over yer, at that old mine, like? Thinkin of explorin it are yew? Ianto shakes his head and doesn't look at her. —No, it's just I . . .

—Ah yeh, yew grew up round yer, didn't yew? Loads-a memories for yew up yer, I suppose.

Marc splutters. —Fuckin Ianto grew up nowhere, Gwenno, mun. He was born a fucked-up adult, he was, if 'adult's' a right term like. Ianto was never a fuckin kiddie, no way. Dragged himself out of that fuckin peat bog over yer, he did.

Gwenno scowls at Marc. —Sod off yew. Ianto's-a only one among yew who makes *me* feel safe today, in that right, Ianto?

With one hand on his rigid chin she gently pulls Ianto's face her way and cranes her neck to kiss him on the lips. Tongueless and with mouth closed but a kiss nonetheless and Ianto's stiff and set body relaxes visibly, his chest deflating, his shoulders softening, and he stares at Gwenno's face a small smile playing around his stubbled lips, soil-stained, for the first time it seems in days.

—I get like this on mushies, Gwenno whispers to his cheek. —Get all . . . *friendly* like. She twirls a finger in Ianto's dirty hair. —Ah, yewer a nice boy really, Ianto, arn yew. Not like all-a others. Not really, like.

Marc shakes his head, his lips pursed. —Christ. That's disgusting.

Gwenno turns on him. —Sooner kiss Ianto than *yew*.

—Yeh. Not what yew said at Llŷr's house last month tho, was it? Oh fuck no. Nothing of-a sort then, oh no. Course, yew were ard pressed to say anything at all, what with yewer gob bein so full an that, aye?

—Up yewer arse. Twat.

She stands and pulls Ianto up beside her by the hand. —Come

253

on, Ianto. Let's get away from this sad fucker. Let's go an explore the cave.

She begins to lead him off downslope towards the disused silver mine and he follows dumbly along for a few yards then stops suddenly digging his heels in and tries to pull her back.

—No, not in yer. I can't fuckin go in yer.

She tries to pull him, but he digs his heels in further. A small trough of scraped-bare mud behind each boot.

—Why not? What's wrong? Are yew scared?

He shakes his head.

—Aw, yer's nowt to be scared of, mun. It's just an old mine, like, it probably comes to-a stop about ten yards in. Let's go an see. Yer might be treasure.

Ianto shakes his head vigorously a mewling sound in his throat and tries to drag Gwenno back up the hill.

—Ianto, mun, what's wrong with yew? What's-a matter like? Let go of my arm, mun. Yewer hurting me!

She yanks her hand free of Ianto's desperate grip and stands there regarding him puzzled, rubbing her shoulder with her right hand. Ianto does and indeed can do nothing but stand there, his jaws working, looking back whimpering at her, his arms hanging limply at his sides, his hands clenching and unclenching rapidly, a tremor in his knees his buttocks tightening to counteract the dilation of his sphincter.

Gwenno's face creases into a smile. —Ah, yewer really that scared? Duw, it's just-a hole in-a ground, mun, that's all it is. Yer's nothin to be scared of. Big baby.

She reaches out and strokes Ianto's face, once.

—God, yewer really fuckin scared, aren't yew? Poor sausage. Yer, I'll tell yew what; I'll go in first an yew follow me in. I'll tell yew if yer's any devils or monsters in yer aye? It'll be alright, honest. Don't yew worry. To show yew yer's nothin to be afraid of I'll go in on my own.

She turns and walks jaunty down the slope. Ianto raises one hand slowly and holds it in mid-air at chest height for a few seconds then drops it again. Behind him for some reason unknown the others stand as one, their hair rising and falling in the breeze, and they and he together watch Gwenno, the back

254

of her blue jeans and grey fleece and hair the colour of a cut, approach the black rectangle at the threshold of which she turns to smile and wave at them and beckon with a hand at Ianto, then she turns again and is engulfed by that oblong darkness upright like a standing grave. For a few seconds her bright hair flickers in the murk then that too is gone.

The wind whistles through the long grass and between the still legs of the people standing like statues, like sentinels, menhirs carved not from rock but from flesh and bone and glyphed with scar and pimple and pockmark. A lone raven soars croaking through the blue air above them and the high sun unveiled once more and brightness washes the mountainside and the dingle and the immense estuary below that too but the cool wind does not cease blowing. A faint splashing is heard from within the old mine. Danny asks of no one in particular what is going on and receives no reply.

There is a high noise in Ianto's throat which he cannot stop. A keening, a heaving. What he knows is that he is about to be stolen from himself perhaps for the final time and that nothing here no mountain or bird or blade of grass and certainly no human can forestall or prevent that horror and there is a maelstrom in his diaphragm and the thin piss of discovery hotly broths his crotch and thighs. For the first time in his life he experiences himself as utterly empty and he would if he could make himself even less, a figure of twig and reed, man of ash or grass or even boneless wraith, mere being of flaccid gas from bodies long rotten. Reduce himself into nothingness.

Another splash comes from the mineshaft, a heavier one this time and turgid as if made by the movement not of water but of mercury and then too a low moan, a rising and falling low moan. For a third time the odd thin voice says: —I'm seein all kinds of weird things up yer, and then there is a glint of grey in the gloom of the mine entrance and Gwenno materialises out of that blackness and stands unsteady in the sunlight, something wrapped around her wet lower leg and boot that looks like a decaying silver eel. She sways for a moment supporting herself with one hand on the exposed taproot of the fallen tree looking with lidded eyes at nothing, then she moans again and buckles

255

to her knees and spews up in the grass. The others instantly run towards her around Ianto, who stands still and stares, observes. He sees them cluster around Gwenno, her on all fours her back rippling as she heaves, Jane and Fran squatting concerned at her side. She points at the mineshaft almost casually and Griff and Ikey and Danny disappear in there and Marc and Llŷr stand watching. Danny re-appears greenfaced with his hand to his mouth and Ikey's face rises in the darkness over his shoulder like a moon to stare for a few moments out at Ianto then it vanishes again. Marc and Llŷr look back over their shoulders at Ianto, their faces set and unreadable, then they scurry backwards out of the way as Ikey and Griff back out of the mineshaft dragging a bloated spongy corpse a foot in each hand. Griff falls flat on his arse as the foot slobbers away in his grip and a cloud of small black flies rise whining and stench spreads and Ianto sees the cheesy bloodless stump ruffled with adipocere mould protruding from the cushioned cuff of the hiking boot in Griff's lap. Griff stares down at it almost paternally for a few moments then he yells and scrambles backwards the foot following him and he yells again louder and stands and the foot falls and splats to the ground in a small splash of milky liquid. Gwenno is now clinging to the fallen tree as if to a life-raft and Fran and Jane are holding each other and Ikey drops the body, leaving it half in and half out of the darkness like some serpent centaur of shade and he steps over it back into the mine. Danny leans and vomits on to the exposed legs of the carcass and Marc and Llŷr watch the dark entrance Llŷr's rifle supported on his shoulder as if at drill and Ikey re-appears with a bundled blue jacket, which he holds up by the arms spread out stinking and dripping for them all to see. He looks wordlessly at Llŷr, who shakes his head rapidly and Ianto can hear his protest, thin but convincing on the lifting wind:

—It's not fucking mine! Ianto took it! It's his! He fucking took it off me, I don't wear it any more, see! *He* does!

He points over his shoulder at Ianto and Ikey nods as if in stern approval and tosses the sodden garment back over his shoulder into the mineshaft and it splashes in the blackness behind him. He strides up the slope towards Ianto, his hands rigid at his sides and splay-fingered and dripping, and Marc and Llŷr fall into step

256

behind him and Danny leans back against the mineshaft wall, his torso heaving, and watches them. Gwenno has her face in her hands and Fran and Jane, still holding on to each other, turn their heads like frightened primates to stare at the standing, static Ianto.

Ianto's feet shift slightly in the small puddle of piss he has produced. Ikey looms in his eyes, growing bigger, Marc and Llŷr at his shoulders like henchmen their faces ashen and drained.

—That's yewer jacket, Ianto, in-a mine like, Ikey says in a voice matter-of-fact and toneless. —Yer's two fuckin bodies in yer as well. What d'yew know about this? One of em's a woman. Half naked like. Looks like she've been fuckin molested or somethin. What in-a name of *fuck* have yew been bastard doin, mun?

Ianto gulps and his lips wobbles. Ikey's face is immense in his, stubbled and pockmarked and bloodshot and behind and to the left of this giant face stand Marc and Llŷr like a pair of Satans. They look utterly alien to Ianto, completely unfamiliar, in no way like themselves. Their green faces split and swim in Ianto's vision. The wind whistles in his ears.

Ikey pushes Ianto's chest and at this contact he whimpers and rocks back on his heels.

—What-a fuck have yew been doin, Ianto, mun? Two dead people likes. A woman's been fuckin raped by-a looks-a things n all. What the *fuck* do yew know about this, Ianto?

All Ianto can do is shake his head. Words are like hiccups in his throat.

—Fuckin pervert, Marc snarls over Ikey's shoulder. Green his face and black his lips like some reptile, some demon, the barrel of Llŷr's gun sticking up behind his head like a thick and twitching antenna.

—It's him, Ikey, Llŷr says. —Fuckin Ianto, mun. *He* did it, mun. Must've.

—Knew it all along, I did, Griff says, appearing suddenly at Ianto's side and sending a jolt through his body. —Fuckin *knew* yer was somethin wrong with this cunt. Fuckin sicko aye. Knew it was only a matter-a time before he did something like this. Too fuckin right, mun.

257

Griff's breath is fetid fire on Ianto's trembling cheek. Ikey's face in his is the size of a mountain, a moon; Ianto can see every tiny crater, every veined tributary, every red delta and blackhead. His eyes scan the ill skin avidly and greedily as if seeking for some refuge there in the cracks and flakes of Ikey's lips or the small shrivelled pips of dried mucus in the tearducts of his eyes.

Ianto finds words, a mere two: —I . . . never . . .

Ikey shoves him again. —Never fuckin what, mun? Never fuckin what? Why's yewer fuckin jacket in that mine? Eh? DID YEW FUCKIN RAPE THAT WOMAN?

The brown grouting of his teeth.

—WHAT THE FUCK HAVE YEW BEEN FUCKIN DOIN IANTO?

Ianto gulps, a sound of collapse, the sound of something deflating or buckling and suddenly Gwenno shrieks:

—IT WAS HIM! IANTO! IANTO KILLED THEM!

Ear-scraping and horrible, ear-splitting and before he knows what he is doing Ianto is screaming too, his hands clasped at his chest as if in prayer and his voice creaking and arid as if in rusted disuse:

—I had to do it! I fuckin *had* to do it! They fuckin *made* me! They wouldn't fuckin leave me alone! They followed me all-a fuckin time! I had to fuckin stop them, they –

—Sick fuck!

—What have yew been *doing* Ianto!

—Did yew kill those people? Did yew fuckin RAPE THAT WOMAN?

Ianto opens his mouth again but only a scream exits, shrieking and deafening like the sounds the warplanes make perhaps a terrible distortion of one affirmative word:

—YYYEEEEEEEEEEEEEEEEEEEEEEEEEEEEEEEEEEEEEEE

And the first punch lifts him airborne and he slams on to his back with the air leaving his lungs in a slow groan like a sigh of relief. He sees the sole of an Adidas trainer raised above him, the sun around it like a halo, one white worm wriggling in its tread, and then there is a detonation in his skull and he is swallowing teeth and blood in swelling blackness. The butt of Llŷr's gun shatters his cheekbone and then his nose once and once again this second time swelling the flesh around his eye, ballooning it, the sky and the mountains and the plunging limbs disappearing to Ianto, becoming lost in a rising flag of red mist black-bordered, the blue sky above and the lone impatient buzzard circling fading, fading. He flops like a beached fish on to his side and sees a small black beetle on its back legs kicking in a dark red puddle and grass stems huge like trees, all this vanishing beneath a spreading blooming blackness and he is turned and dragged aimlessly this way, that way over the ground, his limbs yanked and wrenched and turned in their sockets and a kick bursts his eardrum. He vomits blood. The thick black waters gush into his eyes, gulping his vision and boots stamp on his skull his back his ankles breaking them with the sound of wood snapping and his left arm is fractured over a knee. They kick his ribs until they give and he belches what looks like tar and a mighty boot from someone turns him over on to his back again sightless, gurgling, the sky and the mountains fleeing from him, going. His head is pulled by a female hand until a tussock of his hair comes away in those painted fingers trailing a ragged patch of spurting scalp and his eyes are swollen completely shut revealing to him nothing now, showing to him nothing now but that darkness that has dogged him since the dead lamb hung on his young hands, since the sight-stealer roosted on the twisted tree. His swollen lips burst, the ridged sole of a boot tearing the lower completely off to bare the split and toothless gum and he is hauled down the slope his left leg on the wrong way round gouging the earth with its toecap, although his wrecked face is turned to the sky, his whole body bulging peculiar like a sack of broken bricks his pulled arms stretching to four feet and further as they have left the moorings of their sockets. He is thrown broken into the sky for the second time in his life, the carnage of him splatting into the peat bog face down and sinking, collapsing deeper into that which he was and which he will become, the seepage and trickle of mud, of clay. Dead vegetation and eventual fuel Ianto would one day be were he not to be hauled out of his grave later and laid shattered on to grass beside the fungal couple carried from the mineshaft. To be all three tacked down in forms and folders Ianto's memory and his deeds. Diagrammed and dissected by brains no better than his, for lives no tonic to his pored over and

259

pored over and pored over again. This Ianto is already sinking into the sucking bog below the disused silver mine which keeps his main deed, his big event, brown bubbles bursting around his back under the gaze of his killers and the high wheeling birds, a small yellow flower entangled in the matted hair blood-glued to his smashed skull.

It seems like a heartbeat, but it has taken quite some time to stamp and mangle the life out of Ianto and they float down from the frenzy exhausted, spent, regarding the wreckage of him seething and twitching in the bog. The ruin of him, the shatter of him like a man composite reconstructed by some sick vivisectionist from victims of car crash and industrial crush, an arm where his scapula should be, the vertical set of his eyes swollen, mud-stuffed. Panting and stricken and streaked with dark blood they stand and watch in covenant shocked and silent until the ransacked figure in the swampy ground suddenly begins to buck and twist and astonishingly even seek to drag itself out of the mud's clutch with one tortured, twisted hand and Ikey sighs and says:

—Oh, for fuck's sakes. Give me that fuckin gun.

Llŷr hands it over wordlessly and Ikey snatches it and steps into the bog knee-deep. Looks down at broken Ianto.

—Fuckin rapist. Fuckin psycho. Fuckin pervert . . . yew fuckin stain . . . yew fuckin . . . *mess* . . .

He presses the rifle barrel against the wreck of Ianto's head, the crushed bone sinking with a discernible crunch at the touch of that steel hoop. He pulls the trigger once and the body jerks once matching the nervy reaction of the silent audience, bespattered again with fresh droplets of blood which in a crimson cloud writhing and turning like some hideous jack o' lantern drifts on the light wind over the peat-bog to disperse with a soft hiss on the far bank. Ikey turns to leave, but the tattered scrap of Ianto begins to mewl and whine out of a head the shape of a jigsaw piece and so he turns back to that smashed thing and the noises it's making, mewling like a newborn kitten and he shakes his head and wipes the blood from his face with one rasping hand and shoves the gun barrel deep into the mush of the head and shoots again and the battered mass jerks once and lies finally still

260

and soundless. The gunshots bring someone to investigate from the house of Ianto's childhood, this person in a pristine white England kit, shorts and socks included, peers over the rise at the scene below him then runs back to the house and soon a police helicopter is circling like some giant scavenging bird over the bog and the broken body and the standing staring flock on its banks, all their eyes turned skywards now towards this hovering machine. Figures in dark uniforms and luminous yellow waistcoats hurry over the mountains and fields and up the dingle towards them, some of these converging scramblers in full kevlar body armour and armed with long-sighted rifles. A voice barks instructions through a megaphone somewhere above and if the silent congregation at the edge of the mire, the place where land becomes liquid where people become smoke, hear those distorted mechanical words they give no sign. They simply stand silent and roughly circular and stare down at shattered Ianto. They've done this many times, they have, they've stood like this many times – stood in a rough wide silent circle staring down at Ianto. The only movement is made by Ikey, the dropping of the rifle and the scattering of one hundred and twenty-five small white pills into the bog, where they swiftly dissolve or sink in mud, in blood.

At the dark entrance to the mine, in the shadows under the great bundle of roots of the fallen tree, Gwenno straightens herself out of her tightly curled foetal position and opens her eyes slowly and looks around puzzled at the empty hills, hears the banging rattle of a helicopter and a strange robotic voice in the sky, giving instructions, demanding obedience. She looks over her shoulder at the dead legs protruding from the cold darkness of the mineshaft, sees a big black bird yank a white and rotten ribbon of flesh away from the torn and bloodless stump and swallow it whole, sleek head turned skywards, and she closes her eyes again, turns her face away.

261

—POOR FUCKER.

—Who? Ianto?

—Yeh.

—Shite. Poor fuckin Gwenno, *I* say. Poor fuckin Ikey n all, three bastard years inside, mun.

—Aye, poor fuckin Ianto's victims n all. Schoolboy. A *woman*.

—And her bleedin husband like. Imagin that; seein yewer loved one beaten to death in front-a yew likes. Fuck yew up for life that would.

—Ah fuck all this anyway. Given me a thirst, all this fuckin talkin has. Let's go-a fuckin pub. Llŷr?

—Alright.

—Marc?

—Yeh.

—Danny?

—I don't think so Griff, no. Not at the moment likes. Not really in-a mood. Just want-a sit yer an have a smoke an think for a while like.

—What about?

—Dunno. Just stuff, y'know. Things. Am too bleedin stoned to go to-a pub anyway.

—Yeh well don't fuckin think too much, mun. I know yew, I do; yew'll get all fuckin gloomy an in-a darks an depressed an before we fuckin know it yew'll be back on-a bleedin skag again. Won't yew?

—No I won't. Those days're well fuckin over, mun, I've told yew. All in-a past, they are, those mad times, like.

—Yeh well make sure they fuckin stay yer, that's all I'm sayin.

—Ey, does anyone remember that time at Clarach market when Ianto got on-a bouncy castle? Remember it? Dead fuckin funny it was, see, he –

—Danny, we don't wanter hear it, mun. Heard enough about fuckin Ianto tonight to last me a bastard lifetime I yav. Sick of hearin about that fucker. It's all fuckin over now, innit? Let the bastard rot. It's done.

—Yeh but it's not, tho, is it? Not really, likes. I mean it'll never really be completely over, will it?

—Yeh it will. It fuckin well *is*, mun. *Well* fuckin over. It's all done an bastard well dusted.

—Then how come I keep seen Ianto's fuckin face? Just walkin along or talkin to someone like in a pub or somethin an yer it fuckin is, mun, Ianto's stupid fuckin face. Can't get it out of me fuckin head. See it in me fuckin dreams, I do. It's always bleedin there, mun.

—Aw for fuck's sakes.

—Come on. Leave-a poor cunt to it likes. I've ad just about fuckin enough of this I yav.

—Before or after, Danny?

—Eh?

—Ianto's face. D'you see it before, like, or after we . . . y'know . . .

—Both, mun. Both. I see-a fucker lookin up at the sky like an then I see is eyes all fuckin horrible swollen an bruised. I just can't fuckin help it. I mean . . . Jesus, d'yew all know what we went through, with him? I mean d'yew all really fuckin *know*? D'yew have any idea, d'yew know what it all fuckin *means*?

—Yeh, Danny, we do. Which is why we're goin-a pub to get lashed. Yew wanner sit yer an conjure up Ianto's fuckin face, be my fuckin guest, mun. But if yew wanner come-a pub an get rat-arsed with us, then goan get yewer fuckin coat. What's it to be?

—Erm . . .

—Hurry up, mun. We're not waitin. Look, Marc's already out-a bastard door. An I've got a terrible fuckin thirst on me I yav.

—Erm . . .

—We'll count to three: One . . . two . . .

—Alright. I'll just get me coat an brush me teeth. Just give me a minute.

263

—Alright. One condition, tho, Danny; that yew don't mention that fucker's name once more tonight. We've spoken enough about him for one night an I'm sick an bleedin tired of hearin that fucker's name.

—Whose?

—Yeh. Exactly. Now hurry up an get yewer coat. I'm dyin-a fuckin thirst.

ACKNOWLEDGEMENTS

BIG THANKS TO: Neil Rollinson, who used some of the preceding in his magazine www.boomeranguk.com; all at Cape, especially Robin Robertson for his advice on this one, the other one, and those to come; Brian Evans (*the* man to know when your thirst is bigger than your purse) and his wife Catrin; Ken Grant, Sally Chidlow and the babby; friends and family in Wales, Liverpool, America, Australia, Sheffield, Derbyshire, London, Ireland, Shrewsbury, Lincolnshire, Nottingham, Manchester, Cambridge, wherever you've all ended up; and to Deborah, always and of course.

Take it easy.